JEROME TEEL

THE ELECTION

HOWARD
Fiction

To my wife, Jennifer,
and our three wonderful children,
Brittney, Trey, and Matthew.

ACKNOWLEDGMENTS

I want to express my deepest gratitude to my parents, Carl and Nona Teel, who taught me I could accomplish anything I desired. Without their nurturing, instruction, and commitment to rearing three sons according to God's Word, I never would have had the determination to succeed at anything, including writing this book.

Many thanks to my brothers, Alan and Patrick, and their precious families.

Special thanks to John and Mary Kaye Woods. Their encouragement, support, and friendship are priceless. And to Todd and Rhonda Herndon, who were there when the idea for this book was born.

Special thanks also to Terry Whalin. Terry, you never gave up, and for that I will always be grateful.

And to Howard Books, thanks for taking a risk on a new author . . . and his dream.

CHAPTER ONE

Staples Center, Los Angeles

Edward Burke sat confidently in the Green Room, waiting for his cue to go on stage. *Green is an odd way of describing the room,* he thought. The walls were linen white, and the tightly woven, crushed carpet was slightly darker. Even though he would only be using the room during the Democratic National Convention, he had demanded that it be completely renovated with new furniture. After all, the vice president of the United States expected certain comforts.

Every corner of the room was filled with campaign advisors, aides, and Secret Service agents. Some hoped to ride his coattails, Ed knew. Others genuinely believed in the Democratic party's mission. Whatever their motivations, each person was essential to Ed's presidential campaign—at least that was the way he'd made them feel.

Several aides were speaking on cell phones to other campaign workers who were not fortunate enough to attend the convention. Others huddled in groups of three or four and argued over office space in the future Burke White House.

Ed ignored the bustling activity. *Compartmentalization* was the psychiatric term for his gift. Reclining on a Corinthian leather sofa against the back wall, he felt calm, confident. As he scanned the speech he would deliver, his lips moved slightly with each word. Although the text would be fed to him through teleprompters positioned on both sides of the podium, he didn't want to make any mistakes. Tonight was too important.

His anticipation of the night's events was almost agonizing. He was like a child on Christmas Eve who couldn't wait to open his presents the next morning. Ed wasn't scheduled to make his appearance for at least another hour, but he couldn't relax. He had to see what was happening on the convention floor.

Handing his speech to one of his aides—he didn't know her name—he wove his way through the crowd toward the door to the corridor.

"Mr. Vice President, where are you going?" asked Ed's campaign manager, Benjamin Tobias. The slightly balding Ben always wore a calm expression. But in spite of his outward appearance—short, a little thick in the middle—he was a man who always got things done. The kind of man Ed liked.

"I've got to see what's happening, Ben," Ed replied. "Be back in a minute."

With that, Ed exited the Green Room into the wide, white-tiled corridor. Two Secret Service agents followed like obedient puppies. As Ed entered the hallway, he could hear the roar from the convention hall. As he drew closer, the noise grew louder. Several security guards and convention staffers loitered behind the stage but came to attention as Ed approached. He waved his hand to set them at ease and smiled broadly.

"This is exciting, isn't it?" Ed said to a female intern who appeared nervous.

"Yes, sir," she replied, eyes downcast.

Ed brushed by her with an affectionate pat on the shoulder and climbed the eight metal steps that led to the back of the stage. He peeked through the curtains at the sea of red, white, and blue that covered the convention floor. He had been to every Democratic National Convention since 1980, but this one was different. This year he was the main attraction.

The scene was chaotic. Riotous. It looked like utter confusion. But Ed reveled in it. He inhaled deeply, as if he were smelling the fragrance of a rose, and studied the activity in the convention hall. He saw hats of different shapes, sizes, designs, and colors. He quickly decided his favorite were the straw hats with Burke for President on the bands. Campaign buttons that would one day be collectors' items covered the lapels of the conventioneers. Affixed to wooden handles, large posters with his picture were being waved by thousands of the party's faithful. So many faces he did not know, nor did he care to know.

The DNC and Los Angeles had spared no expense in preparing for this August convention. It had cost $100 million. But Ed thought that was a small price to pay with all the world watching. Everything had to be perfect. A Jumbotron had been installed above the stage. Red, white, and blue bunting was draped from the walls. As he peered through the curtains, Ed saw the vertical signs with the names of all fifty states scattered throughout the crowd. The signs were used to section off the convention floor, and this year the delegation from Tennessee, his home state, commanded the area immediately in front of the stage.

Satellite hookups from every major television network consumed the corporate skyboxes that lined the upper rim of the hall. The news anchors sat with their backs to the convention stage, bright lights in their faces, and talked into television cameras three feet away. Ed knew they were attempting to predict the content of his speech. Most were not even close on their predictions. But a few—those chosen by Ed's campaign to receive the skinny on Ed's speech—would be reasonably accurate.

Immediately below the media skyboxes was the section reserved for the Democratic party dignitaries. Ed scanned the crowd and was pleased to see that every seat was occupied. He would receive a report later from one of his aides, telling him who was actually in attendance, but he wanted to see for himself. Those who failed to attend the convention, *his* convention, would be reminded of that failure. Ed also saw his wife, Millie, sitting on the front row in the middle of the upper section. Ed and Millie had worked their entire lives for the presidency.

As the roll call of states began, Ed stepped away from the curtain and headed back toward the Green Room. Soon he would garner enough votes to receive the nomination for president. Some last-minute preparations were needed before he appeared at the podium for his acceptance speech.

The crowd inside the Green Room glanced up at his return but quickly focused their attention on a television against the back wall as the delegates' votes were counted. Ed watched, too, and listened as a representative from each state announced the delegation's vote. A chill ran along his spine as representative after representative repeated a phrase he had longed for years to hear.

"Mr. Chairman, I am pleased and honored to announce that we cast all our votes for the next president of the United States, Edward Burke."

The roll call continued until Ed's vote tally neared the total needed to win the nomination. With less than ten votes needed to secure the nomination, the Michigan delegation yielded its turn to the delegation from Tennessee. A robust, gray-haired man, who served as the chairman of the Tennessee delegation, strode to a microphone. He paused to allow all the news networks an opportunity to focus their cameras on him before beginning to speak.

"Mr. Chairman," he began. His voice boomed through the sound system with a slightly exaggerated Southern drawl. "The great state of Tennessee is proud to cast all its votes for its native son, Edward Burke."

The horde in the Staples Center erupted into thunderous celebration. Balloons trapped near the ceiling by large nylon nets were released and fell like huge red, white, and blue raindrops. Confetti and streamers cluttered the airspace. Ear-damaging music burst from the mountains of speakers on both sides of the stage.

"Mr. Vice President!" screamed a female aide with a two-way radio in her hand.

Ed could barely hear her above the celebration in the Green Room but liked her determination.

"Mr. Vice President!" she screamed again. "It's time to go."

Ed took one last look in a mirror near the door to make sure his patriotic red tie was straight. This time when he left the room, he had a larger escort. From the top of his black hair to the bottom of his patent-leather shoes, Ed looked presidential—and he knew it. He buttoned the top two buttons of his navy blue suit as he walked briskly toward the ever-escalating roar. The sound drew him much the way the sirens' song lured mariners of Greek mythology to their destruction. His pace quickened, causing his entourage to scramble to keep up. He bolted up the same steps he had tiptoed up earlier and was ready to burst onto the stage when a familiar voice stopped him.

"Not yet, Ed," the voice said calmly. It was Ben. "Just another moment."

The entire convention was scripted down to the very second. Ed's campaign staff knew exactly when the maximum amount of the American population would be watching the convention on CNN or NBC or FOX. Everything had to go according to the script. Everything.

Ben placed his right hand on Ed's shoulder. "Almost." He stared at the synchronized watch on his left wrist and started the countdown. "Three, two, one. Now, Ed. Now," Ben said at the precise second in the script for Ed's appearance. Ben patted Ed on the shoulder, and Ed resumed his march toward the nomination.

The exultation on the convention floor was reaching its climax when Ed finally appeared on stage. The delegates greeted him like he was a conquering hero returning from battle. Ed waved triumphantly to the crowd with both hands and pointed to a few people on the floor, pretending to recognize them. He tried in vain to clap along with the music—but knew he was off beat—and embraced everyone on the platform as he made his way toward the podium to deliver his speech.

The nomination was really nothing more than a formality following the Super Tuesday primaries. The other candidates were out of issues and out of money. Ed had outspent all of them by a cumulative ten-to-one margin. It was impossible for anyone to compete with a vice president who had $50 million in his war chest before the campaign began. There had been ample time for Ed's team to prepare the perfect acceptance speech.

At just the right instant in the script, Ed moved to the podium and motioned with both arms for the crowd to quiet down. Silence quickly descended. Ed smiled. It was as if his audience anticipated the very voice of God. And right now Ed felt close to delivering just that.

Ed began his eloquent speech, prepared by a team of the best writers money could buy. The speech touched on affirmative action, immigration, health care, and the rights of women. Ed talked about saving social security and improving schools. He reached out to the minority voters with his promise of increased urban revitalization. He even highlighted four different people in the audience and explained how their lives were better because of programs implemented by the current Democratic administration. Resounding cheers greeted practically every phrase Ed uttered. His speech was interrupted more times for ovations than any other acceptance speech in the history of the Democratic National Convention.

"Thank you. God bless you, and God bless America," Ed shouted into the microphone as he completed his speech.

He stepped away from the podium and again raised his arms in triumph. The celebration resumed, and the crowd roared with approval, chanting his name for five minutes after the speech ended. On cue, his wife, Millie, moved onto the stage. The two stood proudly, arm in arm, waving to the thousands of supporters they did not know, packed into the Staples Center.

This was their coronation, and nothing was going to stand in their way to the White House.

Hyatt Regency hotel, Miami

The presidential suite had been converted into a makeshift war room. Economic data, poll results, and campaign-contribution reports cluttered every table as Shepard Taylor, the chief campaign strategist for the top Republican candidate, pored over the latest polling data from California.

Just two weeks earlier, in late July, Mackenzie Foster—Mac to his friends—stood on a stage in Philadelphia and accepted the Republican nomination to challenge Vice President Edward Burke in November. Shep knew he'd never forget the climax of that night. It was unlike anything he had ever experienced in all his years in politics, and he was certain the ultimate victory would be theirs. But Ed Burke would be a formidable op-ponent, and Shep searched through the campaign data for any glimmer of hope. He had known Mac a long time—had served as Mac's chief of staff during his current tenure as Senate majority leader. Now Shep was head-ing up Mac's bid for the presidency.

But the march through the primaries had been considerably more dif-ficult for Mac Foster than for Vice President Burke. Mac's campaign funds had been substantially depleted by the time he'd reached the Republican National Convention in July. Pollsters had begun pitting Mac against Ed Burke as soon as it was clear that each man would clinch his respective party's nomination. Shep knew that the results hadn't looked promising for Mac from the very first poll, and he trailed by 10 percentage points even before the Democratic National Convention. With the momentum the vice president would receive from the convention, it was naive to think that Mac could win California's fifty-four electoral votes. So Shep, Mac, and the rest of the campaign team had decided to focus instead on Florida, Pennsylvania, New York, and Texas.

The war room in Miami this warm August night was far from the jubilation in Los Angeles. Mac had asked for it to be that way. The Hyatt would be their headquarters for a few days as Mac campaigned in Florida.

Since it was late, most of the campaign staff had retired for the night. Only Mac and his top two advisors still remained. Following completion of the vice president's speech, they all looked despondent.

"Where is he getting all his money?" asked Jack Bennett, Mac's running mate from Texas. He rubbed his tired eyes under his glasses and fretfully scratched his head through his white hair. Shep could see that the eldest member of the group was exhausted and frustrated.

All of them, and especially Shep, knew Edward Burke would be hard to beat, but no one said it. The economy was strong, and that meant the American people would likely vote to maintain the status quo. Burke was also pro-choice, and unfortunately for Mac, a large segment of the voters agreed with him. Shep knew that the biggest problem, however, was money, or the lack of it. The vice president had it. Mac didn't.

Shep loosened his tie, propped his feet on the glass-topped coffee table, and stared at the ceiling. "He's spending millions and millions on television and radio ads, and it never seems to run out," he mused. "How is that possible?"

"Aside from the campaign funds, the soft money continues to pile up. At this pace he'll have three hundred million to our two hundred million," responded Jack.

Shep listened as Mac and Jack further discussed the vice president's fund-raising prowess. He heard the concern in their voices. Mac was trailing in the polls, but Shep wasn't about to concede defeat. And he knew Mac well enough to know that Mac wasn't about to either. There were still three months until the general election, and anything could happen.

"The other Democratic primary candidates claimed Burke was receiving money illegally, but they could never prove it," Mac began as he paced the room. He stretched his arms over the top of his six-foot-two frame, as if trying to chase the soreness from his muscles, then clasped his hands together on top of his salt-and-pepper hair. "The media likes him, so they're not going to start turning over stones."

He stopped his pacing and turned toward the night skyline just outside the glass doors of the balcony. "Somebody's financing him. That's the only answer. But we'll never be able to prove it. The American people would turn against him if they found out he was selling the presidency to the highest bidder. I'm certain of it from what we've seen and tracked, but how can we prove it?" He shook his head in frustration and pivoted back toward his advisors.

Shep leaned forward in his chair, listening intently. He noticed that Jack followed suit.

"Perhaps we could get a congressional inquiry started," suggested Jack, his brow furrowed in thought. "At least that would create some media interest, and we could put some spin on it after it breaks."

Shep was surprised but pleased when Mac nodded slowly. Shep had worked with Mac a long time and knew that Mac rarely, if ever, authorized the investigation of an opponent. And he always refused to allow an opponent's personal life to become the center of the campaign, no matter how devious his sins. Mac didn't play dirty. He was a straight shooter. Honest. Hardworking. That's why Shep was working day and night to get the man elected to the White House.

"I'll call a couple of friends on the House Judiciary Committee," Jack said.

"I can call in a few favors in the Senate," Mac added.

All three agreed that something had to be done, and soon. They were getting ready to go head-to-head with a vice president with seemingly unlimited financial resources, and there was no way they could compete.

Shep studied Mac. He saw resolve in his strong, firm jaw and a fiery determination—a determination Shep shared—in his rich brown eyes.

"We can't give up," Mac commented, running a hand through his hair. "I firmly believe that God has placed us here, at this point in history, for a purpose. We must win. There is no other alternative."

Shep didn't verbalize his thoughts, but he, too, was convinced that Mac Foster had to win the presidency. After seeing the other option on television tonight, he abhorred even more the idea of Ed Burke winning.

He glanced at his watch. Sleep was a rare commodity, and Shep could tell by the faces of his colleagues that they all needed it.

"We have a big day tomorrow. And if we're going to catch Burke, we all need our rest. Let's finish this discussion over breakfast," Shep suggested.

Mac's two advisers filed out of the presidential suite. Shep suspected that Jack would lie awake, wondering if Mac had any chance of winning. But Shep had other ideas. Even Republican pollsters were reporting that Mac was 10 percentage points behind the vice president. Doubts were beginning to creep in. Mac and his campaign staff needed something big to happen by mid-October, or they had no chance at victory.

And victory, Shep thought, *is crucial. Especially right now.* He loathed the thought of four more years of a Democratic White House. The country's defenses would be depleted, and the United States would be vulnerable to nuclear-missile attacks from as far away as Asia. The probability existed that one or more Supreme Court justices would retire during the next administration, and Burke's liberal appointments would shape the Court for the next thirty years. Shep just couldn't let that happen. The hearts, minds, and souls of the next generation were at stake in this election.

Even so, Mac would not approve of what Shep was about to do.

Shep closed the door to his modest hotel room and hung his suit coat in the closet. It had been a long day and a longer night, and his body felt it. Every muscle ached. He splashed a handful of cold water on his face from the bathroom sink to rejuvenate himself and peered into the mirror. A tired face stared back at him. His once-parted sandy blond hair was now mussed from a hectic day of campaigning. His hazel eyes drooped from exhaustion, and he could feel the rough stubble on his face when he rubbed his eyes to keep them open for a few more minutes.

The clock on the nightstand read 2:00, but it didn't matter to Shep. He had to make the call. He was convinced that the entire campaign hinged on what could be discovered about Ed Burke's campaign fundraising. He scrolled through his PDA until he found the phone number he needed.

Washington DC

The first ring was intertwined into Dalton Miller's recurring dream of being chased by the DC police through the streets of downtown Washington. The second ring jolted him from deep sleep, and he knocked his wireless phone from its resting place. It fell from the nightstand and landed loudly on the floor. His bedmate, the fourth in as many weeks, never flinched.

"Hello," Dalton muttered after retrieving the phone from the floor and opening the lid.

"Dalton," an anxious voice said, "this is Shep Taylor. I'm sorry to call at this hour."

"That's OK," Dalton responded. His brain felt half asleep, and he had already returned to a horizontal position on the bed. But when he recognized the caller and heard the urgency in Shep's voice, Dalton's interest was immediately piqued. Something with a large fee was on the horizon, particularly if Shep Taylor was calling at this hour.

Dalton shook the sleep from his voice. "What can I do for you?"

There was a pause, then Shep admitted, "I need your help."

Dalton smiled. He was known to be the best private investigator in Washington, DC. If information could be found, Dalton was confident he would find it. He could follow an unfaithful spouse and never be noticed. He knew dirt on more senators and representatives than anybody else, and he was proud of it.

"What kind of help?" Dalton asked.

Again a pause. "It involves the vice president and the election."

Dalton sat up. Shep Taylor sounded desperate. Dalton knew the Foster campaign was behind in the polls, but were things really that bad?

"Can you help us?" Shep asked again.

Dalton glanced at the woman lying with her back to him on the other side of the bed. For the life of him, he couldn't recall her name. "Hold on," he added in a voice barely above a whisper. "I need to change rooms."

Dalton left the warmth of his bed and stumbled through the darkness to a small office adjacent to the kitchen. "You realize it's going to be expensive," Dalton informed Shep when he was safely out of earshot of the woman in his bedroom.

"How much?" Shep inquired.

Dalton smiled again. The amount really didn't matter, since his fees were always met. But it was logical to ask the question. "One million, plus expenses."

"Agreed," Shep responded without hesitation.

"I'll also need protection. I am not taking a fall for your guy."

"I'll work on that."

Was there hesitancy in Shep Taylor's voice on that demand? Dalton wondered. But he wouldn't let that issue stand in the way of a large payday.

"Anything else?" Shep asked.

"That's it. Tell me what the job is."

As Shep talked about their suspicions regarding the vice president's fund-raising, the picture became clear to Dalton. Mac Foster's staff needed to know who was funding Ed Burke's campaign, and they needed to know quickly. Dalton was to communicate with Shep, and only Shep. Dalton could not tell anyone who employed him.

"This is important," Shep urged. "I need you to give this top priority."

"I'll get started first thing this morning," Dalton promised.

Hyatt Regency hotel, Miami

After Shep hung up the phone, he was more than ready for bed. His sleep tonight would finally be restful. The best he'd had since Mac clinched the Republican nomination in the April primaries.

CHAPTER TWO

Apollyon Associates, Inc., lower Manhattan

As the presidential election loomed, the Federalists' meetings on the top floor of the Apollyon Associates, Inc. headquarters became more frequent. They had been close to their goal once before, but their technology had not been complete.

Nor had it helped that pictures of their candidate in the arms of a woman other than his wife had appeared in the *Washington Post*. That candidate, John Franklin, was a former governor of Florida. Only a few weeks after losing the presidential election four years ago, he died—apparently of a heart attack. Everyone assumed he succumbed to the pressures of defeat, so no autopsy was performed. If one had been, it would have revealed traces of an obscure Asian toxin known to cause cardiac arrest if taken orally.

The name *Federalists* was a self-appointed title adopted by this trio of American businessmen, but their political beliefs were far from academic federalism. It was more a hybrid of globalism and plutocracy. A one-world government, but controlled by three multinational companies. And not just any companies, but companies owned by the Federalists. Through their companies, they had sufficient resources to control the world's financial markets and its communications. If the Federalists succeeded, they could force every country in the world to submit to their authority. A heady, powerful thought indeed.

"Good afternoon, Mr. Winston," the receptionist said as William Randolph Winston IV entered the lobby through the revolving front doors of the Apollyon headquarters.

Randolph glanced down for a moment. It was still evident that he had been athletic as a young man, but his age was beginning to gain on him. He was slightly overweight, and his black hair was beginning to gray around the fringes. His face was clean-shaven, with the exception of a small goatee. Although he considered himself charming and others agreed, he had never married. A wife and family would have been unnecessary distractions in his trajectory of success.

"Good afternoon," he returned and energetically made his way into a waiting elevator that would transport him to the top-floor conference room.

Randolph Winston was from old East Coast money, and the Federalists' plan had been his idea, born while the three men were classmates and fraternity brothers at Harvard. When his father passed away, Randolph inherited his family's fortune and used it to create a company that ultimately became the exclusive licensing agency for Internet users' identification numbers.

Each time a computer user tried to open an account for Internet access, regardless of what company provided the access, he or she was asked to provide a name, street address, e-mail address, and other statistical information, which was transmitted to Apollyon Associates headquarters via the Internet. Most users provided the requested information without any thought about its ultimate destination. They had no way of knowing that a computer file was being created about them at Apollyon.

In return for providing the needed information, the user would be assigned a ten-digit user-identification number. This number would be transmitted to the user after an account was registered with Apollyon. Each time the user logged in to the Internet, the Internet access provider would ask for the user's number. The number had to be entered or access was denied.

Once the user was logged in, Apollyon was able to track which Web sites the individual user visited, what purchases he or she made online, and the content of e-mails sent and received. This information was then stored in the user's computer file at Apollyon headquarters. Randolph knew that 99 percent of all Internet users were not sophisticated enough to realize how much his company would be able to intrude into their lives through their home computers.

By the time they did realize, it would be too late.

A company intern brought Randolph a cup of coffee while he waited for his two partners. He could relax because his part of the plan was in place. His trip to the West Coast had been successful. He would report to his partners that the technicians at the research and development division had completed the newest software in the Apollyon arsenal. A smile formed as he remembered the clever name he had given the new software: Cannibal.

The access numbers assigned to users could now be required each time they wanted to purchase groceries or gasoline, go to the doctor, or pay their utility bills—whether using the Internet or not. The user number would become the most important set of numbers in a person's life, more important than a social security number, a driver's license number, or a telephone number. It would become a person's signature, or mark, and soon every person in the world would be unable to even purchase basic necessities without it.

That is, if the Federalists accomplished their mission. And Randolph Winston was determined they would do just that.

The opulent conference room at Apollyon was dimly lit at Randolph's direction. He couldn't tolerate much light. He sat at the end of the conference-room table and sipped his coffee. His expensive taste was evident from the décor. The furniture was the rarest antiques. The paintings that lined the walls would make the curators at The Metropolitan Museum of Art in New York envious. Randolph's father had once told him that to *be* successful, he had to *look* successful. Randolph considered the room. He certainly looked successful. His father would have been proud of him.

"Mr. Winston," the receptionist's voice interrupted over the telephone intercom, "Mr. Montgomery is here to see you."

"Send him up," Randolph ordered. Finishing the last of his coffee, he walked toward the conference-room door to meet his compatriot.

Pierce Anthony Montgomery was slightly taller than Randolph, and his navy blue double-breasted suit was tailored to fit his tall frame. Unlike Randolph, Pierce managed to maintain his athletic physique. Racquetball three times a week at the athletic club downtown helped him stay in shape, he had told Randolph. Even though Pierce was nearing fifty, he still combed his black hair from front to back and kept it in place with a styling gel that gave his hair a wet sheen.

Pierce was the founder and controlling stockholder of TransWorld Communications, Inc., the world's largest telecommunications and media conglomerate. Pierce, a self-made billionaire, was confident, bordering on arrogant. He was shrewd. Driven. The current Mrs. Montgomery was his third wife. And Randolph knew she would soon realize, like the ones before her, that Pierce was actually married to TransWorld, or, more accurately, to the Federalists.

Through holding companies, subsidiaries, and foreign corporations, TransWorld had secretly acquired satellites that controlled 60 percent of all the world's wireless communications and 80 percent of all Internet and broadband communication cables. The communication companies TransWorld didn't own were insignificant and would dismantle soon after the Federalists' ascension to power.

Telephone calls from New York to London either traveled through TransWorld's cables or were relayed through TransWorld's satellites. News events that happened in France or South Africa were disseminated through TransWorld's media outlets to the rest of the world. The Federalists had at first planned to isolate allies through TransWorld's infrastructure but then realized that complete isolation would be virtually impossible. But Randolph convinced his partners not to worry about the fact that each country maintained its own secure communications. He had demonstrated that TransWorld could create a temporary disruption in communication among world leaders, giving the Federalists time to fully implement their plan. Creating such a disruption was one key to the Federalists' plan, and TransWorld held that key.

Randolph greeted Pierce as he entered the room. The two men shook hands firmly.

"How are you, my friend?" Randolph asked.

"Fine," replied Pierce civilly. "And how was your trip?"

"The flight was fine," replied Randolph. "We made it to LaGuardia from LA in just under six hours."

"Burke's looking good in the polls. Do you think he can hang on to his lead?"

Randolph winced. Already Pierce had changed the subject to the weakest link in the plan. There was no legitimate chance of success unless the Federalists obtained control of the White House.

"He's scoring points with Hispanic voters with his promise to open the Mexican border to more immigration," responded Randolph, as if Edward Burke was Harvard's star quarterback rather than the man projected to be the next president of the United States. "The African American supporters are ecstatic over his position on affirmative action. He's promising to fill vacant judicial seats with minority jurists and, of course, we will tell him who those will be. The economy is still strong, and that keeps the middle class satisfied. We just can't have any surprises like last time."

The receptionist's voice interrupted their conversation—this time to announce the arrival of Milton Hawthorne McAdams.

Randolph knew it would be more difficult to convince Milton than Pierce that a problem had to be eliminated for the good of the cause. But he also knew Milton believed in their cause as much as, or more than, Randolph did and that he would agree the presidential race was too important to take the risk of being exposed.

Again the elevator doors opened, and Milton McAdams strolled across the hall to the conference room. He was shorter than the other two men, slightly slimmer, and almost completely bald. The few wisps that remained of his prematurely gray hair gave him a dignified, fatherly appearance. He wore a conservative gray suit, white shirt, dark tie, and wingtip shoes.

Milton controlled the largest bank in the world, World Federal Bancshares. Its headquarters were in New York, but it had offices in Tokyo, Hong Kong, Sydney, and London. Over the last several years his brokers had been acquiring large positions in all the world's currencies. Very discreetly World Federal had cornered the market on the dollar, the yen, and the euro. Through its sophisticated maze of subsidiaries, it had acquired more Treasury notes guaranteed by the United States than all other banks and individuals combined.

With these acquisitions came the ability to manipulate the bond market and, therefore, long-term interest rates. Milton had explained to Randolph that it was a simple case of supply and demand. A few days after Edward Burke's inauguration, Milton's brokers would be instructed to begin dumping bonds on the Chicago market, driving bond prices down. Long-term rates would soar, causing widespread panic and selling on Wall Street. Then the Federalists would ride in like white knights to save the world economy . . . at a price, of course. Randolph, Milton, and Pierce had all agreed it was a great plan.

World Federal was also the largest issuer of credit cards. It had for years issued credit cards to unemployed college students. It wasn't as much of a risk to Milton's company as it sounded, since a student's parents would pay the bill, if necessary, to protect their child's credit rating. But Randolph knew that Milton didn't really care whether the debt was repaid or not.

The purpose of issuing credit cards to consumers, whether they qualified or not, was to condition the population to accept that credit cards were the same as currency. Anything could be purchased with a credit card—from groceries to pet food to furniture to automobiles. When the Federalists assumed world control, cash as a form of payment would no longer be accepted.

"Randolph, Pierce, how are you?" asked Milton, shaking hands.

"We are both well," responded Pierce, his voice deep and rich.

"Shall we sit down?" Randolph suggested as he moved toward the table in the center of the room.

Randolph began the meeting by describing the new Cannibal software, the user numbers, and how the software worked into their plan. Pierce and Milton listened intently as Randolph described how computer chips with the Cannibal software could be implanted into Milton's credit cards.

"You see," Randolph explained, "we are close to world supremacy." Pierce and Milton nodded in agreement, and Pierce smiled broadly.

"Everything appears to be in place," Pierce noted after Randolph's presentation. "We are closer than we've ever been to reaching our goal. We can't let anything interfere with our objectives, and we can't take any risks. That being said, what do you think we should do with James Davidson? Do you think he'll keep quiet about us?"

"It was brilliant on our part to have both a Republican and Democratic candidate," Randolph replied. "Davidson came close, but he simply couldn't generate the excitement and support in the Republican party that Burke did among the Democrats. Davidson is of no value to us since he lost the Republican nomination to Foster."

Randolph caught the other two Federalists' eyes as he continued. "There's really no need to keep Senator Davidson around. He knows too much about our plans. I, for one, don't trust him. I think it's time he met a fate similar to Governor Franklin's."

Milton and Pierce were both silent. They looked away from Randolph's penetrating glare.

"We're in agreement then," Randolph announced when there was no debate. "I'll make the arrangements."

"Is that all for today?" Milton asked as he stood to leave.

"We do have one other problem that needs to be addressed," stated Randolph matter-of-factly.

"Go on," insisted Milton as he returned to his seat.

Randolph watched each of his partners intently as he described the last remaining obstacle to world domination and recommended how to eliminate it. He watched carefully for any sign of disagreement. Pierce was of no concern; the man wasn't brave enough to cross Randolph. If there were to be a problem, it would come from Milton.

The room grew momentarily silent when Randolph finished speaking. Pierce's face showed only submission. However, Milton—as expected—appeared concerned. But since Randolph was convinced of the problem's resolution, he refused to be challenged. He set his face in its most unwavering expression to convey an unspoken message to Milton: *On this issue there is no other option. We must follow my recommendation for our own safety . . . and the implementation of the plan.*

"Collateral damage?" Milton inquired. Looking anguished, he rubbed his nearly bald head.

"It will be kept to a minimum," assured Randolph. He discerned Milton's capitulation and knew his message had been received. A small assurance, and the pact would be sealed. "We only desire to eliminate the problem, not create new ones."

Milton stood up, put his coat on, and left the room without saying good-bye to Randolph or Pierce. Randolph knew that nothing else would be said, or needed to be said. The matter was closed. The last remaining obstacles would soon be removed.

After Milton left, Randolph placed a call, dialing the number from memory. Only a few words were spoken. But with those few words, the process to eliminate what the Federalists believed to be their last remaining obstacles was set in motion.

CHAPTER THREE

Reed residence, Jackson, Tennessee

Jake Reed would have preferred to hear the sounds of activity, but that was too much to ask this Monday morning. It was only the second full week of the school year, and his children were not yet accustomed to the early-morning wake-up call after a summer of leisure. He was partially dressed—trousers and undershirt—when he looked at the clock on his nightstand and realized it was already seven fifteen. Jake hated being late.

Rachel, his wife, always awoke before Jake. He slept while she had her morning devotion time and until after she had prepared lunches for the kids. She got the kids started on breakfast, let the dog out for his morning constitutional, and then took a shower. Most days Rachel took the kids to school. But on Mondays she went to a women's Bible study at a local church, and carpool duty fell to Jake. He found Rachel in front of the bathroom mirror, getting ready for the day. Rachel had a running feud with one little twirl of hair in the front, and it always took at least thirty minutes each day to either defeat it or surrender. And Jake knew that surrender was rarely an option.

"Do you think you can help hurry the kids up?" Jake asked Rachel as he squinted over her shoulder into the bathroom mirror and manipulated his necktie. His six-foot-one-inch frame made it easy for him to see himself over her. "We're already going to be late."

"I'm almost ready," Rachel replied. "And then I'll go check on them. Just settle down. You've got plenty of time."

Jake saw her glance at his image in the mirror.

"That tie doesn't match your suit by the way," she added.

"What do you mean it doesn't match?" He frowned.

"I mean it doesn't match. You need to find one with blue in it."

"I don't have time to change." Frustrated, Jake began looking for the kids to evaluate their level of readiness. "Have you even brushed your teeth?" he asked Courtney when he met her coming down the stairs, still in her pajamas. "We're running late."

Courtney was the oldest of the three children. The other two were boys: Brett and Jeremy. Courtney was nine going on nineteen and decorated her room with the latest teen singing sensation. Brett and Jeremy were in the process of redirecting their attention, and inextinguishable energy, from summer-league baseball to schoolyard football.

Courtney had her mother's auburn hair and blue eyes; Brett and Jeremy, their father's brown hair and brown eyes. All three were a deep bronze from a summer of countless hours at the country club swimming pool.

"Dad," Courtney retorted, "I'm way ahead of you. It's the boys who are wasting time."

Jake wasn't crazy about the attitude in her voice, but he realized she was right. Charging up the stairs, he found Brett rummaging through his dresser for his favorite shirt.

"Brett, will you please just put on the clothes Mom laid out for you last night?" Jake said as he watched from Brett's door. He meant it more as a directive than a request.

"But Dad," Brett whined, "I don't like that shirt. It looks like a girl's shirt, and all my friends will laugh at me if I wear it."

Jake knew his response had to be forceful, or they'd never get out the door. "I don't have time to argue with you. Just put it on."

Jake retraced his steps down the staircase and returned to the kitchen. That's where he found Jeremy, still in his pajamas, his face nearly buried behind a big bowl of cereal as he watched the television on the counter.

"C'mon, Jeremy, time to get dressed," Jake insisted as he strode toward the master bedroom to finish dressing. He glanced back. Jeremy never took his eyes off the television.

"Honey, can you help me with Jeremy?" Jake pleaded as he entered their bedroom to heed Rachel's advice and change neckties.

Rachel was now standing in their walk-in closet, selecting her attire for the day.

"We're never going to make it to school on time," Jake finished.

She rolled her eyes at his impatience.

But Rachel had a way with Jeremy, Jake knew. Probably because Jeremy was the baby of the family. Whatever the reason, she was always able to coax him into compliance. So Jake was glad when she slipped her slender figure into a pair of blue jeans and a T-shirt bearing the logo of the Tennessee Titans and went to try some motherly diplomacy on Jeremy and the other two kids.

Finally the children were ready. Backpacks were filled and zipped. Lunch boxes were packed, and everyone appeared to have on clothes that actually matched. Brett needed to run a comb run through his hair, but if that was the biggest omission, then they were OK. They might make it to school on time after all, thought Jake.

"Shotgun," screamed Brett as the children bounded down the steps into the garage.

"But you were in the front seat last time," Courtney yelled.

There was only one way to solve the argument. "Everyone is riding in the backseat," Jake pronounced.

When he glanced at Rachel, who stood at the door, he knew dismay was written all over his face. Rachel gave a wry grin and waved good-bye. He couldn't help but chuckle to himself as he climbed into the driver's seat and saw the kids through the rearview mirror trying to get their seat belts fastened. He reached into the backseat and helped Jeremy with his seat belt, then looked back at Rachel again.

Jake could see Rachel laughing as he backed the car out of the garage. He smiled at her and waved good-bye before pressing the remote control to close the garage door.

Jake drove a four-door Volvo 860 Turbo. Burgundy with tan leather interior. Seat warmers were standard, but they wouldn't be needed for a few more months yet. It was a safe, practical car, but had just enough yuppie in it to impress his friends.

After delivering the children to their assigned destinations, Jake began the short drive to his office. The traffic was lighter than normal for a Monday morning. He had the air-conditioning system set to its highest level, because the August heat was oppressive, and Jake didn't like the feeling of his perspiring back sticking to the leather seat. West Tennessee was in the middle of a summer-long drought, and the clear, blue sky meant at least one more hot and humid day without rain.

The radio in Jake's car was always set to the local talk-radio station. Today's topic was last week's Democratic National Convention. Jake turned the volume down and finished the drive in silence. He preferred to stay away from politics. The hypocrisy made him sick to his stomach.

Jake's office was half a block off the court square in downtown Jackson. Convenient to the courthouse but impossible for clients to find a parking place. He had heard that complaint more than once.

He turned left onto Main Street, which led past his front door. The office was located in a row of buildings with common walls, much like the old part of Williamsburg, Virginia. The exterior was stucco and the color of eggshells. The hunter green front door proclaimed Holcombe & Reed, Attorneys-at-Law on a brass plaque. The building, once a funeral home, still maintained several of its characteristics. Barrett Holcombe, Jake's partner, jokingly told people that dead bodies were no longer kept in the basement, just dead files.

Jake turned left into an alley just past the dry cleaner's, drove along the end of the row buildings, then took another left into the parking lot behind his office. Not many of the office buildings in downtown came with employee parking, and Jake was glad his law firm was one of them. He pulled into the parking space marked Reserved for Mr. Reed. His space was the second one from the back door. Barrett used the closer space.

Jake popped his wireless phone from the hands-free dash mount, grabbed his dictation recorder from the console, and exited the Volvo. The back door to the office required a key for access, and Jake fumbled with his set until he found the right one. Jake had learned early in his career that lawyers never enter through the front door of their own office, for fear that the one client they do not want to see is sitting in the lobby. Once safely inside, he zigzagged through the hallways toward his office in the back right quadrant.

"Good morning, Jake," his assistant warmly greeted him as he rounded the last corner.

Madge Mayfield was in her midfifties. She had been a legal assistant for thirty years and had been working for Jake the last five. She was widowed, slightly overweight, and always dressed professionally, even on casual day at the office. Her brunette hair was peppered with gray, and eyeglasses dangled from a thin chain around her neck.

"Good morning, Madge," Jake replied as he walked into his personal office and hung his coat in the closet. "What do we have this morning?"

"You have a real-estate loan closing for Jackson National Bank at ten and a meeting about probating the Thomas estate at eleven-thirty. There's also a meeting on your calendar at nine this morning with Mr. Jedediah McClellan, but I'm not sure what it's about."

Jedediah McClellan. Jake repeated the name in his head. Everybody who knew him called him Jed. Jake had helped Jed with a workers' compensation claim a few years earlier. Jed had received a nice settlement, Jake got a big fee, and everybody was happy. That's the way Jake liked his fees—big.

"I spoke to Jed last week," Jake remembered. He had set the appointment himself. "He told me he was having trouble with the mortgage on his house. I told him I would take a look at it. I believe the note is held by Jesse Thompson's bank, but I'm not certain. If it is, then Jesse is probably robbing Jed blind. I doubt there's anything I can do about it, except to help Jed file bankruptcy."

Jake didn't plan on his meeting with Jed lasting very long. He had more important things to attend to today. "What else do we have?" he asked Madge as he shuffled through the morning's mail.

"That's it for the morning," she replied. "You have a couple of appointments after lunch."

"Hold my calls, and let me know when Jed gets here. I'm going to try to finish some dictation." He laid the unopened mail on Madge's desk and returned to his office, closing the door behind him.

The interior of Jake's office was tastefully decorated but not too elaborate. A mahogany desk with matching credenza and bookcase rested against the wall opposite the door. The bookcase contained law-school books Jake had never used since then and also displayed pictures of Rachel and the children. Two wingback chairs, supposedly for visitors, were covered with stacks of files. On one corner of his desk sat a telephone and an antique brass lamp Jake had purchased at an estate sale a couple of years earlier. The entire desk surface was cluttered with various drafts of letters, court documents, unopened mail, Post-it notes, and file folders.

The walls in Jake's office were adorned with prints of lawyer-related paintings and pictures drawn by his kids. "The Brag Wall," as lawyers called it, displayed his college and law-school diplomas, and his license to practice law.

T. Jacob Reed had graduated from the University of Tennessee in May 1992. He and Rachel had begun dating while both were sophomores and had married the summer after graduation. Rachel's shoulder-length auburn hair, striking blue eyes, and long legs had made her one of the most desired girls on campus. Jake considered himself lucky to have married her.

After their wedding Jake and Rachel moved to Nashville so Jake could attend law school at Vanderbilt University. He had excelled and graduated magna cum laude in May 1995. There were offers from large firms in Atlanta, Georgia, and Charlotte, North Carolina, and Jake wanted to pursue them. But Rachel persuaded him that Jackson, Tennessee, her hometown, was a better place to raise a family. He knew she was probably right. However, the glamour of the big law firms still intrigued Jake. At times he wondered what it would have been like had he gone to Atlanta or Charlotte.

Barrett Holcombe had been practicing law for twenty-two years when Jake graduated from law school and came to work with him in May 1995. They were both glad when Jake passed the bar exam in July of that year. It was Barrett who taught Jake how to make a comfortable living as a lawyer in a small town. Five years later Barrett offered Jake a full partnership, and their two-man practice had thrived ever since.

". . . and that letter needs to be faxed to Judge Prickett's secretary so maybe we can finalize the court approval later this week," Jake spoke into the dictation machine. "Finally I need to prepare a letter to the attorney for—"

"Jake, Jedediah McClellan is here to see you," interrupted Madge over the phone's intercom.

"OK," Jake responded, turning off the recorder. "I'll be right out."

Jake couldn't believe it was nine o'clock already and wondered if he could finish his appointment with Jed by nine thirty. If so, he'd have time to complete his dictation before his ten o'clock real-estate closing.

Jake left his office and headed down the narrow hall to the front lobby. The old wooden floor creaked with each step. He opened the door to a small but lavishly decorated lobby and found Jed McClellan perched on the settee against the wall near the receptionist's counter.

"Jed," he called, "come on back to my office."

Jedediah McClellan was an imposing African American, six-feet-four and muscular. His large hand, calloused from years of manual labor, engulfed Jake's when they shook hands. Jed was already dressed for his job at the Delta Faucet plant east of town. He wore the company-issued navy blue shirt with a patch bearing his name over the pocket, matching pants, and brown, steel-toed work boots.

Jake knew Jed had played high-school football in Jackson because some of the local die-hard football fans still talked about the catch Jed made to defeat rival Marshall County High School for the conference championship. Jed had blown his knee out his freshman year at the University of Mississippi, so he'd become disposable. He returned to Jackson without completing a college education and began working at one of the local plants. That was almost eleven years ago.

"How are Ruth and the kids?" Jake asked as they entered his office. He removed a stack of manila file folders from one of the chairs.

"They're fine." Jed sat in the now-vacant seat. "But this thing with Jesse Thompson's got me and Ruth down."

When Jake saw the angry flush in Jed's light-brown complexion at just the mention of Jesse Thompson's name, he prodded Jed to tell him the whole story. Jed began by explaining how he had inherited his grandfather's house after the old man's death. Then, several years ago, Jed needed $10,000 and went to First National Bank for a loan. Mr. Thompson said he was glad to help him and asked if he had any collateral. Sure, Jed said, and he told the banker about the house. Mr. Thompson asked Jed to sign a few papers and then gave Jed the money.

Jed didn't know what he was signing. He never read the papers. Ever since then he had been making payments on the loan. But this past spring he'd been out of work for a couple of months and got behind.

"If you missed some payments, then the bank has a right to foreclose," Jake commented matter-of-factly.

"What he's doin' ain't right, and you know it. I swear I didn't know what I was signin'." Jed pounded his right fist into his left hand.

Was Jed's anger directed at Jesse Thompson or at himself? Jake wondered.

He listened as Jed talked about his family and where they would go if they lost their home. He didn't have the money to pay Thompson to stop the foreclosure, and he couldn't borrow it from any of his family. He couldn't afford to rent because that would be more than his payment to the bank, and he refused to consider taking his family to a shelter. When Jed's voice began to crack, he paused to gather himself before continuing.

"Anyway, it was my grandaddy's house, and I ain't lettin' Jesse Thompson get it." Tears welled up in the big man's eyes. He repeatedly wiped them, but several managed to escape down his cheeks.

Jake sat silently, watching Jed. Jake knew he couldn't stop what Jesse Thompson was going to do: foreclose on Jed's house. It may not be right, but it was legal. And nothing was going to change that.

"What do you want me to do?" asked Jake.

"I want you to sue him for me, that's what. He's committin' fraud, or somethin', and I know he can't get away with that."

Jake sighed inwardly. *How are you going to get out of this one?* he asked himself. He couldn't sue Jesse Thompson or First National Bank. Jesse had too much influence in town, not to mention money. The man could easily ruin a lawyer's reputation.

"How do you plan on paying me, Jed? It's going to take a sizeable re-tainer for me to get involved in this mess."

Jed's eyes narrowed. "How much you talkin' about?"

"Five thousand dollars."

"C'mon Jake, you know I ain't got that kinda money. Can't you get your money from Thompson when we win? 'Cause I know we're gonna win."

"Even if you win, I don't think the court is going to make Jesse pay my fee," Jake said in a calm tone.

"If you won't help me, and the law won't help me," Jed announced, his voice rising, "then I'll have to handle things my own way." The muscles on the sides of his face flexed as he gritted his teeth and clenched his fist. "I know where he lives, and if I have to kill him, I will. I'd rather go to jail than let him get away with this."

"Jed, don't talk like that. Someone other than me might hear you, and I know you don't mean it."

"I do too. He ain't gettin' away with this."

Jake knew that Jed could kill Jesse Thompson if he really wanted to. Jed had a history of violence. He had been in a brawl several years ago at the Bad Dog Saloon, where he broke the jaw of a man who was flirting with his wife. Witnesses said that if a couple of men had not held Jed back, he would have killed the guy.

Jake surrendered. "All right, Jed. I'll call Jesse and talk to him. I'm not promising anything, but I'll see if I can convince him to stop the foreclosure. When is it scheduled?"

"Wednesday at noon."

Jake wrote *Jed—foreclosure on Wednesday* on a yellow legal pad so he would remember to call Jesse Thompson later that day. He didn't know what good it would do, since Jesse was known for playing hardball. But then at least Jake could tell Jed that he'd tried.

"Thanks a lot, man." Jed stood up. "I knew you'd help me."

"Don't thank me yet. I haven't done anything. I'll call you when I hear something."

After Jake escorted Jed to the front door, said good-bye, and retreated to his office, Madge informed him that Bob Whitfield was on the phone for him. Jake litigated against most of the insurance defense lawyers in town, and Bob was the epitome of his breed—the man probably billed his clients more hours than any other lawyer in Jackson. But he also had the gift of convincing them it was for their own good. Bob never settled a case until the day before trial. Jake currently had only one case with Bob—*Lillian Scott v. Taylor Trucking*—so Bob had to be calling about that.

Jake had agreed to the representation because Lillian Scott was a single mother of two kids and only in her midthirties. She had become disabled when an eighteen-wheeler had run a traffic light and broadsided her car. She had missed three months of work recuperating, and her medical expenses were well in excess of $35,000. Her case was set for a jury trial next week.

"Bob," Jake said as he answered the phone. "Good morning."

"Good morning, Jake," came the bland reply. "I want to talk to you about this Scott case. It's set for trial next week, and my client is interested in settling."

Jake knew it was too early for Bob to be offering to settle. The trial was still eight days away. That could only mean that Bob's client was pushing to settle before incurring additional fees in final trial preparation.

"I'm not sure Ms. Scott wants to settle," Jake said.

The first rule in settlement negotiations was to never let your opponent know you want to settle. The second rule was to remind them how good your case is. And that's what Jake proceeded to do.

"Dr. Jones testified in his deposition that Ms. Scott has a 28 percent permanent disability to her right leg and may never be able to walk without a cane. She's incurred thirty-five thousand dollars in medical expenses and another ten thousand in lost income. Your client doesn't have enough money to settle this case."

"My client is prepared to make a very reasonable offer," Bob replied. "Of course, your client will have to release my client from any further liability."

"Like I said, I'm not sure Ms. Scott wants to settle, but tell me the offer, and I will talk with her about it."

"I have been authorized to offer one hundred fifty thousand dollars for a full compromise and settlement of Ms. Scott's claim," Bob responded in his best defense-lawyer voice.

A hundred fifty thousand! Jake screamed in his mind. "You know I cannot recommend that offer to my client. It's way too low."

The third rule was to never take the first offer.

"That's all I've got, Jake. Talk to your client, and get back to me before lunch on Wednesday," Bob requested. "After that the offer will be withdrawn."

"I'll talk to her and call you back. 'Bye, Bob."

"Good-bye."

Jake hung up and leaned back in his chair. He smiled with satisfaction as he thought about a big payday just around the corner. He pressed the intercom button.

"Yes," came Madge's voice in response.

"Get Ms. Scott on the phone for me."

In the chaos of the day, while handling the details for Lillian Scott and several other clients, Jake forgot all about his promise to Jed McClellan.

CHAPTER FOUR

Miami International Airport

The Monday 10:00 a.m. flight from Cancun, Mexico, taxied to a stop at gate T-15. The passengers on board reluctantly began to disembark. They slowly made their way up the Jetway and into the concourse that led to the customs gate and the remainder of the airport. Their sunburned skin couldn't hide the displeasure on their faces as reality set in that their Caribbean frolic was over.

The female U.S. customs agent who worked the morning shift had seen the same expressions of shock a thousand times. Most of the passengers were honeymooners or couples returning from a romantic rendezvous. She knew that by tomorrow they would be back to their mundane lives and boring jobs. The cool ocean breezes, sun-drenched beaches, and drinks with little umbrellas would become a distant memory. Only the honeymooners would keep the spark that came with the romantic getaway, but just for a few more months. After that they, too, would fall into a regular routine, and the spontaneity would disappear.

One passenger in particular caught her attention. Although he was dressed just like the other tourists—Bermuda shorts, floral shirt, leather sandals, Oakley sunglasses—the fact that he was traveling alone from a romantic venue made him stand out from the rest of the passengers. Also, his complexion and dark hair indicated he was from somewhere in South America, and most of the other passengers were Americans.

She checked the information and photograph on his passport and found them to be in order. She searched his duffel bag and found nothing suspicious. There was no reason to detain him. As she scanned his passport into the computer, she made sure he stood where the surveillance cameras would record his picture. Then she allowed him to pass through the gate into the main terminal. He quickly mixed with the crowd . . . and disappeared.

En route from Pittsburgh to St. Louis

Ed Burke stared thoughtfully out the small window in the executive cabin as Air Force Two cruised through the air thirty-five thousand feet above Ohio. He reminisced about his first meeting with Randolph Winston, and at the same time he wondered what would happen if he welshed on the deal. Or if that was even a possibility. He didn't reach a resolution before Ben Tobias startled him from his daydreaming.

"We'll be in St. Louis in a few minutes," Ben advised. "Do you need anything before we land?"

Ed turned his attention away from the window. "I'm all right, Ben. Where do we go after St. Louis?"

"We'll spend the night in San Francisco, and then we have several days along the West Coast."

"Are our California numbers still up?"

"Foster doesn't have a prayer in California," Ben said confidently. "You're leading by 14 percentage points."

"Good. That's good. Let me know when we're fifteen minutes out of St. Louis."

Ben returned to the forward cabin, and Ed began to watch the campaign staffers as they scurried around the interior of the airplane, talking on wireless telephones to campaign chairpersons in Texas and California and soliciting endorsements from members of Congress. Ed watched the activity and wondered how much each endorsement cost the Federalists. One million? Two million? Senator Mulvaney from New York probably squeezed them for five million. *Thirty-four electoral votes sure are expensive,* Ed thought. He chuckled to himself and pivoted back toward the window. He really didn't care how much they paid. The Federalists had promised him the presidency, and it didn't matter to him what it cost them.

It had all started back in 1990. Ed had already distinguished himself among his colleagues in the House of Representatives. However, he was from a sparsely populated Southern state, and he knew the Democratic party leaders had no plans to put him on any national ballots. Although he aspired to the Oval Office, he saw no realistic chance of obtaining it and became frustrated.

At the pinnacle of his frustration, Ed was contacted by Randolph Winston. He agreed to travel to New York to meet with the Federalists. They told Ed they needed someone to work with them on several delicate matters but couldn't go into details. Randolph assured Ed that if he cooperated, he would be president of the United States one day.

Edward Burke didn't immediately commit to work for the Federalists. He told Randolph, Pierce, and Milton he'd have to think about it for a few days and talk with his wife. But he left New York that cold winter day knowing what his decision would be. He wanted to be president at any cost, so he sold his soul. And he thought the price was rather cheap.

What Ed Burke hungered for more than anything else was power. Ever since he'd tasted the lifestyle inside the Washington Beltway as a freshman congressman, he had wanted more. The state dinners, the trips to exotic locations, under the guise of congressional research, and the women. Young, beautiful women, who were always willing to satisfy the needs of a congressman. He knew that Millie discovered his infidelity quickly after his first tryst, but he didn't care. And Millie soon began to look the other way.

Soon after his agreement with the Federalists, money was paid to the right people, and Ed was selected as the vice-presidential running mate to presidential candidate Roger Harrison. Four years of national exposure as second-in-command would make him hard to beat in the subsequent election, the Federalists said, and they had been correct. Everything was going according to plan . . .

Now, as the pilot announced their descent into St. Louis, Ed spotted the Gateway Arch. In fifteen minutes he would be shaking hands with supporters—none of whom he would ever see again—who had been paid a thousand dollars each by the Federalists to be in attendance. The television cameras would capture all the festivities and broadcast them around the country on the evening news. The crowd would erupt with applause when the senator from Missouri introduced him as the next president of the United States. It would all be so beautifully orchestrated that someone might believe it was real.

Memphis International Airport

A Latin American man exited Northwest flight 708 from Miami at gate C-25 unnoticed. He glanced at the large round clock over the Starbucks in the concourse. It was 12:15 p.m. He'd gained an hour from Miami, so he set his watch to central time. The television monitors hanging from the ceiling in the waiting areas by each gate broadcast the same *CNN-Airport* news program as he walked up the concourse to the main terminal. He rode the moving walkway toward the ticket counters on the main floor and headed to the exit. The signs overhead pointed to a baggage-claim area down the escalators, but he had no luggage. All the supplies he needed had already been acquired, per his instructions, and were waiting for him in Memphis.

He had changed clothes in Miami, discarding the floral shirt and shorts for a black T-shirt and khaki slacks. Now he exited through the automatic sliding doors into the oppressive humidity and heat synonymous with August in Memphis. He would be glad when this contract was completed. It was hot in Colombia, but not like this.

Crossing over the taxi lane, he headed toward the parking garage, which was primarily reserved for short-term or overnight parking. He could have ridden the shuttle bus to Lot B in the long-term parking area but chose to walk instead. The fewer people he came in contact with, the better. The walk through the parking garage was not very far. He had already spotted the black Chevy S10 pickup, waiting for him in slot 17 as planned.

Glancing around quickly, he reached under the front left fender and retrieved a small metal case held in place by a magnet. Inside the case was a key to the truck, which he used to unlock the door and start the ignition. Once inside, he found a brown envelope under the front seat. Inside the envelope was a map, a picture of his mark, cash, a wireless phone, and a hotel key to room 115 at the Plantation Hotel in Brownsville, Tennessee.

Calmly he exited the parking lot, paid the toll, and merged with the traffic on the I-240 loop around Memphis. The route from the airport to his hotel was highlighted on the map in yellow. He would be at his hotel room, where the remainder of his supplies waited, in forty-five minutes.

The Flying J truck stop, north of Washington DC

It was just past 10:00 p.m. eastern time Monday when Dalton Miller parked his car and walked into the Flying J truck stop at the Powder Mill Road exit off I-95.

The Flying J didn't have the best food in the area, but Dalton knew he wouldn't see anyone from inside the Beltway at this greasy spoon. The sun had disappeared behind the western horizon two hours ago, and the lights inside the diner were dim. Dalton had been here many times and had grown accustomed to the sound of diesel trucks in the parking lot. This environment was perfect for his kind of work. The roar of the trucks made it impossible for someone to overhear a conversation.

An old girlfriend had put him in contact with someone from the Justice Department—a disenchanted junior attorney who was willing to talk. The attorney had agreed to meet with Dalton one time, but after that Dalton was on his own. All Dalton knew was that the attorney's name was Joe.

Dalton glanced down at his clothing. He'd purposefully dressed as though he'd just climbed down from one of the rigs idling in the parking lot. His short stature, robust waistline, jeans, and large belt buckle allowed him to blend in with the other patrons. He covered his brown hair with a white and blue Roadway Trucking cap. He knew the other patrons wouldn't notice him as he nonchalantly entered the restaurant and selected the last booth in the back.

From this vantage point he could see the parking lot through the slits in the vinyl miniblinds and also the front door of the restaurant. He removed a pack of Marlboro Light 100s from his shirt pocket and shook it gently until one cigarette slid partially out. He lit it, took one long, hard drag, and then contributed to the cloud of smoke lingering around the ceiling.

When Dalton was on his second cigarette, Joe entered the truck stop. The young attorney was easy to recognize. He was the only person in the restaurant wearing a necktie . . . and wringing his hands.

Dalton motioned for Joe to join him at a booth against the back wall. A waitress in a pink-and-white polyester uniform, with Betty inscribed on her silver name tag, brought two cups of coffee and disappeared.

"I can't believe I'm here talking with you," Joe began almost before he'd taken his seat. He took one sip of the hot liquid, as if attempting to calm his nerves. "I've never done anything like this before."

Somehow Dalton believed him. He was younger than Dalton had expected. He'd probably graduated from law school less than three years ago and still had grandiose ideas about changing the world, starting with the U.S. Justice Department.

Dalton made it easy for the young man to talk. "You don't have to do this if you don't want to."

"I know, but I want to. I'm sick and tired of these politicians thinking they're above the law."

It wouldn't take much to keep the attorney talking. He was ready to explode.

"I know what you mean," Dalton encouraged. "Those guys think they're better than people like you and me. Somebody has to put a stop to it now, or it will never end."

"You're right. That's why I'm here. I've got something that I think will help put one of those guys in his place." Joe nervously scanned the room.

"Nobody's watching us," Dalton assured him. "And I'm not going to tell anyone that you were here."

Joe reached into his shirt pocket and removed two pieces of paper. He unfolded them and handed them to Dalton.

Dalton scanned through the papers before looking up at Joe. "What is this?"

"It's a copy of an internal memorandum from me to the attorney general." Joe's tone displayed amazement at Dalton's ignorance. "It says that the merger between Apollyon Associates, Inc. and another software company should be challenged because it could create a monopoly, with too much control over end-user Internet access."

"But how does this affect the vice president?"

"The AG told me to bury the memo because the owner of Apollyon was a friend of the vice president, and the vice president had called him to specifically request that the merger go through."

"So the vice president used his influence with the attorney general to get a favor for his friend?"

"That's right."

"What else do you know about Apollyon?"

"That's it. The merger was approved without any problem, and as far as I know, Apollyon has a monopoly on Internet access."

Dalton folded the two pieces of paper and stuffed them into his shirt pocket. "You'd better get out of here before someone sees you." He nodded his head toward the door.

Joe walked out of the Flying J with a bounce in his step, as though a burden had been lifted from his shoulders.

Dalton read through the two pages again. He wasn't sure what information he really had, but at least the memo was a start. He had to find out what he could about Apollyon Associates.

CHAPTER FIVE

Law offices of Holcombe & Reed, Jackson, Tennessee

Jake had hardly slept Monday night, thinking about Lillian Scott's case, and arrived at work on Tuesday the same way he did every other day—in a rush. His cluttered desk was just the way he'd left it. Rachel had complained about his staying late at the office and missing dinner with the kids again last night.

Everything was going to be fine. *"I couldn't help it,"* Jake had explained to her.

She'd merely rolled her eyes.

Lately he knew he'd been making a lot of excuses about coming home late. Rachel was right: work *was* coming before family right now . . . but it was their sole income, after all.

He was certain the *Scott* case was going to settle, and he'd had to meet with Ms. Scott after hours to discuss it. When he did, she wanted to take the $150,000. But Jake convinced her that Bob Whitfield had more money to offer and that they should wait until Wednesday morning, just before lunch, to call Bob and make a counterproposal. He liked making Bob sweat.

Around midmorning on Tuesday Jake was in his office poring over some documents for an impending commercial transaction when Madge knocked lightly on his partially opened door. She informed Jake that Jed McClellan was on the phone, wanting to know what Jake had found out from Jesse Thompson.

Jake winced. How could he have forgotten to make the phone call? "Make something up to buy more time," he instructed Madge. "Tell him

I'm in a meeting, or not in the office, and that you'll make sure I call back before lunch."

Madge nodded her understanding and abruptly left Jake's office.

As soon as Madge left, Jake dialed the number for First National Bank. "This is Jake Reed," he told the bank receptionist. "I need to speak with Jesse Thompson, please."

Jake was well aware of the fact that Jesse Lamar Thompson was hated by most of the people in town, particularly those in the African American community because of his lending practices toward them, and he didn't seem to care. He owned the bank, several gas stations, commercial buildings, and all the judges. Some Southern small towns still had rich white men who ran the town, and Jesse Thompson was the boss of Jackson. He was invincible.

The main office of First National Bank was located on the corner of the court square, diagonal from the offices of Holcombe & Reed. Even though it was only ten stories high, it was the tallest building in Jackson. Jesse Thompson's office was on the second floor, in the back of the building, and immediately above the vault. Jake assumed it was because Jesse wanted to stay out of public sight as much as possible.

Jake began their phone conversation with small talk, hoping to warm up Jesse. He asked about Mrs. Thompson and what Jesse thought about the weather. He talked about the local minor-league baseball team and local politics. He eventually brought up Jed's name and rather sheepishly asked if there was anything that could be done to stop the foreclosure.

"That man's crazy if he thinks I'm stopping the foreclosure," came the harsh reply. "He can pay me what he owes, and that's it."

"Jed is real upset about this," Jake tried. "Do you know the house was once Jed's grandfather's house?"

"I know—and I don't care. It's going to be my house after tomorrow."

"But Jed's got a wife and kids who will have no place to go," Jake pleaded. "Can't you at least postpone it a couple of weeks to give me some time to see what I can do about arranging Jed some other financing?"

"Jake, I'm through talking about this. The foreclosure is tomorrow at noon, and I am not postponing it one minute."

Obviously Jesse wasn't going to change his mind. He didn't have to. Jake had nothing to offer Jesse in exchange for a postponement of the foreclosure. Without any type of leverage over Jesse, Jake could talk until he was blue in the face, and it wouldn't matter. The foreclosure was going forward.

"I'll tell Jed that the only way you'll stop the foreclosure is if he pays you in full," conceded Jake. "But we both know that he can't get that kind of money."

"I guess I'll have me another house, won't I?" Jesse replied sarcastically.

Jake thanked Jesse for his time and hung up. At least he could tell Jed he tried. Maybe now Jed would listen to him about filing bankruptcy. That was really Jed's only choice.

Jake went back to the documents for the commercial closing, trying to forget about Jed, hoping he wouldn't call back. He dreaded telling Jed about his conversation with Jesse.

It wasn't long before Madge interrupted him again. "Jed's on the phone."

This time she hadn't even knocked, Jake noticed. She had to be annoyed.

"It's 12:30, and I told Jed you would call before lunch. He wants to know why you haven't called. You want me to cover for you again?" She wrinkled her nose.

"That's all right. I need to get it over with."

He stared at the blinking light on his telephone for several seconds, hoping it would disappear. It didn't. Finally Jake picked up the phone and pressed the button to connect to Jed.

It was not a good conversation. When he told Jed he'd tried to convince Jesse to stop the foreclosure but Jesse would not listen, Jed became enraged. He accused Jake of siding with Jesse.

Jake assured him that wasn't true. He asked Jed if he'd considered filing for bankruptcy protection. A reorganization bankruptcy would stop the foreclosure and allow Jed the opportunity to get back on his feet.

But Jed didn't think much of that idea. He only became angrier. "That man's a crook!" he screamed into Jake's ear. "I'm not takin' bankruptcy and lettin' him get away with this. I'll do what I gotta do."

The slam of the phone from Jed's end thundered through the line and hurt Jake's ear. Jed was angry, and Jake couldn't blame him. He might react the same way if he were going to lose his home tomorrow.

After Jed hung up, Jake debated whether to tell the authorities about Jed's threats against Jesse. Was it attorney-client communications, or not? Jed hadn't paid him any money, but did that matter?

And then Jake shook his head. *Jed's just hot right now. He'll sleep on it tonight and come to his senses.*

Jake didn't see any need to call the authorities.

Crown Plaza hotel, Detroit

"Our numbers in Michigan are some of our best," Shep informed Mac as they walked along the tenth floor hallway in the Crown Plaza Hotel near the airport. It was just after midnight, and the Foster campaign was winding down after a Tuesday full of automobile-plant tours, a county fair, and a late-night rally. "We're leading Burke by 7 percentage points in this morning's polls. Governor Richards's endorsement today was huge."

"He's a good friend," replied Mac. "He'll do what he can to help."

"I hope we can get help in some other states," Shep said. "We need to make up ground before Labor Day."

Mac and Shep stopped outside Shep's hotel door. "You look beat, Shep," Mac commented. "Why don't you get some rest? We have an early flight to Birmingham. We can talk about this more on the plane."

"That's a good idea. I am pretty tired. I'll see you in a few hours."

Mac continued on toward his suite at the end of the hall as Shep entered his room.

All Shep wanted to do was go to bed. He loosened his tie, kicked off his shoes, and stretched out on the bed. He was too tired to finish undressing. He had barely closed his eyes when his wireless phone rang.

"Shep, this is Dalton. I think I have something." Dalton's voice was unemotional—all business.

Shep sat up on the edge of the bed. His heart pounded from the sudden awakening. He was no longer as tired as he had been five minutes ago. He could only hope that his significant investment was beginning to pay off. "Tell me what you've found," he demanded.

"I spoke with an informant of mine from the Justice Department," began Dalton. "He was telling me about a merger that the vice president requested be approved, even though it creates a monopoly. He said the name of the company was Apollyon Associates. I checked on Apollyon and found out that it's owned by a man named Randolph Winston."

"Randolph Winston?" Shep asked rhetorically. He hastily ran the name through the data bank in his head. "That name sounds familiar."

"It should. He's one of the richest men in the world."

"So Burke does Winston a favor," Shep said thoughtfully, "and in return Winston contributes to his campaign."

"That's the way I have it figured, but I don't have anything concrete yet."

"Good work, Dalton. Let me know what else you find." Shep hung up and thoughtfully scratched the stubble on his chin.

So Burke pushes a merger through for Winston.

But that certainly didn't seem like enough to compel Winston to finance an entire political campaign. Maybe a substantial contribution, but not the whole campaign.

There must be more to it.

While Shep was talking with Dalton, Mac knelt beside his bed to talk to a close friend. It was a nightly conversation he'd begun as a young boy, and one he'd shared with his wife and children ever since they had entered his life. The subject of the conversation covered many topics over the years, and tonight's began with the burden Mac carried from the campaign.

"Holy Father, I don't understand what you have prepared before me or why you are leading me down this difficult path. But I do know that whatever the answers are, you knew them before the world began. I commit myself to your will and know that you are always in complete control of all circumstances."

Mac continued praying for the better part of thirty minutes before climbing into bed. It was almost one o'clock in the morning, and the campaign had an extremely busy next day scheduled. But his nightly conversation with God could not be missed.

Bad Dog Saloon, east of Jackson, Tennessee

"Gimme a bottle of Jack in the black," Jed demanded as he crushed his sixth empty Colt 45 can and tossed it on the floor behind the bar. The bartender complied and slid over a bottle of Jack Daniel's whiskey. Jed's eyes were already bloodshot, and it was time to finish the job. The one hundred dollars he had in his pocket when he arrived provided for a liquid dinner and more. He didn't care how he felt in the morning. He had called Ruth earlier and told her not to wait up. He'd be home when he got there.

The Bad Dog Saloon was a regular haunt of Jed's. He stopped by every Friday after work for a couple of beers with his buddies before going home. It was an old, dilapidated wooden building, but the regulars didn't mind, and the health department stayed away. The outside was painted white, and the windows and doors were trimmed in red. Folklore said that the combination kept evil spirits out. The only spirits the proprietor said he wanted on the inside of the bar were the ones in a bottle. Above the outside of the front door was a large painting of the face of a bulldog. Hence the name.

Jed was the only patron remaining at 2:00 a.m. when the bartender announced that it was closing time. Jed had closed up the Bad Dog on several occasions in his younger days, but never during the week. He staggered out the front door and fell off the small wooden porch onto the gravel and dirt that covered the parking lot. His clothes and body were filthy and smelly from working all day and drinking all night, but he didn't care. He managed to get to his feet and find his way to his pickup.

The bartender locked up at 3:00 a.m. When he saw Jed passed out in the front seat of his pickup in the parking lot, he decided that was the best thing for Jed.

Sleep it off, Jed, the bartender thought as he pulled out of the parking lot onto Highway 412. He would call Ruth later in the morning and tell her where to find her husband.

CHAPTER SIX

Thompson mansion, Jackson, Tennessee

Naomi McClellan had been in the kitchen an hour before Jesse Thompson awoke Wednesday morning at his customary six o'clock. The sun was only half-crested over the eastern horizon, so she knew that Earline Thompson, Jesse's wife, who slept in the bedroom down the hall from Jesse, wouldn't awake for a while yet.

The Thompson mansion was a palatial two-story plantation house northwest of Jackson, just outside the city limits. It took Naomi twenty minutes to drive there from her house in the eastern part of the city. Although no longer an operational plantation, it was still surrounded by the best pasture land in all of Madison County.

"Good morning, Naomi," Jesse called as he entered the kitchen and sat at the head of the table.

Naomi was less than thrilled at Jesse's arrival. She hated him passionately . . . and feared him. Even so, for the last thirty of her sixty years, she had worked at the Thompson mansion. She had tried to find other employment, but all she knew how to do was be a maid to the Thompsons. And the pay was more than she could have made working at a restaurant or a convenience store or a hotel. She had grown accustomed to wearing the white polyester blouse and pants, similar to ones worn by hospital personnel, which Mrs. Thompson required as a uniform.

"Mornin'," Naomi replied. "The newspaper's on the table, and breakfast'll be ready in a minute."

Even at fifty-five Jesse was still an imposing figure. But the years were beginning to catch up with him. His gray hair was thinning on top, and some of his scalp was visible. His face was leathery from years of exposure to the sun, and small wrinkles had developed under his eyes. Brown age spots covered his hands.

The smell of bacon and eggs wafted through the kitchen as Naomi finished cooking the same breakfast she always prepared for Jesse. She sighed inwardly. Her life was relegated to preparing meals and cleaning house for the one man she hated with every ounce in her body. Her plight in finding a job elsewhere wasn't helped much by the fact that she had never finished the third grade and could barely spell her own name. Her husband had left her with a small child, a son, over twenty-five years ago. The last she'd heard was that her husband was living somewhere in Chicago.

She'd been glad when he left. The physical abuse had been unbearable. She still carried reminders of him on her face.

Naomi's life had never been easy, but she didn't mind hard work. She had promised herself years earlier that somehow, some way, she was going to make sure her son had a better life. The women in her family had served the Thompson family for generations, but she was determined to be the last Thompson servant.

Naomi was surprised when Earline entered the kitchen in a huff just after seven o'clock. Earline rarely arose before nine. Her peach-colored bathrobe and white nightgown were wrinkled and unkempt. Her gray-streaked auburn hair was still mangled from the previous night's sleep, and without makeup her skin appeared thin and transparent.

Earline's lips barely moved as she spoke. "A cup of coffee, Naomi." She plopped down in the chair at the end of the table opposite her husband.

Jesse hardly acknowledged Earline's entrance into the room. He didn't lower the newspaper to see his wife, nor did he greet her.

Naomi was well aware that Earline despised Jesse about as much as she did. She'd even heard Earline say on more than one occasion that she wished Jesse were dead.

Naomi prepared the cup of coffee just the way Mrs. Thompson liked it—with two cubes of sugar and a dash of half-and-half—and set it in front of her.

Naomi couldn't help but feel pity for Mrs. Thompson because of the way Mr. Thompson had treated her all these years.

Steam rose from the cup, and Earline blew lightly on the brown liquid to cool it before taking a sip. "Thank you, Naomi."

Naomi knew Earline well. Morning coffee always calmed the woman. After one sip her tone was less threatening.

"Do you want somethin' to eat?" Naomi inquired, knowing the answer would be no. Earline hardly ever ate breakfast.

"Not right now," Earline replied. "Maybe I'll have some fruit in a little while."

Jesse finished his breakfast hurriedly and stood to leave. Evidently he'd already been in the same room with Earline longer than he could tolerate.

"I'm going to check on the cattle before going to the bank," Jesse stated to whoever was listening.

But the comment wasn't aimed at anyone in particular. His words never were, Naomi thought. It was as if, to Jesse Thompson, everybody else was beneath him.

"I'll see you tonight at dinner," Jesse called as he closed the door between the kitchen and the garage.

FBI headquarters, Washington DC

Deputy Director Charles Armacost was in his office deep inside the J. Edgar Hoover Building and had been since five thirty. He liked the quietness of the early morning. No phone calls, no interruptions. It was the perfect working environment, and he was a workaholic.

Just ask his two ex-wives. Charlie had missed his kids' Little League baseball games, ballet recitals, and bedtime stories, and they never forgave him. They were all grown now, and he barely saw them. He had never seen the youngest of his three grandchildren, and the other two only one time—Christmas 1998.

Charlie had spent the early part of his career as a field agent and had frequently relocated from one office to another. He was proud of the fact that he was decorated. It was his investigation that thwarted Lynette "Squeaky" Fromme's assassination attempt on President Ford. He received a commendation for his efforts and had begun to ascend the ladder within the Bureau. Charlie also led the Bureau's part of the invasion of Panama when Noriega was arrested. That ultimately led to his promotion to deputy director, and he would have been named director if the Republicans had regained the presidency in the last election.

Just after seven thirty Assistant Deputy Director George McCullough knocked on the frame to Charlie's open office door.

"Come in," Charlie said without looking up from the report he was reading.

There was a slight hesitation before George entered. "I've got something I think you should see."

Charlie glanced up. He could hear the reluctance in George's voice.

George dimmed the lights and pushed a button on a television remote control that was on Charlie's desk. The bank of television monitors mounted to one wall in Charlie's office switched to a still frame, showing the face of a Latin American in sunglasses.

"Surveillance cameras at Miami International captured this picture of a passenger arriving from Cancun Monday morning," George reported. He pushed the button again, and the monitors switched to another photograph. "This is a file photograph of Raoul Miguel Flores. He's a member of the Hermillo Family in Bogotá. He trained as an assassin under the notorious Carlos the Jackal in South America. We lost track of Raoul after the assassination of President Marcos of Mexico in 2000." George switched the monitors back to the first photograph. "We think this is Raoul. His passport scanned the name of Pedro Gonzales, but we're confident that it's Raoul."

Charlie leaned back in his chair as George went through the presentation. Having anyone trained by the Jackal in the United States was trouble enough. But the Jackal's top prodigy! The thought made Charlie shiver. An assassin of that caliber wasn't hired to murder just anybody. When an assassin such as the Jackal or Raoul made a hit, it was done as a statement, political or otherwise.

Worse, the photograph of Raoul was almost forty-eight hours old. That made Charlie furious . . . and afraid.

"Why didn't we identify him sooner?" demanded Charlie, staring at the row of monitors bearing the image of Raoul.

"The customs agent thought he looked suspicious but forgot to mention it to her supervisors until yesterday afternoon. They pulled the video and sent it to the Bureau office in Miami. We got it this morning."

"Where is he now?"

"We think he boarded a plane bound for Memphis," replied George. "The office in Memphis is reviewing video of all arrivals from Monday."

Charlie rubbed his flattop in anguish. "Let me know what they find."

George left, and Charlie continued staring at the frozen face of Raoul Miguel Flores. He removed his glasses and rubbed the area of his nose between his eyes. "This is all I need," he muttered sarcastically.

Thompson cattle farm, Jackson, Tennessee

The entrance to the farm was approximately two miles from Jesse's house. He owned fifty head of cattle and kept them mainly as a hobby. As he neared the farm, Jesse noticed a small black pickup parked a few hundred yards beyond the entrance to the field. Someone must have had mechanical trouble during the night and left the truck there until it could be repaired. A disabled vehicle on this rural road wasn't unusual. Jesse decided that if it was still there tomorrow morning, he'd call the sheriff and have it towed away.

The gate to the field was locked, just like Jesse left it the day before. He went through a ritual of opening the gate, driving through, and relocking it before proceeding.

The narrow field road was barely more than two worn paths separated by a swath of grass the width of a truck axle. The road led three hundred yards to an old wooden barn with a tin roof. The barn was worn from years of exposure to the elements. Its once brown exterior was now gray and discolored. A layer of rust covered most of the tin roof. Despite its deterioration, the barn still served its purpose of protecting bales of hay and cattle feed from the weather.

As Jesse entered the pasture of green rye grass, he could see the Black Angus already gathering around the front of the barn. *Creatures of habit,* Jesse thought, as the cattle lined up along the feeding troughs. They recognized his truck and knew it was feeding time.

A man lay undetected in a wooded area two hundred yards away, watching as a white pickup rolled slowly toward the barn. Clouds of dust rose up behind the vehicle and then settled softly to the ground.

He glanced at his watch. *7:40. Right on time.*

He looked back at his prey. A man with the same routine was easy to kill. A small hill in the wooded area near the barn provided the best position from which to make the hit. He'd discovered the area the day before when he'd scouted the farm. It had plenty of underbrush to provide cover and was slightly elevated from the target destination.

The camouflage clothing he wore blended precisely with the underbrush, making him virtually invisible. He lay on his stomach near the crest of the rise, peering at his mark below. As he kept his eye on the white truck of his enemy, he reached into a pocket on the outside of his right leg and removed two brass-colored .308 hollow-point bullets.

He thought of every victim as the enemy. It didn't matter that he had never met any of his victims or that he knew little about them. They stood between him and payday, and that made all of them the enemy.

Hardly a muscle in his body twitched as he slowly slid the two bullets into the chamber of his Tango 51 sniper rifle and heard the click of metal against metal. He rarely needed the second but wanted it as a backup. He preferred hollow points because they made a small entry point but an exit hole the size of a grapefruit. With his rifle loaded, he lay motionless, waiting for the precise instant to complete his assignment.

Bad Dog Saloon, east of Jackson, Tennessee

Jed awoke after sleeping slumped over for several hours in the cab of his pickup in front of the Bad Dog.

It was the day scheduled for the foreclosure on his house. A sudden pain stabbed him in his stomach. He quickly chased it away with anger and a sip from the bottle of Jack Daniel's he found in the seat with him.

He had no intentions of losing his home. If his lawyer wouldn't help, he'd just have to convince the great Jesse Lamar Thompson himself to stop the foreclosure.

Jed left the Bad Dog and miraculously made his way across town without colliding with any other vehicles or being stopped by a member of the Jackson Police Department. He took another long, hard drink from the whiskey bottle as he drove along Old Medina Road toward the Thompson farm. It was well known that Jesse Thompson stopped by his cattle farm every morning before going to his office at the bank.

The alcohol in his blood system negatively affected his motor skills, and his old, dented, red Dodge truck swerved from side to side, crossing the centerline of Old Medina repeatedly. He ran off the shoulder on the right-hand side of the road, scattering dirt and gravel, and then whipped the steering wheel to the left, barely avoiding going into a drainage ditch. That overreaction almost caused him to broadside a small black pickup parked on the side of the road. Somehow he managed to straighten his front wheels and avoided hitting the other truck by mere inches.

Jed was going too fast to turn in to the Thompson-farm entrance, but he tried anyway. He came to a sliding stop with the front half of his truck hanging off the shoulder of the road. He wasn't surprised to see that the gate was locked. Jesse had to be there, though, because the white pickup was parked at the barn.

Jed was determined not to leave until he'd convinced Jesse to stop the foreclosure.

CHAPTER SEVEN

Thompson cattle farm, Jackson, Tennessee

The assassin lying on his belly heard the commotion at the entrance of the Thompson farm as a red Dodge pickup pulled up. He thought about aborting his mission, but only for an instant. He had to make the hit today, and nothing was stopping him. He had been in the area too long already and had been seen by too many people. He might have to give his employer two hits for the price of one. First things first, though.

He looked back at his mark. Slowly he raised the Tango 51 to his shoulder and peered through the scope on the top of the barrel. He panned the rifle back and forth from bumper to bumper along the outside of the white truck, waiting on his target to exit the driver's-side door. The rifle was equipped with a suppressor to muffle the sound. No one but the shooter would hear the deadly shot. Through the scope he could see Jesse Thompson sitting in the cab of the truck and knew it would be only a few seconds before his victim got out.

As Jesse sat in his white pickup, he couldn't help but laugh. The host of the talk-radio show was berating Mac Foster over his position on abortion.

The Republicans will never get it, Jesse thought as he turned off the engine. *There aren't enough religious people in the country to elect a pro-life candidate, so why campaign on that issue?* It was so simple. The Democrats had figured that out long ago, and that was why Vice President Burke would be elected president this year.

Jesse chuckled again at Mac Foster's political naiveté and got out of the truck. "Stupid Republicans," he muttered to himself.

The mark was now in the open. The assassin aligned the crosshairs in the scope on the target's head, two hundred yards away. He slid the safety mechanism to Off and patiently waited.

Turn your head a little more to the left, he urged, following his mark through the scope. When the mark unknowingly complied, the assassin squeezed the trigger without hesitation. The muffled sound was barely audible and certainly could not be heard by the person sitting in the truck at the entrance to the farm, whoever he was. The bullet found its intended target, and the mark fell to the ground.

Another easy five million, the shooter thought as he lowered the gun from his shoulder.

He had killed so often that it came without emotion.

Jed, still at least half drunk, saw Jesse as he stepped out of his truck and took a step toward the old barn. Just the sight of the banker enraged Jed even more. He couldn't imagine anyone more ruthless than Jesse Thompson. If Jesse would not listen to him and agree to stop the foreclosure, then Jed would have to use the small .22 caliber handgun in the glove box to convince him otherwise.

Jed firmly believed that Jesse had repeatedly stolen money from African Americans. He had heard the stories of Jesse's bank foreclosing on homes owned by African Americans when they were just a few days late with their mortgage payment. And how African Americans paid a higher interest rate than white people for the same type of loan. It was going to stop, even if Jed had to kill Mr. Thompson.

Jed sat in his truck, his anger swelling by the second.

Then something unexpected happened. Jesse slumped against the side of his truck and crumpled to the ground in a heap. The startled cattle stampeded away, some trampling over Jesse.

Jed rubbed his blurry eyes and looked again. He had to be imagining this. But no, Jesse was still lying on the ground. Jed opened the door to his truck and stumbled out.

"Mr. Thompson!" Jed yelled across the pasture.

No response.

FBI headquarters, Washington DC

George McCullough reported back to Charlie Armacost that the Memphis office had found video of Raoul Flores exiting a plane just after noon on Monday.

"Issue an all-points bulletin to every law-enforcement office within a one-hundred-mile radius of Memphis," Charlie instructed. "Alert the airport, the bus stations, and the train depots. He could be anywhere, but if he's still out there, I want him."

Charlie had a standing meeting with the director at ten o'clock. He decided not to mention Raoul. Not yet anyway. He wanted more information first. Since the director was a political appointee with no experience in the Bureau, Charlie figured that if he mentioned Raoul, the director would tell the attorney general. Then the two of them would decide that the CIA was better equipped to handle the search for an international assassin than the Bureau. Charlie couldn't run the risk that the AG would pull jurisdiction. He'd wait until after they caught Raoul to tell the director about him.

Thompson cattle farm, Jackson, Tennessee

Still lying on his stomach, the assassin peered through the rifle scope at the large unknown man as he exited the red Dodge. Slowly the assassin ejected the empty shell casing from his rifle. It was automatically replaced with the remaining bullet. Mentally he identified the African American as the second mark . . . and he was in the open. The shooter did a quick calculation. The second mark was too far for a clean shot. If he fired now, he probably wouldn't hit the intended target. Worse, it might alert the second mark to his location. He couldn't risk that exposure.

Removing his finger from the trigger, he studied the man. *Only an assassin who makes a mistake gets caught*, he told himself. And the hunter didn't plan on becoming the prey.

His instincts kicked back in. He'd been in much more precarious positions before.

He continued to lie quietly, waiting for an opportunity to escape.

Jed stumbled toward the entrance to Jesse's farm. Once he reached the gate, he stepped on the bottom slat, tried to climb it, and fell over the top, landing on his back with a *thud* on the other side. Struggling to his feet, he began running along the dusty field road toward the place where Jesse lay.

When Jed was within twenty feet or so, he knew instinctively that something was terribly wrong. He stopped dead in his tracks. "Mr. Thompson, are you all right?"

Again, no response.

Jed's breathing was heavy and labored. He walked slowly the remaining twenty feet, whispering "Mr. Thompson" over and over again as he approached. As he drew closer, he could see that the back half of Jesse's head was completely missing, and a pool of blood had collected around what remained. Splattered blood and brain matter covered the front left fender and hood of the pickup truck, streaking its white exterior. Not knowing what else to do, Jed knelt down, grabbed Mr. Thompson's left shoulder, and rolled him onto his back. Mr. Thompson's eyes were open wide but were not seeing. There was a single hole the size of a penny in the middle of his forehead.

Jed's stomach began to churn.

When the assassin realized he hadn't been detected, he saw his chance for escape without having to give away a free hit. Shoving the empty shell casing into his pocket, he ran through the woods toward his parked vehicle on the road near the entrance to the farm. He slowed only to slip between the two strands of barbed wire that formed one section of the fence.

His flight took him past the red truck of the second mark. In order to divert the police authorities' attention, he stopped at the second mark's truck just long enough to place his rifle in the bed. He covered it with the army green tarpaulin already in the truck.

Dashing the remaining one hundred feet to his vehicle, the assassin sped away from the scene. He would not remove his surgical latex gloves until he'd properly disposed of the Chevy S10 and its contents.

Jed McClellan was sweating profusely. The heat and humidity were squeezing him of every drop of hydration, and his heart was racing. The sight of Mr. Thompson lying there with his blood and brains soaking into the ground made Jed want to run, but he couldn't stand up. So he began to crawl away from the corpse. He had crawled only a few feet, however, when he began to vomit violently . . . until he had nothing left to give.

Falling over on his back in exhaustion, moaning and groaning, he stared up at the cloudless blue sky.

After a few seconds he realized something horrible. The person who had killed Jesse Thompson was probably still close by.

Jed stumbled to his feet in terror and staggered to the bed of Jesse Thompson's truck. He braced himself against the tailgate and frantically scanned the pasture and trees in all directions.

Nothing.

Then he heard the sound of an ignition starting. He squinted back toward the road as the small black truck he had almost hit earlier sped past the entrance to the farm. Still clinging to the side of the pickup, Jed made his way to the passenger-side door. He opened it and saw Jesse Thompson's wireless phone on the seat. He dialed 9-1-1.

"What is the nature of your emergency?" the dispatcher asked.

"A man's been shot," Jed replied, still trying to catch his breath. He wiped his face and mouth with the tail of his shirt before continuing. "He's been shot in the head. The whole back of his head's been blown off." His voice became more animated with each phrase.

"Slow down, sir," the dispatcher said calmly. "Please tell me your name."

"Jedediah McClellan."

"Where are you?"

"I'm at the Thompson cattle farm off Old Medina Road north of town."

"Do you know how far it is to the nearest intersection?"

Agitated at the questioning, Jed barked, "No, I don't know. Just send some help quick!"

"Do you recognize the victim?"

"Jesse Thompson," Jed answered. His inebriated mind was finally beginning to register that his enemy was dead.

"Sir, did you say Jesse Thompson?" the dispatcher asked.

"Yes, Jesse Thompson."

"Medical personnel and sheriff deputies are on their way."

Birmingham, Alabama

"Tell me what the overnight national polls show," Mac prompted when he and Shep were safely in Mac's campaign limousine after their early-morning flight from Detroit.

"They still show you trailing by 10 points, sir," Shep replied, knowing that Mac expected the answer. The campaign was stagnant, slowly dying on the vine. They needed something to pump new life into it.

"What have you heard about Burke's campaign financing?"

Shep paused. He knew he couldn't tell Mac about Dalton. Mac would demand that the investigation end immediately. But without the investigation, Shep believed, Mac would lose any chance of overtaking the vice president.

Shep masked his secret by not looking Mac in the eyes. "The Senate may announce that it's conducting an inquiry. That would at least give us something to talk to the voters about."

Mac stared out the window as they passed by modest homes. "It doesn't look good, does it, Shep?"

"No, sir, it doesn't," Shep replied. "But maybe our luck will change soon."

"We're not relying on luck, Shep. If it's in God's plan for me to be president—and I believe it is—then he'll intervene."

There was nothing more to talk about. Shep knew Mac was right. God was in control. Neither spoke until the limousine pulled into a local elementary school for a question-and-answer session with a group of fifth graders.

CHAPTER EIGHT

NBC studio, Rockefeller Plaza, New York

"I met Ed when we were in law school at Yale," Millie Burke said, responding to a question from Annette Stewart of NBC. She was being interviewed on the morning talk show about her best-selling book on the feminist revolution. "He went to college at Vanderbilt, and I graduated from Columbia. That was in 1972. We married in the summer of 1975."

"You maintain a very active schedule, Mrs. Burke. Are you heavily involved in Vice President Burke's campaign?"

"Absolutely," Millie replied. "I can't think of anything better for our country than for Ed Burke to be president." No one would question that she was an essential part of the Burke-for-President campaign. She was intelligent and articulate but also domineering. Very few people crossed her. She was involved in every major campaign decision from fund-raising to speech writing. And she loved it.

In her younger days Millie had been moderately attractive, but never a ravishing beauty. Years of a strained marriage had taken their toll, though, and she struggled to maintain an attractive appearance. She hated to look at herself in the mirror because her body was now the shape of a pear rather than the number eight. Wrinkles encircled her eyes, and her gray-auburn hair always seemed to need attention. Millie's greatest disappointment, though, was that Ed hardly noticed her at all.

After their wedding Ed and Millie had moved to Nashville. Both began working for large law firms that allowed their pursuit of liberal causes. Millie wanted to run for Congress but knew a woman had little chance of running a successful campaign in a Southern state. So she encouraged Ed to run. And he successfully won the seat for United States Congressman for Tennessee's Fifth Congressional District in 1980.

Both Ed and Millie thrived in Washington. He quickly rose in the ranks of the Democrat-controlled House of Representatives. She became a staff attorney for the American Civil Liberties Union. Neither could pinpoint exactly when they had begun to grow apart.

Millie discovered Ed's infidelity during his third congressional term and had confronted him about it. At first he denied it, but eventually he confessed—probably, she ruminated, because it really didn't matter to him what she thought. She considered divorcing him several times, but she liked the Washington environment and the lifestyle that came with it too much to follow through. In the end she chose simply to tolerate his affairs.

By the time they moved into the vice-president's house, Ed and Millie had not slept in the same bedroom, much less the same bed, for years. Ironically, now that Ed was running for president of the United States, Millie was colluding with his staff to keep his affairs secret. She wanted the power of being First Lady almost as much as he wanted to be president. She warned him to stay away from other women until the election was over. They couldn't afford any mistakes. Ed told her that he would, but both knew he was lying.

"Tell me about your book," Annette suggested as the interview continued. All the questions had been preapproved by Millie's staff, so there would be no surprises.

"It's a wonderful book that starts with Betsy Ross and traces the history of the evolution of women in politics through the years," replied Millie. "There are so many women leaders no one knows about. I thought it was time someone gave these women the recognition they deserve."

"You are also one of these women, aren't you, Mrs. Burke?" asked Annette as she pitched another softball.

Millie shook her head sincerely. "I do not belong in the same category with these women." Humility was not her best trait, but she could bring it out when necessary. "I have tried to be a good wife and mother. And being married to the vice president has given me numerous opportunities to speak. With those opportunities, I have tried to educate the public about the impact of women in politics."

"Do you think one day we'll have a female president?" Annette asked.

Millie wanted to say that she planned on being president one day herself but knew now was not the time for such a statement. So instead she replied, "I certainly hope so. I think a woman would do an excellent job. Right now, though, I'm concentrating on my husband's campaign."

Out of the corner of her eye, Millie saw the show's director hold up his right hand, signaling to Annette that five seconds remained until the next commercial break.

Annette began to conclude the interview. "Thank you, Mrs. Burke, for being with us this morning." She smiled broadly at Millie.

"Thank you for inviting me." Millie returned the smile.

"We'll be right back after these messages," Annette said into camera number two as the program went to a commercial break.

The director announced they were off the air, and Millie left the sitting area to meet Zoe Newton, her press secretary, backstage. Millie spoke to the producer and other network personnel for a few minutes before she and Zoe and the rest of her entourage began walking toward the exit.

"How do you think it went?" Millie asked Zoe as they walked along a corridor in the rear of the studio.

"Perfect," replied Zoe. "You appeared confident but not arrogant. Very First Lady–like."

"Good. That's the impression I wanted to convey."

One of Millie's aides opened the exit door, and Millie and Zoe stepped through it into a throng of supporters awaiting her appearance. Millie greeted the crowd warmly and shook hands with several people before climbing into the car that would take her to her next appointment—a luncheon with the White Plains Garden Club. As the group cheered and clapped for her, one female well-wisher yelled, "I wish you were running for president!"

Millie smiled and waved. *One day I will.*

Hilton Head Island, South Carolina

Only a few palmetto trees and the ecological dunes that ran the entire length of the Atlantic side of the island stood between the palatial house and the water's edge. Claudia Duval had finished her daily morning jog thirty minutes ago, showered, and was now enjoying her breakfast of a bagel with strawberry cream cheese and orange juice on the veranda. She had nothing planned for today and decided she would spend the day shopping in Savannah.

The morning tide was almost at its peak as the cool ocean breeze ruffled the edges of her newspaper. Occasionally she looked up at the tranquil Atlantic. She stopped reading to watch the sun separate itself from the eastern horizon and chase away the haze. It would be another glorious day.

The dorsal fins of a school of dolphins were visible as they chased a shrimp boat returning to port with its morning catch. Seagulls, kingfishers, and sandpipers wafted in the gentle wind currents above the ocean's surface.

Claudia sighed. *What a beautiful place.*

Hilton Head had the ability to invigorate her, but its serenity was also relaxing.

The house next door was usually unoccupied, but today Claudia saw a middle-aged man with closely cropped brown hair standing on the balcony that overlooked the pool. She didn't recognize the man, but she waved to be neighborly, and the man returned the greeting.

"Do you think she suspects anything?" a voice from inside the house asked the man on the balcony.

"No," Agent Al Moyers replied. "She probably thinks we're vacationers who have rented the house for the season."

Satisfied that Claudia Duval didn't suspect anything, Al walked back into the upper level of the house. There he found his partner, Agent Bill Osborne, examining the woman next door through binoculars. The night before, while Claudia was out, Al and Bill had planted listening devices in every room in her house. They could now hear every word that she—or anybody else in the house—uttered. After Claudia had returned home, Bill had sneaked into the open garage and attached a tracking device on the underside of her white Jaguar XJ7 convertible. The device would allow them to trace Claudia's car using a Global Positioning System, or GPS.

Al knew that Claudia Duval was thirty-seven years old, married once but divorced, and enjoyed listening to classical music. But the photograph in the dossier did not do her justice. She was beautiful—tan skin, shoulder-length blonde hair that she constantly tucked behind her ears, and intoxicating, deep blue eyes. This would be one assignment that Al and Bill would enjoy.

They watched as Claudia left the veranda and retreated to her bedroom to dress for the day. Thirty minutes later her Jaguar left the garage. Al and Bill allowed her a head start of two minutes before leaving in a Chevy Tahoe that was parked in their garage. Al drove while Bill followed Claudia's car with the GPS in his briefcase. She left the Palmetto Dunes Plantation and turned north on William Hilton Parkway. In a few moments she would cross the bridge that connected the island to the mainland over the Intracoastal Waterway. Al and Bill wouldn't be very far behind.

En route to Savannah, Georgia

Claudia left the island, traveled Highway 17 through Bluffton, South Carolina, and drove toward the city of Savannah, Georgia, which was located barely across the Georgia state line and along the Savannah River. The weather was pleasant, so she drove with the convertible top down, her honey-colored hair fluttering in the warm coastal breeze. Five miles before she reached the Savannah River, she could begin to see the pinnacle of the Savannah River Bridge in the distance. As she drew closer, the bridge began to take on the appearance of tall, white sails of an armada sailing into Savannah Harbor from the Atlantic. She had seen it hundreds of times before, but each time it still took her breath away.

After crossing the bridge and entering the city, she parked her car in a public parking garage on the bluff overlooking the river and traversed the cobblestone steps to the bustling River Street below. At the bottom of the steps an elderly African American sat on a makeshift stool and played his brass saxophone. Claudia stood for a moment, listening to the melody, and then dropped a five-dollar bill in the man's open saxophone case. The music faded away as she ducked in and out of several shops along the cobblestone street.

Claudia had shopped River Street before, but today something was different.

She had an eerie feeling that someone was watching her.

Thompson cattle farm, Jackson, Tennessee

Sheriff Craig West waited in his patrol car at the entrance to the Thompson farm while Deputy Butch Johnson used his department-issued bolt cutters to remove the lock. After the gate was open, the sheriff raced his patrol car, blue lights flashing, through the opening and down the field road toward Jesse Thompson's white pickup. He was followed closely by Deputy Billy Laymon. Craig had instructed Butch to remain at the gate to ensure that only authorized personnel entered the property.

Craig and Billy found Jed McClellan sitting on the ground, leaning against the left-rear tire of Jesse Thompson's vehicle. His knees were pulled up under his chin in an almost upright fetal position. He was less than ten feet from the dead body. Craig stared at the lifeless body of Jesse Thompson for several seconds before he squatted down beside Jed, his face less than a foot away.

"Jed," Sheriff West began, "tell me what happened."

"I don't know, Sheriff," Jed replied in a monotone. His gaze was fixed on a tree across the field. He appeared to be in a trance. "I was sittin' in my truck back there, waitin' on Mr. Thompson, and the next thing I know he's fallin' down on the ground. I yelled for him and started runnin' this way. When I got here, I found him like this. That's all I know."

"Did you hear a gunshot?" the sheriff questioned.

"No, sir," Jed answered, still staring straight ahead.

Billy squatted beside Jed, opposite Craig, and joined the conversation. "You been drinkin', Jed? 'Cause you smell like whiskey."

Jed finally blinked his eyes and cocked his head slightly in Deputy Laymon's direction. "A little last night, but I ain't drunk."

"Billy, get the breathalyzer and check Jed's alcohol level," Craig instructed.

Both officers stood up, and the sheriff peered down at the man who was quickly becoming a murder suspect. "If you're not drunk, then you won't mind letting us test you now, will you, Jed?"

We still know how to handle our blacks in Madison County, Craig thought.

Billy Laymon retrieved the breathalyzer from the trunk of his patrol car and shoved the mouthpiece into Jed's face, demanding he blow into it.

Jed hesitated and then grabbed the breathalyzer with his right hand to steady it. He blew one short breath into the mouthpiece.

As Craig West waited for the results, he turned away from Jed and walked over to the dead body of Jesse Lamar Thompson.

A few seconds later Billy rather cheerfully relayed the result. "It registered .13, Sheriff."

Sheriff West gave further instructions without turning around. "Put Jed in the back of your patrol car," he told the deputy. "And radio Butch to search Jed's truck. Also, call dispatch and have an investigator sent out here. No one comes within a half-mile of this place until homicide is finished. We're going to need a couple of extra deputies to secure the area."

The sheriff turned and watched as Billy forced Jed to stand, cuffed his hands behind his back, led him the few feet to the patrol car, and patted him down before opening the left rear door. Jed climbed inside the back seat without a struggle.

After securing Jed, Billy sat down behind the steering wheel and got on the CB radio to Butch. "SO 2 to SO 6, over," he called into the radio.

"SO 6, go ahead," Butch Johnson blared back.

"Butch, Jed blew a .13 on the breathalyzer. Sheriff wants you to search his truck."

"Roger," Butch responded.

"SO 2 to central dispatch, over," Deputy Laymon continued.

"Central dispatch, over," the female dispatcher replied over the radio.

"Bonnie, will you call Lieutenant Sloan in homicide and tell him that the sheriff wants him out here at the Thompson farm on Old Medina Road? It looks like we got ourselves our first homicide of the year."

After hearing Billy comply with his instructions, Craig crouched his six-foot-two frame over the lifeless body of Jesse Thompson. He removed his hat, revealing his red hair and bushy eyebrows, and wiped the sweat from his face with the back of his right hand and wrist. It sure was hot. His fair skin was going to burn fast under today's scorching sun.

Department procedures prohibited him from touching the body, but that didn't prevent him from examining the fatal wound. Immediately he noticed the precise location of the bullet hole in the middle of Jesse's forehead and how clean the entry was. The dead man's eyes were still open, and that bothered Craig. So he violated his own department's procedure and slowly rubbed his hand over Jesse's face to close his eyes.

He couldn't believe Jesse Thompson was dead. He and Jesse had been friends for thirty years. Jesse had helped him get elected the first time in 1984 and had made sure he was reelected every time since then. Jesse had also supplemented Craig's income with monthly envelopes full of cash, and Craig always complied when Jesse needed him to look the other way or carry out a threat against someone who was causing trouble for Jesse.

Even though Jesse had only been dead about fifteen minutes, the hot summer sun and humidity were not being kind to the corpse. Craig heard footsteps and looked up. Billy Laymon handed him a blanket. Craig used it to cover Jesse Thompson's body.

As directed by the sheriff, Deputy Butch Johnson began his investigation of Jed's old red Dodge truck. He found the driver's-side door still ajar. It creaked as Butch pushed it open wider to look inside. A whiskey bottle in a brown paper sack lay on the driver's-side floorboard. Some of the whiskey had spilled out and formed a puddle around the mouth of the bottle. The bench-style cloth seat was torn in several places, and the vinyl dashboard was cracked above the radio. Even though the door to the truck had been open, the interior still reeked of alcohol.

Butch wiped the beads of sweat from his forehead with his handkerchief before walking around to the rear. The bed contained tools, empty beer cans, and an old spare tire. An army green tarpaulin covered the rest of the contents, so the deputy leaned over to pull it back.

"What is that?" he mumbled to himself in disbelief.

He threw the tarpaulin back further to fully reveal what lay underneath . . . and froze.

He'd found the murder weapon. His heartbeat quickened from the adrenaline rush, and his mouth became dry. He swallowed hard, trying to moisten his throat.

Racing back to his patrol car, he grabbed the CB radio mic and said frantically, "SO 6 to SO 2, over."

Billy and Craig were still crouched beside the corpse of Jesse Thompson when they heard Butch's excited voice over the radio. Billy opened the driver's-side door and responded, "SO 2, over."

"Billy." The deputy's voice crackled loudly over the radio. "You won't believe what I just found. I was searching Jed's truck just like you told me to, and there was this green tarpaulin in the bed. I didn't know whether to move it or not, because I wasn't sure what we were looking for."

"Butch," interrupted Billy, "just tell me what you found."

His interest piqued, Craig joined Billy at his patrol car.

"Like I was saying," continued Butch excitedly, "there was this tarpaulin in the back of the truck, and I pulled it back. You won't believe what was under it."

"Settle down, Butch, and tell me," Billy stated.

"A Tango 51 sniper rifle with a scope and suppressor."

Sheriff West stared at Deputy Laymon. Neither spoke, but the sheriff could see the disbelief on the deputy's face.

Five seconds of shock elapsed.

Then Butch inquired, "Billy, are you there? What do you want me to do?"

Billy raised the mic to his mouth and said, "Hold on." He looked at the sheriff for instructions.

Sheriff West studied Jed, sitting in the backseat of the patrol car. "Tell Butch to tag the rifle and secure it in the trunk of his car. He will need to log it in the evidence room himself. I don't want any chain of custody problems. Then arrest Jed for murder, and take him to central booking. I'll wait here on homicide and the coroner."

En route to Memphis International Airport

The assassin complied with all traffic laws on his trip from the Thompson farm to Memphis International Airport. His flight was scheduled to depart at 10:00 a.m., and he would arrive at the designated gate with only minutes to spare. Just before entering the corporate limits of Memphis, he dialed a preset number on the wireless phone. The call was answered, but no one uttered a sound from the other end of the line.

"He's dead," he stated to whoever was listening and pressed End to disconnect.

The wireless phone, the map, the picture of the mark, and everything else in his possession associated with this contract would be destroyed before he reached the Memphis airport.

CHAPTER NINE

Jackson, Tennessee

Golf was one of Jake Reed's favorite hobbies, although he hardly found time to get away from the office. Today was one of those rare occasions. He had played several of the courses in the area, and the Par 5 fifth hole at the local country club was one he always enjoyed.

The setting around the hole was picturesque. The tee box backed into the shadows of a grove of grand oak trees. Other species of trees stood like sentinels along the beginning section of the hole, and the green, 525 yards ahead, was protected by several deep sand traps. Floral trees and shrubbery flanked the rear of the tee box and likewise behind the green. As he addressed his teed golf ball, Jake scanned down the fairway to a narrow landing that was bathed in early-morning sunlight. *That's where I need to land it.*

High school and collegiate baseball had developed a very natural, fluid swinging motion that helped Jake carry a single-digit handicap. He swung his new driver—one he'd purchased after watching a late-night infomercial that promised greater distance and better accuracy—and heard the *ping* of solid contact with the ball. Looking up, he watched the ball sail at least 240 yards down the middle of the fairway. It landed and rolled another twenty or thirty yards before it stopped.

I might have a go at the green in two today.

Jake twirled the club in his hands as he descended the small embankment back to the waiting golf cart. "This club was the best thousand bucks I've ever spent," he boasted to his playing companion, Steve Herndon.

"Nice shot, you lucky dog," Steve commented as Jake sat in the driver's seat of the cart. "Now if only you could putt," he jabbed.

Jake's wireless phone rang as the golf cart rolled away from the tee box. He glanced at the number on the caller ID. The call was coming from his office.

"This better be an emergency," Jake declared to Steve when he pushed the button to receive the call.

It was Madge. "Jesse Thompson's dead," she blurted.

Jake inhaled. His thoughts ran wild. "What do you mean Jesse Thompson is dead? I just spoke to him yesterday, and he was fine."

"I was just told he was shot this morning at his farm on Old Medina Road," she replied. "The sheriff's department is calling it a homicide. The rumor I hear is that the entire back half of Mr. Thompson's head was blown off. It's so horrible, I don't even want to think about it."

"Do they have any suspects?" Jake asked. He hoped she'd say no, but he had this awful feeling . . .

"They've arrested Jed McClellan," Madge explained. "He's being held at the criminal justice complex."

Jake felt like a heavyweight boxer had punched him in the stomach. Jesse Thompson was dead. *Did Jed really kill him?*

Jake remembered his conversation with Jed from the previous afternoon. Jed was angry, but Jake convinced himself that the man was rational. So he hadn't followed through on his gut instinct to call the authorities.

But what if Jed wasn't rational? He was, after all, desperate, and desperate men did irrational things.

Had Jake been blind to the obvious? Was he unwittingly part of the plot to harm—even kill—Jesse Thompson? How could he have been so stupid?

"I'll get a quick shower at the clubhouse," Jake told Madge. "I'll be in the office in about thirty minutes."

There would be other times to play golf. This matter was too important to wait.

Naval Observatory, residence of the Vice President, Washington DC

Vice President Burke and his entourage left San Francisco just after six o'clock Pacific time Tuesday evening, arriving in Washington at 3:00 a.m.

eastern time Wednesday. The primaries were grueling, but they didn't hold a candle to the endurance test associated with the general-election campaign. Sleep—particularly sleep in his own bed—was a precious commodity. When he finally got to bed at 3:45, he left instructions that he was not to be awakened. No appearances were scheduled until that evening, in Baltimore, only fifty minutes away. There was no need to get up early.

It wasn't long before Ed was dead to the world.

"Mr. Vice President," came the voice of Ed's personal assistant from outside his bedroom door. "Mr. Vice President, are you awake?"

The knock at the door startled Ed out of his dead sleep. His heart raced for a few seconds. He glanced at the clock on his nightstand. 9:52. He knew his top aide would violate his specific instructions only if something was terribly wrong.

"What is it?" he muttered from his bed.

"Sir, there's been a murder," she replied. "And I think you should know about it."

Slipping on the bathrobe that was lying at the foot of the bed, he walked to the door. He rubbed his eyes and yawned, trying to shake off his drowsy state as he opened the door. "Did you say *murder*?"

"Sorry to wake you, sir, but I thought you would want to know. Jesse Thompson was killed this morning."

Disbelief consumed Ed. He staggered backward the few steps to his bed and collapsed on the edge with his face buried in his hands. He and Jesse Thompson had been friends since they were freshmen at Vanderbilt. They stood up in each other's weddings.

Jesse Thompson, dead.

"Are you sure?" Ed asked, hoping he'd misunderstood what was just said.

"We're certain, sir. It happened a couple of hours ago."

"Tell me what you know," he demanded, his vision fixed on the beige carpet beneath his feet.

"Not much at this point," the aide admitted. "He was at his cattle farm and a disgruntled bank customer shot him with an assault rifle."

"Do you know any of the funeral arrangements?"

"Things are still pending," she responded.

"Let me know as soon as you hear something. I will attend the funeral, and I need to schedule a press statement for early afternoon."

"I'll get right on it."

Madison County Criminal Justice Complex, Jackson, Tennessee

A murder in Jackson was rare and usually not newsworthy to anybody outside the Mid-South. But this murder was different. The victim was a personal friend of the vice president of the United States. Reporters from all the major news networks descended on Jackson like vultures. Large white broadcast vans with satellite antennas on their roofs were parked outside the criminal justice complex by the time Jake arrived to see his client.

His client, that is, if Jed wanted his help. Who could blame Jed if he wanted someone else to represent him? Jake knew he hadn't done a very good job to this point. And he still wondered what he could have done to prevent this tragedy. Why didn't he try harder to convince Jesse to stop the foreclosure? Why didn't he tell the authorities about Jed's threats?

Jake shook his head. Here he was, already convicting Jed of the crime, and he hadn't even spoken with the man about it yet.

Jake pulled into the parking lot in front of the red-brick Madison County Criminal Justice Complex and parked his Volvo in a space reserved for attorneys. Only the judges had the privilege of parking inside the secured lot on the north side of the building. Jake entered through the tinted front doors and passed through the metal detector. The elevator carried him to the second floor, where he began his quest for Sheriff Craig West.

Jake soon found the sheriff in the break room, bragging to his deputies about how he knew all the time that Jed McClellan had shot Jesse Thompson.

"Sheriff, I need to see you for a minute," Jake called from where he stood at the door.

"What can I do for you?" replied West, turning toward Jake.

"I need to talk with you about Jed McClellan."

"There's nothing to talk about." West scowled. His hands settled on his hips in a defiant gesture.

Jake didn't like the look West was giving him . . . as if he were sizing up an opponent.

"We got ol' Jed dead to rights, and there's nothing you can do to get him out of this one," the sheriff claimed. "We found him at the murder scene, the murder weapon was in his truck, and I just found out that Jesse was scheduled to foreclose on Jed's house today. That's motive, my friend. Personally, I hope Jed fries. Jesse was one of my best friends."

Jake could tell by the sheriff's clenched jaw that the lawman wasn't going to be of any help. He had no reason to be. After all, he was a suspicious, opinionated man who always thought everybody was guilty of something. And he didn't like Jake very much to start with. Worse, if the rumors about West's and Jesse Thompson's collaborations were true, that was even more reason for West not to be helpful. His income had just been slashed by half with the death of his benefactor.

"Where is he?" asked Jake.

"He's still in booking," West announced. "You can see him in about thirty minutes."

"I want to see him right now," Jake insisted. "I'm his lawyer, and I demand to see my client." He clenched his jaw as tightly as the sheriff's.

West finally relented. "He's down the hall. Interrogation room one." He nodded toward the room.

Jake walked briskly in the direction West indicated and met two detectives in the hallway as they left the interrogation room. "Is Jed McClellan in there?" he inquired.

The first detective smirked. "Yeah, he's in there. Go in if you want. We're through with him."

Jake peered at Jed through the small window in the door. The room was dimly lit and uninviting. A one-way mirror was built into the wall immediately adjacent to the door. Other than a metal table and four tattered chairs, the room had no furnishings.

Jake cursed Sheriff West under his breath for lying to him about Jed still being in booking. Jed looked terrible. He needed a shower and a shave. The booking officer had confiscated his belt and shoestrings. His clothes were wrinkled and unkempt, and he obviously had been crying.

Jake opened the door.

Jed immediately glanced up. "Am I glad to see you," he stated with relief as Jake entered the room.

Jed's smile brightened the dismal room, and that set Jake at ease. He still had to find out what happened, but at least he knew Jed wanted his help.

"You look terrible," began Jake. "Are you OK?"

"I'm OK. Just ready to get outta this place is all. How long you think they're gonna keep me? I need to get home to Ruth. She's probably worryin' about me."

Jake tensed. Now he knew Jed didn't understand what was really going on. Or that he was now public enemy number one and would not be going home anytime soon.

"Jed, Sheriff West told me they found you at the murder scene and the murder weapon was in your truck. Is that true?"

"I didn't kill Jesse Thompson." Jed's voice pleaded for Jake to believe him. "Lord knows I wanted to, but I didn't. I found him like that. His brains all blown out. I don't know how that gun got in my truck. Somebody must have put it there, but it ain't mine."

"Tell me what you remember," Jake instructed as he sat down in a chair across the table from Jed. "Everything."

Jed told Jake about leaving the Bad Dog and driving to the cattle farm to talk to Mr. Thompson about stopping the foreclosure. He stopped at the gate and just spotted the man when he fell. When Jed reached Mr. Thompson, he was dead. Jed saw a small black pickup speeding away. Then he called the police.

"Did you see who was driving it, or anything else about it?"

"No, I just saw the truck."

Sheriff West had conveniently failed to mention the pickup when Jake talked to him earlier. Jake made a note about it. Any glimmer of hope would have to be chased.

"This is a mess." Jake replaced the top of his ink pen and slid it into his shirt pocket. He ran his fingers through his brown hair. "It doesn't look good, Jed. It doesn't look good at all."

"I know, Jake, I know." Jed buried his face in his hands. "But I didn't do it." He looked up at Jake. "You've gotta believe me."

Jake's policy had always been to never evaluate whether his client was innocent or guilty. His job was to take whatever facts he was presented with and turn them as best he could in favor of his client. So he chose not to respond to Jed's last statement. He stood up and rubbed his chin thoughtfully as he paced around the table.

"I anticipate that the DA will seek the death penalty," he contemplated, talking more to himself than to Jed. He crossed his arms over his chest as he continued pacing. "He may offer us a deal to keep you alive if you plead guilty to first-degree murder."

"The death penalty?" Jed turned to follow Jake, who was still pacing around the table. "But I didn't do it. And I ain't pleadin' to nothin'."

Jake stopped at the end of the table opposite Jed. He placed the palms of his hands on the back of the chair and leaned toward the center of the table. The move was designed to show Jed who was in charge. "Jed, listen to me," Jake said forcefully. "I know what it's like to be without a father. Both of my parents died when I was a young boy, and I was raised by my mother's sister. I remember crying myself to sleep at night, wishing I could at least talk to my mom and dad. Jed, you've got to think about your wife and kids. What are they going to do without you?"

"What are they gonna do with me sittin' in prison?" Jed retorted.

He had a valid point. What good would he be to his family if he was incarcerated for the rest of his life at Fort Pillow? He would be alive, but that would be about it. Would that really be living?

"How many cases like this have you handled, Jake?"

Jake removed his hands from the chair back and straightened his body. "Five murder cases."

"Did you get 'em off?"

"Two acquittals, two reduced to manslaughter, and we pleaded insanity for one. He's in Western State in Bolivar. Why?"

"Because I know you're a good lawyer, Jake. You're one of the best 'round these parts. And you can get me outta here."

"It's not that easy, Jed. The evidence doesn't look good."

"But I didn't do it. You gotta believe me. I didn't do it."

Jake rubbed his forehead in anguish. "I'll do what I can, but I can't make any promises. We'll see what the judge says at your arraignment about bail."

A knock sounded on the door, and the two homicide detectives walked in. It was time to take Jed to his cell, they announced. "You two can meet again before the arraignment tomorrow morning," one of the detectives told Jake and Jed.

Jake said good-bye to Jed and assured him he would talk to Ruth. Since murder suspects were not permitted to have visits from family members before their arraignments, Jake said he'd be glad to relay any messages to her.

"Tell her I love her," Jed requested as he left the room with the detectives.

Jake walked solemnly out of the interrogation room and navigated the hallways and stairwells to the front door of the CJC. As he exited, reporters from local and national media outlets jostled for position to be the first to question the attorney for Jedediah McClellan, murder suspect. They blocked Jake's path to the parking lot and stuck microphones and video cameras in his face. The rapid snap of camera shutters was barely audible above the shouts for Jake's attention.

"Are you representing Jed McClellan?" asked a reporter with the FOX affiliate in Memphis.

Jake quickly processed whether to speak with the media. It was a gamble, but he reasoned that he had to begin influencing the prospective jury pool. He would need all the help he could get. Also, it didn't hurt to have some exposure for himself. Lawyers called it free advertising. He held up his hands to quiet the press before speaking.

"I have been retained to represent Mr. McClellan, and I have a couple of statements I would like to make," Jake began. "First, I want to send my condolences, and my client's condolences, to Mr. Thompson's family. He did many great things for this community, and his presence will be greatly missed. Secondly, we hope that the authorities arrest the person or persons responsible for this horrible crime."

"Mr. Reed, does your client claim that he did not shoot Jesse Thompson?" the Fox reporter continued.

"That is correct. My client is innocent, and we look forward to the opportunity to present our side of the case to an impartial jury. Now, if you will excuse me, I have a lot of work to do."

Choruses of "Mr. Reed, Mr. Reed" rang out from the horde of reporters as Jake pushed through the crowd to his car. He knew there would be other opportunities to espouse his client's innocence, and it was critical he check out Jed's story about the mysterious black truck as soon as possible. If what Jed told him about the pickup was true, the murder raised a lot of questions. Jake knew he'd probably never find all the answers, but he had to try. Even if Jed didn't blame him for allowing this to happen, Jake felt some sense of responsibility. There was one immediate benefit from the death of Jesse Thompson, though. The foreclosure on the McClellan home didn't occur. At least Ruth and the kids would have some place to stay while Jake tried to straighten this mess out.

FBI headquarters, Washington, DC

The all-points bulletin from FBI headquarters went unnoticed at Memphis International Airport until it was too late. Raoul Migel Flores used a different passport, prepared by the same Latin American counterfeiter, and applied a disguise before boarding a flight to Mexico City. He would be in Bogotá before nightfall . . . and most likely a lot richer.

Deputy Director Charlie Armacost was furious when he was informed about Raoul's successful escape from the United States. He screamed at everyone from Assistant Deputy Director McCullough to the deputy-in-charge of the Memphis office. He even screamed at a few people who were not even remotely involved in the search for Raoul.

"You're all a bunch of incompetent imbeciles!" he yelled.

After his assault of words on virtually the entire department, Charlie went into hibernation in his office. He noticed on his television monitors that all the news networks were carrying the story of the death of Jesse Lamar Thompson. The murder of a close, personal friend of the vice president was newsworthy, Charlie knew. But it also raised questions in his mind about what had happened and whether the vice president was at risk. He spoke briefly with the head of the secret service and was informed that the secret service would investigate to make sure there was no potential threat to the vice president. It was decided that the Bureau would not be involved with the investigation. The Service would be quickly satisfied that the local authorities arrested the correct man. Any thought of a great conspiracy against Vice President Burke would soon be quashed.

Soon after Charlie's conversation with the Secret Service, McCullough burst into Charlie's office without knocking. "I think we may have discovered what Raoul was doing in the States," George announced. "You know the Thompson murder?"

"I've seen the reports on CNN," replied Charlie. "Why?"

"On a hunch, a field agent from Memphis spoke with the local sheriff about the murder. The sheriff was quite confident they had their man, so the field agent didn't mention anything about Raoul. But the agent asked about the murder weapon. The sheriff told him they had recovered it from the bed of the suspect's truck. Get this. The murder weapon was a Tango 51 sniper rifle. The sheriff knew the suspect and said he was surprised at how good a marksman he was, especially since the guy was drunk at the time. The entry wound was precisely in the center of the victim's forehead. The sheriff said he must have used a hollow point, because the entire back side of the victim's head was blown off."

Charlie sat motionless for a few seconds as he pondered George's report. The modus operandi on the Thompson murder was the same that Raoul Miguel Flores was known to use. The conclusion he drew was that Raoul Miguel Flores was hired to kill a friend of Vice President Burke's. Why? Charlie's mind considered the possibilities. After all, one of the world's greatest assassins didn't work cheap, and he didn't work for just anybody.

"Find out everything you can about Jesse Thompson," Charlie instructed George. "I want to know who his friends were and who he did business with. If he was married, find out about his wife. I want to know if he had any girlfriends. I want to know where he spent his time and money. Put ten men on this if you have to. I want a report Friday morning."

George departed as fast as he'd entered, and Charlie was left alone again. There was only one reason Raoul would be in the States—for an assassination. That was the man's occupation. But could Raoul's plans involve the vice president?

Charlie had hoped to catch Raoul before he hit his mark. But he and George had failed. Now they would have to deal with the fallout.

It was going to be a long few days, maybe weeks. And Director Sanders was certainly not going to be pleased.

CHAPTER TEN

Naval Observatory, residence of the Vice President, Washington, DC

It had been three hours since Edward Burke was awakened and informed of Jesse Thompson's death. A blue and gray podium was erected just outside the front door of the residence. A bank of microphones lined the top of the podium, and on the front was the decorative seal: Vice President of the United States.

Reporters, photographers, and television cameras awaited the vice president's press conference regarding the murder of his friend. Ed walked somberly out the front door of the residence and approached the podium while the *click* of camera shutters filled the air. He wore a dark suit, blue tie, and a stoic expression.

"Good morning," Ed said as he began his prepared remarks. "As I am sure you are aware by now, a dear friend of mine, Jesse Thompson, was murdered this morning. His death has come as a great shock to me and my family. We are all deeply saddened by his passing. I have already personally spoken with Jesse's widow to express my condolences. And I have pledged to her to do all I can to assure that the perpetrator of this crime meets with swift and certain punishment."

Ed concluded his remarks and answered questions from the reporters in attendance. His staff had planted several questions with a few selected reporters before the press conference began, so Ed knew which reporters to recognize. He nodded at one such reporter from CNN.

"Mr. Vice President, do you know any of the details surrounding the murder?"

"At this time it would be inappropriate for me to comment on any specifics. I have been in contact with the local authorities, but I cannot comment further."

Ed nodded at the next friendly reporter.

"Mr. Vice President, do you think this murder could have been avoided if the gun-control legislation you have advocated would have passed the Congress?"

Ed knew that the answer to the question was simply "No." But campaign polls reflected that Ed's message of gun control was being favorably received by the voters, so he needed to close the sale.

"In all fairness it is hard to say for certain that tougher gun-control laws would have prevented this horrible crime. We will never know. However, if I am fortunate enough to be elected the next president of the United States, my number one goal will be to pass gun-control legislation. Until we do, we will have failed to do all we can to prevent such a crime from happening again."

The press conference served Ed's purpose. Anything more would make him appear insensitive and opportunistic.

"Thank you very much," Ed stated as he left the podium and reentered the residence. The furious clicking of camera shutters continued until the front door to the residence was completely closed.

En route to New York

Mac Foster and his top advisors watched Ed Burke's press conference together in Mac's private cabin aboard his campaign airplane. Mac knew it was the only place they could go and have privacy away from the horde of reporters that traveled with the campaign. Mac realized the dilemma he now faced, and he could see it on the faces of his campaign staff. Edward Burke had just appeared on national television and evoked the sympathy of the entire country. It was obvious he was grieving the loss of his friend, but he also appeared strong and in control. At the same time, he was able to capitalize politically on the gun-control issue.

Mac knew his campaign had to react quickly.

"I think we need to immediately extend our sympathy to the vice president and to the Thompson family," Jack Bennett stated, breaking the silence.

"I agree," Mac concurred. "But we don't want to appear patronizing."

It certainly was a precarious situation. Mac was already trailing Burke by a significant margin, so failure to handle this situation properly could result in a death knell for his slim chances at the presidency.

"Let's prepare a press release," Mac began. "It needs to convey our sympathies to the vice president over the death of his friend, and it should state that all campaign efforts will cease until after the Thompson funeral. That will show our concern for the situation and should lessen the damage from Burke's statement."

"I think that's a good decision," Shep commented. "But it will take more than a press release. Burke looked presidential. He was confident. Reassuring. He quieted any concerns of a crisis. This murder could not have come at a worse time for us."

"What do you suggest we do?" Mac asked.

"I'm not sure at this point, but we've got to do something. Issue the press release, and let me think about what else we need to do. I assume you all heard about Senator Davidson?" Shep paused.

"That was terrible news," Mac commented. "Jim and I rarely saw eye-to-eye on most issues, but he was too young to die of a heart attack."

"I'll have someone contact his office and see if there's anything we can do," said Shep.

Reed residence, Jackson, Tennessee

Jake arrived home earlier than usual that afternoon. Jesse Thompson's murder and Jed's arrest made it impossible for him to get any work done at his office. He was emotionally drained.

Choruses of "Daddy's home! Daddy's home!" rang out from Courtney, Brett, and Jeremy as Jake entered the kitchen. The three children hugged Jake around the waist and legs. He reached down with both arms and squeezed them even tighter than usual.

"Daddy, can we play baseball?" Brett asked with glove and bat already in hand.

"Not right now," Jake responded. "Maybe later."

Jake rarely refused to play with his children, but today was an unusual day. Jesse Thompson was dead, and Jed McClellan was in jail for his murder. Jake couldn't rid his mind of the thought that the whole mess was his fault.

Accepting their father's answer, the children ran through the open door and out into the yard.

"Bad day?" Rachel asked as she prepared supper.

"The worst." Jake loosened his tie, removed his suit coat, and draped it over his left arm. He couldn't wait to change clothes.

"I heard about Jesse Thompson on the radio this morning," Rachel said. "Are you doing OK?"

"I'll be all right," he responded. "I just need some time to unwind."

Rachel gave him a peck on the cheek as he walked past her out of the kitchen and toward their bedroom. He finished removing his suit and tie and changed into a pair of blue jeans and a T-shirt.

A few minutes later he was sitting on the couch in the den, waiting for the evening news to begin on television. The children were still outside. Rachel sat down quietly beside him.

The murder of Jesse Thompson and the arrest of Jedediah McClellan were the lead stories on the local television station. The reporter, live in front of the Madison County Criminal Justice Complex, informed the viewers that Jed McClellan was the newest resident at the CJC. Next was the replay of a clip from the impromptu press conference by Jed McClellan's lawyer, Jake Reed.

Rachel placed her right arm around Jake and slowly ran her fingers through his brown hair to relax him. Jake was glad that after years of marriage she knew what it took to relieve his stress. Jake turned his back to her slightly, and Rachel massaged his broad shoulders.

"This is just terrible, Rachel. Jed is a client of mine. I helped him in a workers' compensation case a couple of years ago."

"Do you think he killed Mr. Thompson?" Rachel asked.

"I don't know what to think. Everything points to Jed, but he swears he didn't do it." Jake paused. "Do you know Jed?" He turned his face toward Rachel.

"Not really," she replied. "Except that he grew up in Jackson, too, and that he played football. I remember reading about his high-school games in the paper."

"He's got a wife and two small children. It was horrible what happened to Mr. Thompson, but I can't stop thinking about Jed and his family."

"Can you help him?"

"I don't know," Jake replied honestly. "It doesn't look very good at this point, but I've got to try. If he really is innocent, then I have to do everything I can to help him. I'm not even worried about getting paid. Things are so chaotic and out of control in Jed's life right now. As I saw him sitting in jail, separated from his family, I couldn't help but think about what it would be like if I were separated from you and the kids. Or worse, if something happened to you or one of the kids."

Jake dropped his head from Rachel's gaze and swiped his index finger under his left eye to chase away a tear he felt welling up.

Rachel tenderly, lovingly stroked his hair. "That's not going to happen."

"I love you," Jake whispered.

"I love you too. Everything is going to be OK," she assured him.

Just then Courtney, Brett, and Jeremy barreled through the back door and into the den. They danced around, giggling at the sight of their parents snuggling on the couch.

Brett wedged his way in between Jake and Rachel. "Now can you play with us?" he inquired eagerly.

Jake smiled. "Yes. Now I can play. "

Rachel watched through the open kitchen window as Jake and the kids played baseball in the backyard. Jake pitched and pretended like he was trying to get them out as they ran the makeshift bases after a hit.

"You can't get me, Daddy," Jeremy called, laughing, as he ran across home plate just before Jake tagged him. "Home run!"

"That's a home run, all right," Jake confirmed. "You're too fast for me."

Rachel reflected on how wonderful her life was. She had a great husband, three beautiful kids, and a lovely house. But one concern hung over her daily. It had been years since Jake had attended church with her and the children. He claimed he was a Christian, but Rachel wasn't convinced.

How well she remembered the life-changing event she had experienced soon after she and Jake were married. Jake, too, had been there. She knew that Jake saw what had happened to her and didn't understand why he hadn't shared her excitement. A few days later she had asked Jake to describe his salvation experience. He couldn't, but said he'd been a Christian all his life.

Since then she had prayed daily for Jake to come to know Christ personally.

"Thank you, God, for my husband and children," Rachel said spontaneously as she completed the dinner preparations. She thanked God for providing for all the needs of her family. She prayed for Jed and his family too. And then she added, "And God, please take care of Jake. He's worried about Jed, and I pray that you'll take those worries away. But most importantly, I pray for Jake's salvation."

Madison County Criminal Justice Complex, Jackson, Tennessee

Judge Edgar Prickett held arraignments every morning to handle any arrests from the previous day. So Jed appeared for his arraignment on Thursday morning, the day following the murder.

Jake knew it would be the first of many court appearances for Jed. Jed went from suspect to defendant when he was arrested by the sheriff's department and booked into the Madison County CJC. The district attorney would prosecute and, on behalf of the people of the great state of Tennessee, would use every resource in his office to keep Jed in jail.

The courtroom, like the entire complex, was new. But Jake had been there several times since its opening, so the twenty-five-foot-high ceiling in the courtroom no longer intimidated as it once had. He gave the twelve brass light fixtures, four feet in diameter and each with a white frosted globe, only a fleeting glance. He was focused on getting Jed released on bail.

Jake marched down the center aisle of the courtroom. The rows of seats on either side reminded him of church pews. They, too, were wooden and uncomfortable. On any other arraignment day the seats would have been empty. Today they were bursting with curious townspeople and reporters trying to get their first real look at Jedediah McClellan. Not an empty seat was to be found.

Judge Prickett was already sitting on his lofty perch, surrounded on all sides by a bulletproof wooden casing, in the front of the courtroom. The legal community called the wooden casing a "bench," even though the judge sat behind it rather than on it. Mounted to the floor on a stand three feet to the right of Judge Prickett's bench was the flag of the United States of America. In the same position left of the bench was the flag of the state of Tennessee. A large medallion with the inscription "The Great Seal of the State of Tennessee" hung on the wall above Judge Prickett.

Judge Prickett never fully zipped his robe, so his shirt and necktie were visible. Physically, the judge wasn't a very intimidating man. He stood only five-foot-eight and appeared rather frail. His thin covering of hair was completely white and combed forward. Yet very few people dared to cross him, and those who did regretted it. For the past thirty years he had wielded more authority with his gavel than any other judge in the state.

Local attorneys filled the empty chairs in the jury box on the left-hand side of the courtroom, waiting for their clients' cases to be called. Jake noticed Julie Anderson, the assistant district attorney, sitting at one of the two tables in the front of the courtroom. Although she was barely three years removed from law school, she looked important as she scribbled some notes on a yellow notepad before the arraignments began. On the table in front of her was a banker's box, crammed full of thin manila folders. In each folder were the charges pending against each criminal defendant being arraigned that day. Jake knew that one of the folders bore the name of Jedediah McClellan.

Jed's wife, Ruth, and his mother, Naomi, sat on the pew immediately behind the bar that separated the spectator seats from the area of the courtroom where the attorneys, defendants, and judge were located. The two ladies clutched tissues, and Ruth repeatedly dabbed her tissue against the corners of her deep brown eyes to dry the tears before they ran down her face. Naomi's chin was firm, resolved. Only occasionally did she need to dry the few tears that welled up in her eyes.

Jake had gone to see Ruth soon after he left Jed the previous day. He tried to explain to her what was happening to Jed, but it was difficult for her to understand. When he saw her now, he recalled their conversation of the previous afternoon.

"But, Jake, why? Why is Jed being held? He'd never do this," Ruth said. *"And what am I going to tell the children? How can I tell them their daddy can't come home? And why he can't come home?"*

Even now Ruth's pleas rang in Jake's mind. When he gave her Jed's message—*"I love you"*—she cried even harder.

Jake wondered if Ruth and the kids had cried themselves to sleep.

Now he leaned over the bar and whispered to Ruth and Naomi, "I'm going to do the best I can to help Jed. Hopefully Judge Prickett will set a bail we can afford."

"We've raised ten thousand dollars from family and church friends," Naomi responded, her eyes and voice hopeful.

Jake had to tell her the truth. "I doubt that will be enough, Ms. McClellan. That will only purchase a hundred thousand dollar bail bond, and Judge Prickett will likely set bail much higher than that." Seeing the dejection on the women's faces, he added, "But I'll try. I'll try to get his bail down to one hundred thousand dollars."

Jake moved to the table opposite Assistant DA Anderson. He watched as the court security officers led a line of inmates from the holding cell into the courtroom. They were all dressed in orange jumpsuits, with Madison County CJC printed on the back. Their hands and feet were shackled to the hands and feet of the inmates in front and in back of them. They wore shoes without shoestrings that resembled bathroom slippers.

Jake saw Jed in the back of the line. The stubble on his face was visible across the room, and his eyes were bloodshot and swollen. He looked confused and out of place. He was chained to a young white male with tattoos covering both arms. The white inmate, who had probably been arrested on some drug-possession charge, more resembled a murder suspect than did Jed.

As the courtroom deputy began calling the various cases from the docket one by one, in chronological order, each defendant entered a plea of either guilty or not guilty. If a defendant pleaded guilty, the judge scheduled a sentencing hearing to follow in a few days. If he pleaded not guilty, the district attorney recommended bail, and the judge usually followed the DA's recommendation.

"*State of Tennessee versus Jedediah McClellan*," called out the courtroom deputy from her seat next to the court security officer.

Jed, still shackled to the other prisoner, stepped forward from the line of inmates as best he could.

Jake walked to the podium separating the table for the criminal defense lawyers from the one for the prosecution. "Jake Reed for the defendant, Your Honor."

"How does your client plead, Mr. Reed?" Judge Prickett inquired.

"Not guilty," Jake answered firmly.

"All right," the judge commented. He then faced the prosecution table. "Bail recommendations?"

"The People request that the defendant be held without bail, Your Honor," stated Assistant DA Anderson. "He is charged with first-degree murder in the vicious slaying of Jesse Thompson. We may amend later to increase the charge to capital murder."

Jake knew that last statement was for him. He received the message loud and clear. "Your Honor, my client is a lifelong resident of this county. He is not a flight risk. He has family here and doesn't even own a passport. We request that bail be set at one hundred thousand dollars."

"I can't let him out, Mr. Reed," Judge Prickett said without hesitation. "Bail is denied, and the defendant is remanded to the criminal justice center." He banged his gavel a little harder than usual for the dramatic effect. "Next case," he barked.

As Jed stepped back into line with the other inmates, he glanced at Ruth and his mother.

Jake was glad it was only a brief connection. Anything longer would have caused an eruption of emotions that none of them could have controlled.

After Jed and the other inmates were led back to their cells, Jake ushered

Ruth and Naomi into a side room in the rear of the courtroom before they exited into the hallway.

"Ruth, Ms. McClellan," he began, looking back and forth between the two women, "I know this is difficult, but I need you right now. More importantly, Jed needs you. He's in there all by himself, and he needs you to be strong."

"It's hard to be strong," Ruth said, almost in tears again. "What are me and the kids supposed to do? Jed is all we have, and now I can't even talk to him."

"Ain't no black man gonna get a fair trial in Madison County, and you know it," Naomi said, waving her index finger at Jake. "Only God can help Jed now."

"I'll be honest with both of you," Jake said. "I don't know what will happen to Jed. I don't know if a jury will find him guilty or innocent. And if he's found guilty, I don't know what his penalty will be. What I do know is that Jed needs all three of us right now." Jake eyed each woman individually. "So this is not the time for your emotions to get the best of you. When we leave the courtroom, there will be several television cameras and newspaper reporters waiting. We are going to walk out that door and tell the world that Jedediah McClellan is innocent of this crime," he stated very calmly but sternly. "I need you there beside me, showing your support for Jed."

After their brief meeting Jed led Naomi and Ruth out of the courtroom and into the horde of reporters.

"Mr. Reed, what do you think about the judge's decision to hold your client without bail?" came the first question.

Hot white lights burned from the remote television cameras, virtually blinding the trio. Jake stepped ahead of Ruth and Naomi to shield them.

"We are certainly disappointed, but not surprised," Jake responded quickly. He took control of the press conference. "However, we are confident this is only a temporary setback and that justice will prevail in the end. Mr. McClellan will soon be home with his family, where he belongs."

"Mrs. McClellan," another reporter asked, thrusting the mike Ruth's direction, "how does it feel to be married to a man who is accused of murder?"

Before Ruth had time to answer, Jake interrupted. He felt the need to protect Ruth, as if she were his wife. "Mrs. McClellan has no comment at this time. Please excuse us."

Grasping one of Ruth's arms and one of Naomi's, Jake pushed his way through the crowd.

He had a lot of work to do on the case. And he was worried. Would he be able to save Jed's life, no matter what he did?

Whether Jed was innocent or guilty, the outcome didn't look good.

CHAPTER ELEVEN

Hilton Head Island, South Carolina

Claudia Duval had been reared in a small town in north Mississippi. She'd been captain of the cheerleading squad, a member of the debate team, and an honor student. To the other students in her high school, she appeared to have everything together.

But how well Claudia knew that appearances could be deceiving. Her friends couldn't see how much she hurt on the inside. The pain had begun when her father died suddenly when she was nine. She had no brothers or sisters, so his death left her and her mother, Charlotte, all alone.

When her mother began working two jobs to make ends meet, she and Claudia drifted apart. By the time Claudia was a teenager, she and her mother were engaged in a bitter war of wills, and their relationship deteriorated virtually beyond repair. Claudia couldn't wait until her high-school graduation when she could move out of the house.

She was barely out of high school and only eighteen when she found the quickest road away from her mother. His name was Jimmy Simpson. He was a nice young man from all appearances, but it didn't take long after their marriage for Claudia to realize her mistake. They were both young and immature, and Claudia didn't really love him. She'd simply married him out of spite toward her mother.

Claudia and Jimmy had been married for less than a year when she found him with another woman. The divorce was simple. They had no assets to divide or debts to allocate. Claudia resumed using her maiden name.

That was eighteen years ago, and Claudia hadn't been involved in a serious relationship since. Of course, there had been other men in her life, but she could never make a real commitment.

After her divorce Claudia moved back home with her mother. That, too, was a mistake, but Claudia was stuck. She had no money and no other place to go. The fighting resumed, and Claudia moved out for good a couple of summers later. Over the next couple of years she visited her mother infrequently, and the visits were rarely pleasant. It wasn't long before Claudia stopped trying.

Claudia hadn't been to her mother's home in the last fifteen years. Their relationship had deteriorated so far that the last time Claudia had even spoken to her mother via phone was Christmas Day, ten years ago.

Not long after they last spoke on the phone, Claudia's life took a turn for the better. She moved to Hilton Head Island just prior to the local real-estate boom and obtained her real-estate license. Every year for the last five she had been a multimillion-dollar producer for her agency.

Six months ago she had met Hudson Kinney at a black-tie party at the yacht club in Sea Pines. He was fifteen years her senior, but he made her laugh. Quickly she became attracted to him, believing she had found the one man who could truly make her happy. He was a commercial real-estate developer from the Northeast and spent practically every weekend on Hilton Head. After he met Claudia, his trips became more frequent. Within a few weeks he convinced her to move into the house he owned in the Palmetto Dunes Plantation on the east side of the island.

It was Friday morning at Hilton Head, and Claudia again stood on the veranda, drinking a cup of her favorite flavored coffee. Hudson had arrived late last night and would leave again Monday morning. She treasured every moment she had with him.

Early morning was Claudia's favorite time of day. She took pleasure in the serenity that washed in with the ocean's waves. It wasn't long before Hudson joined her on the veranda. She knew he loved this place as much as she did. He often told her that the sound of the ocean crashing onto the beach and the gentle breeze relaxed him. For the few days he was there every week, he was able to forget about his hectic business and the stresses that accompanied it. Claudia and Hudson affectionately called their home "Eden," because it truly was their paradise. As they gazed out over the tranquil Atlantic Ocean, Hudson gently stroked Claudia's long blond hair.

"Is that our guy?" Agent Bill Osborne peered through his binoculars from a window in the house next door to the romantic-looking couple.

"I think so," Agent Al Moyers responded. He focused the lens of the 35mm camera on the balcony next door and snapped off several photographs.

"Let's keep an eye on them."

Jackson, Tennessee

Air Force Two touched down at McKellar-Sipes Regional Airport in Jackson just after 9:00 a.m. on the Friday following Jesse Thompson's murder. The funeral was scheduled for ten o'clock, and Vice President Burke had agreed to give the eulogy.

As Ed and Millie exited the airplane, they were greeted by several local Democratic politicians, as was customary everywhere Ed went. The local politicians would escort the Burkes to the funeral. An opportunity to be seen with the popular vice president could not be missed, Ed mused wryly.

Secret-service agents had arrived on Thursday to map the vice president's route from the airport to the funeral service and back. Air Force Two would be in the air again by noon. Ed and Millie were also accompanied on the trip by Ben Tobias. Since the election was just over two months away, Ed knew his campaign manager needed every moment with him.

The motorcade left the airport and turned east on Airways Boulevard. Ed had been told that thousands of people, hoping for a glimpse of the vice president, were standing in the August heat along the route to the funeral home. The sight was indeed impressive.

It confirmed what Ed knew to be true. The polls conducted by his pollsters Thursday night indicated his lead over Mac Foster had grown to 15 percentage points. Eighty percent of those polled stated they felt Vice

President Burke was a man of compassion but also a man of principle. The results of the polls showed that the voters wanted a president who was a great leader, but also a president with feelings. Ed had convinced them he was that man.

"The polls look good, Mr. Vice President," Ben commented as the motorcade crossed over the Highway 45 bypass that encircled Jackson and raced toward downtown.

"I agree, Ben," Ed replied. "They do look promising. But we need to make sure we don't lose this momentum. I want to have the largest winning margin in the history of presidential elections."

"Let's not get too greedy," Millie advised. "An appearance of arrogance will turn these people against you." She pointed out the window at the people who lined the street. "Continue to look statesmanlike, but show some humility."

"You're right, Millie," Ed agreed. "Foster is scrambling to do the correct thing in the wake of Jesse's death, and nobody is listening to him. We need to keep the people's attention on our campaign. We also need to make sure that Jesse's murderer stays in jail, at least until the election is over. Ben, find out who the prosecutor is, and have him ride back to the airport with us after the funeral."

The motorcade pulled into the parking lot of George A. Smith & Sons Funeral Home in downtown Jackson at approximately 9:45 a.m. Two secret-service agents ushered Ed and Millie into the building. Ben remained in the limousine to make phone calls.

The crowd that had begun arriving at the funeral home at 8:30 a.m. was still growing when Ed and Millie arrived. Ed knew that most of the people were not there to pay their respects to Jesse Thompson. They were there to see the vice president. However, the typical campaign signs were nowhere to be seen. Instead, the signs held by the throng of Burke supporters contained words that expressed the people's sympathy for Edward Burke: "We Love You, and God Bless You."

Ed had the voters right where he wanted them, and he knew it.

He and Millie seized the moment, stopping on the top of the concrete steps leading to the front door of the funeral home. They turned and waved to the mass of people as if to say, "Thank you."

Ed knew the touching scene would be replayed repeatedly throughout the country on the evening news.

The funeral service was conducted in the chapel adjacent to the funeral home. The small chapel was furnished with several rows of padded church pews. Flower arrangements lined the walls and the space behind the casket. For obvious reasons the casket was closed, and an American flag was draped over it. A recent eight-by-ten photograph of Jesse Thompson sat on top of the casket among a large spray of roses.

Ed and Millie sat on the front row of the chapel beside Earline Thompson. Ed slipped his arm around Earline and gave her a gentle hug. "How are you making it, Earline?"

"I'm doing fine." Her chin lifted in a determined gesture. "It was so good of you to come."

"Millie and I wouldn't miss it. Jesse and I were friends for a long time."

The organist began to softly play "Amazing Grace" as a minister approached the pulpit. Although Jesse Thompson had not attended a church service in twenty years, he still considered himself a member of Highland Avenue United Methodist Church. Reverend Ronald Holmes, the pastor of that church, would conduct the funeral service.

"We are here today to pay tribute to Jesse Lamar Thompson," Reverend Holmes began.

Ed listened as Reverend Holmes said a few complimentary things about Jesse and then read a few verses from the Bible. In closing, he reminded those in attendance how important it was to make sure their eternal affairs were in order.

After Reverend Holmes finished his prepared remarks, he invited Vice President Burke to deliver the eulogy. Ed somberly made his way to the pulpit. He shook hands with Reverend Holmes, who then settled into a chair behind the pulpit.

Ed grabbed the top of each side of the pulpit like a Southern revival preacher about to deliver a fire-and-brimstone sermon. "Friends, we have lost a very dear person and a leader in this community with the death of Jesse Thompson. Jesse and I were friends since we both were students at Vanderbilt. I remember . . ."

Ed continued his eulogy for several minutes. He was very melancholy.

Not once did he mention punishment for Jesse's killer or the presidential campaign. His remarks were appropriate and delivered humbly.

The voters would trust him even more.

While Ed gave Jesse Thompson's eulogy, Ben Tobias tracked down DA Drake Highfill. Drake was in attendance at the funeral, his secretary told Ben. Upon hearing that, Ben slipped quietly in the back door of the chapel as Ed's eulogy was coming to an end and asked a sheriff's deputy to identify Highfill. The deputy pointed to a man sitting on the left side of the chapel, six rows from the front.

After Ed concluded the eulogy, the funeral director asked that everyone stand as the pallbearers carried the casket containing Jesse Thompson's body to the waiting hearse for transport to Riverside Cemetery. Earline Thompson, accompanied by Ed and Millie, followed the pallbearers up the middle aisle and out the door in the rear of the chapel.

As the remainder of the crowd exited the chapel, Ben approached Drake Highfill.

"Mr. Highfill," Ben greeted him, extending his right hand, "I'm Ben Tobias, Vice President Burke's campaign manager. Your secretary said I could find you here."

"Nice to meet you, Ben." Drake shook the extended hand.

"Vice President Burke asked if you would be kind enough to accompany him on his return to the airport."

"I'd be glad to," responded Drake enthusiastically.

Ben and Drake waited in Ed's limousine as Ed and Millie said goodbye to Earline Thompson and apologized for not being able to attend the graveside services. Within a few moments Ed and Millie entered the car through the rear driver's-side door.

"Mr. Vice President," Ben stated, "this is Drake Highfill. Drake is the prosecutor you were asking me about earlier."

"Drake." Ed clasped Drake's outstretched hand. "Nice to meet you. This is my wife, Millie."

"Mrs. Burke," Drake acknowledged, "it's a pleasure to meet you." He returned his attention to Vice President Burke. "I'm sorry about the loss of Mr. Thompson. As I'm sure you know, an arrest has already been made, and my office is vigorously prosecuting."

"That's what I want to talk to you about," Ed stated as the motorcade exited the funeral-home parking lot and began the return trip to the airport. "Drake, I want to make sure that everything is done to ensure that the criminal who committed this heinous act is prosecuted to the fullest extent of the law."

"I assure you, Mr. Vice President, that we are doing everything we possibly can. In fact, Judge Prickett denied bail at yesterday's hearing."

"Good. That's good. We certainly do not need this animal back on the street. Before we leave, Ben is going to give you a telephone number where I can be reached day or night. I want you to call me if there's anything I can do to assist you. If everything goes well, perhaps I can find a position for you in my administration."

"I would like that," Drake responded almost gleefully.

The motorcade returned to McKellar-Sipes Regional Airport precisely on time. Ed, Millie, Ben, and Drake exited the limousine and walked across the tarmac to the waiting Boeing 747. Ed thanked Drake again for his assistance, and then he, Millie, and Ben boarded Air Force Two.

Drake Highfill stood on the tarmac. He watched the vice president's plane take off and bank toward the North. The Burke campaign was scheduled to resume in Chicago. Drake could hardly control his excitement as he thought about Vice President Burke's promise of an administration position.

All he had to do was get a conviction.

CHAPTER TWELVE

The Flying J Truck Stop, north of Washington DC

Late Friday evening Dalton Miller again visited the Flying J on I-95. He was still chasing the lead he received from the attorney known as Joe but wasn't finding much useful information on his own. It was time to cast his net wider.

The weather was terrible—a torrential downpour—as he ducked in the front door of the restaurant. Closing his umbrella, he stood it in the corner by the door. Betty, his regular waitress, motioned for him to sit in his usual booth in the back of the restaurant. Even though Dalton didn't know anything about Betty—other than she was tall and had bleached-blond hair—he liked her. She kept her mouth shut.

Sliding into his regular seat by the back wall, he wrung his hands to warm them as Betty set a cup of coffee on the table in front of him. He used it to chase away the chill from the rain.

The place hadn't changed much since his last visit, he thought. Probably hadn't changed in the last fifteen years. Dalton polished off his first cup of coffee in short order.

He was on his second cup and second Marlboro when George McCullough entered the truck stop. George, too, had been caught in the blowing rain. A puddle formed around his feet as he stood just inside the door. Removing his hooded raincoat, he hung it on the rack by Dalton's umbrella. Then he anxiously scanned the room until he saw Dalton waving at him from the booth in the back corner.

It had been a few months since Dalton had seen George. Contact too often was risky. As the agent approached, Dalton noticed that his limp was more pronounced, but little else had changed. His sandy-blond hair was closely cropped, his face was strong, and it was evident he still had a regular exercise regimen.

"Good afternoon," Dalton said as George sat down across the table from him.

"Good afternoon," George replied.

Betty appeared from the kitchen and walked over to their table. "What'll ya have, hon?"

"Coffee," George replied, shivering. "Black."

Betty retreated to the kitchen.

"How are things at the Bureau?" Dalton asked.

George McCullough had served as Dalton's contact within the FBI for the last three years, so Dalton knew the assistant deputy director well. Now that George was in his midforties, he rarely saw any real action with the Bureau anymore. It was unfortunate, Dalton thought. For a long time George had been one of the best field agents in the Bureau.

But that all changed when George had taken a bullet in the right thigh during a raid on a drug-smuggling operation in Miami. The wound had ended his field career. Dalton knew the injury still bothered George occasionally. Particularly on cold, rainy days like this one.

George had moved to Bureau headquarters in 1990 and had been there ever since. He was putting in his time behind a desk, analyzing reports from the front lines. Dalton knew George longed to return to the field, where the action was.

But Dalton knew the reality. Such a move was now impossible. George was too old. The only thing that gave the man the opportunity for some excitement again seemed to be his infrequent visits with Dalton. Or at least that's what George had told Dalton on one occasion.

"Things are busy," George responded, without giving away any specifics. "Who are you working for today?"

Dalton rolled his eyes. "You know I can't tell you that. The names of my clients are confidential."

George calmly dried the remaining moisture from his hands with a napkin Betty had left. "I'm not going to give you anything unless I know where it's going," he insisted.

"Let's just say that it could have national implications."

George glared at Dalton. "What is that supposed to mean?"

"It means I can't give you any names, but what I'm looking for could have an impact on the presidential election."

Betty delivered George's coffee and quickly disappeared again.

"What do you need?" George took a sip of coffee and peered at Dalton over the rim of the cup.

"Have you ever heard of a company called Apollyon Associates?"

"Not really." George rolled the coffee mug between his hands. "Why?"

"I can't answer that yet. Do some snooping and see if anything looks interesting."

"OK, I can do that." George nodded slightly. "I'll let you know what I find."

"What else is going on at the Bureau?"

Dalton could see the hesitation on George's face. It wasn't anything new for George to be reluctant. Dalton often fished for additional information from George. Sometimes George bit, and sometimes he didn't. Dalton hoped that today was one of those days where George would willingly take the bait.

And it was.

"Deputy Director Armacost thinks the murder of Jesse Thompson in Tennessee is suspicious," George said.

Dalton had seen a clip from Burke's eulogy on the evening news, so was vaguely familiar with the event to which George referred. "How so?"

George leaned in to the middle of the table and motioned for Dalton to do the same. "The local authorities recovered a Tango 51 sniper's rifle from the scene. Our field agent doesn't think there's any way possible that the man arrested could have fired the shot."

"A sniper's rifle? Who do you think did it?" prodded Dalton quietly.

"The MO is that of an assassin from Bogotá."

"Do you have any idea who hired him?"

"Not at this point." George's voice was barely above a whisper. "We're still investigating."

"What does Director Sanders say about it?"

"You'll find this interesting," George stated. "Armacost hasn't told him yet."

"Why not?"

"I don't know," George responded. "And I'm certainly not going to tell Sanders if Armacost isn't."

"That is very interesting." Dalton leaned back in his seat thoughtfully. "Keep me posted."

Dalton glanced at his watch. More than fifteen minutes together at a time was risky for George, so Dalton motioned to Betty to bring him their check.

The rain slacked up slightly, and both men made a dash for their vehicles.

When Betty bused the table Dalton Miller and his friend had just left, she smiled.

Her usual one hundred dollar bill was pinned under Dalton's coffee cup.

It was no wonder he was her favorite customer.

Marriott Marquis Hotel, Manhattan

Late Friday night Mac Foster, Shep Taylor, and Jack Bennett huddled in Mac's suite at the Marriott Marquis Hotel at Times Square in Manhattan. Senator Ted Mulvaney, Mac's counterpart from New York State, was an outspoken critic of Mac. Mulvaney's attacks caused Mac to spend more time and money in his home state than he needed to. It was unfortunate, but he couldn't afford to lose his home state.

"I thought the press release was effective," Jack stated. Mac knew that Jack was referring to the statement they had released following Jesse Thompson's death.

"That won't be enough," Shep commented confidently. "I know none of you wants to hear this, but Burke is killing us. If we don't catch a break soon, we can hang it up. Our own polls show that his lead has increased from 10 points to 12 points in the last two days. We have got to do something."

Mac was as frustrated as Shep and Jack were. After all, he was running a positive campaign, with everything aboveboard. Straightforward and honest. He espoused conservative positions on issues such as income-tax cuts, increased military spending, and welfare reform. He was staunchly pro-life, the only position he could take on the issue because of his personal beliefs. Yet despite all this, he was only polling at 70 percent among likely Republican voters. What was going on?

Mac was also exhausted. The campaign trail had been grueling, and it was beginning to show. He had lost weight. The gray was taking over the black in his hair even more. His lower back ached constantly. But all the exhaustion, pains, and aches would be worth it if he and his staff could just figure out some way to win. Mac loathed the thought of Ed Burke, with his skewed principles, sitting in the Oval Office.

"What do you suggest we do?" Mac asked Shep.

"I've given a lot of thought to that over the last few days. I think we need to do two things. First, we need to lure Burke into a nationally televised debate. If we can, we might be able to expose his fund-raising prowess. It may be difficult to get his campaign to agree to a debate since he's leading, but we need to try."

"I like that idea," Mac replied. "Let's get some people working on that first thing in the morning. What's the second idea?"

Shep hesitated. "I know you may not like it, but I think we need to get Shannon out in the public."

Shannon was Mac's wife. They had met when Mac was chief of staff for John Abrahms, governor of New York. Shannon was an administrative assistant in the attorney general's office. They had fallen madly in love, married in 1978, and soon had two children, Joseph and David. Shannon worked hard behind the scenes in Mac's campaign, but he had always tried to protect her from the media.

"No," Mac replied forcefully. "Absolutely not. There's no way I will allow Shannon to be placed under that microscope. I'd rather lose the election than do that."

"If you don't do it, you will certainly lose," Shep stated confidently. "By putting Shannon out there, I believe we can stop the bleeding. We may even pick up some points. She's attractive and well spoken. The public has only seen her on a limited basis. She is one of our best assets, and I think it's been a mistake not to have utilized her talents more before now."

"I agree with Shep," Jack said. "We need to play all our cards, and she's one of them."

"I don't like it," Mac stated.

"I think you need to consider it," Jack urged. "This election is too important. If we don't give it our best shot, we may all regret it in ten years. Worse, the entire country may regret it."

Mac stood up and strode over to the window. He could see the bustle on Broadway below, and the thousands of people who littered the sidewalks on both sides. They appeared to be walking aimlessly in many different directions . . . the wrong directions.

They need leadership. Leadership to take them in the right direction.

Mac wanted to provide that leadership. He'd been called to provide that leadership. He couldn't turn back now.

"Will you at least talk with Shannon about it?" Shep inquired.

Mac could tell that Shep was trying to close the sale.

"I think she's stronger than you give her credit for being," Shep added.

"OK," Mac relented. He exhaled deeply, still staring down at the mass of lost souls below. "I'll talk with Shannon."

Jackson, Tennessee

Attending church on Sunday morning was part of life for most of the people in Jackson, particularly Naomi McClellan. She thought it was a crime not to go. For as long as she could remember, she had been attending worship services at Mount Hebron CME Church every Sunday. Naomi had convinced Ruth to come with her today—and to bring the children.

The services were already under way when Naomi, Ruth, and the children—Derrick, nine, and Tosha, six—arrived. Naomi parked her blue 1989 Buick Century in a vacant spot not far from the church. They could hear the congregation singing as they exited the car and headed along the sidewalk to the front door of the church.

Ruth had dressed Derrick and Tosha in the best clothes they had.

Naomi took each child by the hand, and Ruth followed closely behind. Derrick was big for his age, thought Naomi, and he reminded her of Jed at the same age. The top of Derrick's head was nearly to Naomi's shoulder.

It won't be long before he's a grown man, Naomi thought. *And this mess is makin' him grow up sooner.*

Tosha was petite like Ruth and had her soft skin. Naomi noticed how pretty Tosha was in her red knee-length dress, ruffled socks, and white shoes.

I'm gonna do everythin' I can to make sure your life is better than mine has been.

The quaint, yellow-brick church had been constructed in 1935, eleven years before Naomi was born, and it was the center of so many memories for her. As a child she had attended Sunday school in one of the classrooms in the rear of the building. More importantly, when she was twelve, she had knelt at the altar in the front of the sanctuary and accepted Jesus Christ as her Lord and Savior. As an adult she had spent many glorious days of worship at the church.

Tosha pointed, eyes wide, to the stained-glass window above the front door. Jesus Christ was pictured in a white robe with a golden halo above his head. His arms were extended in love as blood dripped from the palms of his hands.

Naomi looked up toward the pinnacle of the roof, to the simple steeple that bore a plain white cross. Of all her loved ones, Naomi knew she was the only one who understood its significance. And her heart grieved at the realization.

Over the last several days, since her only child had been charged with murder, Naomi had felt every emotion imaginable. From fear to hate to sorrow to fear again. The sight of the old church soothed her. It welcomed her like an old friend.

She sighed and grasped the children's hands again. Climbing the fifteen concrete steps that led to the front door, she and the children entered the church foyer, with Ruth trailing behind her. An elderly gentleman greeted them with a warm smile and handed Naomi and Ruth each a bulletin. He patted the children on the head and gave each of them a piece of peppermint candy. Then, quietly opening one of the doors that led from the foyer to the sanctuary, he ushered them in.

The high, vaulted ceiling was supported by beautiful, old beams made of solid oak and stained with a deep brown varnish that made them shiny. Golden rays of sunlight beamed through the many arched windows. Row after row of pews with burgundy seat pads lined both sides of the center aisle. The table in front of the pulpit was inscribed with THIS DO IN REMEMBRANCE OF ME.

The sanctuary was filled to capacity. The parishioners, dressed in their best clothes, displayed vibrant bursts of color—red, green, and yellow. The choir loft was packed with singing, clapping choir members in ornate, lavender robes. The congregation on the main floor was standing and waving their arms as they sang a spiritual.

Naomi's eyes met those of Reverend Monroe Douglass, the longtime pastor of Mount Hebron, as they entered the sanctuary. He was behind the pulpit flashing his contagious smile and being very animated like the rest of the congregation. When his eyes met Naomi's, he motioned for the organist and pianist to stop playing as everyone in attendance turned to see Naomi and her family in the back of the sanctuary.

"Brothers and sisters," Reverend Douglass began. He looked sympathetically at the McClellan children and clasped his hands together in front of his chest, as if he were praying. "We have some special guests with us today."

Shouts of "amen" rose from several members of the congregation.

"Very special guests," Reverend Douglass repeated.

The "amens" intensified.

"Sister Naomi has with her today her daughter-in-law, Ruth, and two grandchildren, Derrick and Tosha. Now we all know the travesty that has beset Naomi's son, Jedediah. He needs us now. His family needs us. Sister Naomi needs us."

Reverend Douglass's voice grew louder and louder with each phrase, and the chorus of "amens" likewise crescendoed.

"We, as brothers and sisters in Christ, must do everything we possibly can to help this family," Reverend Douglass instructed. "The first thing we can do is pray for them. Sister Naomi, bring your family down here to the altar."

Naomi grabbed Ruth's right hand and tugged her toward the altar. Derrick and Tosha hesitantly followed their mother and grandmother down the center aisle. At Reverend Douglass's direction all four of them knelt at the steps that led to the pulpit, lowered their heads, and closed their eyes.

Reverend Douglass's vibrant pastoral robe appeared to consume the area immediately in front of the pulpit as he stood between the two kneeling women. He placed one of his hands on Naomi's right shoulder and the other hand on Ruth's left shoulder. Then he raised his face toward heaven, closed his eyes, and began to pray.

"Dear Lord . . ." The reverend's deep, rich voice echoed throughout the sanctuary. "We know you are almighty and merciful. We do not know why sometimes we are faced with difficult challenges in our lives, but even then we know that you are with us . . ."

It was a prayer Naomi needed to hear. She was a strong woman—mentally, physically, and spiritually. She had always relied on God to provide for her needs, no matter what happened. But having Jed charged with murder had shaken her like nothing else, to the very core of her being. She had spent countless hours since Wednesday on her knees praying for her son . . . and for his lawyer.

But now she rested, bathed in the words of peace and comfort as Reverend Douglass called upon God to take care of Naomi and her family during this terrible ordeal. To comfort Jed.

Naomi began to cry. She could feel the presence of the Holy Spirit as Reverend Douglass prayed. A calming peace swept over her. She did not understand why things happened the way they did, but she knew that whatever the outcome, God was with her and was in control.

She also realized something else: in order to save her son, she would have to sacrifice herself.

CHAPTER THIRTEEN

Jackson, Tennessee

Jake awoke in a cold sweat at 4:00 a.m. on the Monday following Jed's arrest. He had spent every waking moment since last Wednesday on Jed's defense and had forgotten about Lillian Scott's case.

He rolled onto his back and grimaced at the ramifications of his singular focus. He had failed to respond to Bob Whitfield by noon last Wednesday. That meant the $150,000 offer had expired. Jake wanted to call Bob right then, even if he had to wake the guy up by screaming, "We accept! We accept!"

But Jake knew it would be futile. The offer had expired on Wednesday. It was as simple as that. He wanted to call Lillian Scott and apologize but knew that was not practical either.

Jake lay in his bed wide awake for an hour, worrying. *Practicing law is stressful enough without mistakes like this.*

Finally he decided he couldn't go back to sleep. Rachel would have to handle the kids by herself this morning. With everything going on, he knew she'd understand.

He took a shower, threw on a pair of khaki slacks and a golf shirt, and headed to his office. At this time of day the phones wouldn't be ringing, and there would be no interruptions. He would be able to think. And think was what he needed to do.

It was just after six o'clock when Jake arrived. He unlocked the back door, and the security alarm began beeping. He punched in the access code on the security panel to disarm it and went to his office.

When he sat down at his desk, he noticed that some of his file folders were not where he'd left them on Friday.

The cleaning-company employees probably moved them when they cleaned over the weekend, he figured. Maybe he'd have Madge put in a phone call later to tell them not to rearrange anything on his desk.

But in the long run such little things didn't matter. He didn't have time to worry about some manila folders being rearranged. Madge would be there in a couple of hours, and he needed to have a game plan before she arrived.

FBI headquarters, Washington DC

It was eight o'clock, and Deputy Director Armacost had been at the office for an hour and a half. All weekend he had thought about the report on the Thompson murder and come up with the same conclusion: there was no other connection between Edward Burke and Jesse Thompson other than the obvious facts. They had attended Vanderbilt University together. Burke had gone into politics and Thompson into banking. Both were tremendously successful. Burke had become the vice president of the United States, and Thompson was a multimillionaire. Neither man had any ex-wives—or any kind of criminal record. Bureau agents couldn't find a history of drug use with either man.

Other than occasional phone calls, the agents had also been unable to find very much communication between Burke and Thompson over the last several years. Burke had a small loan at Thompson's bank, which he paid regularly by personal check. Thompson contributed the maximum $1,000 to every one of Burke's campaigns. There was nothing unusual in the report.

Charlie was deep in thought, analyzing the Thompson murder, when FBI Director Saul Sanders knocked on the frame to his open door. The knock startled Charlie, and he quickly hid the Thompson report in a manila file folder.

"May I come in?" Sanders asked.

Charlie loathed Saul Sanders. He was a political appointee of President Roger Harrison and had made numerous mistakes. A federal prosecutor from New York, Sanders had lost his bid for the Senate against Mac Foster in 1996. Somehow he'd ended up with his FBI job.

Charlie couldn't correct all of Sanders's mistakes, and that made him angry. Charlie believed the Bureau had suffered under Sanders's administration because of his lack of experience. The influx of illegal drugs from outside the borders of the United States had increased. Domestic violence was on the rise, and organized crime was making a resurgence. Charlie hoped that historians would identify Sanders as the worst FBI director in history.

But right now he was Charlie's boss, whether Charlie liked it or not. Charlie knew he himself was the only high-ranking Bureau official retained from the prior administration. He would have been gone, too, but Director Sanders had retained him because he needed someone with experience.

"Sure," Charlie responded. "You want some coffee?"

"That's OK. I'll only be a few minutes." Sanders sat down in a chair across the desk from Charlie. "Tell me what you know about the Jesse Thompson murder," he stated forcefully.

Charlie really shouldn't have been surprised that Sanders knew about the Thompson investigation, but he was. He tried hard to look like he really didn't know anything, but he knew it was too late.

"Not much," replied Charlie, deciding to cover himself. "He was a friend of the vice president and was shot by a disgruntled customer. Why?"

"Are we investigating?"

"Not really," Charlie lied. "The Secret Service is lead on this one because of the connection with the vice president. We don't have any jurisdiction over the local authorities because the crime occurred completely within the borders of the same state. Why do you ask?"

Sanders rubbed his chin. "No reason in particular." He studied Charlie. "I heard the victim was a friend of the vice president and thought maybe we had some involvement in the investigation. That's all."

Each man sat in silence for a few seconds.

Charlie could tell that Sanders was measuring him . . . and above all, making sure Charlie knew he was watching. Charlie met the director's gaze with as much determination and confidence as he could muster.

After what seemed like an eternity of awkward silence, Sanders finally stood up to leave. "Let me know what you find out," he stated as he left Charlie's office.

"I will."

He's up to something. I know it.

Just what Sanders was up to, Charlie didn't know, but he would find out. Saul Sanders never came to his office unless there was a reason behind it, and certainly not at this hour of the day.

I'll have to be careful, Charlie realized. Someone in his department was a mole for Saul Sanders, but whoever it was would one day regret it.

Charlie didn't like being ambushed. If Sanders had summoned Charlie to his office, he would have had time to prepare, and the element of surprise would have been lost.

Charlie refused to let Sanders have the upper hand, even if the man was his boss. So he followed the heavyset man out into the hall, watching as he strode arrogantly toward the elevator with smug satisfaction written all over his face.

Charlie was enraged that Sanders had walked into his office without a warning from his secretary. When he was certain Sanders was safely out of hearing range, he charged into Marcia Naylor's work station. Her gray-paneled cubicle was immediately outside the entrance to Charlie's office.

"How dare you do that!" Charlie screamed.

"Do what?" Charlie's secretary cowered from the unforeseen attack.

"Allow Director Sanders to walk into my office without warning me."

"I tried to stop him, but he wouldn't," she defended. Her voice quivered in fear.

"If it happens again, you're fired," Charlie threatened. He shook a firm index finger in her face.

Then he stormed back into his office and slammed the door.

Law offices of Holcombe & Reed, Jackson, Tennessee

Madge arrived at the office just after eight, and Jake was lying in wait for her like a hunter waits for his prey. She was barely in the office when the attack began.

"How dare you be late," he accused. "Especially when so much is going on."

Madge set down her purse. She started to open her mouth, then abruptly shut it again.

"And how dare you let me forget about Lillian Scott's settlement!" he continued. The stress of the past five days had so built up inside that he could hardly see past it. "It's your job to remind me of things . . . of important matters, like the Scott case. But you didn't. So instead, I've been awake since four o'clock worrying about it. I have a good mind to fire you!"

Jake faced off against Madge, his hands jammed on his hips. He was daring her to respond, to defend herself.

Madge was tough, so he wasn't surprised when she attacked back.

"*I'm* not the lawyer," Madge countered, her hazel eyes narrowed to slits. "*You* are. Remember? If you want to fire me, then do it."

He backed down a little and took a breath. "You know I've been spending every hour since Wednesday working on Jed's case. It's your job to remind me about all my other files. I can't have things getting out of control like this."

"And I won't be treated like this," Madge fired back, punctuating her speech with angry gestures that sent her glasses swinging widely on their chain. "I don't need this job anyway."

Jake stared at her. He knew Madge needed her job. Just as he knew that nobody else would work for him. He was a demanding boss. Sometimes he took on clients that were equally or more demanding, and the result was enormous stress on him and his staff. Madge too often was on the receiving end of rants from him or a high-maintenance client. But she was tough and could handle the pressure, he knew.

Still, there was no benefit to berating Madge over the Scott case.

"Forget it." He waved a dismissive hand and began to bark out instructions. "The Scott trial is next week, and we have a lot of work to do. The file is in the conference room. I made a list of witnesses who need to be subpoenaed. Start with that, and bring me the deposition of the defense's expert witness. I need to file a motion to exclude part of his testimony."

Jake plopped down in his chair and began dictating a draft of a pretrial motion into his tape recorder. He only spoke a few words before his mind wandered and he laid the recorder on his desk. As he sat there alone, he began to realize that Jed's case was affecting him like no other case had.

You've never lost control of your emotions like this, he told himself.

But ever since Wednesday he'd been riding an emotional roller coaster. Several thoughts ran through his mind. *What could I have done differently to prevent this from happening? What did I miss when I talked to Jed last Monday?* But the one thought that troubled him the most was, *What if I couldn't come home to my wife and kids?*

He clasped his hands behind his head and leaned back in his chair. *You've got to get control of yourself.* He'd never threatened to fire Madge before. Sure, there'd been times when he was stressed and on edge, but he'd never threatened Madge with her job.

He hung his head. Madge was right. She didn't have to take it. She wasn't the lawyer—he was.

And he'd have to find a way to do something he wasn't good at. Apologize.

He exhaled a heavy sigh and then started dictating again.

Five minutes later Madge was back in his office with the doctor's deposition and a separate piece of paper. She laid the deposition on his desk and handed him the single sheet of paper.

"I think you need to look at this," Madge said, a little smile creasing her lips. "It just came over the fax machine."

Jake glanced at the paper. He could tell from the name of the law firm at the top of the page that it was a letter from Bob Whitfield. He held his breath and began to read silently.

Dear Jake,

You did not respond to my offer by last Wednesday, and I assume by your silence that it was rejected. Therefore, my client has authorized me to increase our offer to $250,000. This is our last offer. Take it or leave it.

Sincerely,
Robert H. Whitfield

Jake looked up at Madge and smiled. For once Bob had failed to see the obvious. Jake had spent so much time with Jed the last several days that he had thought of nothing else. Bob had to know it because Jake had been on every news broadcast the last five nights in a row. But instead of going for the kill, Bob Whitfield had given Jake new life. Bob should have realized there was no way Jake could prepare for the Scott trial by next Monday, but he didn't.

Jake had just learned something about Robert H. Whitfield, Esquire. Under all the bluff and bravado, Bob was weak.

Jake thought about calling Bob and telling him that Ms. Scott would take nothing less than $300,000. Then he decided he'd better not push his luck. He'd just had his hide pulled from the fire. Ms. Scott had authorized him to settle for $175,000. She'd be ecstatic over $250,000.

Jake wrote *Agreed* on the bottom of Bob's fax, signed his name, and handed it back to Madge. "Fax this back to Bob."

Madge eyed him with that same funny smile as she took the fax.

"And Madge?" he called.

She turned around and poked her head back into his office.

"I'm sorry about before."

Madge raised an eyebrow.

"I was just blowing steam, you know? It's been a long five days," Jake tried.

She wagged her head. "Don't worry about it. I know it's been tough. But thanks anyway."

After Madge left, Jake leaned back in his chair and propped his feet up on his desk. Jake's part of the Scott settlement would be just over $80,000. Somebody had to be looking out for him, he thought, but he wasn't sure why. For just the briefest of moments he was able to relax, to forget about Jed McClellan. He quickly calculated that he would clear about $50,000 after splitting the fee with Barrett and covering overhead expenses.

How was he going to spend the money? he asked himself. Certainly he'd invest some of it. After that, perhaps a trip with his family. Or maybe they could buy a new car. There were so many possibilities. He needed to call Rachel and tell her the good news. Everything was finally back in the right order . . .

A minute later his daydreaming was interrupted by the receptionist's voice over the intercom. "Jake."

Jake glanced at his watch. 8:45. The short respite had been nice, but now it was back to reality. He'd have to wait a little longer before sharing the good news with his wife. "Yes, what is it?"

"Ms. Naomi McClellan is here to see you."

Jake paused. He didn't have an appointment with Naomi McClellan but, after all, she was Jed's mother. She probably needed a shoulder to cry on, so to speak, and Jake needed to talk with her about Jed's case anyway.

"OK," Jake agreed. "I'll have Madge show her back."

As he waited for Naomi's arrival, Jake wondered whether she realized that at best Jed would spend the rest of his life in jail. Fate had already been unfair to Naomi McClellan, Jake knew. Her father had probably been executed by the Klan, and her husband had deserted her. Naomi didn't deserve another tragedy.

But nobody ever said life is fair, Jake thought, shaking his head.

His office door opened, and Madge ushered Naomi McClellan in.

"Please sit down." Jake pointed at one of the chairs. "May I offer you something to drink?"

Naomi wore the same worn blue dress with a white collar and five white buttons marching down the front that she had worn at Jed's arraignment.

"I'm fine," Naomi replied politely. She sat where Jake had indicated and set her purse on the floor beside her. Her face looked tired and worried. "Thank you anyway."

"How are Ruth and the kids doing?" Jake asked as he sat back down behind his desk.

She sighed. "Terrible. Just terrible. I'm not sure how much more Ruth can take. She hardly sleeps. Tosha cries for her daddy all the time, but Derrick thinks he needs to be the man of the house. He thinks he needs to take care of Ruth and Tosha. Protect them. I'm afraid Ruth's gonna have a nervous breakdown if Jed don't come home soon."

"How are *you* doing?" Jake asked sympathetically as he studied her.

Naomi had birthed Jed and nurtured and raised him most of his life without the help of any spouse, Jake knew. And now he saw the glimmer of determination in her eyes. As if she would be willing to trade places with

Jed in an instant, even if that meant living out her life in jail . . . or dying in his place. He marveled at her courage.

"I'm OK," Naomi answered, but tears began to stream down. "It's tough, you know, but I'm gonna make it." She forced a smile. "The folks at the church have been good to me, and I know God's in control. We're gonna be OK."

The words fell flat against Jake's ears. Perhaps he'd heard them too much when he did attend church. And then, in his line of work, he'd seen too many things out of control to believe there was a God who was in control anymore.

"I'm doing everything I can for Jed," Jake assured her. "You know that, don't you?"

"I know," she replied.

Then her expression changed to one Jake couldn't quite identify.

"Do you have any children, Mr. Reed?" Naomi asked.

"Call me Jake, and yes, I do. Rachel and I have three kids."

"Would you do anythin' you could to protect 'em?"

"Absolutely. Rachel and our kids are the only family I have."

She looked at him quizzically. "Would you sacrifice your own life to protect them?"

"Of course I would, Ms. McClellan," Jake replied. "They're my children. But that's a strange question. Why did you ask it?"

"There's somethin' I need to tell you," Naomi said. "I don't know if it will help or not, but I think you need to know." She paused, one hand twisting a button on her dress. "It's difficult for me to talk about. I've spent thirty years hidin' from the truth, but it found me. I've never told anyone about this, not even Jed."

"What is it, Ms. McClellan?" Jake prodded, giving her his full attention.

Naomi took a shaky breath and averted her eyes. It was clear she didn't want to look Jake in the face. "Jesse Thompson is Jed's father," she said quietly.

Over the years of his practice Jake had learned to expect the unexpected. Despite the best pleas or threats, clients never told him everything. A personal-injury client would lie about prior injuries. A criminal defense client would lie about prior arrests. When the truth came out—and it usually did—there was always more damage to the case than if the client had been truthful on the front end.

As a result Jake had become cynical. He'd learned to hold himself back from getting involved with clients. He thought he was prepared for anything.

But nothing could have prepared him for the news Naomi McClellan just delivered.

Jake didn't realize he was staring at Naomi until she glanced at him. The slight movement of her head caused Jake to blink. "I don't understand," Jake said finally, cutting through the tension in the room. "How could Jesse Thompson be Jed's father?"

Naomi continued to fumble with the middle button on her dress. "He raped me," she replied without emotion.

Jake felt something kick in his gut. Sadness? Anger? Disbelief? He lowered his head for a minute, supporting his chin with his fist.

Was it true? If so, he was amazed even more at this older woman's courage. *How difficult it must be for her to talk about this.* He suspected it was a secret Naomi had planned to carry to her grave. But now Jake knew. And he didn't want to add any more to her embarrassment by asking further questions. So he waited for her to continue.

"I remember the day like it was yesterday. I had been working at the Thompson house only a few weeks. Mrs. Thompson had gone to town, and I was in the bedroom makin' up their bed. Mr. Thompson came in, threw me on the bed, and raped me."

When Naomi was silent for a few seconds, Jake asked, "Did you tell anybody?"

She sighed. "In those days blacks didn't have no rights. If I had gone to the police, they would have just laughed at me. I never even told my husband. He was light-skinned, like Jed. He thought Jed was his son."

"Why did you keep working for Jesse Thompson?"

"I was a young black woman. I had little schoolin'. Where else was I gonna work? I needed a job then—and especially five years later, after my husband left. Mrs. Thompson paid me well. Treated me well. So I stayed.

It never happened again, and I never even told Mr. Thompson that Jed was his. I was afraid to."

Jake rubbed his chin thoughtfully. The story was unbelievable. But if it was true—and only a blood test or DNA testing could confirm its truth—Jesse Thompson was the father of the man accused of murdering him!

"Ms. McClellan, you know that if I tell your story, the world will soon know your secret, don't you?"

"I know." She lifted her chin.

"There will be a lot of questions." Jake caught her eye before he continued. "It's not as if you're accusing a common criminal of rape. This is Jesse Thompson you're talking about. You'll be called a liar, and nobody will believe you. Everywhere you go in town, people will be pointing at you and whispering."

"I've thought about all that."

"Are you willing to take that chance?"

"I don't care what happens to me. I'll do anythin' to help Jed."

Jake would have a lot more questions for Ms. McClellan later. Right now he needed to decide how to use this information to help Jed. "Ms. McClellan, I need to think about what you have told me. And how this information could impact Jed's case. To figure out how to reveal it to anybody else."

Naomi must have sensed his hesitation. His struggle to believe her story. "I know it's hard to believe, but it's true," she insisted. "Jesse Thompson is Jed's father."

"We've got to prove that with more than your word, and that may be difficult."

How am I going to get a sample of Jesse Thompson's blood?

"I understand," Naomi said. "I'll do whatever you need me to." She picked up her purse. "I've taken up enough of your time. You've got other things to do."

"You can stay as long as you like," Jake offered. And he meant it.

"I know, but I really need to go."

Jake understood. He was the only person in the world who knew her secret, and she had to escape from his presence.

"Good-bye," she said softly and left.

He stood to shake her hand and then watched as she walked down the hall toward the reception area.

How brave she is, he thought again. *Not only for telling me and risking scorn, but also for working every day, all those years, for the very man who had violated her.*

He wondered. Could he have done such a thing? And what about if it had happened to his wife? Or his daughter?

Jake shook off his heavy thoughts and closed the door.

Jake hadn't been able to uncover any information about the black pickup Jed described to him immediately after his arrest. Every place Jake turned had been a dead end.

Now Naomi McClellan had just offered the first real break in the case, and he had a lot of work to do.

New York City

The first interview Shannon Foster had ever done was conducted before a live audience at a studio on Broadway in New York City, but was being taped to be replayed at the designated time slot. She sat on the stage at the bottom of the amphitheater-styled studio with Lori Curry, the show's host. Lori was an attractive, petite brunette, and her show was watched in millions of homes across the country.

Shep watched from just offstage.

After introducing Shannon to the audience, Lori asked, "How long have you and Senator Foster been married?"

Shannon smiled. "We had our twenty-eighth wedding anniversary in June. And it's been the most wonderful twenty-eight years of my life."

A rousing round of applause erupted from the audience as congratulations for the longevity of Mac and Shannon's marriage.

"Twenty-eight years!" Lori exclaimed. "You don't look old enough to have been married that long. I've got to know your secret."

Applause mixed with laughter arose from the audience.

Shannon chuckled lightly and crossed her legs at the ankles. Shep thought she appeared almost embarrassed by the compliment, but that wasn't bad, either.

It was clear that everyone in the studio recognized that Shannon was very attractive. Her blond hair showed no signs of graying. Her green eyes were still intoxicating, and her face was wrinkle free. Shep knew she exercised regularly, and it showed. Her taut, five-foot-six frame made her appear thirty-five instead of fifty-five. If any middle-aged man saw the show, he would be envious of Mac Foster.

"Seriously," Lori resumed after the applause died down, "you're a very beautiful woman, and I'm glad you're able to be with us on the show. Tell me, Mrs. Foster, as First Lady, what would be the number one thing you'd like to accomplish?"

"I have always had a special place in my heart for children," responded Shannon. "I believe there is so much more we can do for our children. They are our future, and we need to educate them, love them, and protect them."

"Do you anticipate having an active role in your husband's presidency, should he be elected?"

"Oh, I doubt it. My husband is very capable of running the country without my help," Shannon quipped.

The audience laughed.

She's scoring a few points for the Foster campaign, Shep thought. *We did the right thing.*

"Mrs. Foster," Lori continued, "tell us a little about Senator Foster."

"He's a wonderful man," Shannon began. "He's an excellent husband and father and lives out his faith in God in everything he does." She gazed thoughtfully at the audience. "Let me tell you a story about my husband that will show you what I'm talking about. One Christmas when our children were small, Mac and I were talking about what to get them for Christmas. Mac suggested something that actually became a family tradition: that we contact one of the local civic organizations and get the names of some underprivileged children who needed toys and clothes. Our kids had the best time buying toys and clothes for those other children.

And we continue that tradition to this day, even though our kids are now in college. Mac is always thinking of others . . . and what he can do to help them."

Shep continued to watch Shannon's interview from his position, stage left. To him the interview couldn't have gone better. Shannon was genuine and sincere. She appeared very First Lady-like. He knew her national television debut would put some life back into the Foster campaign—and right when it was so desperately needed.

The question that remained was how it would play in the polls.

The task of winning the presidency still seemed almost impossible, but they had taken a big step in the right direction.

And Shannon Foster, bless her, had carried out her part well.

CHAPTER FOURTEEN

En route to Dallas–Fort Worth International Airport

Mac Foster loved fall, and the long Labor Day weekend meant that autumn was just around the corner. The leaves on the trees would soon start changing colors, and Saturdays would be filled with college football games. Kennedy liked sailing; Ford played golf; and George H. W. Bush brought horseshoes to the White House. When he became president, Mac told Shep, Saturday afternoons would be set aside for watching college football.

"Labor Day also means there are only two months left before the election," Shep reminded Mac that Friday as they cruised toward Dallas–Fort Worth International Airport on the Boeing 747. "And we are still trailing by ten points in our own polling."

Mac nodded. "I know. But the campaign is a long way from being over. Everything will come together in God's timing, not ours."

"I'm sure you're right. By the way, we did get a little bounce in the polls from Shannon's interview."

Mac appeared thoughtful. "I still don't like the idea of her being exposed to the media. But I have to admit, she did a great job." Mac stood to stretch his tired legs and walked around the cabin. "Shep, I watch our campaign workers and some of them have defeat written all over their faces. But you never do. Why is that? Why do you always seem so positive?"

"It's the same thing you just said. I'm convinced that God has a plan, and part of that plan is for you to become president. With that kind of outlook, how could I be anything other than positive?"

Shep meant what he said, but he also knew he wasn't being entirely forthright with Mac. Shep had a sudden urge to spill everything about Dalton Miller's investigation but suppressed the words before they erupted from his mouth.

Now is not the time, he reminded himself. *Let Dalton get some clear proof first.*

"We're almost to DFW," he noted. "You probably need to get ready for your speech."

"You're right." There was a twinkle in Mac's eye. "See what you can do about spilling some of that positive attitude on the rest of the staff, will you?"

The campaign plane landed at Dallas–Fort Worth International Airport just after noon. A platform was erected on the tarmac for a quick speech, and then the motorcade would be off to a "Texas bar-b-que" campaign rally. Mac had to carry Texas. Without Texas he had no chance of winning. He had already spent a lot of money in Texas and would spend a lot more before November.

The crowd at the airport was boisterous and completely pro-Foster. The Texas governor, a Republican, met Mac as he descended the stairway from the airplane. The governor had announced his endorsement for Mac during the primaries and had been campaigning hard for him in Texas. Hundreds of supporters were waving Foster-for-President signs. Thunderous applause and cheers greeted Mac as he stepped up to the podium in a red-and-black-plaid shirt and jeans. He motioned for the crowd to quiet down, and the noise softened to a small roar. Shep stood just to the side of the platform, stage right, and soaked in all the applause and cheers. He smiled slightly in anticipation as Mac stepped to the microphone, because Mac always began his speeches the same way.

"Friends, it is time for a change!"

The crowd erupted again. Mac backed away from the podium and triumphantly raised his arms. The campaign rally planners arrived a few hours before Mac at every stop and always did an excellent job of whipping those in attendance into a frenzy. The television cameras recorded every cheer, and Shep hoped that a clip from the rally would be on the evening news on all the national networks.

Shep watched as Mac continued his speech. His wireless phone was set on vibrate because he knew he wouldn't hear a ring amidst the cheering. He felt the vibration and checked the caller ID. It was Dalton.

Shep stepped farther away from the rally so the noise would not interfere with the conversation. He raised the clam shell to his right ear and covered his left with his left hand to block the crowd noise. "Hello."

"Shep, this is Dalton."

"I haven't heard from you in a couple of weeks. I've been worried."

"I've been busy," Dalton stated.

"On our project, I trust."

"Of course," Dalton replied. "I haven't quite put my finger on it, but there's something out there. I told you about the Randolph Winston connection."

"Right."

"Well, my contact at the Bureau tells me that they smell something fishy about the murder of the vice president's friend in Tennessee."

"What does he mean?"

"I'm not sure. He tells me that it looks like a hit rather than a murder by a disgruntled customer like everybody is saying. The shot was too clean from too far away. They say there's no way the guy who's been arrested could be that good. Everything points to a known Colombian assassin."

"Do they think the vice president hired a hit man to take out his own friend?"

"They're not sure," responded Dalton. "They can't find any other connections. No large sum of money is missing from Burke's account, but it's hard to track every penny of campaign funds."

"Does the Bureau know about Winston?" asked Shep.

"I don't think so, and I didn't mention it."

"Good. Let's keep it like that for a while. What else do you have?"

"Get this." There was a little more excitement in Dalton's voice. "Deputy Director Armacost is covertly conducting the investigation into the Thompson murder, and he has not told Director Sanders anything about it. What do you make of that?"

"Obviously Armacost is convinced there's something to the assassination theory, but I don't know why he hasn't told Sanders. Perhaps he's waiting until he has more to go on."

"Or perhaps he's hedging his bets," Dalton said, answering his own question.

"What do you mean?"

"Armacost is the only holdover from the previous administration. Everyone else was sent packing, but not Armacost. Why? I don't know, but for some reason he doesn't trust Sanders."

"You think he might want to share his investigation results with us?" hoped Shep.

"Either that, or he might be planning to go straight to the vice president. Depending on what he finds, he could use it as a bargaining chip to get the director's job."

"Did your contact say what Armacost planned to do next?" Shep paced back and forth as he considered the information.

"They can't put too many men on this, or Sanders will smell something. Other than a phone call by one agent from the Memphis office, the Bureau has not performed any field investigation. Two agents are being sent in by the end of the week."

"I think you need to go too," directed Shep. "See what you can find, but don't let anybody with the Bureau see you there."

"I thought you might say that. I'm booked on the first flight to Memphis in the morning. It's the closest major airport to Jackson."

"Do you know anything about the lawyer representing the man accused of killing Thompson?" Shep knew that Dalton always did his homework.

"Only a little at this point. His name is Jake Reed. He's in his midthirties and married with three kids. His parents died when he was young, and he was reared by family members, mainly an aunt who died three years ago. He went to college on a partial baseball scholarship and worked odd jobs to make up the difference. That's where he met his wife. She put him through law school, and he finished fifth in his class at Vanderbilt University in Nashville."

"Sounds like he's determined to succeed. What are his politics?"

"As best I can determine, he's apolitical. He voted in the last three presidential elections, but not in any primaries. It's impossible to tell whether he has any loyalties, and if so, where they lie."

"Any skeletons?"

"None that I've found."

"You better get going," Shep said as he drew the conversation to a close. "Let me know as soon as you hear anything new."

"I'll do that."

"And, Dalton, hurry," Shep pleaded. "We're running out of time."

Shep placed the phone in his left inside coat pocket and returned to the platform to hear the conclusion of Mac's speech. He had heard it so many times before that he could give it himself from rote memory.

". . . and ladies and gentlemen, I want to be your next president!"

The crowd roared its approval as Mac waved his arms victoriously and left the platform for his waiting limousine.

Shep entered the back of the car opposite Mac. He still couldn't tell Mac what was going on. Perhaps he never would, but the future was beginning to look brighter, and that was the important thing. His biggest concern was time. Whatever Dalton found would be useless if he found it after the election was over.

"Shep, you look troubled about something," Mac stated when Shep sat down across from him. "What is it?"

"Nothing, sir," Shep lied. "Nothing."

Pinecrest Club, outside Jackson, Tennessee

It had been ten days since his meeting with Naomi McClellan, and Jake still had not told anyone else her story, including Rachel. He was convinced, at least, that Jesse Thompson had raped Naomi. He couldn't imagine that any woman would voluntarily subject herself to the ridicule and scorn that would come from falsely accusing a dead man of rape. The question he struggled with was whether Jesse was in fact Jed's father. Jake didn't doubt that Naomi believed it, but he had to be certain. Naomi was married at the time, so her husband could also be the father.

Jake had to find out for sure. He knew that DNA testing, or even a simple blood test, could prove almost conclusively whether Jesse was Jed's father or not. Getting blood or a hair sample from Jed was easy enough, but Jesse was dead. The only place Jake could find a sample of Jesse's blood would be in the evidence room at the sheriff's department.

The Labor Day weekend was just beginning. It was early Friday evening, and Jake was on a mission. As he pulled into the parking lot of the Pinecrest Club on Highway 70, west of town, he cringed. What a stark contrast his Volvo was to the motorcycles and pickups with rebel flags in the rear windows. The rectangular club building was constructed of concrete blocks, painted white, and trimmed in green. A sign on top displayed a picture of mountaintops and a pine tree growing from the highest point. All windows in the building were covered from the inside by confederate flags.

Jake probably wouldn't have been welcomed at a place like the Pinecrest under any circumstance, and the fact that he was the lawyer of a black man accused of killing a white man didn't help matters. His palms were sweating as he reached for the doorknob. He could only guess what his wife would say when she found out he'd died at the Pinecrest.

When he stepped inside, everyone stopped what they were doing and stared at him. All he could see through the cigarette smoke were angry faces with shaggy, unkempt beards immediately above sleeveless shirts bearing some type of motorcycle logo. Every arm boasted at least one tattoo, and every foot was covered with a cowboy boot.

I bet there's no tassel loafers in this crowd, Jake thought. *But at least no one's wearing a white cloak and pointed hat.*

"I'm looking for Billy Laymon," Jake said to the bartender.

The bartender had been drying a glass beer mug when Jake entered, and he was still holding it in his hand. The stub of a cigar protruded from the right corner of his mouth, which was surrounded by a long beard and mustache. His nose was crooked.

Perhaps from a barroom fight?

The bartender never said a word. He simply indicated with a jerk of his head that Billy Laymon was in the back of the room.

The room was still deathly silent. No cards were being shuffled, and no billiard balls were being racked. There was not even any music playing. Jake had no idea what hell was like, but as he walked farther into the interior, where the light of day never reached, he decided hell had to be better than the Pinecrest.

In this crowd, even if he tried to make an escape, he'd have no chance. The roughnecks would be all over him. It was safer to find Billy and get his business done than try to run. He could feel every eye in the room on him as he walked through the smoke in the direction the bartender had indicated.

Finally he saw Billy sitting at a table in the back corner playing poker. "Billy, I need to talk to you." Jake looked at the other men standing nearby, trying to determine where an attack might come from.

Billy waved a dismissive hand at his playing partners. "It's OK, boys. I can handle it."

Loud music, louder talking, and cussing arguments over poker games resumed immediately, as if Jake wasn't even there.

"What do you want, lawyer?" Billy asked sarcastically.

Jake sat down in a chair across the table from Billy. "I need your help on the *Jed McClellan* case."

"I ain't helpin' you get that Negro off," replied Billy through gritted teeth.

"Billy, I don't need much help, and nobody will ever know you were involved."

"Whatever it is, I ain't doin' it," Billy responded emphatically. "You need to get out of here before I turn some of these boys loose on you."

"I was hoping you would agree to help me voluntarily," Jake said. "But if you want me to tell your wife about your girlfriend down in Memphis, I will."

Even though the room was gloomy and swirled with smoke, Jake could see the fright on Billy's face. Billy had no way of knowing that a law school classmate of Jake's represented the girlfriend's husband in their divorce. When Jake had heard about it, he decided he would save that card to play on ol' Billy some time, and now was the time. Everybody in town knew that Billy's wife was someone to be reckoned with. She'd have Billy's hide if she found out about his affair.

Billy's disposition went from anger to sheer fright. Jake could see the pulse in the lawman's temples from across the table. Billy glanced anxiously around the room to make sure nobody else had heard Jake's words.

"That's right, Billy," Jake continued in a calm tone. "I know all about it. I even have copies of photographs out in my car right now. You want me to show them to you?" Jake partially rose from his chair.

"No, that's OK," Billy snapped.

In that instant Jake knew he was completely in control. Billy would agree to anything Jake wanted.

"Are you ready to help me?"

Billy relented. "What do you want me to do?"

Jake didn't tell Billy about Naomi McClellan's story. He simply told Billy that he needed a sample of Jesse Thompson's blood from the evidence room.

"I can't do that!" Billy exclaimed.

Billy's reaction garnered a couple of looks from the patrons nearby, so Jake waited until everyone resumed their meaningless activities before continuing.

"Sure you can, and you will," Jake directed.

"That's tamperin' with evidence."

"Don't take the whole thing. Just swab off some and bring it to me."

"How do you suggest I do it without anyone seein' me?"

"You're a smart guy." Jake smirked. "Figure it out. I don't care how you do it. I just need a sample, and I need it next week."

"You don't give a guy much time, do you?"

Jake's mission was accomplished. He stood up and pushed his chair under the table. "See you next week, Billy."

There was a swagger in Jake's step as he strode back through the crowd. He'd been inside the Pinecrest and lived to tell about it. He bet there were very few people who could make that claim. He stopped just before opening the door and scanned the inside of the club one last time.

"Nice place you've got here," Jake commented to the cigar-chewing bartender as he closed the door and left.

Crown Plaza hotel, Manhattan

"Is everything ready for tomorrow's campaign rally?" Ed Burke asked as Ben Tobias entered Ed's suite on the top floor of the Crown Plaza on the corner of 8th Avenue and 48th Street. The posh presidential suite would be Ed's home for a couple of days. Only the best would do for the vice president.

A rally had been scheduled in Central Park for Saturday morning. Labor Day weekend was a great time to gather big crowds.

"Right on schedule," Ben replied. He consulted his watch. "It's almost midnight, and I think the construction crews plan to stay through the night if they have to in order to finish erecting the stage and speakers."

"Good, that's good," Ed muttered loud enough for Ben to hear it. He poured Ben and himself a gin and tonic, and handed Ben his tumbler as they moved into the sitting area of the suite.

"How are the polls looking?" Ed asked as they sat down, facing each other across the coffee table.

"Couldn't be better," Ben answered. "We're showing a 14 point lead, and I heard that Foster's polls are showing him trailing by 10. Either way, you're well in front. Trailing on Labor Day will be impossible for Foster to overcome. And, even better news, contributions continue to increase. Foster will never be able to catch us on spending."

The Federalists are doing their part, Ed thought. Money was pouring in from all corners of the country.

"Is Senator Mulvaney going to be on the platform with me tomorrow?" Ed asked. "I want to do everything we can to win New York."

"He'll be there. He has no affinity for his counterpart in the Senate, so he'll do everything he can to make sure Foster doesn't win. Mulvaney will whip the one hundred thousand or so people at the rally into a frenzy for you."

Ed couldn't help but chuckle at the thought.

"It looks like you're going to get your wish," Ben continued. "A landslide is a real possibility. The polls show that Foster is only leading in Michigan, Mississippi, and New York."

"I like the sound of that," commented Ed. He placed his empty glass on the marble coffee table, stretched out on the couch, and closed his eyes. "I hope everything after the election is as easy as winning has been."

"What are you talking about?" Ben replied. "You're going to be the best president in history." He grinned.

"That's not what I meant."

"What did you mean then?"

Ed had carried the Federalists' secret for several years. There were times when he'd wanted to tell Millie, but he never did. Their marriage was not strong enough. He desperately wanted to share his burden with someone, and Ben had become a close friend and confidant. At that moment, Ed desired to tell Ben about his pact with the Federalists like he'd never desired anything before.

But as his mind grappled with the secret, reality struck. Ed knew Ben hungered for the same power he did. But he doubted Ben would approve of his agreement with the Federalists. This was not the right time to discuss it. He had to win the presidency first.

"Never mind," Ed replied.

"Ed, if there's something I need to know, then tell me," Ben cajoled.

"It's nothing really." Ed yawned. "I'll tell you about it later. By the way, see what you can do about those last three states. I want to crush Foster."

"I've been thinking about that very thing. Foster has been begging for a debate. I think we should give it to him."

"Why do you think that?" Ed sat back up on the couch. "We're leading. You know as well as I do that the only person a debate can help is the one who's behind."

Ben smoothed a few wisps of hair over his balding head. "This may be one of those exceptions to the rule, because I think you'll eat him alive. His extreme right-wing positions will be displayed for the whole country to see. Your lead coming out of the debate can only increase. It's a no-lose situation."

Ed liked the sound of that. He wanted to win every state, and win big. That would be a mandate, he told himself.

"Let's do it," he decided. "Call his staff, and get it scheduled."

CHAPTER FIFTEEN

Sanders residence, Arlington, Virginia

Saul Sanders was very cautious to maintain the lifestyle of a federal employee. He refrained from driving expensive cars or wearing $3,000 suits. He had every penny of the $10,000 Randolph Winston paid him every month tucked away in a secret account in a bank in Nassau.

Saul made sure he didn't communicate with Randolph while in his office at the J. Edgar Hoover building. In a few months Randolph would have a line directly into Saul's office, and he wouldn't care who knew they were talking. But for now the secrecy had to be maintained.

Randolph always called at precisely 8:00 a.m. every Saturday. A separate telephone line had been installed in the study in Saul's house in Arlington, Virginia, and only Randolph had the number. The phone bills were sent to a post-office box in Arlington, where they were gathered by a courier and forwarded to Randolph for payment. Saul didn't particularly like getting up early on Saturday mornings, but for $10,000 a month, it was a minor inconvenience.

"Armacost is looking into the Thompson murder," Saul told Randolph shortly after their weekly briefing began. "But he hasn't found anything yet."

"Why is Armacost interested in a murder in Tennessee? Does he think there's more to it than the local authorities have found?"

"I don't think he's looking for anything in particular," responded Saul. "He's just looking. It's not every day that a friend of a vice president is murdered. Armacost is always a little suspicious. But I think he'll give up soon."

"Let me know if anything new comes up. We can't have any surprises this close to the election."

"I will," Saul assured Randolph. "There's nothing there for him to find, and like I said, he'll pull the agents off in the next few days."

Saul knew he couldn't tell Deputy Director Armacost to stop an investigation that really didn't exist, particularly since he technically didn't know anything about it. He and Randolph had decided it was better to let Charlie Armacost conduct his investigation and leave Jackson as soon as possible. Randolph was satisfied that no disruption in the Federalists' plan would come from the Thompson murder.

First Baptist Church, New Orleans

It impressed Shep that Mac Foster made it a priority with his advisors that the entire campaign staff attend a church somewhere every Sunday, regardless of where they may be geographically in the country. It wasn't always practical, but Shep made a concerted effort to comply with Mac's request. Mac had told him that he thought it was important for people around the country to see his faithfulness to what he believed. And Mac needed the weekly refill.

On the Sunday before Labor Day they were in New Orleans at the First Baptist Church, and all Mac's top advisors were present and accounted for. Shep sat on the third row, middle section, and Jack Bennett sat beside him. Mac was on the row immediately in front of them with the family of the church's pastor, Dr. Dawson McGregor.

The morning worship services were almost over, and Shep couldn't wait to get back on the campaign trail. His whole life revolved around Mac Foster's campaign for the presidency.

Politics was in Shep's blood. He had run for a seat in the New York State Senate in 1988 but had been beaten when the local newspaper printed lies about his being an alcoholic. He swore he would never run for office again himself but would do all he could to get people with conservative values elected to every public office.

Not long after that he met Mac Foster. Their alliance became successful almost immediately. Shep guided Mac to a seat in two U.S. House of Representatives elections and to the Senate in 1996, when he'd defeated Saul Sanders, current FBI director, for the open seat.

The driving force behind Shep was one issue: abortion. To say he hated it was an understatement. He abhorred it. The thought of one more innocent unborn baby being murdered sickened him.

It had all started for Shep in 1986. His wife, Sarah, had a miscarriage, and her physician said she would never be able to have children. So Shep and Sarah decided to adopt a child. When they brought Jonathan home, it was one of the happiest days of their life. During the process of the adoption Shep learned that there were hundreds of prospective adoptive parents waiting to adopt a child, but not enough children. He was against abortions before that time, but became even more so when he realized that every abortion was unnecessary. He committed himself to doing everything he could to stop the senseless killings. And the best thing he could do was to help put a pro-life president in the White House.

So when Mac decided to run for the presidency, Shep was right there. He was prepared to do whatever it took for Mac to win. The ends justified the means with Shep. And right now the "end" was that Mac Foster had to win the presidency. That was why he'd had to hire Dalton Miller, and Shep wasn't ashamed of it.

Shep had hardly heard anything the pastor said during his sermon. His mind was churning as he thought about how they could overcome the deficit to Burke. Finally Dr. McGregor gave the benediction and dismissed the congregation. Mac, his Secret Service detail in tow, exited the church first, with Shep and Jack following closely behind.

"Is there something you're not telling me?" Jack asked Shep as they bounded down the concrete steps in front of the church.

Shep turned toward Jack. "What do you mean?"

"I mean, I see you talking on the telephone all the time, but I don't know to who. You're always optimistic, even when we're trailing by 10 points. What's going on?"

"I'm just trying to keep the troops encouraged."

"There's more to it than that, Shep," Jack said, his hazel eyes probing. "Tell me what it is."

Shep considered his dilemma. The time was not right to tell Jack about Dalton since the PI really hadn't found anything of substance yet. And the more people who knew about him, the more chances that Mac would find out and shut down the entire investigation. Shep could not let that happen. It was their only chance.

"Let's just say you can never tell when something might break," Shep replied. He changed the subject of the conversation as they reached one of the Suburbans waiting to transport them to their next stop. "But enough about that. I finally got confirmation from Burke's people that they'll agree to do one debate."

"How did you do that?" Jack asked. "I thought his staff had been telling our people they wouldn't even consider it."

"They had been, but Ben Tobias called me last night to tell me they want to hold a debate as soon as possible. I don't know why the sudden change, but it may be one of those breaks I was talking about. I'm going to get it scheduled as quickly as I can. We need something to change the momentum of this campaign."

Hilton Head Island, South Carolina

Claudia and Hudson strolled hand-in-hand along the pristine shoreline just behind Eden. The morning tide gently splashed on their bare feet. The Labor Day weekend marked the end of the vacation season at Hilton Head, and the island was remarkably desolate in the weeks that followed. Most of the remaining inhabitants were either permanent residents or those few wise souls who had discovered the ideal time of the year to visit the island.

As they walked, Claudia and Hudson met a woman on a bicycle. Her yellow Labrador retriever followed close behind. A hundred yards from the water's edge, a flock of kingfishers skimmed the wave crests in a perfect, straight-line formation, searching for breakfast. Six or eight sandpipers accompanied Claudia and Hudson, occasionally poking their beaks in the sand for a mussel. A man stood waist-deep in the Atlantic with his rod and reel, fishing for ocean perch. Several joggers passed them.

Claudia and Hudson continued their leisurely pace as the cool ocean breeze wafted across their faces.

It seemed like it was only yesterday that Hudson had arrived, but it was already Tuesday morning and time for him to return to New York. Claudia longed to go with him, but she knew their relationship could not be public yet. That was OK with her. He assured her that before too long the whole world would know, but the timing was not right. He promised to take care of her and love her, and that satisfied her. Claudia loved him, too, and had stopped inquiring long ago about when the right time would be. Their time together was too precious to her to disrupt it with petty questions.

There was something different about Hudson this trip, though. He seemed distant. Worried. Claudia had noticed it when he first arrived and thought it would disappear as the weekend progressed. It hadn't.

"Is something bothering you?" Claudia asked now, hoping she could help.

Hudson stopped walking. He turned her toward him and tenderly brushed her hair away from her face. "I cannot tell you what it is, but it has nothing to do with you."

"I'm worried about you. I've never seen you like this."

"I'll be all right," he assured her. "Soon everything will be OK, and I'll explain it all to you. Promise me one thing, though."

"Anything." She squeezed his hand.

"Promise me that no matter what happens, you'll always love me."

"Hudson, you're scaring me."

"Just promise me, Claudia."

"I promise."

She wrapped her arms around him as Hudson drew her body close in an embrace.

"What do you think they're talking about?" Bill Osborne asked Al Moyers. The camera in Bill's hands made a rapid *click* as he took photographs of Hudson and Claudia in quick succession.

"I don't know," replied Al. "This transmitter isn't working very well.

I can't hear them over the sound of the ocean." He was holding a device that looked like a radar gun used by a police officer or state trooper and was pointing it at the couple who had stopped to hug on the beach.

"That's OK," Bill stated. "I think we have enough photographs and other recordings to file a report."

"I agree," Al said. "Let's get started."

Sheriff's department, Jackson, Tennessee

"Mornin', Timmy." Deputy Billy Laymon walked into the outer office of the evidence room bright and early on Tuesday. Deputy Timothy Henderson sat behind a green metal desk, reading the sports page from the morning newspaper.

Deputy Henderson's office was not much larger than a jail cell and was sparsely decorated. A map of Tennessee hung on the wall behind the desk, and a four-drawer metal filing cabinet stood in one corner. Other than one picture frame containing a photograph of his wife and child, and a large desktop calendar, his desk was completely clean.

"Mornin', Billy," Timmy responded. "What can I do for you?"

Billy began his rehearsed lines. "Remember that drug bust we made earlier in the summer on that guy named Toliver?"

Timmy looked up from the newspaper. From his puzzled expression, it was obvious he was trying to recall the arrest. "Was that the one where he swallowed the bags of marijuana?"

"That's the one," Billy answered.

"Yeah, I remember. What about it?"

"The preliminary is coming up next week, and I'm testifyin'. I need to look through the evidence for a few minutes."

Billy hated to lie to Timmy, but it wasn't a complete lie. The preliminary hearing was scheduled for the following week, and he was scheduled to testify. The part that was a lie was that he needed to look at the evidence. Billy knew the evidence in that case like the back of his hand. But he'd picked the Toliver case because alphabetically it would be close to the Thompson file in the evidence room.

"All right, Billy," Timmy said. "Sign in."

He pushed a clipboard with the sign-in sheet clipped to it in Billy's direction. Billy signed the sheet of paper and wrote down the time of day, 8:35. Timmy unlocked the door to the evidence room with a set of keys he removed from the top drawer of his desk. Opening the door, he pointed toward the right-hand side. "The Toliver case is over there."

"Thanks, Timmy," Billy said as he entered. "I'll only be a few minutes."

Timmy propped the evidence-room door open with a rubber doorstop and returned to his morning paper. The evidence room was thirty feet deep and fifty feet wide. It contained twenty rows of gray metal storage racks. The floor-to-ceiling racks stood parallel to each other and extended almost wall-to-wall. A space of three feet remained between the ends of the racks and the walls for visitors to walk. Narrow aisles separated the racks, providing barely enough room for one person to view the contents of an evidence box.

Billy walked to the end of the room where files beginning with the letter *T* were located. In his mind he recited the alphabet slowly as he scanned the name on each box until he reached *Thompson*. His heartbeat rapidly increased as he slid the box containing the evidence from the Thompson murder out into the aisle between the storage racks. Billy was far enough away from the open door that Timmy could not see him. But that also meant he could not see Timmy.

"Did you see that game Saturday night?" Billy called out to Timmy, to make sure he was still in the other room.

"Yeah, that was some game," Timmy answered from the outer office. "I was just reading about it in the paper. Did you know that Morrow threw for over three hundred yards?"

Billy opened the top of the box and found the manila envelope containing the blood samples removed from the side of Jesse Thompson's truck. "Yeah, I know," he called back to Timmy. "We watched the game on Mark's big screen. Have you ever been over to his house?"

"No, why?" Timmy responded curiously.

Billy opened the envelope and removed one of the plastic bags. Inside the bag was a piece of cardboard with some of Jesse Thompson's blood smeared on it. He reached into his pocket and removed another plastic bag. Inside the second plastic bag was a cotton swab, which he used to remove some of the blood.

"His den is painted solid orange," said Billy with a chuckle. "That really is somethin' to see. My wife would kill me if I painted our den orange."

"Did you say Mark's den was orange?" Timmy said, his voice sounding louder . . . and closer.

Billy's heart beat even faster, if that were possible. *He's coming this way!* Frantically he began putting the Thompson evidence box back together.

"Billy, did you say Mark's den was orange?" Timmy asked again. Billy could hear the other deputy's footsteps as he passed the aisle containing the *S* files and turned into the aisle where Billy was.

"That's right, Timmy, orange." Billy pushed the box containing the evidence back into place just as Timmy reached him. "Ain't that somethin'? An orange room."

From the inquisitive look on Timmy's face, Billy knew he needed to escape before Timmy prolonged the conversation.

"Thanks, Timmy," Billy said with a slight slap on Timmy's shoulder as he passed him. "I've got to go."

Billy left the evidence room and walked straight out the back door of the sheriff's department building without stopping. He was so nervous, he thought he'd vomit before he got to his patrol car. Once inside the car, it took a few moments to calm down. He closed his eyes and drew a shaky breath.

A knock sounded on the driver's-side window. It was one of the other deputies, returning from patrol duty.

Startled, Billy rolled down the window.

"Everything OK in there?" the deputy asked.

"Sure," Billy said. "Just kinda tired today. Spent all day at the lake yesterday, and it's catchin' up with me."

He turned the ignition to start the car, waved at the other deputy, and exited the parking area.

He and Jake had made prior arrangements about where Billy would leave the plastic bag containing Jesse Thompson's blood, so Billy drove straight to the drop location.

As he approached the location, Billy called Jake's office.

"Good morning, Holcombe & Reed," the receptionist answered.

"This is Deputy Laymon with the sheriff's department. I need to speak with Mr. Reed."

When the receptionist placed him on hold, Billy disconnected the call. He knew that the prearranged signal had been given to Jake. He simply left the bag as planned and drove away as fast as he could.

CHAPTER SIXTEEN

Law offices of Holcombe & Reed, Jackson, Tennessee

"Did you notice that someone rented the old jewelry store across the street?" Madge asked as Jake entered the back door of the office around ten o'clock. He was returning from retrieving the package Billy Laymon had left for him.

"No, I didn't," Jake said shortly. He didn't trouble himself with such trivial matters. He walked into his office and unlocked his filing cabinet. Inside the top drawer of the filing cabinet was a manila envelope containing a plastic bag with a strand of Jed McClellan's hair, which he had obtained surreptitiously over the weekend when he visited Jed. He placed the plastic bag from Billy in the same envelope and closed the drawer. A lab in Memphis was sending a courier to pick up the envelope later today. They had promised him he'd have the results as soon as possible.

"Mrs. Alexander, who owns the building across the street, said the new tenant also rented the upstairs apartment," Madge persisted as she walked into his office just as he was locking the filing cabinet.

Ellen Alexander was a client of Jake's. He had helped her probate her late husband's will a couple of years ago. The old jewelry-store building across the street from Jake's office was part of the assets Mrs. Alexander had received from her husband's estate. She had been trying to rent it for several months.

"What?" Jake replied. He really hadn't been paying attention before now. But something Madge said was catching his interest.

"The store across the street," Madge reminded him. "Mrs. Alexander said the tenant also rented the upstairs apartment. They paid cash up-front for a six-month lease."

That's odd, Jake thought. Nobody paid for the whole lease on the front end, and certainly not with cash.

"Did she say who the tenant was?" Jake asked.

"No. She just said it was two men, and they were going to remodel it into an interior design business. They covered all the front windows so nobody can see in during the renovation."

"Two men living together in an apartment above an interior-design business?" Jake asked sarcastically. "That's just what we need."

The building across from the offices of Holcombe & Reed was a perfect location from which to conduct the clandestine investigation. The Bureau had been glad to pay $9,000 for a six-month lease. The two agents would probably be there less than a month, but the landlady had refused to agree to a lease shorter than six months. They had negotiated with her like real businessmen for appearance purposes but would have paid whatever she wanted.

Agents Ronald Boyd and Jerry Simon had been sent to Jackson from the New Orleans office. They were loyal to Deputy Director Armacost, and he had personally selected them for this assignment because their accents would blend with those of the local residents.

Ron and Jerry had been involved in busting one of the largest money-laundering schemes in the Southeast. Ron had infiltrated the Capris, a New Orleans organized-crime family that owned the Paradise Island riverboat casino. Jerry had posed as a drug kingpin from Houston, with ties to South America, who had a need to run money through the casino and then to an untraceable account in Panama City. The Capris had liked the idea and sent millions of dollars of their own money to Panama as well. Cash from the casino was loaded into a small plane in New Orleans and then flown to Panama City, where it was deposited into an account set up by the Bureau.

The Capris family never did figure out why the airplane was able to make it safely to Panama City and back every time, when other planes with illegal shipments couldn't. The $100 million that was in the account when the Capris family was arrested was used to fund other FBI under-cover operations, including the $9,000 given to Ellen Alexander.

Ron and Jerry had hung Opening Soon signs on the outside front of the old jewelry store right away. Since the locals had heard the rumors about the interior-design business, it was inevitable that someone would try to peer in the front windows. It was impossible, though, because the agents had covered the windows immediately with thick black paper.

Early in their assignment the agents planted small, wireless transmitters, or bugs, throughout the offices of Holcombe & Reed and tapped the telephones. There wasn't a sound that could be made in the law offices that the bugs wouldn't pick up, and Ron and Jerry had to hear every sound that came out of Holcombe & Reed. In the two weeks they'd been there, they'd heard nothing unusual. The Jed McClellan trial was the most talked-about topic, but even those conversations were nothing other than typical trial preparation. At most, Ron and Jerry would stay through the trial in case something important happened; then they would disappear as mysteriously as they'd arrived.

Just then another curious local pressed his face against the glass in the front door, trying desperately to see what was going on inside. Jerry laughed. When would the townspeople realize they couldn't see in?

After trying to peer in the front door, Dalton Miller walked casually back to his car, which was parked two blocks up from the old jewelry store. He knew FBI agents were in town, and he had finally found them. They were watching Jake, but they didn't know that Dalton was watching them. He drove past the Holcombe & Reed offices just as the van from River City Laboratory was pulling up.

Madison County Criminal Justice Complex, Jackson, Tennessee

At the preliminary hearing regarding the case of *State of Tennessee v. Jedediah McClellan*, Jake had discovered that the sheriff deputies at the crime scene had searched Jed's truck without obtaining a search warrant. Deputy Butch Johnson had testified that the gun was covered by the tarpaulin and was not in open sight in the back of the truck. Jake saw Assistant DA Julie

Anderson cringe when Butch stated that he had removed the tarpaulin to see the gun. Jake believed that was an illegal search, and the other defense attorneys waiting in the courtroom that day for their clients' cases to be called agreed with him. If the gun was inadmissible, then the DA would have a hard time convicting Jed of murder, especially capital murder.

The preliminary hearing had been held the week after Jed's arrest, and Jake had filed a motion to suppress the discovery of the gun the following day. The motion had been scheduled for a hearing before Judge Prickett this morning, the Monday following Labor Day. If Jake could somehow convince Judge Prickett to exclude the murder weapon from the evidence presented to the jury, then he might have a shot at an acquittal.

Jake entered the meeting room through a door that connected the holding cell to the courtroom. He wanted to talk with Jed before the hearing. Jed was dressed in the same orange jumpsuit that he'd worn to the arraignment and the preliminary hearing. It had been several days since Jake last saw Jed, and he immediately noticed the changes. Jed's hair was even more shaggy and unkempt, and his eyes were sullen. He evidently hadn't shaved for a while, and he had lost weight. It had been almost a month since his arrest, and confinement in the CJC was beginning to take its toll.

Jed sat in a chair at the small wooden table with his back toward the door. He stared blankly at the concrete block wall across from him. He hardly acknowledged Jake's entrance.

Jake took the chair at the end of the table, to Jed's right. In all the time that had passed since Naomi's confession, Jake had never told Jed who his father was. He wouldn't unless he had undeniable proof from the DNA testing. Even then, if it was true, what had happened was something a mother should tell her son personally first. Before it got out in public. Even if it might swing the court's decision about Jesse's trial.

"Jed, if we win this hearing, we will be in a better position to reach a plea bargain with the DA."

Jed never took his eyes off the concrete wall. "I ain't pleadin' guilty to somethin' I didn't do." His voice was deliberate.

"Jed, we've talked about this before. If they convict you, there's a chance you could be sentenced to death," Jake said firmly.

"I don't care," Jed fired back. "I didn't do it, and that's it."

"Jed, you're being unreasonable. Think about Ruth and the kids. If I can plead you to manslaughter, and you only have to serve eight years, then you should take it."

Jed finally looked at Jake. "If Judge Prickett throws out the gun"—he began to sob brokenly—"can you get him to set bail?"

"I'll try."

"You've gotta get me out of this place," Jed begged. "I've gotta go home to my wife and kids."

Jake knew his client was looking for a little hope. The man needed something to hold on to. Would it be so bad to give Jed what he needed, right now?

After all, Jake reminded himself, *Jed probably wouldn't be in this situation if it weren't for you.*

This whole case seemed to be spinning out of control, and Jake liked to be in control. He didn't like to ask for help from anybody. Even going to Billy Laymon under the table had gone against Jake's grain. He'd spent almost a month working on the case, doing everything he could to get Jed out, but nothing was working. Maybe today their luck would turn. After all, it was clear that everyone in the previous hearing had considered the search of Jed's truck illegal. So the judge would have to grant Jake's motion to suppress the murder weapon, wouldn't he? And without that proof it was possible that soon this whole nightmare would go away.

But Jed McClellan couldn't wait. He needed encouragement *now.*

"Without the gun Judge Prickett might even dismiss the whole case," Jake blurted out.

It wasn't a complete lie, but it wasn't the truth, either, and Jake knew it. Chances were very high that Judge Prickett would rule to suppress the evidence, due to the illegal search, but it was doubtful he'd dismiss the case. Yet Jake was compelled to keep his client's hope alive.

Jed straightened in his chair. A glimmer of relief shone in his eyes. "Do you really think so?"

"It's possible," assured Jake. "But we've got to win this motion first."

There was a knock on the door, and a court security officer popped his head in. "The judge is ready for you, Mr. Reed."

When Jake and Jed were both seated in the courtroom, the deputy called out, "*State of Tennessee versus Jedediah McClellan.* Motion to suppress filed by the defendant."

"All right, Mr. Reed," said Judge Prickett. "Let's hear what you've got."

Jake rose from his chair behind the defense table and approached the lectern between the two tables. "If it pleases the court, we are here today on the defendant's motion to suppress certain evidence obtained by the sheriff's department in violation of my client's constitutional rights. The prosecution relied on this evidence in indicting my client for this murder and will seek to introduce said evidence to the jury at trial."

Jake continued, very eloquently explaining to the judge why the gun, the alleged murder weapon, should be excluded from the trial. He reviewed the facts about how Deputy Johnson removed the tarpaulin to expose the gun without obtaining a search warrant. Jake referenced the judge to numerous cases decided by both the supreme court of the State of Tennessee and the Supreme Court of the United States. Those cases, he argued, were similar to the *McClellan* case and required the Court to suppress the gun as evidence.

Judge Prickett sat in his large leather chair behind the bench in the front of the courtroom. He listened very politely, but Jake could sense the judge wasn't really paying attention. Had he made up his mind before the hearing?

". . . and that is why we believe that the court should rule that the gun is inadmissible," concluded Jake. He returned to his chair behind the defense table and sat down beside Jed. He gave Jed an encouraging pat on the back as Judge Prickett turned to District Attorney General Drake Highfill.

"General, do you have anything?" asked the judge.

Drake Highfill rose from behind the prosecution table and buttoned the top two buttons on his three-button suit coat before approaching the lectern. He held his head high as he walked. His shoes glistened from a recent shining, gold-engraved cuff links were visible beyond his coat sleeve, and his suit and shirt were fresh from the cleaners. His skin was so tan that he had to be making regular visits to a tanning salon. Everything about Drake was perfect . . . and it made Jake sick to his stomach.

It was absurd how important Drake tried to look, Jake thought. Only in Drake's own mind was he important. His position as lead prosecutor in the three-county district could easily be wrested away from him at the next election, and then Drake would be nothing.

"Your Honor, the present case is clearly distinguishable from the cases cited by counsel for the defendant. The defendant could not possibly have had a privacy right in the contents of the bed of his pickup. The items in the bed of the truck, including the tarpaulin, were in plain view. Since the tarpaulin was in plain view, then it could be removed to expose what was beneath it. The investigating officer did not violate the defendant's constitutional rights when he discovered the murder weapon."

Ten minutes later, when Drake concluded his argument, Judge Prickett was ready to render his decision. "Gentlemen, I've read your memoranda and listened to your arguments. You each did an excellent job presenting your respective sides of the case. The court is of the opinion that the sheriff's department did not violate the defendant's Fourth Amendment right against unreasonable searches and seizures. Therefore, the court finds that the defendant's motion to suppress should be denied." With no further explanation Judge Prickett banged his gavel and turned to the courtroom deputy. "The court will stand in recess," the judge announced as he abruptly left his lofty perch and disappeared to his chambers.

"All rise," the courtroom deputy commanded as Judge Prickett exited the courtroom.

Just before the bailiff led Jed away to the holding cell, Jake leaned over and whispered to Jed, "It'll be OK. We can get this overturned on appeal if we have to." But Jake wasn't confident about that.

Drake began smugly answering questions from reporters even before he left the courtroom.

Meanwhile, Jake hustled out of the criminal justice complex to avoid the reporters' questions. He was stunned at Judge Prickett's decision. Before the hearing he'd been fairly certain—even cocky—about Judge Prickett's agreeing with his position on the gun. Even now he believed that Judge Prickett's decision was wrong.

The ruling had taken Jake by complete surprise.

Now Jed was on the fast track to death row, and it was all Jake's fault.

For the first time Jake could remember, his client's fate was almost completely out of his control. And he didn't like the feeling.

CHAPTER SEVENTEEN

Fogelman Center, University of Memphis

Shep Taylor and Ben Tobias had spoken several times by telephone following Ed Burke's decision to debate Mac Foster. Details had to be worked out. The time. Place. Moderator. Town-hall format, questions from the moderator, or questions from the candidates. Shep tried to negotiate the best arrangement he could for Mac, but Ed had the lead and the leverage. Shep finally had to concede to almost everything Ed wanted. The date was set for the last week of September.

The auditorium at the Fogelman Center had only 150 seats, and most of them were filled with reporters from the different news agencies, print and television. The few remaining seats were taken by supporters loyal to Ed Burke. Only a handful of Mac Foster's supporters were permitted in the auditorium.

Shep, Jack, and Shannon sat on the front row on the right-hand side of the auditorium. Admittedly, Shep was nervous, and he could see nervousness on the faces of Jack and Shannon, too, since they believed the entire campaign rode on this debate. Shep had completed an interview with FOX News a few minutes before the debate began. He had conceded that Mac had to do well during the debate. Otherwise, they would be unable to close the gap before Election Day.

Ben Tobias and Millie Burke sat on the front row on the left-hand side of the auditorium. Their smug expressions made Shep's blood boil.

The auditorium was constructed in an amphitheater style. Each row of seats was slightly elevated above the one in front of it. The room was completely dark, except for the stage area, which was flooded with hot white lights. Two identical podiums, blue top over gray base, stood approximately ten feet apart. Each podium was draped with a banner of red, white, and blue bunting and held one microphone. The moderator sat at a table on the front of the stage, facing the candidates, with his back to the audience. On the front of the stage, between the moderator's desk and the audience, stood a bank of three television cameras, their lenses directed at the podiums. Hidden behind the blue curtain that covered the rear wall of the stage was a single camera that focused on the moderator. Every movement, every gesture, every word spoken on stage would be broadcast around the world.

"Good evening," the male anchor from CNN stated to both the audience watching the debate in the auditorium and those tuning in by television. He had been chosen as the moderator by the Burke campaign. "Welcome to this first, and only, debate of this presidential election. I'm Barry Cannon from CNN, and I will be the moderator tonight. The candidates have agreed to certain ground rules, so before we begin the debate, I want to go over those with you."

Barry explained the rules for the one-hour debate, rules that were dictated by the Burke campaign. Then Barry introduced the candidates. Ed entered from stage left; Mac from stage right. Each wore a dark suit. Ed's tie was red. Mac's was royal blue. They met in the middle of the stage, shook hands briefly, and retreated to their respective podiums. Each candidate gave a brief opening statement, highlighting the strengths of his campaign and attacking the weaknesses of his opponent's. To Shep they sounded like trial lawyers trying to persuade a jury to side with their client.

Then the questioning began. "Mr. Vice President," Barry said, "our world faces an enormous amount of political unrest. As president, what will you do to protect the United States from future attack?"

Shep could tell that Ed was prepared. Without hesitation he eloquently explained his foreign-policy philosophy. He talked about increased spending for NATO and reducing the number of American troops in the Middle East. The United States must work with other countries to build a global military under NATO, he advised. He explained that the United States had to continue spreading democracy throughout the world.

Then Barry directed the same question at Mac. He, too, was prepared. Mac had statistics about how depleted America's armed forces were. He compared the smaller amount of military spending under the current Democratic administration against the larger amount of military spending in previous Republican administrations.

Mac's knowledge of foreign-policy matters surprised Ben and Millie, Shep noticed. A small sense of satisfaction came over him as their smugness slowly began to disappear.

"We live in a different world than our parents did, Barry," Mac said as he continued to display his mastery of foreign-policy issues. "Our parents never had to contend with terrorists. There are a tremendous number of people, in several different countries, who despise Americans. We can do very little to change their perception of us, but we can take active steps to protect ourselves from any attack they may mount. Unlike Mr. Burke, I think we must first increase our intelligence so we can defuse potential terrorist attacks before they happen. Second, we must continue to solidify relations with our allies, such as England and Israel. And lastly, I think we should continue our policy of never negotiating with terrorists and never backing down when we are threatened."

The questioning then turned to economic policy. Again, Mac held his own. He was as fluent in discussing financial markets as Ed. They had their differences. Mac proposed a tax cut. Ed didn't. Ed wanted to spend more money on welfare issues. Mac didn't. But by and large, each man demonstrated an in-depth understanding of the American and world economies.

For forty-five minutes Ed and Mac went toe-to-toe like two heavyweight boxers. Neither made any mistakes, and neither landed any knockout punches. Shep could hardly control his excitement. Mac's performance was exactly what the campaign needed.

"It is now time for our candidates to ask the other candidate one question," Barry advised. "Senator Foster, we'll begin with you."

"Thank you, Barry," Mac replied. "My question for Vice President Burke concerns fund-raising. Mr. Vice President, reports circulated during the primaries that you were accepting illegal campaign contributions. Is that true or not?"

A collective silence fell over the crowd in the auditorium. Shep leaned forward in his seat to get a better look at Ed Burke's face. If Ed denied the truth of the assertion, he would be lying. Shep wanted to see Ed's face as he lied.

Ed smiled slyly. With the entire nation on the edge of its collective seat, Ed dramatically reached under his podium and slowly retrieved a stack of papers. Shep could see that it was a computer printout of some type. Hundreds of sheets of paper that stood at least a foot high. Ed placed the printout on the top of the podium and ran his hand across one end of it. The ruffling sound echoed through the quiet auditorium.

"Senator Burke." Ed tapped the top of the stack with the index finger of his right hand. "This printout contains the names of contributors to my campaign. This one only goes through the letter C. I have nine more printouts just like this one in my office. So no, I have not received any illegal contributions. The hard-working people of these great United States are funding my campaign."

Ed didn't blink. He didn't grimace. He didn't flinch. His body language gave no indication that he was lying.

Shep slumped back in his seat, deflated. Mac's question had backfired.

Then it was Ed Burke's turn to ask his question. Shep knew that Ed would ask the one question the entire Foster campaign team feared. That's why he had tried desperately to prohibit direct questions between the candidates. But Ben Tobias had been adamant that there would be no debate unless the candidates were permitted to ask each other one question. Everybody with the Foster campaign knew what Burke's question would be, especially Shep. And they knew what Mac's answer would be.

"Senator Burke, there will probably be at least one Supreme Court justice who will retire during the next administration, and maybe as many as three. I want to know, and I think the American people have a right to know, whether, as president, you intend to appoint jurists to the Supreme Court who will vote to overturn *Roe v. Wade*."

Mac didn't hesitate before responding. "I absolutely intend to appoint justices to the Supreme Court who will overturn *Roe v. Wade*. I would hope that you would do the same thing, Mr. Burke. It is time for the senseless killing of unborn children to stop."

Although Shep agreed wholeheartedly with Mac personally, he also realized that the Burke campaign had accomplished its goal: painting Mac

Foster as an extreme right-wing religious fanatic. The voting public cared little for the differences between where Mac stood on foreign policy and economic issues, and where Ed stood.

The damage had been done to the Foster campaign . . . and Shep feared the blow was lethal.

Apollyon Associates, Inc., Lower Manhattan

Randolph pressed the button on the remote control, and the screen on the television in the Apollyon conference room went dark. He, Pierce, and Milton sat quietly in the dimly lit conference room. They didn't care to see the television journalists analyze the debate. Burke for President was an unstoppable train, and the Federalists were driving it. It was time to move forward.

"Things are going extremely well," Randolph announced and swiveled in his chair to face the others. "I don't see any possibility that Burke can lose. I think it's time we begin to finalize the details."

"I agree," concurred Pierce as he stretched out his long legs in front of him. "We need to be prepared to place things into motion immediately following the inauguration in January."

"Let's not be too hasty," commented Milton. "I agree that we need to be prepared, but the election is still six weeks away. We need to remain cautious."

"Cautious?" responded Randolph. "There's no need to be cautious. Victory is ours."

"That type of confidence will be our demise, my friend," Milton replied. "Tell me what's happening with the investigation in Tennessee."

"What do you mean?" Randolph inquired.

"Is the FBI still investigating the Thompson murder?" Pierce asked, appearing annoyed that he'd been kept out of the loop.

"Saul Sanders told me there are two agents in Jackson," Randolph explained, "but they shouldn't be there for much longer."

"I hope not," Milton replied, rubbing his hands together. "But we need to keep our eye on that situation."

Randolph scowled. "Saul assures me he's monitoring it and that we have nothing to worry about."

"Still," Milton continued, "I'm worried about what is going on there. I don't like the fact that the FBI is investigating. It makes me uneasy."

"Stop worrying," Randolph assured Milton. "We're six weeks away from the election, and everything is under control."

"Randolph's right," Pierce said. "What's going on in Jackson, Tennessee, is not important. We must maintain our focus on the task in front of us. Let's forget about everything else and focus our attention on implementing our post-election strategy."

"I hope you're right, Randolph," Milton said as the conversation began to conclude. "But I'm afraid we're making a monumental mistake by ignoring it."

After the meeting Milton McAdams took his leave first. As Randolph watched the dignified banker exit, he sat back, fingers interlaced thoughtfully, and frowned.

CHAPTER EIGHTEEN

Law offices of Holcombe & Reed, Jackson, Tennessee

Early October brought welcome relief from the heat in West Tennessee. September had not been as hot as August, and October's temperatures were really quite pleasant. Jake drove to his office with the driver's-side window down for the first time since late spring. The large trees lining North Highland Avenue were beginning to turn different shades of brown, yellow, and red. It made him wish that his occupation permitted him to work outdoors.

Jed McClellan and his case was practically all Jake had thought about since mid-August. He was convinced that his error in judgment had started the sequence of events that had led to Jed's serious predicament. After all, if Jake had phoned the authorities when he'd first heard Jed make a threat toward Jesse Thompson, Jed probably would have been called in for questioning instead of getting drunk and then driving to Jesse's farm. Jake felt sick. He'd endured many sleepless nights just thinking about it.

Worse, Jake's defense of Jed had met roadblocks at every turn. Bail had been denied and so had the motion to suppress. The writing was on the wall for Jed. Jake decided it was time to seek a plea bargain.

He dialed the number for District Attorney Drake Highfill's office. "This is Jake Reed," he announced when the receptionist answered the phone. "I need to speak with Drake Highfill."

"Hold please," the receptionist responded. "I'll see if he's available."

After a few seconds Drake Highfill was on the line. "Jake. What can I do for you?"

"I want to talk with you about the *Jed McClellan* case."

"What is there to talk about?" Drake said, his tone haughty. "Judge Prickett denied your motion to suppress."

"I know," Jake replied. "But I want to talk with you about a plea bargain."

"Jake, this is an open-and-shut case . . ."

"I disagree with you. I think you should consider manslaughter in the first degree."

"Why?" Drake retorted. "Give me one reason I should consider that!"

The silence was deadly, and Jake knew it. He couldn't think of any leverage he had to use against Drake to pry a plea bargain from him. Jed had been found at the murder scene. The murder weapon had been in the back of Jed's truck, and Jed had motive.

"You can't think of one, can you?" Drake answered for him. "I'm not even willing to discuss life without parole with you."

Before his conversation with Drake, Jake thought he at least would get Drake to agree to first-degree murder. If he had, Jed would serve a minimum of twenty-five years, but he wouldn't be put to death. Without a plea bargain, Jake was certain Jed would die. After he hung up the phone, Jake realized just how desperately he needed a break.

Madge knocked on his door and interrupted his sulking. "The receptionist said there's a Belinda Llewellyn here to see you. Does she have an appointment with you?"

"I don't think so. Did she say what she wanted?"

"She said she was Wanda Lacy's daughter. Do you know who that is?"

"I know Wanda Lacy. She's a client of mine."

"She's not a client anymore. Ms. Llewellyn said she was here to talk to you about her mother's estate."

"Estate? I didn't know Ms. Lacy died." Jake clasped his hands around the back of his head, leaned back in his chair, and closed his eyes. He really didn't have time to meet with Ms. Llewellyn. Every ounce of his being had to be focused on saving Jed.

"You want me to tell her you can't meet with her?" Madge asked.

"No," he responded after a couple more seconds of silence. He opened his eyes again and released his head. "I owe it to Ms. Lacy to see if I can help. Bring her back."

Wanda Lacy had been a long-time client of Holcombe & Reed. She was elderly, eccentric, and wealthy. Jake had helped her with her estate planning a few years ago but hadn't seen her much since then. Wanda lived in a modest white-brick, ranch-style house on Old Medina Road, not far from Jesse Thompson's farm. She had slowly become a hermit following her husband's death and had rarely been seen outside of her house other than in her garden. Jake heard the rumor that she buried one thousand tin cans with one thousand dollars in each of them in her backyard. He also heard about some teenage boys who tried to find a few of those tin cans two years ago and were met with a couple of shotgun blasts from the kitchen window. With his preoccupation on Jed's case, Jake hadn't noticed Wanda Lacy's obituary in the newspaper last Sunday.

Belinda Lacy Llewellyn was forty-nine, overweight, and had glaringly artificial red hair. Wanda had told Jake years earlier that Belinda had moved to Connecticut thirty years prior and had only visited Jackson once a year since then, at most.

"I'm sorry to hear about your mother," Jake said as Belinda entered his office. "She was a wonderful woman."

"She's in a better place now," Belinda replied. She sat in one of the leather chairs across the desk from Jake. "Mother always said that when she died, she hoped God would give her a garden to work in heaven. I bet she got what she wanted."

"I bet she did too," Jake said politely. He had never thought of Ms. Lacy as a religious woman. "What can I do for you?"

"I was going through some of Mother's things after she died and saw where your office had prepared her will. The family would like for you to handle the estate for us."

If circumstances were different, Jake would have jumped at the opportunity to probate the estate of Wanda Lacy. The estate would be large, and that would mean a large fee. But he just couldn't take that responsibility with Jed's case looming.

"Ms. Llewellyn, I'll be honest with you," Jake began. "I'm extremely busy right now, and I'm afraid I cannot devote the amount of time to your mother's estate that will be necessary."

"I understand, but we really wish you would consider it," Belinda insisted.

Like her mother, Belinda was persistent. And, Jake also realized, she couldn't get access to her mother's money unless an estate was probated.

"We don't know any other lawyers in town," Belinda explained, "and it appears that you took good care of Mother's affairs."

"I really can't," Jake said again.

"I have all of Mother's papers with me," Belinda continued. "Would you at least look through those?"

Belinda removed a large envelope from her satchel and handed it to Jake. Reluctantly he opened the clasp and removed the documents inside. The will was one he had prepared. He also found life-insurance policies and bank records.

He sighed inwardly. *It will take someone the better part of a day to make heads or tails of all these documents.*

The last items in the package were three photographs.

"What's this?" Jake asked as he pulled the photographs from the envelope.

Belinda shrugged. "We're not sure. Mother was quite a shutterbug. She kept a full darkroom in the house to develop her own photographs. Most of the photographs we found were of flowers or other plants from her garden. They were scattered all throughout the house, but none appeared to be of any significance. The pictures you're holding seem to be the only ones she wanted to keep. We found them among her personal papers, as if they had some importance."

Jake looked closely at the 8 x 11 inch photographs. They were black-and-white and grainy, but in the first photograph he could clearly see the images of two pickups parked near a fence. One truck looked like Jed McClellan's Dodge. Immediately Jake recalled Jed's story about a black pickup at the murder scene. Had Jed been telling the truth? Jake had given up on that thread because he hadn't been able to find any other evidence to corroborate it.

Jake's pulse quickened. *Could this be the mysterious truck?*

The other truck in the photograph sure looked like Jed's. He slid the first picture to the back of the stack and exposed the second photograph. It, too, was grainy, but Jake could make out the image of a man standing near the back of one of the trucks. It appeared as though the man was placing something in the bed of the truck. Jake couldn't make out the face of the man, though. Perhaps it could be enlarged?

Jake hastily turned to the third photograph. The quality wasn't much better than the other two, but the scene was different. It contained the image of the rear of one of the trucks. It was as if Ms. Lacy was intentionally trying to photograph the rear of the truck for some reason . . .

And then it hit Jake. *That's it! She was trying to photograph the license plate!*

He squinted at the white area on the back of the truck in the picture but couldn't make out the numbers.

Jake looked up from the photographs. His mind was racing. *Could Jed have been right all this time? Could he have been framed? If so, who would frame Jed, and why?*

Belinda broke his concentration. "Mr. Reed, are you all right? Do those photographs mean something to you?"

"They might, Ms. Llewellyn. Do you mind if I keep them?"

She answered with another question. "Do you think you'll be able to help us with Mother's estate?"

Jake wasn't certain of the value of the photographs, but they were certainly worth making a small promise to Belinda. "I'll take a look at what you have here and get back to you."

"Thank you, Mr. Reed. I'll call you later in the week and see how things are progressing."

"That will be fine. I have another client scheduled in just a few minutes, and I really need to conclude our meeting."

After Belinda left, Jake scrutinized the photographs and pondered the mystery truck and the timing of the revelation.

Would these fuzzy photos be the break he needed to get Jed out of this mess?

Agents Boyd and Simon in the old jewelry store across the street from Holcombe & Reed recorded every word of the conversation between Jake Reed and Belinda Llewellyn.

"They may not be anything," Ron said to Jerry, "but we better get a copy of those photographs just in case."

They retrieved the photographs from Jake's office during the night and scanned them into their computer. The scanned images were uploaded into Deputy Director Armacost's computer at FBI headquarters.

The originals were returned before anyone arrived for work at the offices of Holcombe & Reed the next day.

FBI headquarters, Washington DC

The photographs of Raoul Miguel Flores and the pickup he was driving were waiting on Charlie Armacost's desk when he arrived at his office. The photos were enhanced and enlarged by technicians in the lab in the basement of the Hoover Building. They clearly showed Raoul and a pickup with Kentucky license plates. The plates were traced to a tobacco farmer in central Kentucky who had reported the truck missing a few days before the murder. Another dead end.

The photographs confirmed that Raoul was at least at the Jesse Thompson murder scene. They weren't conclusive, but they likely proved that Raoul had carried out the assassination. But at least two questions remained. Who had hired Raoul, and why? Charlie decided there was only one way to find out. They had to find Raoul.

Funds such as those recovered from the Capris Family were never reported to Congress and never accounted for by the Bureau. Those monies were used to fund covert operations in venues around the globe, including Bogotá, Colombia. It was time for some help, and Charlie knew where to find it. He dialed the number for the unofficial FBI agent in Bogotá.

Juan Martinez was a native-born Colombian. His birth parents were upper-middle-class by Colombian standards. His father was a high-ranking judge who opposed the militarization of Colombia. Both his mother and father were gunned down on an ordinary traffic-clogged street in Bogotá in February 1980. Juan was a baby at the time, and miraculously his life was spared. A group of nuns reared him until he was ten. One of the nuns contacted somebody in the States, who contacted somebody else, until one day Charlie Armacost was knocking on the front door of the convent. That was sixteen years ago.

Juan had lived in America for eight years—learning English and being trained as an FBI covert agent. He had returned to Bogotá with a new identity and had infiltrated the Hermillo Family. Slowly he worked his way up the ranks of the cartel, while at the same time secretly informing the FBI of the cartel's cocaine-manufacturing activities. More than one drug lab had been destroyed as a direct result of Juan's information.

"Juan, this is Charlie," the deputy director said to his prodigy after Juan answered the encrypted call. "I need your help."

"What can I do for you, my friend?" responded Juan.

"Do you know an assassin named Raoul?" asked Charlie.

"I know he works for the Family. I have only met him on a couple of occasions. Why do you ask?"

"We've tied him to a hit here in the States that may have a direct relation to the presidential election. If it does, it's crucial that we find out who hired him. That's where we need your help."

"I understand. I'll see what I can do."

"And Juan—"

"Yes?"

"I need you to report directly to me. And only to me. I may have a mole in the Bureau, but I don't know who it is yet. The fewer people who know, the better at this point."

Juan's voice was calm. "I understand. I'll call you in a few days."

Assistant Deputy Director George McCullough entered Charlie's office just as he finished his telephone call with Juan. "Anything new on the Thompson murder?"

Charlie still wasn't sure whom he could trust. Someone was leaking information to the director. Was it George? Until the mole was revealed, Charlie had to be very careful.

"Nothing really," he replied. "We may pull out of there in the next week or so."

"We can't give up just like that, Charlie," George insisted.

"We're not finding anything. There's no need to continue if we aren't getting any leads. The local authorities may have the right man in custody."

"Why don't we give it at least through the end of the month?" George suggested. "If we don't find anything, then we can pull out."

"OK, let's give it to the end of the month." Charlie changed the subject slightly. "What are you hearing from the director's office about the investigation?"

George looked confused. "I thought Saul didn't know anything about this investigation."

Good, thought Charlie. The mole probably wasn't George.

"He knows all right," Charlie said. "He came in here the other day asking about the investigation. I told him nothing was going on, but I'm pretty sure he knew I was lying."

"How did he find out?"

"That's a good question. I have a leak somewhere, and I may need your help to plug it."

"You know you can count on me."

Charlie studied George's eyes. He watched his facial expressions. He'd been in the Bureau long enough to be able to tell, without the aid of a polygraph machine, when someone was lying. "Look at these photographs Ron and Jerry sent me."

CHAPTER NINETEEN

Law offices of Holcombe & Reed, Jackson, Tennessee

River City Laboratory faxed the results from the DNA testing to Jake on the Thursday of the second week of October. The results were conclusive. Jesse Thompson was Jed McClellan's father. Jake was the only person in the world who knew it, except for Naomi McClellan. Jake struggled with how to use the information for Jed's benefit. Perhaps his partner would have some ideas.

Barrett's office was upstairs and in the back of the building. It was directly over Jake's office below, and somewhat larger. Being the senior partner had some perks.

Jake headed upstairs and knocked on Barrett's door.

"Come in," Barrett called.

"Do you have a minute?" Jake asked as he entered the office.

It was decorated with mounted animal heads. Barrett liked the great outdoors, but he kept his trophies at the office because his wife wouldn't let him display them at home. Barrett's favorite, Jake knew, was a moose head from a kill in Alaska.

"Sure. Have a seat." Barrett smiled and gestured toward a chair.

Barrett's office was neat and orderly—a definite contrast to Jake's. The guest chairs weren't cluttered with manila file folders or court documents. Every book was in its place on the shelves behind his desk. Even the top of the eighteenth-century partners' desk was clear of debris and clutter.

Over the years Jake had come to appreciate Barrett as more than a law partner. He was fifty-eight, and for the last eleven years he had been Jake's mentor. Barrett had taught Jake the things a lawyer doesn't learn in law school. Things like how to treat a client with respect and how to negotiate without flinching. Above everything else, Barrett and Jake were friends, and Jake trusted him implicitly.

From the first time they had met, Jake knew why Barrett was so successful in law. He was an imposing figure—easily six-foot-five and 275 pounds—both in a courtroom and in his office. His quick mind and deep voice commanded attention from everyone within earshot. Barrett maintained the same military-style haircut he'd acquired nearly forty years earlier in the Marine Corps. Only now the flattop was mostly gray.

Barrett removed his reading glasses when Jake entered the room and gave Jake his full attention.

"I need some advice on the *McClellan* case," Jake began. "You know Judge Prickett denied my motion to suppress."

"I heard that," Barrett said. "How did Jed take it?"

"Not good. I'm really worried about Jed. He didn't look well when I saw him last. I don't know how much more of this he can take."

"Do you think Drake can convince a jury to sentence Jed to death?"

"That's what scares me the most," Jake admitted. "You know how I despise losing control of a situation. So I spoke with Drake about a plea, but he refused to even talk about the possibility. Since then I'm beginning to find some helpful leads, but I'm not sure it's going to be enough."

"What type of leads?"

"Wanda Lacy passed away the other day, and her daughter came to see me. She brought some pictures that appeared to show someone else was at the murder scene."

"That sounds promising," Barrett remarked.

"I know. But the murder weapon was found in Jed's truck, and he certainly had motive."

"Keep at it," Barrett encouraged. "The photographs might create reasonable doubt with a jury. Maybe you'll catch another break like the photographs."

"Maybe I have already," Jake continued. "Jed's mother came to see me the week after he was arrested with a shocking story. You're the first person

I'm telling this to, and I don't know any way to tell it other than to come right out and say it." He paused for a second so Barrett would understand the import of his next statement. "Naomi McClellan told me that Jesse Thompson was Jed's father."

Barrett's eyes grew wide. He was obviously startled. "You've got to be kidding! Jed's *father?*"

"I know." Jake shook his head slightly. "I was skeptical at first, but the DNA test just proved it was true."

"DNA test? Where did you get a sample from Thompson?"

Jake avoided the issue. "It's not important. What is important is deciding what to do with this information. I doubt it will be admissible. Do you have any suggestions?"

Barrett paused, his face thoughtful. "Why don't you sue Thompson's estate for a child's share? Jed and his children are heirs of Jesse Thompson, right?"

"Right."

"That means he's entitled to part of the estate."

"Do you think that will work?"

"You certainly have grounds to make the claim. And proof with the DNA testing. I suspect Mrs. Thompson will take the position that Jed can't profit from his alleged crime, but she might want to reach a financial settlement to keep word of this from getting out. And she might even try to influence Highfill for you. Who knows?"

Jake thought about Barrett's suggestion. Jed was a blood descendant of Jesse Thompson, and that meant he was entitled to inherit money from Thompson's estate. Thompson was probably worth $15 million dollars when he died. Jed could make a claim against part of that, and Mrs. Thompson would probably settle.

"Who's representing the estate?" Jake asked Barrett.

"I believe Bob Whitfield is the estate's attorney."

Jake lifted an eyebrow. "Bob Whitfield? Are you sure?"

"I'm sure," assured Barrett. "I was in probate court the day the estate was opened. The judge adjourned for a few minutes so Bob could go into chambers to swear in Mrs. Thompson as the personal representative."

Jake thought about how Bob Whitfield handled the Lillian Scott case and smiled. "I wonder what they would do to keep this quiet?"

Agents Boyd and Simon rewound the tape of the conversation between Jake and Barrett and played it again. Jake clearly said that Jesse Thompson was the father of Jed McClellan, the prime suspect. They dubbed the recording into the computer's hard drive, logged in to the Internet, and sent a secure e-mail with the recording as an attachment to Deputy Director Armacost. He would be able to hear it for himself in a few minutes. This assignment was finally beginning to get interesting.

Jake stood behind Madge as he dictated the letter to Bob Whitfield over her shoulder.

When she heard him say that Jesse Thompson was Jed McClellan's father, she stopped typing and turned around. "What did you say?"

"I'll explain later. For now, just type."

After a couple of revisions the final text was ready to be faxed to Bob Whitfield.

Dear Bob:

Attached you will find a copy of a DNA report prepared by River City Laboratory from Memphis. You will see that the results of the test conclusively prove that Jesse Thompson was the father of Jedediah McClellan. As such, my client, Jedediah McClellan, and his children are entitled to receive a large distribution from the Thompson estate. Also, I believe that it is worth something to Mrs. Thompson for this information to be kept confidential. Please let me know what

your client is willing to pay or do for our
silence.

Sincerely,

T. Jacob Reed

In less than an hour after the letter was faxed to Bob Whitfield, the receptionist informed Jake that Whitfield was on the phone.

"Jake, this is Bob Whitfield. We need to talk."

"I thought you might say that."

"I think I have more to offer you than money," Bob said coyly.

"What does that mean?"

"I can't discuss it over the telephone. Meet me at the Downtown Grill at six o'clock tonight. I'll be in the booth in the far back."

"I'll be there."

The Downtown Grill, Jackson, Tennessee

The Downtown Grill was located three blocks west of the court square in Jackson on Shannon Street. It was one of the locals' favorite eating establishments. The Grill, as most everyone called it, was a two-story building with a yellowish wooden exterior.

The Grill was already beginning to fill for the evening meal when Agent Ronald Boyd entered at 5:45 and asked the hostess where the restroom was located. She directed him toward the back of the restaurant. No one was sitting in the last booth closest to the restroom. *I bet that's where they're planning to meet.* As he walked by the booth, Ron very discreetly stuck a small transmitter underneath the table.

After he was in the rest room long enough to look like he'd actually used it, he walked out and saw a man and a woman sitting at the last booth. He smiled. He'd guessed right.

The meeting would begin in just a few minutes.

He walked toward the front door of the Grill just as Jake Reed entered.

Jake Reed was standing just inside the entrance of the Downtown Grill, scanning the crowd for Bob and Mrs. Thompson, when he overheard a conversation.

"Aren't you one of the men who's opening the interior-design business?" one of the waitresses asked a black-haired man.

"I am," replied the man. "We hope to be open in a few weeks."

Now is as good a time as any to meet a neighbor, Jake thought. He stepped over toward the newcomer and extended his hand. "I'm Jake Reed. I have the office across the street from you."

"Ralph Jones," the man said and shook Jake's hand without meeting his eyes. "It's nice to meet you, but I really must be going. Will you excuse me?"

"Sure. I didn't mean to hold you up."

Jake watched as Mr. Jones quickly exited the restaurant. The man had an athletic build, and his hand was calloused.

Odd. I would have suspected a softer hand from an interior-design consultant, Jake thought briefly.

Then he turned back to the main dining room and saw Bob Whitfield sitting in the back booth with a woman who looked like Mrs. Thompson. The seat closest to the back wall was left empty for Jake, and he preferred that seat anyway. It gave him the opportunity to see who came in the front door of the restaurant.

"Hello, Bob," Jake said as he sat down. "Hello, Mrs. Thompson. I didn't expect to see you here."

"I didn't expect to be here when I awoke this morning either, but here we are," Earline stated, exhibiting a forced smile.

Earline Thompson was doing quite well, Jake thought, for a woman whose husband had been murdered only seven weeks ago. The period of grieving had been short, Jake heard. The day after her husband was buried, she swept into First National Bank to inform all the employees that she was now in charge. Rumor was, she told the staff that her father had built First National Bank anyway, and now it was time to run it the way her daddy had meant for it to be run.

"I had my suspicions about Jesse and Naomi, but Naomi never told me about it," Earline continued. "What did she tell you?"

"That Mr. Thompson raped her, and that Jed was Mr. Thompson's son," replied Jake without hesitation.

Earline's lips tightened. "I guessed years ago that Jesse raped her, but I wasn't sure whether Jed was his son or not. Now I know for sure."

How could you continue to live with him if you knew? Why didn't you go to the authorities? You come from one of the most influential families in the county. The authorities would have listened to you, he couldn't help but think.

"What is this meeting about?" Jake asked, looking back and forth between Bob Whitfield and Earline Thompson for an answer. "I really need to get home."

"You know the law doesn't allow Mr. McClellan to profit from his crime," Bob said in his best lawyer's voice.

"That's true," Jake replied. "But his children might, and you're assuming he gets convicted."

"You're a good lawyer, Jake, but I doubt even you can win this one."

"We'll see," Jake said, his gaze steely. "But win or lose, I suspect Mrs. Thompson doesn't want word getting out about Mr. Thompson and Naomi McClellan." Jake looked at Earline. "Isn't that right, Mrs. Thompson?"

Earline studied Jake briefly, and then turned her eyes back to Bob.

"I'm going to ask you one more time," Jake said, growing irritated. "What's this meeting really about?"

"Go ahead," Bob urged Earline. "Tell him."

"After I became president of the bank," Earline explained, "I started looking over some records, and I found these." She slid an envelope full of documents across the table to Jake.

"What's in here?" Jake asked without opening the envelope.

"Those are bank records regarding several accounts for F-PAC, a Democratic political-action committee. As best I can tell, F-PAC was laundering money under different names through the bank for the last two years. Jesse was skimming money from the accounts."

"What good does this do Jed?" Jake asked.

"It gives you a defense to the murder charge," suggested Bob Whitfield.

"You can prove that someone else had motivation to kill Jesse Thompson, and that might create reasonable doubt with the jury."

"Are you offering to give me these records in exchange for my keeping quiet about Mr. Thompson and Naomi McClellan?" Jake inquired. "Because if you are, I'm not biting. Mr. Thompson was worth at least fifteen million."

"We thought you might say that. So I'm prepared to pay one million in addition," Earline added. Her voice grew soft. "Naomi McClellan didn't deserve what Jesse did to her all those years ago. This should go a long way toward rectifying that situation. I wish Naomi still worked for me. But with her son accused of killing Jesse, it just wasn't possible for her to continue. Looking back, I'm surprised she stayed as long as she did."

"I don't know, Mrs. Thompson," Jake said. "I need to talk this over with Ruth and Ms. McClellan."

"What is there to talk about?" inquired Bob, rolling his eyes in disgust. "This is a great deal."

Jake remembered the *Lillian Scott* case. He knew Bob always had more money on the table.

"All right. I'll tell you what." Jake took control of the conversation. "You put two million dollars in a separate account with the McClellans' names on it only, give me those records, and then I'll keep your dirty secret quiet."

Mrs. Thompson looked at Bob and nodded slightly.

"Agreed," Bob said.

"And release the mortgage against Jed's house," Jake continued.

"You drive a hard bargain, Mr. Reed," Earline said with a small smile. "Agreed."

Jake took the envelope full of documents and left the restaurant. He was back in control, and it felt great.

Even better, things were beginning to look up for Jed and his family. He might still be charged with murder, but at least his family wouldn't lose their home and they'd be taken care of financially for the rest of their lives.

And Jake still held two other cards that might impact Jed's

case—proof of Jesse Thompson's money laundering and Wanda Lacy's photographs.

Who knew what might happen when he brought those to light?

Agents Boyd and Simon, both wearing headphones, sat in the back of a white van in the parking lot of the Downtown Grill. They had heard every word spoken by Jake, Earline Thompson, and Bob Whitfield. Ron hurriedly wrote down *F-PAC* while Jerry moved to the driver's seat. They returned to the old jewelry-store building and phoned Deputy Director Armacost, who was, as usual, in his office late.

"We recorded a conversation between Jesse Thompson's widow, her lawyer, and Jake Reed," Ron announced. "Mrs. Thompson gave Reed some records concerning a political organization called F-PAC. We don't have a copy of those records, but we'll try to get them."

"We looked at F-PAC early in the investigation," responded Charlie. "We didn't find anything at that time, but maybe we missed it."

"Mrs. Thompson and her lawyer certainly thought there was some connection between F-PAC and the Thompson murder, based on those records," Ron stated.

"See if you can get a copy, but stay out of sight," instructed Charlie. "Somebody knows you're there."

Dalton Miller finished the last bite of his filet, grilled medium-well, as Jake Reed, Earline Thompson, and Bob Whitfield left the Downtown Grill. He paid the waitress with a nice tip for arranging the table he had requested, second from the back, and then exited the restaurant.

Once he was back in his hotel room, he dialed Shep Taylor's cell phone.

"Shep, this is Dalton. Can you talk?"

"I'm by myself. Go ahead."

Dalton told Shep about the conversation he'd overheard and the money laundering at First National Bank in Jackson for F-PAC. He also told Shep that the FBI had heard it too. He'd watched as an agent bugged the table.

"We're getting close," Shep said. "And the election is getting close too. We've got to break some news soon. Can you get a copy of those documents?"

"I'll see what I can do, but let me tell you something else," continued Dalton. "It turns out that the guy they arrested for shooting Thompson is really his son. Reed has a DNA test that proves it."

"DNA? How did he get a blood sample from the dead guy?"

"I don't know. He's resourceful, I'll give him that." Dalton chuckled. "He convinced Mrs. Thompson and her lawyer to pay his client two mill to keep quiet."

"I like this guy. What do you think he'll do next?"

"Maybe nothing. He's got what he needs. He might try to get a plea bargain for his client, but I bet he's got enough to get the charges dismissed. I'd say he's done for a while."

"He's our best lead. We can't let him quit yet. It may be about time for you to introduce yourself to him."

Dalton scratched his cheek. "I was thinking the same thing. I'll try to see him the first of the week, but I've got to be careful. The Feds have him wired tight, and they don't know I'm here."

"Speaking of the Bureau, what are you hearing from them?"

"They got some photographs from our boy that clearly show the assassin they suspected was at the murder scene," Dalton responded. "I think they're looking for him now."

"Is the director still in the dark?"

"He knows the investigation is going on, but the deputy director is keeping as much from him as possible. There's no love lost between the two of those guys, that much is for sure." Dalton gave another chuckle. "My contact tells me that somebody is keeping the director informed, but the deputy director hasn't found the mole."

"I may need to make a personal visit to Armacost," said Shep. "He may be on our side." There was a pause, then, "I've got to go. Someone's knocking on my door. Let me know how your meeting goes."

Dalton hung up the phone. He knew he had a lot of work to do, and he was running out of time.

Loews Denver Hotel, Denver

Shep opened his hotel room door and found Mac Foster on the other side.

"Who were you talking to?" Mac asked, evidently spotting the cell phone in Shep's hand.

Shep desperately wanted to tell Mac everything about the investigation. The words screamed in his mind. He wanted to share his burden—and his elation—with someone. But he knew Mac would not stand for anything covert going on. Shep had to maintain his silence . . . for now.

"Just checking on Sarah and Jonathan, sir," Shep responded.

Law offices of Holcombe & Reed, Jackson, Tennessee

Jake left The Grill and drove straight to his office. Rachel and the children would have to wait a few more minutes. The documents from Earline Thompson had to be placed safely under lock and key before he went to bed. By the time Jake returned to his office from the evening meeting with Earline and Bob Whitfield, the parking lot was empty except for Barrett's red four-wheel-drive pickup. Jake parked next to it and strode toward the back door of the office. As he opened the door, he bumped into Barrett, who was just leaving.

"You've got to see this," Jake said.

"What is it?"

"It's the information that Earline Thompson and Bob Whitfield wanted to give me in exchange for keeping the rape quiet."

"Is that all you got?"

"That and two million dollars." Jake grinned.

"Two million!"

"Let's go back to my office and take a look at these. I'll explain everything to you."

Once they were in his office, Jake removed the F-PAC documents from the envelope. He and Barrett scanned through the documents for several minutes, attempting to decipher the information. As they did so, Jake gave a blow-by-blow account of his meeting with Bob and Earline.

Most of the documents were ledgers with handwritten entries. The entries identified millions of dollars deposited into dummy accounts at First National Bank. The entries also identified millions of dollars being paid from those accounts into another account with a customer name of F-PAC. Most of the money made the transition safely, but the ledger records reflected that thousands of dollars from each transaction were being deposited into another account labeled *Jesse Thompson*.

"So that's what he was doing," commented Barrett thoughtfully. He was studying the last few documents in the stack. "Jesse was skimming money."

"That's what Mrs. Thompson said. I can't wait to see Highfill's face when I show him these. When he sees that someone else had motivation to murder Jesse Thompson, he'll have no choice but to at least talk about a plea."

"Are you going to tell Jed about the money?"

"I think I'll wait and surprise him, Ruth, and Naomi, with the dismissal papers and the money at the same time." Jake beamed a broad, satisfied smile at his partner.

"Come on, counselor." Barrett handed a stack of the F-PAC documents back to Jake. "We've both had a busy day. Let's go home."

"That's a good idea." Jake took the documents from Barrett and put them in the manila envelope with the others. He unlocked one of the filing cabinets in his office and inserted the envelope into Jed's file, right in front of the photographs of Raoul. Jake agreed with Barrett. It had been a busy day. And a long one. He would hardly see his children before it was time for them to go to bed.

CHAPTER TWENTY

Sanders residence, Arlington, Virginia

Saul Sanders had begun to dread the weekly Saturday telephone calls with Randolph Winston. There had been no significant news the last three weeks, and he could sense the anger in Winston's voice. But today would be different, since Charlie Armacost's agents had been busy.

Saul had been up before dawn, anxiously awaiting Winston's call. When the phone rang, Saul jumped. He looked at the clock on his study wall.

Eight o'clock. Randolph sure is punctual.

"Saul," Randolph commanded. "I hope you have some news for me today."

"I do. But you aren't going to like it. Our friends in Tennessee have been busy."

The moment of silence hung heavy.

"I thought you said Armacost was going to abandon that investigation," Randolph said. "Yet it's been nearly two months now, and his people are still there."

Saul tried to defend himself. "I thought he would leave soon, but now it looks like his guys are going to be there awhile longer. They've uncovered some information."

"Have you heard anything about Burke or us?"

"Not yet, but you better be careful," Saul warned.

"What do you mean?" Randolph's voice was threatening.

"Attorney Reed has discovered that Jesse Thompson was the father of the man who's been charged with the murder."

"How did he find that out?" inquired Randolph.

"I don't know, but that's not the half of it. It gets worse."

"Go on."

"He has pictures of an assassin named Raoul Miguel Flores at the crime scene."

"Armacost now thinks an assassin was involved in the murder of Jesse Thompson?"

"That's what it looks like."

"Has Armacost connected the assassin with whoever employed him?"

"Not yet, but it gets even worse than that. Armacost's agents overheard a meeting where Thompson's widow gave Attorney Reed some documents referring to F-PAC."

"That is a problem," Randolph agreed. "Those documents might link us to Thompson and Burke."

"Do you know anything about the assassin?" Saul asked.

"The assassin's not important at this point. I'm worried about what Jake Reed might be planning to do with those documents."

"You should be worried. It appears that he continues to turn over stones that I didn't know existed. Who knows what he might find under the next one? He's quite resourceful."

"So he is," Randolph responded slowly, as if deep in thought. "Don't do anything yet. I need to talk with Pierce and Milton. I'll get word to you about what to do with Mr. Reed."

"I'll await your instructions."

"Good," Randolph replied. "What about the other matter you're handling for us?"

"We keep an eye on both of them twenty-four hours a day, seven days a week. He visits her every weekend, but we haven't seen anything suspicious yet."

"Keep watching them. There's something there that we're missing. I can't figure it out, but he's up to something. I can't afford any mistakes at this point, and I'm concerned that he could be trouble."

"I've got some of my best people on it. If it can be found, they'll find it. I'll let you know if we see something out of the ordinary."

Apollyon Associates, Inc., lower Manhattan

Randolph Winston hung up the phone and gazed out the window of his office. Complete control of the world was only three weeks away. Any interference would not be tolerated, and Jake Reed was becoming an interference.

Law offices of Holcombe & Reed, Jackson, Tennessee

It was a cold and rainy Sunday night. One solitary streetlamp hung from the rear corner of the building near the alley. It illuminated only a fragment of the parking lot and a portion of the street that ran behind the building. The steady rainfall and storm clouds blocked the light from the moon, further increasing the blanket of darkness. Occasionally a lightning bolt flashed, momentarily illuminating the entire parking lot. Its light would trick the streetlamp into thinking it was daytime. The lamp would extinguish itself following the lightning strike, and the few seconds that followed were the darkest of the entire night.

Dalton Miller stood under the small overhang that covered the rear entrance to the office. It was just past midnight, and Dalton knew no one would be inside the building at this hour. His dark clothing, the murkiness of the night, and the rain made him practically invisible. He stood with his back to the door and constantly looked in all directions. He had to get in and out as quickly as possible, without being seen.

Dalton wasn't worried about the door lock. It would be easy enough to manipulate. The security system was the problem. He couldn't find any exterior wiring that he could use to disarm it. He would only have thirty seconds once he entered the building to identify the code and enter it into the keypad near the back door. One last look around the parking lot, and he was ready for action. He inserted a small, flat, metal locksmith tool into the keyhole of the doorknob and twisted it to the right until he heard the metal pin retract from the door casing. He leaned against the door with his right shoulder, preparing for entry. He slowly counted to three in his head, then swiftly pushed the door inward to open it and stepped inside.

The keypad immediately to the left of the door began beeping, warning Dalton of his deadline to enter the access code. Dalton mentally marked on his digital watch where the indicator would be when the thirty seconds to enter the code would expire. He removed a hand-held computer from his pocket and clamped it to the front of the keypad. On the outside of the computer were red numbers that rapidly began deciphering the access code. The first number locked on 1. Then the second on 4. 1 again. The last was 9. Dalton removed the computer, and punched 1-4-1-9, Off, into the keypad. It went silent.

Dalton had staked out the Holcombe & Reed offices often enough over the last several weeks that he knew exactly which office was Jake Reed's. He retrieved a compact flashlight from his coat pocket and quietly maneuvered the hallway in the building until he reached a door with T. Jacob Reed on the narrow brass plaque.

Agents Boyd and Simon were asleep in the upstairs apartment across the street from the Holcombe & Reed offices. Rarely was there any activity at Holcombe & Reed after business hours, and never after midnight. As a precaution, though, they always set the surveillance equipment to sound an alarm if a noise was detected during the night. The alarm startled both of them when it activated. It was the first time it had sounded since they had arrived in Jackson. Ron, the first agent to assume his position in the darkened downstairs surveillance room, quickly donned a set of headphones.

"Do you hear anything?" Jerry asked as he entered the room a few seconds after Boyd.

"Not yet," Ron whispered. He focused his eyes on the floor and concentrated on the silence coming through the headphones. Jerry peeled back a small section of the paper covering the windows in the front of the old jewelry store. He scanned up and down Main Street for any signs of activity. Nothing. He peered through a pair of binoculars at the law offices across the street and examined every window for any movement. Nothing. Maybe the surveillance equipment had malfunctioned.

Ron pushed the red buttons on the receiver to designate which room in the Holcombe & Reed offices he wanted to listen to. Front lobby. Conference room. Jake Reed's office. "Wait a minute," he exclaimed, but still at a whisper. "I think I hear something."

Dalton was careful to replace the papers on Jake Reed's desk and the items in the drawers precisely as he looked for the F-PAC documents. When he didn't find anything in either of those places, he moved to the credenza behind the desk. It was filled with manila and expandable file folders containing court documents and correspondence, but no F-PAC documents. Two putty colored four-drawer filing cabinets stood in the corner of the office near the closet. One was locked, and the other was not. Dalton quickly looked through the unlocked one, hoping to get lucky. Nothing. He removed the same locksmith tool he had used earlier and easily unlocked the remaining filing cabinet. Finally, in the third drawer from the top, he hit pay dirt.

"There's definitely someone in there," Agent Boyd stated to Agent Simon. "Do you see any lights?"

"If there are any lights on, they have to be in the back." Jerry continued to scan the law offices across the street through his binoculars. "I can't see anything from here."

"You better go check it out. Take a radio, and circle around to the back. I'll keep you posted on what I hear."

Dalton spread the F-PAC documents across the top of Jake Reed's already cluttered desk, and examined them with his flashlight.

Shep will be ecstatic to see this.

He removed a slender silver camera from his pocket and began snapping photographs of each page. There were ten pages in all. It took only a few seconds, and he placed the documents back in the filing cabinet precisely where he'd found them. He suspected the FBI had the office wired and took a moment to look for the small transmitters. One was under the lamp stand on the desk. Another in the telephone. A third was under the guest chair near the door. He had all the information he needed. It was time to leave.

"Everything is silent now," Agent Boyd spoke into his radio. "He may be leaving. Are you near the back door yet?"

"Almost," Agent Simon responded. "I'm in the alley beside the cleaners. I'll be there in ten seconds." He sloshed around the rear of the building that housed the cleaners and into the Holcombe & Reed employee parking lot.

Dalton stopped at the rear door to reset the alarm before exiting. Every precaution was necessary to make sure that his presence in the Holcombe & Reed offices would go unnoticed. He knew the puddles of water on the floor that formed when he entered the building would evaporate before the employees arrived for work. The alarm was the only variable remaining. He punched 1-4-1-9, Set, opened the door, and backed out, closing the door behind him.

Just before the door latched, and without warning, Dalton was struck violently in the back of the neck. It felt like he had been rear-ended by an eighteen-wheeler. The force of the blow caused him to fall forward into the partially closed door and onto the hard linoleum floor immediately inside the door. He was stunned for a second but rolled to his back in time to see the silhouette of a man pouncing on him like a cat on its surprised prey.

"Who are you?" the voice from the unknown man demanded from the darkness as his body landed on Dalton.

Dalton raised his right forearm and shielded his body from the onslaught. The two men rolled savagely on the floor, swinging their closed fists wildly. The other man managed to land a punch to Dalton's face, and

Dalton felt the warmth of blood streaming from the open wound. The keypad for the alarm system began beeping again. The thirty seconds permitted to exit the building after the alarm was set had almost expired.

Dalton struck his attacker in the left temple, dazing him. Dalton finally had enough of his wits about him and landed another blow, this time to the man's diaphragm. When the man slumped to the floor, gasping for air, and curled up into a fetal position, Dalton struggled to his feet. The security alarm began to wail from the outside speakers just as Dalton reached for the doorknob.

As he dashed out the door into the downpour, he could hear the assailant's groans. Just then a bolt of lightning streaked across the sky, providing Dalton with enough light to see that the parking lot was empty. Then blackness descended again.

Agent Boyd heard the commotion through Agent Simon's radio, and raced from the jewelry store building to the rear of the Holcombe & Reed offices. He tried to open the rear door to the offices, but it was locked from the inside. Jerry's moaning was barely audible through the constant siren blaring from the alarm system.

"Jerry, are you in there?" Ron knew his voice was probably swallowed by the sounds of the rain, the thunder, and the siren. He listened again at the door. More moaning sounds. He stepped back from the door and kicked at the knob with his right foot. The door began to give way. He kicked again, and the door burst open.

He found Jerry lying on the floor immediately inside the door.

"Are you OK?" Ron said as he knelt down.

Jerry managed to raise himself to his knees. "I think so." He grimaced with pain.

"Come on." Ron grabbed Jerry under the right arm and tried to lift him to his feet. "We've got to get out of here. The police will be here any minute."

Jerry struggled to his feet, and Ron assisted him out into the rain, around the cleaners, and across Main Street. They had just entered the front door to the jewelry-store building and locked it as three police cars with sirens sounding and blue lights flashing slid to a stop in front of the Holcombe & Reed offices.

"Were you able to make an identification?" Ron asked Jerry when the door was closed. He peered through the crack Jerry had created earlier in the paper covering the front windows and watched the police officers scurry around the law offices across the street.

Jerry Simon lay down gingerly on an old sofa in the downstairs floor of the old jewelry store. He covered his eyes with his left forearm and gritted his teeth as he responded to his partner's inquiry.

"I couldn't see anything." He struggled to keep his breath. "I know it was a male, but that's all."

Ron continued to peer through the window at the activity across the street. "Somebody else is watching Attorney Reed," he commented thoughtfully. "But we don't know who." He replaced the paper over the small opening and turned to Jerry. "Can you make it upstairs? I'll send Armacost a report from there."

"I think so."

Ron assisted his partner to his feet and up the dusty staircase to the second-floor apartment. Jerry gratefully sank into bed in one of the two bedrooms. But Ron doubted his partner would get much sleep. The rest of the night was bound to be painful.

After Jerry was as comfortable as he would get, Ron logged in to the computer and sent Charlie Armacost a coded e-mail. When deciphered, the message would inform the deputy director that someone other than the FBI was watching Jake Reed. That meant, most likely, someone else was interested in the Jesse Thompson murder.

Dalton made it safely to his car three blocks west of the Holcombe & Reed offices. He was bleeding and soaked, but he knew he would survive. He reached into his pocket and removed the slender silver camera he had used to photograph the F-PAC documents. He was relieved that he hadn't lost it during the melee. He examined his right cheek in the rearview mirror and pressed a white handkerchief against the gash in an attempt to stop the bleeding.

"Shep is going to owe me for this," he muttered.

After driving back to his hotel room and sneaking in the back entrance, he showered and dressed his wound. He then loaded the digital film from the camera into his laptop computer and e-mailed the images of the F-PAC documents to Shep. After the transmission was complete, he unplugged the computer and climbed into bed. His body ached from the fracas with his unknown assailant, and it was time for several hours of hibernation.

CHAPTER TWENTY-ONE

Law offices of Holcombe & Reed, Jackson, Tennessee

Jake arrived for work at eight fifteen Monday morning and found an old, dented, white cargo van parked near the rear door of the building. Wilson's Remodeling was emblazoned on the van doors. Jake greeted the young, muscular proprietor as he walked through the opening where the door used to be.

He wasn't surprised to see the repairs being made. He and Barrett had been summoned to the office at 1:00 a.m. by the Jackson Police Department. They had searched throughout the office to determine whether anything was missing, damaged, or destroyed. After a rather exhaustive search, they determined that the only damage was to the back door. The few drops of blood on the floor near the door had been collected for testing at the Tennessee State Forensic Laboratory in Nashville. The police officer in charge surmised that the intruder cut himself when he kicked the door in, and the alarm had frightened him away. A report would be filed with the police department, and an investigator would be assigned to the case. The chance of finding the culprit was slim, Jake knew.

"What happened last night?" Madge asked as Jake walked past her into his office.

"Someone tried to break in," he responded from the interior of his office. "Barrett and I couldn't find anything missing, but you and the other employees should double-check." Jake returned to Madge's desk. "I also need you to contact Jackson National Bank and set up an interest-bearing account in the name of Jed and Ruth McClellan. I'm expecting a wire transfer later today."

Madison County Criminal Justice Complex, Jackson, Tennessee

Monday mornings were the only visiting time permitted at the Madison County CJC for inmates awaiting trial on capital murder charges. Ever since Jed's ordeal began, Ruth McClellan religiously was the first person every Monday to enter the visiting area as soon as the doors opened to visitors. Just as religiously, Jed was always waiting on her at the last viewing window on the right.

On the third Monday in October, Ruth entered the room, sat down in the chair, and removed from its cradle the telephone that was mounted on the wall to her left. A bulletproof window separated Jed and Ruth, and the telephone was the only way they could communicate. It didn't matter to Jed that every word of their conversation was being recorded.

"How are the kids?" was Jed's first question.

"They're doin' as good as can be expected," was Ruth's usual response. Then she hung her head. "I don't know how much more of this I can take, Jed."

Jed could see that Ruth was crumbling. He knew she was fragile—that she could handle only a certain amount of anxiety—and could see she was way past her breaking point. The stress of explaining to their children, time after time, why their father wasn't coming home was unbearable, she told him. The neighbors constantly asked questions. When she went to the grocery store, the other customers pointed at her and whispered.

She was also having a difficult time keeping the household bills paid, she told him. The money she received from her part-time job and the generosity of the people at Naomi's church only went so far. She'd had to apply for welfare assistance, and that broke her pride.

"I know, Ruth, but you've got to hang in there. The trial is the first week of December, and this nightmare's gonna be over."

"I don't know if I can make it." Tears streamed down Ruth's face. "The kids still cry all the time. I cry all the time. We don't have no money. How are we gonna make it?"

Jed tried to reassure Ruth. He wanted to take her in his arms and comfort her, but the glass wall prevented it. It was a transparent, immovable barrier that separated him from the woman he loved. He could only talk to her, and Ruth needed more than encouraging words.

"I know it's tough," Jed told her. "Just be strong. We're gonna be all right."

He reached out his hand and put it on the glass, getting as close to her as he could. He saw her shiver, saw her gulp back a sob.

"I can't do it, Jed." Her voice was louder than a conversation tone, but not a scream. "I just can't do it."

And with those few words Ruth slammed the phone back in its cradle and ran, crying, from the visiting room.

Jed wanted to chase after her, but all he could do was scream her name into his end of the telephone. "Ruth! Ruth! Come back!"

It was no use. She was gone. There was nothing Jed could do.

He had never felt as helpless as he did at that moment. Slowly he replaced the telephone receiver in its cradle on the wall beside him, staring despondently through the glass wall at the chair where Ruth had been sitting.

After a couple of minutes he realized she wasn't coming back.

His return to his cell was the longest walk he'd ever taken.

Jackson, Tennessee

Jake didn't often get the opportunity to sleep in on a Tuesday morning, but he took advantage of it when it presented itself. Rachel took the children to school, and Jake lay in bed until after eight o'clock. He had received confirmation yesterday afternoon that the $2 million agreed to by Mrs. Thompson had been transferred into an account for the McClellans, without any strings attached. The money would allow Jed and his family to live very comfortably the rest of their lives. All that was left was to get the murder charges against Jed dismissed.

As far as Jake was concerned, the case was over. He had made some mistakes along the way, but everything was working out in the end. Jed didn't kill Jesse Thompson, and Jake now had everything he needed to prove it. He had been under a lot of stress since mid-August, but now a great weight had been lifted from his shoulders. He felt relaxed, rejuvenated, and a little bit lazy. It was almost ten o'clock when Jake finally walked through the repaired back door of Holcombe & Reed. He didn't have any appointments scheduled for the day, and he didn't plan on staying at the office very long.

Madge was in her usual position, immediately outside the door to Jake's office. He stopped at her desk and thumbed through the morning's mail.

"There's a gentleman here to see you," Madge said. "I tried to explain that you might not be in all day, but he insisted on waiting for you."

"Did he say what he wanted?" Jake replied. He continued shuffling through the envelopes of unopened mail.

"Not really," Madge responded. "I managed to get him to tell me that someone in his family was involved in an automobile accident, but that was about it."

Jake placed the mail back on Madge's desk. He knew she would open the envelopes later and place the contents in the appropriate files.

"Why do some people think they can just walk in off the street and meet with a lawyer?" Jake muttered as he poured himself a cup of coffee. It was one of his pet peeves. People didn't go to a doctor without making an appointment. Why did they think they should get to see an attorney without an appointment?

But that kind of thinking wasn't likely to change anytime soon.

"All right." Jake sighed. "Show him back," he told Madge. "I'll see if I can refer him to somebody." He headed back to his office to wait for Madge and the man without an appointment.

In a few moments Madge entered with the man, who introduced himself as Sammy Walker. Mr. Walker had a bandage on his right cheek and carried a briefcase. Jake guessed that it contained an accident report, medical records, and an insurance policy or two.

"Mr. Walker, what can I do for you?" Jake asked. He pointed Mr. Walker toward a chair, and then sat down behind his desk.

"It's about my daughter," Mr. Walker began. He laid his briefcase in his lap, opened it, and removed a yellow legal-size notepad. "She was injured real bad in a car wreck a couple of months ago, and we need a lawyer." He scribbled something on his notepad.

"I certainly represent people who are injured in auto accidents, and their families, but I'm afraid my plate is full right now," Jake explained.

"I understand," said Mr. Walker. He held up the notepad so Jake could read it:

YOUR OFFICE IS BUGGED.

Jake's eyes widened, and he began to examine the room.

Mr. Walker kept talking. "We hear you're the best in town, and we want the best for our little girl." He caught Jake's eye and motioned with his hand that they needed to keep the conversation going.

"I wouldn't say that I'm the best," Jake stuttered, trying to sound modest but distracted by wondering where the bugs were. "We just try to do the best we can for our clients."

While Jake was talking, Mr. Walker stood up, stepped to the front of the desk, and lifted the antique lamp. He showed Jake a small transmitter attached to the bottom.

"That's all we can ask," Mr. Walker stated. "Would you please consider taking our case?" He wrote another message on his notepad:

MEET ME AT HIGHLAND PARK AT 10:30.

Jake nodded his understanding. "Let me get some information from you."

He asked the man several questions about the fictitious daughter and her injuries. They carried on the charade for thirty minutes to make sure that whoever was listening would be convinced the meeting was legitimate.

"I've taken enough of your time," Mr. Walker said as he stood to leave. "I hope I hear from you real soon."

"You can count on it."

When Mr. Walker left, Jake consulted his watch. *10:08.* He paced in his office with his door closed for a few minutes while he waited to leave. It would only take five minutes to reach Highland Park from his office.

As he paced, he tried to figure out who could have possibly bugged his office, and why? He knew the answers lay with the mysterious man who was waiting at Highland Park.

Finally it was 10:20. The twelve minutes that had elapsed between the time Mr. Walker left and the time Jake left the office felt like an eternity. As he headed toward the back exit, he announced to Madge, "I have an errand to run. I'll be back in a while."

Highland Park was rather desolate at 10:30 on a Tuesday morning in October.

Mr. Walker was sitting at a faded red picnic table under one of the wooden pavilions on the south side of the park. As Jake walked in his direction, Mr. Walker turned around on the bench and leaned back against the table.

"What's this all about?" demanded Jake, even before he sat down. "And who are you, and how did you know my office was bugged?"

"Slow down, Mr. Reed," Mr. Walker said calmly. "My name is Dalton Miller. I can't tell you who I work for, but let's just say that the two of you are sort of on the same side."

"That's comforting," Jake said sarcastically as he sat down across the table.

"Your office was bugged by the FBI."

"The FBI!" exclaimed Jake.

"That's right, the FBI. They've set up shop across the street from you at the old jewelry store."

"Why are they watching me?"

"They're interested in the Thompson murder. They think there's more to it than it seems on the surface."

"I don't understand."

Mr. Miller placed his elbows on the top of the table and leaned in toward the center. "Look, I know about the photographs, the DNA, and the money. So does the FBI. That's where I got my information. The man in the photograph is Raoul Miguel Flores, a known assassin and a member of the Hermillo Family in Bogotá."

"An assassin? In Jackson? Who would hire an assassin to kill Jesse Thompson?"

"That's what the FBI is trying to determine. That's also what I'm trying to figure out. My boss thinks it has something to do with the presidential election. We just can't quite put our finger on it."

Jake stared up through the tree branches. The things Mr. Miller was describing were simply too bizarre. The truck in Wanda Lacy's photographs had been used by an assassin who had killed Jesse Thompson. The FBI was investigating the murder and had bugged his office. Now this mysterious man was telling him that it all pertained to the presidential election?

"I still don't understand why you're telling me any of this," Jake stated, his gaze returning to Mr. Miller.

"We need your help," Mr. Miller replied matter-of-factly.

"You need my help? What can I do?"

"You're the link. Nobody can know of my involvement, or the involvement of my boss. We don't know if we can trust the FBI. So that leaves you."

"What makes you think I'll help you?" Jake retorted. "I don't even know who you are, really. At the office you told me your name was Sammy Walker, and now you tell me it's Dalton Miller. I'm not sure I believe any of what you're telling me, and I know I don't trust you."

"Let me tell you something, Mr. Reed. You have children, right?"

"That's right."

"Do you want them to grow up in an America that's free, or in one that's controlled by an elite few? Because if Edward Burke wins the presidency, that's exactly what will happen."

Jake waved his hands in confusion. "What are you talking about?"

"I'm talking about the presidency of the United States of America," Mr. Miller insisted. "And you"—he gestured toward Jake with animation—"you have the ability to affect the outcome of the election. If my employer is right, and this murder has something to do with Vice President Burke, then don't you think the American people should know that?"

"I guess so," responded Jake.

"You guess so?"

Dalton's hand gestures became even more animated. "If Burke will have someone murdered whom he thinks stands in his way of getting the presidency, what do you think he'll do once he becomes president? And Jesse Thompson was supposedly a friend of his."

Dalton Miller made a good point, Jake realized. Thompson and Burke were friends, but how did Jake know that Burke had him killed? Perhaps Mr. Miller's boss, whoever he was, had killed Thompson. Jake still wasn't sure he believed any of this. It all seemed unreal.

"I don't want to help you," Jake finally said. "I don't want to help anybody. The FBI has bugged my office, or so you say. You could have done it for all I know. You're obviously following me. I just want to be left alone."

"Where is your sense of patriotism?" Mr. Miller inquired. "You have the ability to influence the future of America for the better. All you have to do is make a couple of phone calls, leak some information to the press, and the course of history is changed."

"I don't want to change history. I've done my job. I've recovered some money for my client, and I have obtained enough information to clear him of murder charges. If you want to change history, then do it without me. You obviously know as much as I do."

"That's true." Mr. Miller's voice was calmer than before. "But the news would have a lot more credibility if it came from a source other than my employer."

"Look, I'm not helping you, and that's final," Jake said angrily. He stood and started to leave. "You tell your employer, whoever he is, to leave me alone."

Mr. Miller backed off. "I can understand your position, Mr. Reed. Here is my number." He handed Jake a card with his cell-phone number printed on it. "Call me anytime."

Even though Jake knew he'd never use the number, he took the card and placed it in his wallet. Then he strode back to his car, leaving Mr. Miller under the pavilion.

As Jake drove back to his office, his emotions ranged from anger to fear. A million thoughts raced through his mind, and none of them were pleasant. How much did the FBI know about him? Was it really the FBI? Who else was watching him? Why did he care who won the election?

Jake usually drove like a maniac everywhere he went. This time, however, he was obeying the traffic laws, and then some. He had to think. And the only quiet place he had was the inside of his car.

How did he know that this character was even telling the truth about the FBI? Perhaps Dalton Miller was not who he said he was and was just trying to scare Jake. But scare him from what? It didn't make sense. Jake already knew about Jesse Thompson's crime against Naomi McClellan. That had been settled. He had the photographs from the crime scene, but obviously Mr. Miller knew about them as well. What was he missing?

Jake decided to check out the new interior-design business across from his office. He had to find out whether the FBI was there or not. That would answer a lot of questions. He drove past the front of his own office and turned onto an alley across the street from the dry cleaners. The alley led to a parking lot in the back of the building that housed the old jewelry store.

A small porch with a shingle-covered roof protruded from the back of the building. It provided a dry area for deliveries through the back door of the business. The door was a metal fireproof door with a peephole. Jake scaled the four concrete steps leading to the back door and pressed the buzzer used by delivery personnel. The man Jake met at the Downtown Grill opened the door.

"Hello," Jake said, "I have an office across the street." He indicated the direction with his hand. "We met a few nights ago at the Downtown Grill. Mr. Jones, I believe?"

"Oh, yes," the man replied. "What can I do for you?"

"I thought maybe I could come in for a few minutes and see what you're doing in here."

"We're not open yet," the man said politely.

"I know," Jake replied. "But I thought you might let me come in and have a look around. The landlady is a client of mine, and she asked me to make sure everything was going OK."

"Everything is fine," the man assured him. "We plan on opening in a few days."

Jake tried to look over the man's shoulder. It really didn't appear that very much activity was going on in the building. Cobwebs hung in the corners, and he couldn't see any new furniture.

"You sure have a long way to go to get this place ready to open," Jake said, still straining to see inside.

The man smirked. "You're right, and that's why I really must be going. So if you will excuse me . . ."

He tried to close the door, but Jake leaned hard against it to keep it open.

"Are you sure I can't come in for a moment?" Jake stood on his tiptoes in an attempt to look over the top of the man's head. "Mrs. Alexander really wants me to make sure that you're not busting holes in the walls or doing other structural damage."

"Tell Mrs. Alexander that everything is fine. Now I really must go," the man said as he pushed Jake back and closed the door.

Agents Boyd and Simon watched through one of the rear windows in the building as Jake drove away.

"That was close," Jerry said. "It's probably about time we pulled out of here."

"I agree," Ron concurred. "Let's call Armacost."

CHAPTER TWENTY-TWO

Cincinnati, Ohio

The Foster for President caravan landed in Cincinnati. Shep knew they were losing campaign workers in all corners of the country and campaign funds were being spent faster than they could be raised. At this rate the campaign would end up $10 million in debt. Top campaign officials told Shep that Mac would, in fact, lose New York and that other big states like California and Florida were also lost causes. The decision was made to concentrate on the Midwest and to try to make a respectable showing in November. Everyone was finally coming to grips with the reality that they could not overtake Vice President Burke.

Everyone except Shep.

Dalton called just after one o'clock. Shep was speaking with some campaign staffers at an office on Front Street near Three Rivers Stadium when his wireless phone rang. He walked away from the group before answering.

"Did you get the e-mail I sent with the F-PAC documents?" Dalton asked.

"I did. I'm trying to find out who is running F-PAC. That might be exactly what we're looking for. I wish we had those documents back when we debated Burke. They may have changed the outcome of the debate. I'm afraid we may still need our friend there in Jackson. Did you get the opportunity to talk to him?"

"I talked to him this morning," Dalton replied.

"And?" Shep asked.

"And he refused to help."

"Refused?" Shep grabbed the back of his neck in frustration. "Did you explain to him America needs him, not to mention our campaign?"

"I explained that to him," Dalton replied. "But he still refused. He wants to be left out of this. He thinks he has accomplished his goal of clearing his client's name, and he does not care what happens in the election. He doesn't think it's a concern of his."

That's what is wrong with this great country of ours, Shep thought. *Nobody wants to get involved. The people who should be serving the country are too afraid of being ridiculed by the media to run for office.*

"Stay there a little while longer, Dalton," Shep said after a few moments. "He may change his mind. But I'll also need to think about how to break this news to the press without him if he won't cooperate. Call me in a couple of days."

Hilton Head Island, South Carolina

There were some weekends over the last six months that Hudson had not been able to come to Eden. He told Claudia he was in the middle of closing a deal on another piece of commercial property or that he had a meeting that couldn't be rescheduled. But he always called to tell Claudia he wouldn't be there. It was Tuesday, and Claudia had not heard from Hudson since last Monday. To say she was worried was an understatement.

When she heard the *B-r-ring*, Claudia answered the phone on the glass-top nightstand in the master bedroom immediately. She hoped that it was Hudson.

"Hello."

"Claudia?" asked an unfamiliar voice on the other end of the line. It sounded like the voice of an elderly man. It was one she had heard somewhere in her past, but she could not match it with a face.

"Yes," Claudia replied. "Who is this?"

"This is your uncle Samuel."

Samuel Joyner was Charlotte Duval's older brother and only sibling. He lived three houses down from Charlotte in Claudia's hometown. His daughters, Kathy and Susan, had been two of Claudia's dearest friends when she was a teenager. Like the rest of that chapter of her life, though, she had long since closed the book on them as well.

"Uncle Samuel." Claudia hesitated. "I haven't talked to you in years."

"It has been awhile," he said kindly.

"How did you find me?"

"It wasn't easy, but I finally tracked you down. How are you doing?"

"I'm fine. How is your family?"

"Everyone is doing fine," Samuel replied.

"Kathy and Susan. How are they doing?"

"They're doing great. Both are married and have children."

An awkward silence descended.

Samuel broke in again. "Claudia, let me tell you what I'm calling about."

"What is it?" Her heart was racing with dread.

"It's your mother."

She stiffened. "What about my mother?"

"She has pancreatic cancer. The doctors have only given her a few months to live."

After all these years, hearing someone mention her mother was disturbing.

Claudia sat down on the edge of the king-size bed and stared at the floral comforter. She had thought about her mother often over the last ten years but could never bring herself to phone. The emotional scars were too deep. And the longer Claudia went without calling, the easier it became not to. She hadn't been home to Mississippi in fifteen years.

"Cancer?" she asked. "What am I supposed to do about it?"

"Nobody expects you to do anything," Samuel said. "I just thought you would like to know. That's all."

"Thanks for telling me, but I really don't see how it concerns me."

She could hear the catch of breath on the other end of the line.

"She's your mother, Claudia. Won't you at least come and see her before she dies?" Uncle Samuel prodded.

"She was never a mother to me," Claudia snapped back. "Just because she gave birth to me doesn't mean anything. There's a lot more to being a mother than that." All these years of carrying anger, and it was beginning to escape. "Besides, she has never made an attempt to contact me. Why should I bother?"

"I didn't call to argue with you about this." Uncle Samuel was maddeningly calm. "I just wanted to make sure you knew. That's all. You can come if you want to."

After she and Samuel said good-bye, Claudia continued to sit on the edge of the bed. She hadn't talked to her mother, much less anyone else in her family, in the last ten years. Her stomach ached, and she knew it was due to the stress of the few minutes she had spoken with Samuel.

Why is this happening now? she agonized.

For the first time in her life, Claudia Duval was happy. Her life with Hudson was wonderful. Financially, she was satisfied. The last thing she wanted was to see her mother. To dig up all the old wounds, the old arguments. She didn't need that kind of turmoil in her life.

She refused to go home.

Her mother—who really wasn't a mother anyway—could just die without her.

Agent Bill Osborne rewound the tape from the telephone conversation between Claudia and Samuel. The male voice clearly stated that Claudia's mother "had pancreatic cancer."

"What do you make of that?" he asked Al Moyers.

"I think Ms. Duval has a lot of problems. Not the least of which is that the man she thinks is Hudson Kinney is not really Hudson Kinney."

Bogotá, Colombia

Raoul Miguel Flores slapped the back of his friend as they left the Restaurante Kurnik on Avenida 127 in Bogotá. It was early Sunday morning, just after midnight, and the restaurant was closing. They had spent the last three hours eating, drinking, and partying with several other members of the Hermillo Family. Raoul's car was parked in an alley on the north side of the restaurant. He laughed loudly as his friend told one last joke, and then they parted ways.

Carefree, Raoul strolled around the corner of the building and into the dark alley. He reached into his pocket and removed his key ring. Two keys, a BMW medallion, and a remote-entry control dangled from it. The medallion glistened under the streetlamps as he playfully twirled it around his index finger. As he neared his car, he pushed a button on the remote entry and heard the familiar sound of his German-made BMW 740IL unlocking.

He was within five feet of the car when he was grabbed from behind and shoved to the pavement. The assailant landed on top of him with his knee in the lumbar area of Raoul's back. A small caliber pistol was thrust into the base of his neck. He had no choice but to surrender.

"Don't move," the assailant demanded in Spanish. "Don't move, or they'll hardly recognize your face when they find your body."

"OK, OK," replied Raoul. "What do you want?"

"Slowly move your right hand behind you," the assailant instructed.

Raoul complied, and the assailant grabbed his arm and twisted it, palm side up. He tied one end of a plastic restraint to Raoul's right wrist.

"Give me your other hand," he demanded of Raoul.

Again Raoul complied, and the assailant attached the remaining loop of the restraint to Raoul's left wrist. The gun was still pressed hard into the back of Raoul's head.

"My wallet is in my front pocket," Raoul said. "Take it and leave."

"It is not your wallet that I want," the assailant replied.

"Then what do you want?"

"Look at the great Raoul," the assailant said in a kind of crowing tone, as if savoring the moment. "The great assassin has been trapped."

"Who are you?" Raoul demanded.

"That's none of your business," the assailant growled. "You don't talk unless I tell you to. Understand?" He grabbed Raoul's hair and slammed his head against the hard concrete. "Tell me—who hired you for the hit on Jesse Thompson?"

"Jesse Thompson? I don't know what you're talking about."

The assailant pulled Raoul's head back, and slammed it into the concrete again. Blood began to rush from a large gash on Raoul's forehead.

"Let's try this again. Who hired you?" the assailant growled.

"Go to—"

Before Raoul could finish his defiant response, the assailant grabbed the index finger on Raoul's left hand, and in an instant snapped it just below the second knuckle. Raoul screamed out in pain.

"Tell me," the assailant warned, "or I'll break the one on your right hand."

Raoul was right-handed. He knew that a broken index finger on the right hand would significantly hamper his livelihood. So he quickly complied. "All I know is the name Winston."

"Winston who?" the assailant demanded.

"I don't know. Just Winston."

"I found you this time," the assailant threatened, "and I can find you again. If you're lying, or if you tell this Winston about our encounter, I'll hunt you down and kill you. Do you understand?"

"Yes."

The pressure on Raoul's back lifted. By the time Raoul dared to struggle to his feet, there was no sign of his assailant.

The Lowell Thomas State Office Building, Jackson, Tennessee

Jake had spent the remainder of the previous week contemplating his conversation with Dalton Miller and his confirmation that the old jewelry store was not being remodeled. In fact, he hadn't seen any activity there since he had tried to enter through the back door. He had also scoured the Holcombe & Reed offices until he was satisfied that all the bugs had been removed. He was now back on track and focused on getting the charges against Jed dismissed. He decided to surprise District Attorney General Drake Highfill with a personal visit. What he had to say couldn't be said over the telephone.

The Lowell Thomas State Office Building was located six blocks south of downtown Jackson, just off Auditorium Drive, and across the street from the Carl Perkins Civic Center. Three state employees rode the elevator with Jake, and he watched the numbers above the door light up as the elevator ascended past the second floor. It reached the third floor, and the doors opened to a reception area for the district attorney's office. Jake exited the elevator and stopped at the receptionist's desk.

"I'm Jake Reed, and I'm here to see Mr. Highfill," he told the young lady sitting behind the desk.

"Please have a seat over there." She pointed to a group of chairs in the waiting area. "And I'll let Mr. Highfill know you're here."

Jake sat in an oxblood imitation-leather chair near the window that overlooked the parking lot below. In the several times he'd been here before, he'd never noticed how terrible the view was. He picked up a *U.S. News & World Report* sitting on the table in front of him and thumbed through the pages as he waited on Drake.

Drake was meeting with his chief assistant district attorney, Harvey Orman, when the receptionist knocked on his office door.

"Come in," Drake stated dramatically.

"Mr. Highfill," she said as she opened the door, "Mr. Jake Reed is here to see you."

"Thank you." Drake nodded. "I'll be with him in just a few minutes."

As the receptionist left, closing the office door behind her, Drake turned back to Harvey. "Jake Reed is here to talk about Jed McClellan. Since Judge Prickett denied the motion to suppress, I have no intentions to plead that case. I have already told Jake as much. Is there anything we're missing?"

"I don't know of anything," responded Harvey. "I think we've got Jed dead to rights. It's an open-and-shut case."

"Good." Drake was convinced he was in a no-lose situation. "Ask the receptionist to show Jake back to my office. I want to make him squirm a little."

Harvey left the office to comply with his boss's instructions.

Soon Jake was walking down the corridor leading to Drake Highfill's office. He could see the haughty DA standing in the doorway, waiting for him. They exchanged some professional pleasantries and shook hands quickly. Jake always thought Drake more closely resembled a Wall Street lawyer than a Southern Democratic district attorney with his Armani suits, gold tie tack, matching cuff links, and wingtip shoes. Seeing Drake reminded Jake how little he liked the man.

Drake's office had not changed much over the years. It was still small and cramped, but everything was in order. The documents and folders on top of Drake's desk were organized in neat piles. A small credenza behind the desk was covered with picture frames of various sizes. Some of the photographs were of Drake's family, but others showed Drake with different politicians.

"Please sit down," Drake said to Jake, indicating a worn-out leather sofa directly in front of the desk.

Jake complied as Drake sat in his chair behind the desk. Over the years Jake had learned to sit on the front edge of the old sofa when he visited Drake. The sofa sagged in the middle. If Jake sat in the middle, it gave the perception that Drake was peering down on him from behind the desk. And Jake didn't like that at all.

"What can I do for you?" Drake inquired patronizingly.

Jake was blunt. "I want to talk to you about the Jed McClellan case."

"I guessed as much," Drake replied smugly. "I don't know what there is to talk about. I've already told you that I'm not going to plea-bargain this case."

"I'm not interested in a plea," Jake announced. "I want you to agree to dismiss the charges against Jed."

Drake laughed out loud. It was a deep laugh. One that Jake wouldn't forget. "Did you say dismiss the charges?" Drake looked incredulous.

"I did," Jake replied. His expression never changed.

"Why?" Drake said, continuing to laugh. "Judge Prickett denied your motion to suppress. Your client had motive to kill Jesse Thompson. He was found at the murder scene, and the murder weapon was found in his vehicle. Ballistics matched the bullet to the gun. And, even if all that wasn't true, I still would not be inclined to dismiss the charges. Jesse Thompson was a close friend of mine, and I intend to do everything I can to make sure Jed gets a lethal injection."

"I think you should reconsider your position," Jake stated. "To continue to prosecute Jed is a huge mistake."

"A mistake!" Drake laughed again.

Jake reached down beside the sofa he was sitting on and retrieved his briefcase. He laid it in his lap and slid the locks to the outside. The case popped open, and Jake raised the lid and removed the contents. He tossed them onto the middle of Drake's desk, closed his briefcase, and returned it to its place on the floor.

Drake picked up the contents of Jake's briefcase and began examining the items.

"Those are copies of photographs from the murder scene," Jake explained when he saw the confusion on Drake's face. "And those documents are evidence that Mr. Thompson was involved with a political action committee called F-PAC. He was skimming money. Someone else obviously had motive to kill Jesse Thompson, and someone else was at the scene at the time of the murder."

"Where did you get these?" inquired Drake.

Jake could sense the momentum of the negotiations shifting in his favor. Drake was no longer laughing.

"That's not important at this point," Jake insisted. "What *is* important is that this will give the jury reasonable doubt about my client's guilt. That means acquittal."

Jake knew that Drake certainly couldn't risk a jury acquitting Jed McClellan. That would be political death. He had aspirations beyond the district attorney's office, and a conviction of the murderer of Jesse Thompson would provide a springboard to a higher office.

"I can't consider dismissing the charges without knowing where you obtained this information," Drake demanded.

"I can't tell you that."

"You know Judge Prickett will order you to provide me with that information."

"If he does, then I'll decide whether to comply or appeal that decision. Right now I'm not willing to disclose my sources."

Drake gritted his teeth and glared across the desk at Jake. "If you're not willing to provide me the names of the people who gave you these photographs and documents, then we don't have anything else to talk about. You can find your way out, can't you?"

Jake stood up to leave. "Think about what I said, Drake. Continuing to prosecute Jed is a huge mistake."

"Good day, Counselor," Drake replied sternly.

Neither offered his hand as Jake left the room.

Jake strode to the elevator, pleased that he'd been able to verbally slap the smugness off Drake's face that he saw when he first entered the DA's office. He knew that at this very moment Drake was pacing in his office, trying to determine how to keep a jury from seeing the exculpatory documents about F-PAC, and the photographs. It was no use, Jake knew, because the documents and photographs were relevant and would be admitted into evidence, despite Drake's best objections.

A few days ago Jake thought he'd lost complete control over the outcome of Jed's case. Now he was convinced that Jed would be acquitted.

CHAPTER TWENTY-THREE

Atlanta, Georgia

Election Day was fifteen days away. The Burke for President campaign made a stop in Atlanta for a rare joint appearance with Ed's vice presidential running mate. Although they'd never talked about it, Ed was certain that his running mate had also sold his soul to the Federalists.

Ed's motorcade left Hartsfield-Jackson Atlanta International Airport and proceeded north on I-75 toward Olympic Park. All access ramps were blocked by patrol cars from Atlanta's Metro Police Department, and all streets that crossed over I-75 were cleared of traffic and pedestrians.

The motorcade was led by six Atlanta police officers on motorcycles. A similar battalion brought up the rear. In-between were six black bulletproof Chevrolet Suburbans carrying Secret Service agents and Burke for President campaign officials, and one black bulletproof limousine. In the limousine with Ed were Millie and Ben Tobias.

Ed sat in the rear of the limousine, reviewing his prepared speech for today's campaign rally. Millie gazed out at the throngs of people that lined the motorcade route. "Edward, I hope none of these people really know where you stand on the issues," she commented playfully.

"I hope so too," Ed responded without looking up from his speech. "I want them to vote for me."

Ben was reviewing favorable polling data when his wireless telephone rang. "Ben Tobias," he answered, rather absently. Then, "Yes, Vice President Burke is here."

Ed looked up.

"Mr. Vice President," Ben said, handing the phone to Ed, "it's Drake Highfill."

Ed laid his speech papers on the seat beside him and removed his reading glasses before putting the phone to his ear. "Drake, this is Ed Burke. How can I help you?"

"Mr. Vice President, I know you're busy, but I thought this was something you might be interested in."

"I'm listening. Go on."

"Jake Reed just left my office. He had photographs from the Thompson murder scene showing a second vehicle and a man other than Jed McClellan. He also had documents from Thompson's bank concerning an organization called F-PAC."

"Did he say where he got the photographs or the other documents?"

"No," replied Drake. "I pressed him, and he refused to tell me."

"Did he say anything else?"

"That was it, really. He was trying to use it to convince me to dismiss the charges against McClellan, but I refused."

"Did he mention my name?"

"No, sir. Your name never came up."

"Good. Let's keep it that way. If you hear anything else about this, call me immediately."

When Ed closed the phone, he noticed that Millie and Ben were staring at him.

"What was that all about?" Millie demanded.

Ed handed the phone back to Ben and smiled reassuringly at both of them. "Nothing I can't handle," Ed assured her. "I just need to make a call later."

"I hope you can handle it," Millie snapped. "The election is a little over two weeks away, and we certainly don't need any surprises."

Ed turned his head away from Millie and Ben. He looked out the window at the throngs of people. At their blurred faces as the motorcade raced by.

They can never know about the Federalists.

Ed's suite at the Ritz Carlton in the posh Atlanta suburb of Buckhead provided solitude from the raucous scene in Ben Tobias's suite where his top advisors, including Millie, were planning strategy and campaign stops for the homestretch. He couldn't stop thinking about his conversation with Drake Highfill. What Drake had told him about another murder suspect didn't bother him. Ed didn't care who was convicted for Jesse's murder. The part that caused him great concern, though, was what Drake had said about F-PAC.

The Federalist used F-PAC to provide funds for his campaign. That link between Ed and the Federalists couldn't be exposed. It would destroy him even at this late date in the campaign. He had intentionally avoided any contact with the Federalists during the campaign, but this was serious. It was time to violate that cardinal rule.

Apollyon Associates, Inc., lower Manhattan

Randolph Winston had called Pierce and Milton to the meeting to discuss what to do about Jake Reed.

"The election is fifteen days from today," Randolph began. "Mr. Reed must be dealt with, and I, for one, think he should be eliminated."

"No," refused Milton. "Your handling of the last problem has jeopardized our plans. I will not acquiesce in Mr. Reed's murder."

"You don't understand, Milton," Randolph charged. "If Reed provides any of this to the Republicans—or worse, the media—before the election, then we run the risk of being exposed."

"That's not a risk I'm willing to take," Pierce stated as he joined the conversation. "I have too much invested in this to risk losing it."

"I don't see the risk," Milton countered. "Reed doesn't understand the significance of the information he possesses, other than the fact it helps his client's case. He has no reason to give it to the media."

Just then the phone in Randolph's office rang on his direct-in-dial line rather than through the answering service. Very few people had access to that number, and because of that, Randolph decided he needed to answer the call. The discussion about what to do with Jake Reed ceased as Randolph answered the call.

"Randolph, this is Ed."

Randolph grew stern. "Ed, you know it's dangerous for you to call me." Randolph glanced at Pierce and Milton, who showed concern at the mention of Ed Burke's name.

"I know," Ed replied. "But we have a problem that we need to talk about."

"Wait a minute, Ed. I'm here with Pierce and Milton. Let me put you on the speaker."

Randolph pressed a button on his telephone to activate the speakerphone option so Pierce and Milton could hear Ed, and vice versa.

"What's the problem?" Randolph asked after Pierce and Milton had exchanged greetings with Ed.

"I received a call today from Drake Highfill, the prosecutor on the case involving my friend Jesse Thompson."

"We've been following that situation," responded Randolph. "What did Highfill have to say?"

"He told me that the lawyer defending the animal accused of killing Jesse was in his office today showing him some documents about F-PAC. Those documents link you to me. We can't let them get out."

"That's just what we're talking about," Randolph stated. "We're trying to determine the best course of action to take."

"Did Highfill say what Reed planned to do with this information?" Milton asked.

"Not really," replied Ed. "I got the impression that Reed was using them to get his client some kind of deal. Personally, I hope that animal fries."

"I think Pierce, Milton, and I need to talk about this some more, Ed," Randolph stated.

"I don't want any problems with only fifteen days to go," Ed informed his benefactors. "You promised me the presidency, and I expect you to hold up your end of the bargain."

"We want you to be president as well," Pierce defended. "There's too much riding on this for anybody to make a mistake. Randolph, Milton, and I will decide what to do."

"Highfill also said that Reed had pictures of someone else at the murder scene," Ed stated. "Any truth to that?"

"We're checking on that as well," Randolph replied. "But you really must let Pierce, Milton, and me handle this. You don't need to talk to Highfill any more about it, and you certainly don't need to call Mr. Reed."

"I understand," Ed replied. "I just hope you take care of it, and soon. We don't need any problems this late in the game. And I wish you would find out what you can about another person being at the murder scene." With that, Ed said good-bye.

Randolph, Pierce, and Milton returned to discussing how to handle Jake Reed.

"Now will you agree to eliminating him, Milton?" Randolph asked.

"I still don't believe that to be necessary," Milton defiantly argued. "He doesn't realize the importance of the information. He only sees it as a bargaining chip to use against the prosecutor. If we kill him, then suspicions will rise, and someone will discover that he was murdered because of this information."

"But that discovery won't occur until after the election," Randolph fired back. He glared at Milton. "We won't care at that point, because we'll have everything we need."

Milton drew himself up to his full short height. "That doesn't matter to me, and you don't know that for sure. I cannot agree to another murder."

"Can we at least threaten him or blackmail him?" Pierce inquired. "We only need his silence for a short while longer."

"I'll agree to that," Milton replied, looking at Randolph for conciliation.

"I don't like it," Randolph stated. "But if that's what you want, then that's what we'll do. I'll call Sanders tomorrow and give him instructions."

Madison County Criminal Justice Complex, Jackson, Tennessee

The Monday following Ruth's last visit was the day that Jed broke. There wasn't anything special about the day. It was significant only because it was a Monday, and Ruth always visited on Mondays. Except for this Monday. He had been in the Madison County Criminal Justice Complex for seventy days. Or was it seventy-one? he asked himself. He couldn't remember. It didn't matter anyway. He was leaving tonight—one way or the other.

Jake Reed had told him that he could plead guilty and the DA would not seek the death penalty. But Jed couldn't convince himself to do it. He was innocent, for goodness' sake, and no one seemed to be listening to him. His mind was made up. He couldn't spend one more day in this place. It was either freedom . . . or death. There was no in between as far as Jed was concerned, and it appeared that the option of freedom had faded away. Judge Prickett had denied the motion to suppress, and the gun would be admitted into evidence. Jake told him that they would have grounds to appeal any verdict, but what good was that?

Jed was only permitted one visitor per week, other than his lawyer. The days between visits by Ruth seemed to be getting longer. And she didn't visit today. It was the first visiting day she missed since his incarceration. Her absence was even more troubling because of the way she left last Monday. Crying. Broken. Distraught. Jed hadn't seen his children since the day before his arrest, and to make matters worse, now his wife wasn't visiting.

He felt all alone.

He was all alone. He was isolated from the rest of the prison population in solitary confinement. He was allowed one hour a day in the recreation yard and spent the other twenty-three hours of the day in his jail cell, alone.

Jed's accommodations were worse than miserable, and that added to his loneliness. His cell was cramped—ten foot by ten foot. The walls in the rear and side of the cell were made of white concrete blocks surrounding reinforced steel. The front wall consisted of iron bars from floor to ceiling, with a sliding door constructed of iron bars in the middle. Even the ceiling was made of impenetrable concrete.

The furnishings were equally depressing. A twin-size metal bed frame bolted to one of the side walls substituted as the bed. It featured a four-inch-thick pad, which the warden called a mattress. Attached to the rear wall were a stainless-steel sink and a stainless-steel toilet.

And that was it.

No pictures on the wall.

No recliner.

No television.

Jed couldn't take it anymore.

He preferred to have a rope, or something like it, but would have to make do with what was available. Jed tied the ends of his bed sheets together, draped it over the pipe running through the ceiling for the sprinkler system, and made a noose at the end.

FBI headquarters, Washington DC

Deputy Director Charlie Armacost arrived for work on Tuesday at his usual time of 5:30 a.m. He sat in his office deep inside the J. Edgar Hoover Building, again scrutinizing the photographs of Raoul at the murder scene, and the documents obtained by Agents Boyd and Simon.

He was beginning to have that intuitive feeling that comes from twenty years in the Bureau. He knew that the murder of Jesse Thompson was more than just a murder. What he didn't know yet was the identity of the person who had ordered the hit. He had called Agents Boyd and Simon back from Jackson after Jake Reed had surprised them. He couldn't afford exposure at this point in the investigation. The timing couldn't have been worse, though.

Charlie laid the photographs on his desk and leaned back in his chair. Everything he had so far was pointing toward the vice president. Could Edward Burke be a murderer? Could he have ordered the assassination of his longtime friend? If so, why? Charlie knew he didn't have all the pieces to the puzzle, and the ones he did have weren't fitting together very well. He was missing the link between them.

His telephone rang, and he noticed the call was coming in on his private number that only a few agents in international countries knew. It had to be Juan.

"Juan," Charlie said as he answered the call. He laid his glasses on his desk and rubbed his sore eyes.

"Hello, my friend," Juan responded.

Charlie checked the number. Juan was calling from his apartment in the northern section of Bogotá. The call traveled through three different telephone circuits before it rang to Charlie's desk. Charlie knew the call couldn't be traced. But, just in case, their conversation was encrypted.

"Have you found Raoul?"

"Yes. He and I had a professional meeting of sorts."

"Did he say anything?"

"He said the name of the man who hired him was Winston."

"Winston?" Charlie asked rhetorically. "Did he say anything else?"

"That was it."

"Are you certain he was telling the truth?"

Juan chuckled. "I'm certain."

"Good," Charlie replied. "Let me know if you hear anything else."

Juan hung up, and Charlie pushed the intercom button on the telephone. He dialed Assistant Deputy Director McCullough's office.

"George," he said when the assistant deputy director answered the call. "I need you in my office immediately."

In less than thirty seconds George was at Charlie's door. "What is it?" he inquired as he entered the room.

"I have a name I need you to check out. You're the only one, other than me, who will know this name, and we need to keep it that way. You need to handle this personally. I'm still not certain who we can trust."

"Does it have to do with the Thompson murder?" George asked.

"Perhaps, and that's why you must keep it top secret. The name is Winston, and that's all I have. Just that one name."

"Do you know how many people there must be in the country with Winston somewhere in their name?"

"I didn't say the assignment would be easy. It has to be someone with unlimited wealth. Start there. Let me know what you find."

Madison County Criminal Justice Complex, Jackson, Tennessee

The guard on duty found Jed at 6:00 a.m. Tuesday when he made his rounds. There was a note lying on the bed addressed to Jed's wife. He apologized for all the pain and agony he had caused, and asked her to forgive him.

FBI headquarters, Washington DC

Saul Sanders consulted his calendar when he arrived at his office. It was Tuesday, and the presidential election was exactly two weeks away. Maybe then he could get rid of that thorn in the flesh, Armacost. *Things will be better when the Federalists are in charge.* Saul saw the light flashing for his private line. Only Randolph would be calling it, and Saul knew it had to be urgent. He closed and locked the door to his office before answering it.

"Saul," Randolph began when Saul answered the phone. He didn't have the time or the courtesy for an appropriate greeting. "Our problem is larger than we thought."

"What do you mean?"

"Reed is using the photographs of Raoul Miguel Flores and the F-PAC documents for negotiations with the prosecutor. It won't be long before Reed shows those to somebody who will know what they mean. We can't take the chance that he does that before the election. If he does, it won't be long before that road leads to us. We must act quickly."

"Do you want him eliminated?" inquired Saul eagerly. He wanted to make certain that Randolph recognized his loyalty.

"I do. But Milton and Pierce wouldn't agree to it. Milton thinks that Reed only wants to help his client and doesn't know the significance of the information. All we need is to make sure he doesn't show it to anyone before the election. We need you to help us with that."

"I have just the man for the job," Saul responded.

"Good. We need to move quickly before he discusses it with anyone else."

"I'll call my contact as soon as we hang up."

"And Saul, I need you to do one other thing for me," Randolph said.

"What is it?"

"I need you to eliminate the other problem we've been watching."

CHAPTER TWENTY-FOUR

Jackson-Madison County General Hospital, Jackson, Tennessee

Somehow, miraculously, Jed survived. The bed sheets were not strong enough to break any bones in his neck. He had fallen unconscious and hung from the sprinkler pipe, his toes barely touching the floor, until the guard discovered him. Jed was still unconscious.

Jake parked his car in the parking garage south of Jackson-Madison County General Hospital and entered through the revolving door that led to the main lobby. He stopped at the information desk across from the entrance and asked the volunteer working there where he could find the McClellan family.

After receiving directions, Jake found Ruth in the waiting room outside the critical-care unit. She was sitting alone on a yellow vinyl couch with her face buried in her hands, sobbing.

"What happened?" Jake asked as he sat down beside Ruth and placed his arm around her.

"Sheriff West said he tried to commit suicide," Ruth answered. She laid her head on Jake's shoulder. "I just can't believe it. The last time I saw him was last Monday in the visitin' room."

She raised her head from Jake's shoulder and righted herself on the vinyl couch. "I didn't stay the whole time, and I left cryin'. I didn't even visit yesterday. I just couldn't take it no more." She hesitated. "This is all my fault." Ruth buried her head in her hands again and sobbed. Jake didn't know how to comfort her. He simply placed his hand on her back and patted it.

Jake knew Ruth wasn't to blame. If anybody was to blame, he was. If he hadn't been trying to be a hero, he could have prevented Jed's suicide attempt. All Jed had needed was some realistic hope. Why hadn't he told Jed about Jesse Thompson being his father? Or about the $2 million he'd squeezed from Mrs. Thompson? If he had, would Jed still have attempted suicide? He wouldn't have had a reason to.

Jake's plan had been to tell Jed this morning about the photographs, the money, and about his meeting with Drake. But, in his attempt to control every minute detail, he had waited too long. And that delay had resulted in Jed's current condition.

"What are the doctors saying?" Jake asked when Ruth's weeping subsided.

"They're not sure if he'll live. If he does, he'll prob'ly have brain damage from the lack of oxygen. It's still too early to tell." She wiped her eyes with the tissue she was clasping.

"I'd like to go see him," Jake said.

"I think that'd be great."

Jake stood with Ruth, and they walked past the nurses' station and down the sterile hall toward Jed's room. The entrance to each room looked identical to the one next to it, but it was easy for Jake to identify Jed's room before reaching it since it was the only room in the hospital with a sheriff's deputy posted on either side of the door. The deputies recognized Jake and nodded permission for him and Ruth to enter Jed's room.

Jake followed Ruth into the room. Jed was unconscious, with an IV in each arm and a tube down his throat to help him breathe. In his mind Jake searched for words to describe Jed's appearance, and he kept going back to the same description.

Jed looked dead.

Were it not for the regular *beep beep* of the monitors, Jake would have thought Jed really was dead.

Certainly, his spirit was gone. Physically, he may have been lying in that hospital bed, but spiritually, he was dead. He had lost hope and given up. It was as simple as that, Jake knew.

Naomi was sitting in a chair by the side of Jed's bed. When Jake gently touched her on the shoulder, she looked up at him and smiled. She seemed to have a strange peace about her, and he couldn't understand why. With everything that had happened in her life, how could she be at peace?

Then Jake remembered something Naomi told him when she was in his office. *"God's in control. We're gonna be OK."*

Looking at Naomi, Jake realized for the first time that his life was missing something. He had filled his life with money, his law practice, and even his family. But there was still something missing. Naomi had no personal possessions to speak of, yet she was at peace. Jake knew she was poor. Her only child was accused of murder, and now he was lying in a hospital bed almost dead. How could she be so peaceful? What was it that she had that Jake didn't?

Jake asked himself if it really could be her belief in God. He knew all about the Christian faith. He even told anyone who asked that he was a Christian. But the thought of God being in control of every event that takes place seemed implausible to him. If God really was in control, then why did horrible things happen to good people like Naomi McClellan?

No, Jake finally told himself. *There must be some other explanation for Naomi's peace.* He was not ready to accept Naomi's notion that God was in control.

He looked back at Jed's listless body. The sight of him lying there barely alive was sickening. Jake couldn't even approach the side of the bed. He turned away and started to leave the room. Ruth touched him on the arm, and he gazed into her face.

"We're going to make it through this, you know," she assured him.

"I know, Ruth, but I should have seen this coming, and I didn't."

"Don't blame yourself. I don't, and I know Jed don't. You just keep workin' to clear Jed's name."

He started to tell her about the money but decided against it. It didn't really matter at the moment. Jake knew Drake Highfill wouldn't go to trial against an unconscious man. It was time to close the file on the *Jedediah McClellan* case, at least for a while.

"I'll check on you again tomorrow, Ruth," Jake said as he left the room and walked toward the front door of the hospital. The closer he got to the exit, the quicker his steps became. He had to get out of there.

Reed residence, Jackson, Tennessee

Jake arrived home just past six o'clock. The kids had no doubt already eaten supper without him, again. He pulled into the garage, put the car in park, and laid his head against the steering wheel, trying to gather himself before he went inside. He didn't want his children to see that their daddy had been crying. He was supposed to be strong, not weak, he kept reminding himself. He had to at least act like there was nothing wrong, even when there was. After a few minutes of isolation he was ready to face his family.

Jake knew that the sound of the opening door would signal his children that he was home. It did, and they raced to greet him before the door was completely closed. As they hugged him around the legs and waist, he felt the warmth of their bodies. He knelt down so he would be at eye level with them.

"How was your day at school, Courtney?" he asked.

"It was good, Daddy. I got an A on my math test."

"I knew you could. I told you that all you had to do was take your time." He pulled Courtney close and gave her an extra squeeze.

"What about you, Brett?" Jake asked as he turned his attention to his middle child. "Did you have a good day?"

"I didn't have to go to the principal's office." Brett announced.

That was how Brett measured whether a day was good or bad, Jake knew. He grinned.

"Jeremy, did you have a good day at kindergarten?"

"It was fun. We painted with our fingers."

"And how was your day?" came a voice from behind the children. It was Rachel, and Jake was glad to see her.

"Terrible," Jake replied.

"What happened?"

Jake glanced around at the children, who were listening to every word their parents were saying.

"I'll tell you later . . ."

By eight thirty the children were bathed and in bed. Jake sat with Rachel on the couch in the great room. The only light in the room came from a small lamp on top of the Wurlitzer piano.

"So tell me why your day was so terrible," Rachel prodded.

"Jed McClellan tried to commit suicide today."

She gasped. "How? Why?"

"He tried to hang himself by making a noose with the bed sheets in his cell. I'm not sure about the why, but I suspect it was because Jed couldn't stand the thought of another day in the CJC." Jake swallowed hard. "And it's my fault."

Rachel's brow creased. "That's ridiculous, Jake."

"It's true. It's my fault that Jed is lying in the hospital on his death-bed." Jake didn't tie the bed sheets together and make the noose for Jed, but he certainly didn't do enough to stop it either. He began to weep and was finally able to release his pent-up emotions, which now fully erupted. Jake sobbed uncontrollably.

Rachel moved even closer and put her arms around him, holding him as he cried. "You can't blame yourself for what happened to Jed," she said softly after a few minutes. "He's a grown man and made his own decision."

Jake wiped his eyes with the palms of his hands. "You don't under-stand. Jed came to me before any of this started and asked me to help him with a problem he was having with Jesse Thompson. I didn't really believe Jed would do anything to Jesse. So I didn't try very hard to help. Then the other day I discovered some information that helped Jed, and I haven't told him yet. If I had, he probably wouldn't have tried to kill himself."

Her voice was solemn. "You can't be sure, Jake. You don't know what's in a man's mind. You've done the very best you can to help Jed."

"I went to see Jed today at the hospital after I heard about the suicide attempt," Jake said, still trying to compose himself. "He looked awful. I don't know if he's going to live or not. What will I do if he dies? I'll always believe I was responsible for his death."

"Stop blaming yourself," Rachel instructed sternly. "Did you see any of Jed's family at the hospital?"

"Ruth was there, and so was Jed's mother."

She lifted an eyebrow. "Are they blaming you?"

"No," Jake admitted.

"That's what I'm talking about. They're not blaming you, and you shouldn't blame yourself either."

Jake thought about Rachel's admonishment, and he also thought about seeing Naomi at the hospital. What was it about that sixty-year-old woman that intrigued him so much?

"It was strange, really," Jake explained, awe in his voice. "Jed's mother seemed completely at peace with the situation. She wasn't blaming anybody. I can't understand how she can be so calm."

"Maybe the doctor told her that Jed was going to be OK."

"No, the doctor told them he wasn't sure if Jed would recover. She was in my office the week after Jed was arrested and said something that has really stuck with me. She said, 'God's in control. We're gonna be OK.'" Jake thought about Naomi's words. "I can't comprehend what that means," he admitted.

Jake and Rachel talked for over an hour. Jake needed it. Before he realized it, it was ten o'clock.

"Let's go to bed," Rachel suggested. "A good night's rest, and you'll be able to think more clearly."

"That sounds great." He was tired. "You go ahead, and I'll be there in a few minutes. I want to watch the news first," he said as he reached for the remote.

Rachel changed into her pajamas and knelt beside their bed, as she did every night.

"God, I don't always understand why things happen, but I know that everything that happens fits into your plan. That's why I know you're in control of what has happened to Jed. I pray you will be with Jed and his family. And God, I pray that you will take care of Jake too. Give him strength, and help him through this time. But, most important, I pray that Jake will accept Jesus Christ as his Lord and Savior."

Jackson-Madison County General Hospital, Jackson, Tennessee

Naomi looked around room 8 in the critical-care unit as she entered for the last visiting time of the day. The front wall to the room was solid glass, and Naomi could see the hospital staff at the nurses' station. She knew the transparent wall was so that the staff could have visual contact with Jed at all times. The head of Jed's bed was on the rear wall and monitors flanked either side. Naomi sat in a green vinyl chair to Jed's left.

The room was quiet with the exception of the regular *beep* of the monitor attached to Jed, recording his vital signs. Naomi wasn't sure what purpose the monitor served medically, but the constant sound confirmed to her that Jed was still alive.

She pulled her chair closer to Jed's bed and peered over the cold, metal rail into his seemingly lifeless face. A tube ran from his nostrils, around the back of his head, and into a valve in the wall behind the bed. Oxygen constantly flowed from the tubes into his nose. A larger tube protruded from his mouth into a similar valve behind the bed. Naomi couldn't see the end of the tube that was in Jed's throat. But the doctor told her that Jed had damaged the passageway leading from his mouth to his lungs when he hanged himself, and he needed the tube to help him breathe. Naomi took Jed's big, calloused left hand and placed it in hers. She squeezed it, trying to help Jed hang on to what little life he had remaining.

As she studied Jed, she didn't see a grown man lying there. All she could see was the little boy she used to hold in her lap and sing songs to. She remembered how she cried the first day Jed went to school and how she cried again when he didn't want to go back the next day. She remembered his first Pop Warner football game and when he started high school. Naomi also remembered Jed's high-school graduation and how proud she was of him. Jed was the first McClellan to get his high-school diploma . . .

Although Naomi knew her son couldn't hear her now, she talked to him. "How'd we get here, Jed? What happened to you, to us, along the way that you wound up in this hospital bed? If I could, I'd trade places with you. It ain't right you lyin' here dyin'. You're still so young and got so much life left. Ruth and the kids miss you. You've gotta fight for them."

Naomi rested her chin on the top of the bed rail and stroked the side of Jed's face with her right hand. "Please wake up, Jed," she begged. "Please."

Naomi recalled the doctor's telling Ruth and her that he wasn't sure Jed would ever wake up again. If he did, the doctor wasn't sure what condition his mind would be in. Jed had gone a long time with little, if any, oxygen to his brain, the doctor had told them.

Naomi knew there was only one way that Jed would wake up and be all right—and that was through God. She closed her eyes and offered a simple prayer. "Lord, take care of Jed."

A single tear escaped from Naomi's eye and gently fell on Jed's big hand.

CHAPTER TWENTY-FIVE

George Bush Intercontinental Airport, north of Houston, Texas

Shep wanted to keep his involvement in Dalton's investigation a secret until after the election, if not forever. If the PI's efforts proved fruitless, then Shep wouldn't have the embarrassment of having to explain to the campaign staff how he had failed. If Dalton's efforts were fruitful, then victory would be theirs, and Mac wouldn't really care how it happened. But Jack prodded him often after their conversation at the church in New Orleans. Each time Shep refused to say anything, but with each prod his resistance diminished.

Shep didn't like the idea of telling Jack. The more people who knew, the more chances there were for Mac to find out. Even at this late date Shep knew that Mac would demand that all covert activities cease. Shep couldn't let that happen. Dalton was their only hope.

The campaign was back in Texas. The latest polls Shep received indicated a slight increase for Mac in the Lone Star State, with the margin there narrowed to 8 points. Shep knew that, mathematically, Mac had no chance of winning the presidency, even if he carried Texas. The electoral college and the popular vote were both completely in Edward Burke's column. But Texas was a large state, and if Mac could carry it, the final tally on Election Day wouldn't be nearly as embarrassing.

The Foster for President Boeing 747 was parked on the tarmac at George Bush Intercontinental Airport on Highway 59, north of Houston. In the final two-week marathon the campaign would hit five cities a day, trying to rally the Republican voter base for a final push to Election Day. Shep watched Mac from the airplane as Mac stood on a platform below, giving his best fire-and-brimstone speech. His voice was tired and hoarse, but his energy was endless.

"The race isn't over!" His voice boomed into the microphone over the crowd noise. It was one of the larger crowds the Foster campaign had seen in the last few days.

"We're not giving up, and neither should you!" he shouted again. The crowd roared its approval.

Soon Jack joined Shep in the passenger cabin of the airplane, and both watched Mac through the small oval windows.

"He really is something," Jack stated in admiration. "He doesn't have a prayer of winning, and still he's out there, giving 110 percent."

It was time, Shep realized. Time to let Jack in on his secret. "He still has a chance," Shep said, keeping his gaze fixed on Mac.

Jack turned to scrutinize Shep. "You keep saying that, but you never tell me how that's possible. And, in fact, it can't be possible with only two weeks remaining until Election Day. We're too far behind."

"Do you remember the night we were in Miami, watching Burke's acceptance speech?" Shep asked, still keeping his eyes on Mac.

"Yes," Jack said slowly.

Shep could feel Jack's stare. "We talked about Burke's campaign fund-raising."

"I remember," Jack replied. "But nothing ever came of it."

"That's not exactly true."

"What do you mean?"

Shep turned away from the window and faced Jack, who was looking at him like an eager puppy wanting a morsel. "I mean something has come of it." He paused to make sure Jack would hear his next statement clearly. "I hired a private investigator."

"What?" Jack yelled. Then, looking around, he lowered his voice. "You hired a *private investigator*? Are you crazy?"

Shep raised his hands, palm side toward Jack, defending himself. "You've been begging to hear this. Just listen to me. I hired an investigator. You remember the murder of Burke's friend in Tennessee in August?"

"Vaguely," Jack responded.

"It turns out it was an assassination."

"Assassination? What are you talking about?"

Shep told Jack everything he knew about the Jesse Thompson murder and the connection to F-PAC. He promised to show him the F-PAC documents later.

"What does all that mean?" Jack asked.

"It means we're close," Shep insisted. "If we can tie F-PAC to Burke, then we've got him. Without that connection, we have nothing."

"We've got to tell Mac," Jack stated.

"No!" replied Shep. "Mac cannot know now . . . and maybe never."

"Why?"

"Because he'll tell us to end the investigation, and the investigation is the only thing we have that might save us." Shep glared at Jack. "You cannot tell Mac anything about this. If anybody tells him, *I'll* tell him. But only when the time is right."

When Shep heard the music from the local high-school marching band that was brought in for the rally, he knew Mac's speech was over. He and Jack separated into different areas of the plane.

In just a few moments Mac and Shannon boarded the plane, and Mac found Shep in the galley.

"Anything new?" Mac inquired.

"Not really, sir," Shep replied.

"It was a great rally. I wish all the crowds could be that big."

"It was a great rally." Shep grinned. He could tell Mac was still experiencing an adrenaline rush from the rally's energy. "You're going to make a great president."

"Thanks for the encouragement. Where is our next stop?"

"San Antonio. We'll finish up Texas today, and then go back to Albany for the night. We have a lot of stops to make between now and Election Day."

"It will be good to go home," Mac commented. "If only for one night."

Hilton Head Island, South Carolina

It had now been a little over two weeks since Hudson's last visit, and Claudia still hadn't heard from him. Not a word. To say she was worried would be an understatement. She constantly recalled their conversation on the beach one morning several weeks ago. She was terrified, and rightfully so, that something terrible had happened to him. It was so unlike him to not even call between visits.

Claudia sat by the glass-top kitchen table, half-heartedly picking at her lunch: a bowl of she-crab soup. She hadn't had much of an appetite in several days. It was impossible to worry and be hungry at the same time. She took only a few spoonfuls of the soup before pushing it away and standing up.

She paced to the large triple-wide window in the great room that overlooked the vast Atlantic Ocean. The ocean and sky seemed endless.

Her worries crescendoed after all the days with no word from the man she loved. *Where can Hudson be? Why hasn't he called? Has something happened to him?*

Her thoughts were interrupted by a knock at the front door.

Perhaps that's him, and he's forgotten his key!

She hurried to the front door, anticipating seeing Hudson on the other side.

But when she opened the front door, a young man in a blue uniform stood there. The name tag over the pocket of his shirt indicated that he was with an island courier service.

"Are you Claudia Duval?" he asked.

"I am," she replied. "Why do you ask?"

"I have a package for you." The young man handed Claudia a small, padded manila envelope. "Please sign here." He thrust a clipboard at her.

Claudia took the envelope, signed the clipboard, gave the courier a tip, and closed the door. She looked at the return address. It was from Hudson. She tried to rip open the envelope with her hands, but the flap was sealed by a metal clasp and three layers of Scotch tape. She finally located a metal letter opener in the top drawer of the desk in the study adjacent to the great room. She slit the top crease of the envelope and poured its contents onto the kitchen table. A tiny key and a single, tri-folded sheet of paper fell out. She unfolded the paper and began to read.

My Dearest Claudia,

I am so sorry that I have not contacted you sooner, but I have feared for your safety. I have lied to you. My name is really not Hudson Kinney. It is Milton McAdams. And I have done some terrible things. Not me personally, but I agreed that they should be done.

Let me explain. I belong to a group called the Federalists. When I agreed to join, everything was fine. But now I deeply regret my involvement. I haven't contacted you because I was afraid that if they discovered our relationship, then your life would be in jeopardy.

The enclosed key is to a storage locker at the airport in Atlanta. I don't think anything will happen to me, but if it does, please take the contents from the locker and deliver them to Attorney Jake Reed in Jackson, Tennessee. He will know what to do.

Claudia, please know that I love you, and that I did not intend for any of this to happen. I hope to be able to contact you in a couple of weeks, and I hope you can forgive me.

All My Love,
Milton

Claudia picked up the brass key and brought it close to her face. The round head of the key was covered with red plastic, and on it was inscribed *T-25*.

Her life had just been thrown into utter confusion. The last six months with Hudson had been a complete lie.

Once again, Claudia was all alone. She had no friends or family to talk to, and now no Hudson.

Nothing made sense.

"Can you tell what's going on?" Agent Moyers asked.

He and Agent Osborne had watched the courier come and go. They also watched Claudia read the letter and saw her reaction.

"I have no idea what's happening," Bill replied. "There was obviously something in that letter."

"Stay alert," Al stated. "Anything could happen."

CHAPTER TWENTY-SIX

Manhattan

Despite his Irish name, Milton McAdams loved Italian food. The best Italian restaurant in Manhattan was Carmine's on 44th Street between Broadway and Eighth Avenue. The food was delicious, and the waiters were typically New York rude. The restaurant was always packed and noisy. Carmine's didn't provide its patrons with menus. The offerings of the day were written on a chalkboard by the front door, and the customer was expected to be prepared to order when he sat down at his table.

Milton arrived at the restaurant just after eight o'clock on Wednesday evening. He was a regular customer, and the proprietor always had a table for him. He followed the hostess into the main dining area. She led him to the booth in the back-right corner of the restaurant. A Ben Franklin always garnered him his favorite table. The deeper Milton walked into Carmine's, the more it took on the appearance of a quaint eatery in the old section of Rome. A single candle illuminated the red-and-white-checkered cloth on his table. Italian paraphernalia covered the interior walls, and photographs of the proprietor's ancestors hung alongside red, white, and green flags.

Another chalkboard bearing the evening's menu hung on a wall near Milton's table, and he glanced at it as the waiter approached. Milton selected the *bola pasta*, accompanied by a glass of red wine. He wished Claudia were there with him. By now she would have received his package, but he couldn't call to check on her. It would be taking too much of a risk.

Milton noticed a man and a woman sitting three tables away. They appeared to be from out of town and were enjoying some of the world-famous

Manhattan cuisine. They laughed, talked, and laughed again. Occasionally one of them glanced in his direction, and he politely smiled.

The waiter delivered his pasta, and Milton savored his meal as long as he could. But when the evening grew to be nearly nine o'clock, he realized, reluctantly, that it was time to leave. He finished his pasta, paid the waiter, put on his cashmere topcoat, and left the restaurant. He had previously instructed his chauffeur to pick him up precisely at nine o'clock at the corner of Broadway and 44th. Milton walked the half block along the dirty sidewalk and through the blowing exhaust, created by the underground subway system, to the scheduled destination. He saw his limousine two blocks away and waved, signaling the driver to pull the car forward to where he was standing.

The huge Jumbotron at the south end of Times Square captured his attention. While it broadcast an MTV music video, a stock-market ticker ran around the bottom of the screen, displaying closing stock quotes from the NYSE and NASDAQ markets in red letters. Milton watched for the World Federal symbol, although he knew the day's closing price. Cacophony filled the brisk night air. Cars honked, people shouted, and neon lights flashed. To an outsider Times Square looked like chaos, but not to Milton.

He turned from watching the stock-market ticker and glanced up and down Broadway as he waited on his limousine. Milton loved Manhattan almost as much as he loved Eden. Each place was special to him. Manhattan was exciting, fast-paced, and unpredictable. Eden was relaxing, comfortable, and serene. But Eden had one advantage over Manhattan. It had Claudia. And that was where Milton wanted to be.

Two more weeks, he encouraged himself. *Two more weeks and this whole ordeal will be over. Then you can go home to Claudia.*

The idea of world dominance he'd agreed to had been altered, and there was no way of reversing courses. He knew the problem was Randolph. Milton didn't think that Pierce had noticed it yet, but Randolph had changed. He was different than he'd been when the concept of the Federalists originated. Randolph was now obsessed with the Federalists, but his obsession appeared to have nothing to do anymore with saving the world. The last time the Federalists were together,

Milton had seen something in Randolph . . . in his eyes. It was something Milton had never seen before. He couldn't quite put his finger on it, but it was definitely evil. It made him shiver even now, thinking about it.

Two more weeks, he told himself again. He was prepared to allow Randolph and Pierce to have the Federalists, and he would never tell a soul about them. All he wanted to do was wake up every morning next to Claudia.

FBI agents Sam Chambers and Teresa Markham left Carmine's immediately after Milton McAdams. Their assignment from Saul Sanders was clear. Milton McAdams had to be eliminated tonight.

"I don't think he knew we were watching him in the restaurant, but it's got to be done before he gets in his car," Teresa advised. Her vision was fixed firmly on the back of their target, now twenty feet in front of them. "We may not get another opportunity."

"I know," Sam replied. "You keep a look out for NYPD. I'll make the hit before he gets in the car."

Teresa and Sam stayed a safe distance behind, following their mark to the corner of 44th and Broadway. Pedestrians streamed through the crosswalk, hurrying to cross Broadway before the signal changed. Milton stood immediately to the right of the entrance to the crosswalk. Pedestrians passed behind him on the sidewalk, one or two bumping into him. Sam methodically made his way through the crowd until finally he was standing directly behind Milton. He knew Teresa stood twenty feet away, constantly scanning the crowd for the blue uniforms of NYPD street cops. She would give a signal if one appeared.

Milton saw his limousine had stopped at the red light at 45th and Broadway, behind a yellow cab. When the traffic light changed to green, several straggling pedestrians increased their pace to complete the trek across Broadway before being struck by the oncoming traffic. The cab accelerated slowly. Milton's limousine was immediately behind it, casually making its way to the pickup point.

"Can't you go any faster!" the male passenger screamed at the Ukrainian immigrant driver of Cab 57 from the Yellow Cab Company. The driver hardly understood any English, but the passenger hoped his tone would convey his message. He leaned forward again, shouting through the small holes in the bulletproof window separating the front seat from the backseat. He wanted to make sure the driver could hear him. "I've got to be at the corner of 34th in five minutes!" The acceleration from the driver's response caused the passenger to fall back into the tattered rear seat of the cab.

Chambers inched closer to Milton. He placed his right hand in his coat pocket and gripped the cold metal from the .38 caliber Smith & Wesson pistol, equipped with a silencer. He placed his index finger along the trigger and angled the barrel of the gun at Milton's back. As he began to pull the trigger, he saw Cab 57 barreling down Broadway in the lane closest to the sidewalk and relaxed his trigger finger. He wouldn't need to fire his gun after all. As the cab sped through the intersection at 44th, Sam nudged Milton in the back with his right shoulder. Milton lost his balance on the curb and stumbled into the street, right into the path of the oncoming vehicle.

As the cab careened violently toward Milton, he screamed, and the pedestrians who remained on the corner screamed. The sounds were engulfed by the swirl of noise that blew through Times Square.

Sam watched calmly as the front bumper of the cab struck Milton immediately below the waist and his body flipped into the air, landing on the hood and front windshield of the car. The impact shattered the windshield. The driver of the cab slammed on the car's brakes, and Milton's body rolled wildly off the front of the cab. His cashmere topcoat was still wrapped around him as his lifeless body landed on Broadway and slid to a halt against the curb. Blood began to stream from every orifice of Milton's head, running into the metal street gutter that led to the underground storm drain system.

The whole event had lasted less than five seconds.

Sam congratulated himself. Nobody would see anything in it but a horrible accident. He and Teresa had accomplished their mission.

The Ukrainian driver of the cab leaped from the driver's-side door and rushed to Milton's body. He frantically called for help in his native tongue, but no one responded.

"Where are you going?" the cab's passenger yelled out the window as the driver exited the car. "I'm already late!"

He smacked his fist into the backseat cushion and exited the car through the driver's-side rear door.

After slamming the door, he hailed another cab. "I don't have time for this," he muttered as the second cab pulled away from the scene.

Pedestrians gathered around Milton's corpse, gawking at the spectacle of a dead man lying in the middle of Times Square. Because the NYPD utilized officers on horses and bicycles to patrol Times Square, two NYPD officers on bicycles were at the scene within a minute. One officer radioed his precinct office, requesting medical assistance and additional officers, while the other officer began questioning the multitude of onlookers. Homicide detectives would also question spectators later, but every witness would tell the same story. It was a horrible accident.

Sam and Teresa disappeared into the crowd and walked north on Broadway, away from the scene. Within an hour they would be on an airplane out of LaGuardia to DC and would personally give Saul Sanders their report.

Hilton Head Island, South Carolina

After she read Milton's letter, Claudia ran through a multitude of emotions—from anger to confusion to sadness and back to anger again. She finally lay down on the sofa in the den and passed out from the exhaustion of the emotional roller coaster she had ridden over the last several hours.

Agents Osborne and Moyers stood on the balcony of the house next door. The full moon glistened off the calm waters of the Atlantic Ocean, and the blue light from the television in Claudia's house was visible through the clear night sky. It was the only illumination in the entire house, but it cast enough light into the great room that Al could see Claudia lying on the sofa through his binoculars.

"Do you think she's dead?" Bill asked Al. "It's 9:58, and she's been like that for a couple of hours now."

"She's alive. I didn't see her take any pills or anything." Al paused before giving his next report. "She's moving. Something must have awakened her."

Startled from her sleep, Claudia abruptly sat up on the sofa and looked wildly around the room. Seeing nothing out of place, her pulse began to return to normal. She softly rubbed her swollen eyes. Her mouth felt like it was filled with cotton, so she stumbled toward the kitchen to retrieve a bottle of water from the refrigerator.

She had not been watching the television, but as she walked by, something caught her eye. It was a picture of Hudson! She frantically found the remote control and increased the volume. She sat back awkwardly on the arm of the sofa, her attention focused intently on the news broadcast.

As a female reporter from *FOX News* spoke into the camera, the phrase BREAKING NEWS flashed in red letters beneath her face. Over her left shoulder was the picture of Hudson.

"*FOX News* has learned that billionaire Milton McAdams was killed in a bizarre accident in Times Square," the reporter said. "Mr. McAdams was the principal shareholder in World Federal Bancshares . . ."

"What was that?" Bill asked.

"She screamed," Al said. He continued to watch Claudia through the binoculars, then realized, from her horrified stare, that something on television had her riveted. "Quick, turn on the television. What do you see?"

"They're talking about some guy getting killed in Times Square," Bill replied. "Hey, wait a minute. That's our guy. Milton McAdams. The reporter just said that Milton McAdams was run over by a cab in Times Square."

"We better call Sanders."

Apollyon Associates, Inc., lower Manhattan

Randolph paced around his office. He had received confirmation five minutes ago that Milton was dead. It had been a difficult decision, but in Randolph's mind it was the correct decision. He and Pierce didn't need Milton. They could exert enough control over the world through their two companies that World Federal had become unnecessary. More importantly, Milton was weak, and there was no place for weakness in the Federalists. Now that he was out of the way, the only remaining variable was Jake Reed, and he would be neutralized soon.

Randolph's pacing was not from worry. He had nothing to worry about. He could smell victory, and that caused elation to consume him. He walked back and forth in front of his desk in quick, choppy steps. In two weeks the election would be over, and everything would be in place for Randolph to be dictator of the world. He could hardly control his excitement.

The first-floor security guard's voice over the intercom interrupted his pacing, and he stopped just in front of his desk.

"Mr. Winston, there's a Mr. Pierce Montgomery here to see you."

"Send him up," Randolph ordered.

Randolph was certain that Pierce had by now heard of Milton's death. Randolph hadn't sought Pierce's approval before deciding to kill Milton, and now was not the time to discuss it. He returned to his pacing, but this time his steps were slower and more deliberate. He was thinking.

It took only a few minutes before Pierce burst into Randolph's office. "What is going on?" Pierce demanded.

His usually meticulously pressed clothing was wrinkled and untucked. His silk tie dangled from around his neck, untied. It looked like the man had been sleeping in his clothes.

"What are you talking about?" Randolph stopped pacing again.

"Don't patronize me, Randolph," Pierce warned. "You know what I'm talking about. Milton is dead."

"I know he's dead, but there's nothing we can do about that now. The plan will still succeed."

"How can you be so calm about this? Didn't you hear me? Milton is *dead*."

"Pierce, I know he's dead," Randolph replied, his emotions completely under control. "I received confirmation of it a few minutes ago."

"Confirmation? What do you mean *confirmation*? You would only need confirmation if—" Pierce halted midthought.

Randolph raised his eyebrows slightly. He saw the look on Pierce's face when the revelation struck him.

"If you had something to do with his death," Pierce concluded. His eyes narrowed. "Did you kill him?"

It was no use lying to Pierce, Randolph decided. And he didn't really care whether Pierce agreed with the decision or not. In fact, Randolph had already decided that if Pierce wasn't careful, he would be next.

"Yes, I killed him," Randolph said proudly. "He was a weak link, and we could not afford for it to break."

Pierce tugged at his tie. "How could you do this?" He exhaled loudly. "Milton was our partner, our friend. He was one of us."

"It was easy," Randolph responded with an evil grin. "Friend or no friend. Nothing is going to stand between me and world supremacy." He glared at Pierce, preparing for his partner's next verbal assault, but his glare was distracted by the ringing of his phone. It was his private line, and he assumed it was Saul Sanders.

He pushed the button to activate the speakerphone. "This is Randolph Winston."

"Randolph, this is Saul Sanders. I think we have something here that you need to know about."

"Go on," Randolph insisted. He talked to the telephone but stared at Pierce as if he thought Pierce might physically attack him.

Saul reported to Randolph everything Osborne and Moyers had seen—from the package Claudia had received to the hysterical screaming.

"Did you say something about a key?" Randolph asked.

"She received a small key. The agents on the ground said it looked like a bank lockbox key or an airport locker key, but they were looking at it through binoculars."

Milton! Randolph screamed in his mind. He was enraged. Even dead, Milton was still causing problems. He had hidden something important somewhere.

Whatever it was, Randolph had to have it.

"Saul, tell your guys to find out whatever that key leads to. Milton probably hid something that can haunt us, and I need to find it. Once they get it, bring it to me, and then eliminate her too."

"I understand," Saul replied.

"Good. This is important, Saul. Keep me posted twenty-four hours a day," he instructed, then pushed the button on the telephone to terminate the call.

Pierce was still standing in the doorway of the office. His expression was one of contempt. "What was he talking about?" demanded Pierce.

"Shut up, Pierce." Randolph returned to his pacing. "I need to think, and this does not involve you."

"Doesn't involve me! Have you completely lost your mind?" Pierce's voice was angry and nearly frantic. "I am part of the Federalists, and Sanders was talking about Milton. I demand to know what he was talking about."

"Pierce, if you don't shut up, you'll wind up like Milton!" Randolph shouted. "I told you I have to think!"

"You're crazy, Randolph," Pierce said solemnly. "We're finished. I don't want to have anything more to do with you."

Randolph watched as Pierce strode toward the door and exited.

Then Randolph returned to his pacing.

CHAPTER TWENTY-SEVEN

Foster residence, Upstate New York

It was just after midnight on Thursday. Mac and Shannon were returning to their home in upstate New York for a rare few hours of sleep in their own bed. Their neat, white two-story Victorian was not far from the banks of the Hudson River, near the state capital of Albany. As they approached, Mac spotted their house in the distance through the automobile's window. He continued staring at it as the image grew, until finally the car came to rest immediately outside the front door. Mac and Shannon waited until the Secret Service detail took their positions around the perimeter of the house. Even though he had no chance of winning the election, he was still entitled to Secret Service protection until the election was over.

Mac and Shannon exited the armor-plated black Suburban that had become their family automobile over the last several months. The autumn night sky was clear, and the brisk air hit Mac's face, momentarily chasing away his drowsiness. As he gazed at the millions of stars above him, he realized anew his own insignificance. Mac clasped his right arm around his wife's shoulders, pulling her close to him. They walked somberly up the gray wooden steps that led to their front door.

Mac was finally coming to terms with the fact that the presidency was probably out of his reach. But he still had no plans of quitting—even though the final days of the campaign would probably be meaningless.

Outwardly he remained energetic, hopeful. But in his quiet moments, he'd begun to doubt his belief that God's plan for him was to become president of the United States.

Perhaps I was wrong.

For Mac the desire to be president didn't evolve out of a need for power. In fact, he preferred to stay out of the limelight. But he had pursued the presidency because of the changes in American society he had witnessed over the past thirty years. He remembered the era when mothers and fathers reared their children with instruction and discipline, and the children obeyed and respected their parents. A time when taking the life of an unborn child was considered murder rather than a medical procedure, and *euthanasia* was a term used in conversations about animals, not people.

Once inside the house Shannon lightly kissed Mac and went upstairs to their bedroom while Mac retired to his study. His private study provided a haven for him when he was troubled. The rich pecan-wood walls and hardwood floors welcomed him like an old friend. A navy leather settee occupied one corner of the room, and a small reading light illuminated the top of Mac's antique desk. The bookcases behind the desk were filled with as many books as Mac could possibly squeeze into them. Books authored by Lewis, Eliot, Hemingway, Faulkner, and others.

There had been events in his life, both good and bad, that had caused Mac to retreat to the security of this room. The death of his father. The birth of his first child. The first time he lost an election, and the first time he won one. Each time this old friend helped him renew his inner peace. He knew he was faced with one of those events again tonight.

He sat down in the antique wooden swivel chair that matched the desk. Casters allowed the chair to roll between the desk and the credenza. The chair squeaked each time Mac changed sitting positions. On the desk in front of him was a brown leather-covered Bible that had been his father's. Mac opened it and silently read a familiar passage from the fourth chapter of the book of Philippians.

It was not the fear of losing the election that troubled Mac. It was much deeper than that. He had long since learned to be content, no matter what circumstances he faced. What troubled him tonight was the thought that four more years and a whole generation of youthful innocence would be lost. Could America survive if she lost the hearts and souls of this generation? How many more single-parent homes would be created? How many more unborn children would be lost? The answers to those questions troubled Mac deeply, even though he knew that God would ultimately be victorious.

Mac rubbed his eyes, stretched his arms out, and yawned. It was getting late. He checked his watch. *Two o'clock.* He would only get a few hours sleep before it was time to leave again, but the quiet time in his study had been just what he needed.

The door to his study opened, and Shannon tiptoed in. Mac was glad for the company—glad she was still awake.

"Why don't you come to bed?" she suggested.

"That sounds like a good idea." Mac closed his Bible and patted its front cover before standing up. He was convinced that God would remain in control, even if he lost the election, and that everything was going to be all right.

FBI *headquarters, Washington DC*

"May I come in?" Assistant Deputy Director George McCullough asked as he knocked on the metal frame to Deputy Director Armacost's office door.

It was early Thursday morning, and George knew Charlie would already be sitting at his desk.

"Sure," Charlie responded. "Have you found something?"

George entered Charlie's office, closed the door, and sat in a chair across the desk from Charlie before beginning his report. "It took me a couple of days, but I believe so. It turns out that the *Winston* Raoul referred to is William Randolph Winston IV."

It was a name George had run across when he'd investigated Apollyon Associates, Inc. weeks ago at the suggestion of Dalton Miller, but he wasn't about to tell Charlie about Dalton.

"I've heard that name before," Charlie stated.

"You should have. He's one of the richest men in the world. He's the majority stockholder in Apollyon Associates, Inc. That company holds all the rights to Internet-access user-identification numbers."

"An Internet company? Why would he hire an assassin to kill a small-town banker?"

"I asked myself the same question. So I kept digging. I found some very interesting information about Mr. Winston and Vice President Burke."

"Like what?"

"Vice President Burke assisted Mr. Winston by railroading through the Justice Department a questionable merger. Winston now has his software in 80 percent of the world's computers."

Charlie bristled. "Those railroad jobs happen all the time. I hope you've got more than that."

"I do. It seems that Vice President Burke has also shown some interest in two other companies: World Federal Bancshares and TransWorld Communications, Inc. TransWorld is controlled by Pierce Anthony Montgomery, and World Federal Bancshares is controlled by Milton Hawthorne McAdams."

"McAdams?" Charlie frowned. "Did I see something about him on the news?"

"I'd say so. He was killed in a freak accident in Times Square last night. Only I'm not so sure it was an accident. The only person who was watching McAdams when he allegedly stumbled out into oncoming traffic was his limousine driver. He told NYPD that it looked to him like McAdams was pushed. NYPD has cameras all over Times Square, and they're reviewing the tapes as we speak."

"OK," Charlie began thoughtfully, leaning back in his chair.

George had seen that pose from Charlie before and knew it meant that the gears in Charlie's mind were turning.

"Burke helps Winston, Montgomery, and McAdams," Charlie theorized. "Burke's friend in Tennessee is killed by Winston. Then McAdams is killed in an accident that may not be an accident."

"That's not all. Winston, Montgomery, and McAdams were all fraternity brothers at Harvard. They've known each other for years."

George watched as Charlie continued leaning back in his chair, chewing on the end of his ballpoint pen. "What are they up to?" Charlie wondered out loud.

"The only name Raoul told Juan was Winston," Charlie began. "I bet he's calling the shots. The election is week after next, and Burke is comfortably ahead. For some reason Winston needs Burke in the White House, but why?"

"That's what I was hoping you could figure out," George responded.

"Let's put some tails on Montgomery and Winston but keep your cards close to your vest. I don't need Sanders finding out. There's still something there with him that I can't quite put my finger on, but I'll figure that out too."

"I'm on it," George announced as he left Charlie's office to carry out his boss's instructions.

Marcia Naylor, Charlie's secretary, couldn't hear what had been discussed in Armacost's office, but the two men had been scurrying around like a couple of chipmunks the last few days. "Anything exciting happening?" she asked George as he exited Charlie's office.

"Nothing really," he threw back as he headed down the hall. "It just involves the vice president."

Marcia didn't know whether George was telling the truth or being patronizing. But the comment caught her attention nonetheless.

Hilton Head Island, South Carolina

Claudia awoke to an overcast, rainy morning. Without looking at her bedside clock, she'd never have known it was already nine o'clock. It was barely light outside. The low line of gray clouds that blanketed Hilton Head Island prevented the sun from announcing the arrival of the morning.

Even though it was later than she usually awoke, Claudia had little desire to get out of bed. Death does that to those who are left behind, and Claudia was no different. But even worse for Claudia, she was suffering in isolation. There was no one to console her. She had nothing to hold on to. Nothing in which she could find comfort. When she had finally gone to bed after the late news, she had tossed and turned until well past three before she finally fell asleep. And the sleep that came was restless.

This morning, after several minutes of lying awake in her bed, staring through the bedroom window at the depressing sky, she realized her sleep was gone. She decided to get up, not knowing exactly what she would do once she dressed. Her reason for living was gone. There had been other times in her life when she had fallen into a mire of self-pity, but none of them had been as deep as this one. She wondered if she could ever recover.

Claudia peered through the great-room window at the steady rain that pecked at the surface of the ocean. She noticed the beach was empty. No joggers. No fishermen. No signs of life. The emptiness added to her loneliness and depression.

Eden—her Eden—was no longer paradise. She turned from the window and slowly retreated to the kitchen, not knowing where to go next, what to do with her life.

"She's awake," Moyers announced as Osborne entered the upstairs room that had become their center of operations. The two agents alternated shifts through the night to make sure one of them was awake every minute. Saul Sanders had phoned at midnight with new instructions, and their surveillance of Claudia Duval had intensified.

"I don't understand why we can't simply break in, take the key, and finish her." Bill yawned and stretched his arms over his head. His shift had ended at 5:00 a.m., and the four hours of sleep had not been enough to completely chase away his fatigue.

"Because that's not what Sanders told us to do. Besides, we've got to find out what the key opens, and only she can lead us to it."

"What is she doing?" Bill asked.

"Not much. Sitting at the kitchen table, slowly stirring a cup of coffee. It doesn't appear she's going anywhere anytime soon."

Jackson-Madison County General Hospital, Jackson, Tennessee

Naomi McClellan was told by the hospital staff that a living will would have solved the problem. If Jed would have signed that kind of legal document when he was conscious and sane, then he could have decided himself whether he wanted life-sustaining measures to remain in place if he were ever in a coma. If Jed's doctor made the determination that Jed was only being kept alive by artificial means, and Jed had previously executed a living will saying he wanted no life-sustaining measures, then the artificial life-sustaining measures could be discontinued. In more crass terms, the process was referred to as "pulling the plug."

But Jed didn't have a living will. And Naomi didn't like the thought of one anyway. It was like taking matters out of God's hands. Jed's doctor had just told Ruth and Naomi that he hadn't been able to detect any brain activity since Jed was admitted to the hospital two days ago. The doctor couldn't be sure, though, until he tested Jed by disconnecting the respiratory equipment to see if Jed could breathe on his own. And that could not be done without a living will.

So the hospital personnel had stabilized Jed to where he could be moved to a private room on the seventh floor. Naomi now stood with Ruth at the foot of Jed's bed. Reverend Douglass had been there a few minutes earlier and offered a prayer, seeking a miracle from God. Naomi was convinced that only a miracle would save Jed now. She knew that each day he went without awakening, the slimmer his chances became to awake at all, and particularly to awake without substantial damage to his brain.

FBI headquarters, Washington DC

As he often did, Charlie Armacost ate lunch in the cafeteria located in the basement of the J. Edgar Hoover Building. The food was terrible, but the location was convenient. He refused to be away from his office for any sustained period of time. Particularly today. Anything could happen, and he had to be ready. He even cut his lunch break fifteen minutes short.

Charlie rode the elevator from the basement to the fifth floor and made his way through the meandering hallway of white walls and gray industrial carpet to his office suite. He constantly ran the information from the investigation through the computer in his head, trying to make all the pieces fit, but something was still missing.

What is it?

He passed his secretary's work station and empty chair and opened the door to his office.

A startled shriek rose from behind his desk. His secretary, Marcia Naylor, was holding a set of documents and photographs.

"What are you doing?" Charlie demanded.

"I-I'm l-looking for those documents you wanted me to send to LA," she replied.

But it was obvious to Charlie from her demeanor that she was lying.

"Give me those." Charlie pointed at the items in Marcia's hands.

She hesitated, and then reluctantly surrendered her possessions.

Charlie quickly realized what they were: copies of the F-PAC documents and photographs of Raoul at the Thompson murder scene. He shuffled through the items to make sure nothing was missing, and then looked up at her again. "What were you doing with these?"

"She was getting them for me," a voice responded from behind Charlie.

Charlie pivoted and saw Saul Sanders standing in the doorway.

"For you?" Charlie growled. He was dumbfounded. Sanders's mole had been right under his nose the whole time. "Both of you get out of my office," he demanded.

Sanders smirked. "You're over your head, Armacost. You can't stop what's happening. This thing is bigger than you. It's bigger than the FBI. And, as soon as it is over, you're finished. Come on, Marcia."

Marcia hurried past Charlie and through the door to the safety beyond Sanders.

Charlie's anger burned hotter as he watched the two walk toward Sanders's office. As soon as he could no longer see them, he called for George McCullough.

George responded immediately. He was always at Charlie's beck and call. "What is it, Charlie?" George inquired as he dashed into Charlie's office.

"Sanders. I now know that he's into this up to his neck with Winston. And I want to take him down. Whatever it takes, I want Sanders to go down with this. Pull out all the stops. Ed Burke can't win this election. If he does, the world as we know it will no longer exist."

"It's that bad?" George asked.

"It's that bad."

CHAPTER TWENTY-EIGHT

Jackson-Madison County General Hospital, Jackson, Tennessee

Jake's weekly Thursday morning appearance in bankruptcy court ended at eleven forty-five, and that allowed him to keep his commitment to visit Jed in the hospital every day during lunch. The daily visits didn't completely eliminate his feelings of guilt, but they helped—at least for one brief hour in the middle of the day.

Jake pulled into the west parking lot and began circling through, looking for an empty space. It took five minutes to find one, and then Jake entered the hospital through the automatic sliding doors.

The deputy-sheriff sentinel no longer stood at attention outside Jed's room since it had become apparent to all concerned that Jed couldn't escape. Jake could hear Naomi's and Ruth's voices as he neared room 741.

"Jed," he heard Naomi say through the crack in the door, "this is your momma. Can you hear me? Squeeze my hand if you can hear me."

"This is Ruth, Jed. Open your eyes for me. Let me see your eyes."

Jake knocked lightly on the door, and the pleading stopped.

"Come in," Ruth called.

Jake pushed the door open, wide enough to walk in, then closed it behind him. Naomi was standing on the right side of Jed's bed and Ruth on the left.

"Jake," Naomi said, "it's so good to see you."

"Hello, Ms. McClellan. Ruth." Jake nodded in the direction of each woman. "How is he doing today?"

"Not good." Ruth seemed despondent. "The doctor said they ain't seen no brain activity since they brought Jed in." She was talking to Jake but looking at Jed. She gently ran her hand up and down Jed's arm.

"The doctor told us to talk to him as much as we could to see if we could get some kinda response," Naomi explained. "But so far we ain't seen nothin'."

Although Jake knew the report was realistic, it wasn't what he wanted to hear. Somehow he'd hoped for the impossible . . . pleaded with the heavens for the impossible . . . that Jed would be awake when he arrived, and everything would be OK.

"Did the doctor say how much longer before Jed will wake up?" Jake asked.

"He's not sure he ever will," Naomi replied. "He may be like this the rest of his life, but we ain't givin' up on him."

Jake saw the resilience in both women's faces. Their determination. Their courage. He believed them when they said they weren't going to give up.

"The two of you are a lot stronger than I am," Jake commented. "I don't know what I would do if something happened to my wife or one of my kids. I don't think I could handle it as well as the two of you have handled this."

"You have to remember that God is in control, and that everything happens for a purpose," Naomi responded without hesitation.

Jake heard what Naomi said, but he didn't understand it. He refused to believe that anything good could come from Jed's attempted suicide. How could it? Jed was near death. Medically he might even be considered dead. And that meant his young children were without a father, Ruth was without a husband, and Naomi was without her only child.

Jake couldn't see anything good about it. "Ms. McClellan, are you saying you think God caused Jed to attempt suicide?"

"God didn't cause it," she said swiftly. "But there's some purpose for it. We may never know what it is, but God will use this for the good of his kingdom."

Jake still couldn't understand what Naomi was telling him. God didn't cause Jed to attempt suicide, but he would use it for some common good? That didn't even make sense. Couldn't God see the pain that Jed's family had endured? If he truly was a merciful God, then he would wake Jed up right now and answer the prayers of these two women.

Jake wanted to shake his head in disbelief and raise his fist to the heavens in frustration—that God could just sit by and let all this happen.

Instead he eyed Naomi. It was clear in her expression that she believed every word she'd said. There was no need to prod her any further.

"I've got to get back to the office," Jake finally said, breaking the silence. "I have some phone calls to return."

"Thanks for comin' by," Ruth said. "I'll tell Jed you were here."

After Jake left the room, he hesitated outside the door before walking to the elevator. He heard Ruth and Naomi resume their pleas for Jed to awake.

Hilton Head Island, South Carolina

By midafternoon Thursday the cold drizzle and gray clouds moved offshore, and rays of sunshine began to brighten the dismal weather conditions on the island. The sunshine was also an antidote to what ailed Claudia, starting the slow healing process within her. Just as life returned to the beach behind Eden, it also began to return to Claudia. The self-imposed feeling of loneliness, although not gone completely, began to disappear. She could see a way out of this valley of despair.

She walked onto the veranda and was invigorated by the cool breeze that had moved in after the rain. She inhaled the fresh sea air, and her mind began to clear. The depressive thoughts that had haunted her since last night were replaced with thoughts of survival. She wasn't going to be beaten again.

Each time she had faced a difficult situation in the past—her failed marriage to Jimmy, her relationship with her mother—her only defense had been to run. Even when Uncle Samuel called about her mother's cancer, Claudia refused to even consider going to see her.

Somehow she thought that if she hid, her problems would go away. She was beginning to realize that problems never go away. They would affect every minute of her life. Every decision she'd made in the last twenty years had been made because she was running from one problem or the other. But not this time. She wasn't going to run this time. Even if she was scared.

Claudia went back inside and picked up the letter that Milton had sent with the key. She read it again. If she truly was going to win this time, she knew there was only one thing to do.

Reed residence, Jackson, Tennessee

In the early hours on Friday morning, Nick Herod sat in his car two blocks from Jake Reed's house on Magnolia Lane. He looked around for any signs of life. He was a hired thug, a mercenary, and had no convictions about any assignment he received. He'd spent two years on Rikers Island in the late 1980s for some petty larceny crimes. The prosecutor, Saul Sanders, had offered a light sentence in exchange for Nick's handling of some "delicate matters." Nick had agreed. During the last fifteen years he had completed several "assignments" for Sanders. The pay was always good, and Nick enjoyed the work. So he was eager when Sanders called with the latest assignment.

All the lights in the Reed house had been out for over an hour, so Nick was certain everyone was asleep. He closely watched all the neighbors' houses, to make sure they could not see him either. He unscrewed the bulb in the dome light before he opened the door. After easing the door shut, he disappeared into a grove of trees in front of a house two doors up from the Reed house. He was clothed from head to toe in black, so it was virtually impossible for anyone to see him.

Stealthily he made his way from tree to tree through the adjoining yards until he reached the southeast corner of the Reed house. Staying in the shadows, he slid along the brick exterior to the back of the house until he reached the control box that operated the alarm system.

Slowly he opened the door to the box, exposing several wires of different colors. He smiled to himself when he recognized the wiring configuration from one of the many he had studied. He ran the small wires through his fingers until he found the yellow one. One swift snip with a pair of pliers, and the alarm system was disabled. There would be no call to the police to report his intrusion.

Nick then moved to the double French doors that led to a back patio and retrieved a pack of locksmith tools from his pocket. He removed a slender, flat blade from the pack and, just as quickly as he'd disarmed the alarm system, he unlocked the French doors. Stepping inside, he quietly closed the doors behind him.

Nick found himself standing in a small study on the main floor. He knew the interior of the house from a set of blueprints he'd obtained from the local building department the previous day. It was a good thing. The books and pictures in the room were barely discernible in the faint moonlight that shone through the window panes of the French doors.

Nick moved swiftly to the door leading to the rest of the house. He knew the master bedroom was on the main level, and that the children's bedrooms were upstairs.

The stairs to the second level were just outside the study door. Nick began to ascend the steep staircase slowly and methodically. One step at a time. His right foot followed by his left. The interior of the house was almost completely dark. He had memorized the number of steps—eighteen in all—from the blueprints and now counted them in his head as his right foot landed on the next step.

Thirteen.

Fourteen.

Fifteen. As he put his full weight on the step, a loud *creak-k-k* vibrated from under his foot.

Rachel elbowed Jake in the middle of the night. "Did you hear that?"

"Hear what?" he mumbled, mostly asleep.

"That noise."

"What noise?"

"That creaking sound on the stairs," Rachel said, now shaking Jake violently. "I think someone is in the house."

He woke slowly. "There's no one in the house. This is exactly why I had that expensive alarm system installed. So you wouldn't think someone was in the house."

"Just go look this one time," Rachel begged. "Please."

"If there was someone in the house, the dog would be barking," Jake said, thinking he had found a way to satisfy Rachel that would keep him warm and cozy in their bed.

"I didn't bring the dog in before we came to bed," Rachel reminded him. "Please, Jake," she pleaded. "Go and look."

Jake lay there with his eyes closed, hoping she would either give up, or go look herself. He knew there was no one in the house, and he did not want to get up.

She nudged him again.

"Oh, all right," he said in a resigned tone.

Jake slung the bed covers back, got out of his warm bed, and put on his bathrobe. He barely opened his eyes as he began walking down the hall to the family room. He checked every room on the lower level of the house. Nothing. He was convinced that Rachel was crazy and that he would never get back to sleep. He thought about not going upstairs, but he knew Rachel would ask if he'd checked the children's rooms when he returned to bed. Then he would have to get up again. He might as well save himself the trouble. The kids probably needed the covers pulled up again anyway.

Nick heard steps and hid in the linen closet at the end of the upstairs hallway. He pulled the door closed but left a crack between the door and the doorjamb so he could peek out. Nick saw a man in a bathrobe as he reached the top of the stairs.

He's walking this way, Nick thought. *If he opens this door, I'm going to have to kill him to get out of here.*

Jake looked in every room, and all the kids were sound asleep.

I knew there was nobody in the house. One of these days Rachel is going to start listening to me.

He had checked on Courtney last. Her room was the last one on the right at the end of the hall. He closed the door to her room and turned back toward the hallway. As he did, he noticed that the linen closet door was slightly ajar. He pushed it from the outside until he heard the click of the pin sliding into the metal plate in the door-frame casing.

Rachel was sitting up in the bed when he returned to the bedroom.

"Everybody is fine," Jake reported as he removed his robe.

"Did you check everywhere?"

"Everywhere," he confirmed.

"Did you go upstairs?"

"Of course I went upstairs."

"I swear I heard something," Rachel said.

"One of these days . . . ," Jake muttered and climbed back into bed.

Her tone was icy. "Oh, shut up."

Nick was sweating profusely in the cramped linen closet but resolved to stay for fifteen minutes after Jake left before he opened the door. He pressed a button on the side of his watch that caused the backlight to illuminate. *3:30*.

When the self-imposed fifteen minutes of confinement had elapsed, Nick edged the door open and peered down the hall. He could see no one. He walked carefully to the balcony that overlooked the family room. He listened for any sounds that might indicate someone was awake downstairs. Nothing.

Turning back toward the bedrooms that lined the opposite side of the hall, he opened the last door on the right. His instructions were specific.

CHAPTER TWENTY-NINE

Hilton Head Island, South Carolina

Claudia had slept better Thursday night than the night before, but still her sleep was not completely restful. She couldn't rid herself of the horrible image she'd seen on the news of Milton's body lying on Broadway in Manhattan with a white cloth covering it. Each time she closed her eyes, she saw it. She tried to replace it with an image of Hudson's charming face, but it was impossible. And so was any more sleep.

She resolved to comply with Hudson's last request, but it all seemed like a jigsaw puzzle. A thousand-piece jigsaw puzzle at that, and she was missing five hundred of the pieces. She decided that the contents of the locker at Hartsfield and Jake Reed, whoever he was, held most, if not all, of the remaining pieces to the puzzle. To restore her own sanity, she had no choice but to go.

By seven o'clock she had showered, dressed, and packed a bag. She tucked the key to locker T-25 safely in the front-right pocket of her blue jeans, and the letter from Hudson in her duffel bag. The drive to Hartsfield-Jackson International Airport in Atlanta would take about four hours, she figured. She purchased an e-ticket online and printed out her boarding pass for the 12:50 p.m. Northwest flight bound for Memphis. From there she would take a rental car to Jackson and look for Jake Reed.

Claudia exited from the house into the garage. She pressed a button mounted on the wall beside the door, and the garage door began to retract, opening to a beautiful, sun-drenched morning. She threw her burgundy duffel bag into the backseat of the Jaguar and got in behind the wheel. She hated to leave but convinced herself that she had to honor Hudson's last request. She backed out of the garage, hesitated before backing into the street, and looked at the place that had been her personal Eden.

Who owned it now that Hudson was dead?

Would she ever be able to return?

It doesn't matter, she told herself. *Everything about this place has been a lie.*

She eased out of the driveway, drove past the security gate that limited access to the Palmetto Dunes Plantation, and merged onto Queens Folly, which led out of the plantation. The Spanish moss dripping from the branches of the tall trees that stretched across the narrow two-lane road gave the appearance that Claudia was driving through a dimly lit tunnel. In a few minutes she reached William Hilton Parkway and turned north toward the bridge that crossed the Intracoastal Waterway and provided access to the mainland.

When Claudia reached the outskirts of Savannah, she exited I-95 onto I-16 north toward Macon. The area of Georgia between Savannah and Macon was less populated than the northern part of the state. Only a few small towns dotted the landscape near the interstate. The sparse scenery made an already long and mundane drive even longer. But Claudia didn't mind.

Then, about sixty miles south of Macon, she had a strange feeling. She couldn't explain it, but it was similar to what she'd experienced while shopping in Savannah. It was the feeling that someone was following her. She took inventory of the vehicles around her. There were only four. A gray Mercury Sable in front. Red minivan with Ohio license plate in the lane beside her, and slightly ahead. In the same lane, and behind her, was an eighteen-wheel tractor-trailer. In her driver's-side mirror she caught a glimpse of a gray Chevy Tahoe behind the semitractor.

Nothing seemed suspicious. Perhaps she was being overly cautious because of what had happened to Hudson. But that was understandable. If her suspicions about Hudson's death were correct, it was possible that whoever killed Hudson may also be planning to kill her. She convinced herself that she needed to be careful.

En route to Macon, Georgia

"Don't get too close," Osborne instructed. Moyers was driving the gray Chevy Tahoe, two vehicles behind Claudia's Jaguar. "We don't want her to get suspicious."

Al rolled his eyes. "I know. I know."

"Why don't you pass her?" Bill suggested. "That way she won't think we're following her, and we can still track her with the GPS."

Al accelerated the Tahoe an additional five miles per hour and moved into the inside lane of I-16. It took only a few seconds before the Tahoe overtook the semi-tractor and pulled parallel with Claudia's Jaguar. Claudia's natural reaction caused her to look into the window of the passing vehicle.

"That man looks familiar," Claudia mumbled to herself. "I wonder where I've seen him before."

When the vehicle passed her, Claudia noticed the South Carolina license plate.

Probably saw him on the island.

Reed residence, Jackson, Tennessee

While Jake showered Friday morning, Rachel was in the kitchen preparing breakfast for the two boys. It was already seven o'clock, and school started in an hour.

"Have either of you seen Courtney?" Rachel asked as she poured two glasses of milk.

"No, Mom," replied Brett. "Her door was closed when I came down."

"Me neither," Jeremy said as he continued to watch the television on the kitchen countertop.

"She needs to hurry, or all of you will be late for school."

Rachel walked out of the kitchen into the family room and then to the base of the staircase leading to the second level of the house. "Courtney," she called out.

No response.

"Courtney, answer me," she said, a little agitated.

No response.

"Courtney, don't make me come up there. We're in a hurry."

No response.

Rachel growled under her breath and began stomping up the stairs. As she continued stomping down the hallway to Courtney's bedroom, she could hear the boys in the kitchen giggling at the thought of Courtney getting in trouble. When she reached Courtney's bedroom, she grabbed the doorknob and flung open the door, ready to give Courtney a piece of her mind.

Jake was half-dressed, shaving in front of the bathroom mirror, when Rachel screamed. He had heard her scream before when one of the boys, usually Brett, came home with a frog and startled her.

But this scream was different. It wasn't a startled scream. It was terror-stricken.

Jake dropped the razor beside the sink, wiped the remainder of the shaving cream from his face, and began running toward the sound. He ran through the den and up the stairs to Courtney's bedroom, where his wife was still screaming hysterically and pointing at Courtney's bed.

Jake looked in the room and saw Courtney lying bound and gagged on the bed. Her fragile arms and legs were each tied to one of the corner posts. Her eyes were pleading for help. Jake raced to her bedside and frantically began to free her from her bonds. He removed the gag in her mouth first.

"Mommy!" Courtney wailed. "I want my mommy!"

Rachel collected herself and ran to Courtney as Jake moved next to untie the ropes from her feet and hands.

"There was a man, Mommy," Courtney described through her tears.

"What, honey?" Rachel prodded.

Finally all the ropes were untied.

Rachel scooped Courtney up in her arms and sat on the bed, rocking Courtney back and forth in her lap.

"There was a man in my room last night, and he tied me up." Courtney buried her face in Rachel's chest as Rachel stroked her auburn hair.

"Did he hurt you?" Jake asked, his mind leaping to the worst possible scenario.

"No, Daddy," she said from the security of her mother's arms. "He didn't hurt me, but I was real scared."

Courtney's whole body was shaking in trauma. Her face had lost all color. Jake examined her wrists and ankles and saw that they were raw from the ropes rubbing against them as she struggled for freedom.

Jake joined Rachel and Courtney on the bed. Jake's mind raced as he held them both. Someone had violated the sanctity of his home, and that angered and scared him.

"Who could have done this?" Rachel asked in Jake's direction.

Jake shook his head. "I don't know."

And then it hit him—the suspicions as to why it had happened.

As Jake continued to hold the two most important women in his life, he noticed a single sheet of paper on the nightstand by Courtney's bed. Jake grabbed the piece of paper and frantically read the words.

See how easy it was to get into your house? Are you scared? If you tell anybody what you know about the Thompson murder, we'll do more than scare you next time. Do you care about your pretty little girl? What about your sons, or your wife? If you do, then do what we say, and nobody else gets hurt.

He handed the note to Rachel and slid Courtney from Rachel's lap to his. Jake watched Rachel's face as she scanned the words.

"What does this mean?" she inquired.

"I don't know. But I'm going to find out." Jake pressed Courtney's head firmly against his chest and wrapped his arms around her. "It's OK, honey. Daddy's going to take care of you."

Those words were some he wished he could have heard his own father say. So many times, as a young boy, Jake had longed to climb into his own father's lap and feel the protection and security from that haven. But Jake's father and mother had died before he'd had much of a chance to get to know them. Only a few memories of them still lingered.

When Courtney was born, he had sworn to himself that he'd sacrifice everything to take care of her. It was the same promise he'd made when Brett and Jeremy were born. Now, as he sat on the edge of Courtney's bed, holding her, he realized he'd failed miserably.

Gingerly he inspected the bruises and abrasions around her wrists and ankles again. *Who could have done this to my innocent, delicate daughter?*

A large tear from each eye ran over his chin and fell onto Courtney's soft hair.

"I was so scared, Daddy," Courtney mumbled again. "I thought he was going to kill me, and I couldn't scream because he had my mouth covered."

Jake squeezed Courtney again. "It's OK now, baby. Mommy and Daddy are here, and we're not going to let anything happen to you ever again."

Rachel stroked Courtney's hair and said softly to Jake, "We need to call the sheriff's department and get Courtney to the hospital."

Just then Brett and Jeremy ran into the room. "What's all the screaming about?" Brett asked excitedly.

"Nothing to worry about," Jake assured them. "Everything is OK now. Both of you come over here and give your sister a hug."

"Why?"

"Just because, Brett. Courtney needs it."

Brett and Jeremy complied, and Jake and Rachel continued to sit on the bed with Courtney on Jake's lap. Jake reached his left arm around the backs of the two boys and pulled them closer. Rachel's right arm curled around their backs as well. Together the members of the Reed family formed a small circle, with Courtney in the middle.

Perhaps for the first time Jake understood why the family hug was so important. He sat motionless, for what seemed like hours.

Holding those precious lives in his arms.

Feeling the awe and the responsibility.

Battling the mix of dread and gratefulness that Courtney was not hurt worse . . .

And then it was over. It had lasted only a few seconds, but they had been frozen in time.

Jake knew that Jeremy had lasted as long as he could before he began squirming for freedom.

"Let me go," Jeremy finally demanded.

"OK," Jake said and kissed each of the children on top of the head. "Everything's going to be fine," he told Rachel. "I'll take the boys back downstairs and call the sheriff's department. You stay here with Courtney."

Jake escorted the boys down the stairs and ushered them into the kitchen with instructions to finish their breakfast. When they were settled, he retreated to his study and closed the door. He settled into the chair behind the antique desk and stared at the picture of his family that had been taken last summer at the beach in Destin, Florida. A precious blue-eyed daughter smiled back impishly.

He groaned. The thought of something happening to Courtney was unbearable. He rubbed his face with both hands to collect his thoughts and took a deep breath. It was time to call Sheriff West.

The phone only rang once before the dispatcher at the sheriff's department answered.

"This is Jake Reed. I need to speak to Sheriff West."

The next voice on the phone was Sheriff Craig West, Jake's arch enemy.

"Sheriff, this is Jake Reed."

"What can I do for you?" responded Sheriff West sharply.

Jake told Sheriff West as many of the details as he could remember. By the time he finished, Jake could sense that Sheriff West's attitude had changed, and he was listening intently. Jake knew that he and Sheriff West had many professional differences, but this was different.

"I'll be right over," Sheriff West responded without hesitation.

Ten minutes after his phone conversation with Jake, Sheriff West arrived at the Reed house with two other patrol cars close behind. All three cars pulled into the driveway of the blue two-story colonial without any sirens or flashing lights. He knew the neighbors would find out soon enough that a crime had been committed, but there was no need to alarm them this early in the morning. An ambulance arrived a couple of minutes later.

Jake greeted the sheriff as he approached the front door. Sheriff West really hadn't cared very much for Jake Reed over the years. They'd clashed often in professional circles.

But today there was something different about the man. He was visibly shaken. His home had been violated. Sheriff West knew that the emotional turmoil of such an incident was incomprehensible to most people—until it happened to them—but he understood it. He had seen it plenty of times before. Today he saw it in Jake. Today he would try to help Jake understand what had happened. Today Jake and the sheriff were on the same side . . . for the first time.

Sheriff West stood beside Jake and watched as the emergency medical technicians assisted Courtney onto the gurney and loaded her into the rear of the ambulance. Rachel climbed in with her, and Jake gave Courtney a kiss before the EMT closed the door. He had to stay with the boys until Rachel's parents arrived, he said.

The two men returned to the house, and Sheriff West listened as Jake repeated the details of the break-in to him and the other investigating officers. The sheriff went upstairs so Jake could show him where the intruder had left the note.

For the next two hours the deputies dusted for fingerprints, took photographs, and looked for evidence. Sheriff West suspected they would find nothing incriminating.

Macon, Georgia

Claudia reached Macon, Georgia, at 10:30. She needed to fill both the tank in her car and the tank in her stomach. The three-hour drive from Savannah, and the rhythmic sound of the road, had allowed her to momentarily forget about Hudson. Now her appetite had returned, and it wasn't long before the hunger pangs were more than she could tolerate. She merged from I-16 onto I-75 north and took the Riverside Drive exit in Macon. She found an Amoco gas station and a Wendy's side by side.

She entered the Wendy's. In line in front of her was a young couple with a little blond girl who couldn't have been more than four or five years old. She hung onto the rail that directed the customers toward the cashier, lifted her feet off the floor, and gently swung back and forth underneath the rail.

"How many more hours before we're home?" the little girl asked her mother.

"About four more hours, sweetheart. Now please quit swinging. You're going to fall and hurt yourself."

They must be on a family trip of some kind, Claudia thought to herself.

The scene caused Claudia to recall the one fond memory of her childhood . . .

It was in the summer of 1970, before her father died . . .

Claudia was nine when the three of them took a family vacation in Eureka Springs, a town in northern Arkansas, in the Ozark Mountains.

When they arrived at the small motel outside of town, Claudia noticed that the swimming pool had a waterslide attached to it. At first her father refused to get in the pool. *"We have other things to do,"* he had said. But she persisted and her father finally relented and agreed to swim with her. She must have slid down one hundred times into her father's waiting arms. Meanwhile, her mother relaxed in a lounge chair at the side of the pool and laughed and cheered with each splash . . .

That was the last time Claudia recalled her mother laughing. Her father died the next winter, and then things began to deteriorate between her and her mother. Claudia had never really thought about it until now, but it must have been extremely difficult for her mother following her father's death.

"Ma'am, may I help you?" the cashier asked. "Ma'am?"

The cashier's voice awakened Claudia from her daydreaming, and the images of the family vacation from long ago vanished. She placed her order, to go, and in five minutes was back in her car. She drove around the back of the restaurant to exit the parking lot, and something caught her attention. It was the gray Tahoe with South Carolina plates that had passed her outside Savannah.

It's just a coincidence, she convinced herself.

She glanced at the truck again and, for a split second, it seemed that the man in the passenger seat was studying her.

"I know him from somewhere," she mumbled again. "But where?"

"Let's sit here in the parking lot another minute or two," Moyers told Osborne. "We know she's going to Atlanta. The GPS will keep up with her."

The two agents watched the blip on the screen of the GPS monitor as Claudia's Jaguar crossed over I-75 to the northbound access ramp, then proceeded north on I-75 toward Atlanta. They waited another minute before leaving the parking lot. They needed to stay close enough to react when she led them to whatever it was that Milton McAdams had left behind.

Jackson-Madison County General Hospital, Jackson, Tennessee

Sheriff West found Jake and Rachel in examination room 5 in the ER. Courtney, who was in bed in the room, was still crying. He motioned for Jake to step into the hall.

"How's she doing?" Sheriff West asked and nodded at the examination room.

"She's going to be OK," Jake responded. "Some bruising and the rope burns to her wrists and ankles are the only physical injuries. She should be healed in a few days. The emotional scars will take longer."

"I hope she gets better real soon."

"Thanks, Sheriff. I appreciate it. What did you find at our house?"

"It looks like a real pro, Jake," Sheriff West began. "The alarm system was bypassed. The monitoring company thought it was still working, but it was disarmed. Our guess is that he picked the lock on the French doors in the study and made his way upstairs. He left no fingerprints. The place is clean."

Sheriff West hesitated, wondering whether he would get a straight answer to his next question, but he asked it anyway. "Do you have any idea who would have done this?"

Jake's face was tense. "No, Sheriff, I have no idea. I showed you that note, but I don't know who would threaten me about the Thompson murder. Jed is still here in the hospital, and the case has slowed down."

Sheriff West had a feeling Jake wasn't being entirely truthful, but he didn't press any further. After all, how would he feel if some thug had done this to *his* daughter?

"We're going to clean up. We should be out of the house within the hour," the sheriff stated. "I think it would be a good idea for me to assign a few deputies to watch you and your family for a few days."

"I'd appreciate that, Sheriff. I know it would make Rachel feel better."

"I'll station one deputy outside your daughter's room to monitor visitors who may come in, and a patrol car will be in the parking lot. Another patrol car will be posted outside of your house twenty-four hours a day. Also, we bagged the note and checked it into the evidence room. Let me know if you get any other threatening letters or phone calls."

"I will, Sheriff. Thanks for everything." Jake extended his hand.

The animosity Sheriff West had for Jake had eroded away. He no longer viewed Jake as a high-priced villain. Rather, he saw Jake as a father and a husband, and as someone who cared deeply for his wife and children. Today they were not adversaries, but allies. They desired the same thing—to capture the person who had violated the Reed home.

Jake and Sheriff West shared a warm handshake.

As Sheriff West turned to leave, he paused. "And Jake."

"Yes, Sheriff."

"Take care of that little girl."

Jake smiled. "I will. You can count on it."

CHAPTER THIRTY

Hartsfield-Jackson International Airport, Atlanta

Claudia arrived at the airport in Atlanta at 11:30 and parked in the nearest lot to the main entrance. Removing the burgundy duffel bag from the backseat, she locked the Jaguar and followed the crosswalk into the main entrance of the airport.

Then she began looking for the locker storage area.

"OK, she's in," Agent Osborne told Agent Moyers. "Let's go."

The two FBI agents quickly exited their Tahoe and followed Claudia's path into the airport. There was no transmitter on Claudia's person, so they had to maintain visual contact of her. They spotted her as she stepped onto the down escalator that led to the underground tram. From there she could go to the other concourses. They had to reach her before she got on the tram, or they might lose her.

When Bill and Al reached the bottom of the escalator, they saw Claudia standing on the platform, waiting for the tram. Bill was certain she had not spotted them. He walked past Claudia and stood with the other passengers waiting to board one car in front of Claudia's. He motioned for Al to take a position at the waiting area one car behind Claudia's.

Claudia removed the key from her front pocket and looked at it again. *T-25*. As she clutched the key tightly, her heart began to beat more rapidly with the anticipation that the contents of the locker would answer her numerous questions.

Just then the computer-generated voice gave its warning that the tram was arriving. "Stand back. The doors are opening."

Claudia put the key back into her right-front pocket and waited for the doors to open. Practically all the passengers exited the car and streamed en masse toward the escalators that led up to the main terminal. Claudia waited for all the passengers to exit and the ones in front of her to board before she stepped into the middle car of the tram, a split second before the doors closed.

The computer voice repeated its admonishment, but this time with a slight variation. "Stand back. The doors are closing."

Claudia rode the tram until it reached the atrium area of the airport and exited at that stop. The lockers were between the two sets of escalators that provided access to the boarding areas above. Claudia quickly located the row labeled *T* and began counting the lockers until she reached 25. Taking the key from her pocket, she slid it into the keyhole in locker T-25 and turned the key clockwise until she heard a click. By this time her palms were clammy. She glanced in all directions to see if anyone was watching her.

Satisfied no one was watching, she slowly opened the small door and removed the contents: two medium-size manila envelopes. The first envelope, labeled in Hudson's scrawl with the name *T. Jacob Reed*, felt as if it contained a videotape. The second envelope was addressed to her. It was thick and felt as though it was stuffed with documents. She wanted to rip open the envelope addressed to her, to see if she could find the answers to her many questions. But she resisted the temptation, deciding that discretion required her to wait until she was in a more secluded location.

Claudia stuffed both envelopes into her duffel bag and turned to wait for the returning tram. She had her head down, still trying to arrange the envelopes in her bag, when she bumped into someone. "Excuse me," she said, glancing up at her victim.

"That's quite all right . . . Ms. *Duval*," the man replied.

Claudia was startled. How could this brown-haired stranger know her name? She looked more closely at his face. And why was he smirking?

She moved backward two steps and studied the man again. Then she noticed there was a second man with him.

"I know you," she said, placing her hand over her mouth. "You're the man from next door."

"That's right, Ms. Duval," the first man said. "We've been watching you for weeks, and now you're coming with us."

"I'll take that," his black-haired partner said as he took Claudia's bag from her.

The two men each gripped one of Claudia's biceps. She tried to liberate herself, but it was of no use. Their hold was too tight.

"Let me go," she growled at her stalkers as they practically dragged her toward the tram that had just arrived. "I've done nothing to you."

"Settle down, Ms. Duval," the second man instructed.

Claudia could feel the strength of his grip increasing around her arm.

"If you make another sound," the man added, "we'll kill you right here."

Those words paralyzed Claudia. No further sound could come from her throat. Her mind raced as she tried to calculate her escape. She couldn't break free and run. Their grip on her arms felt like she was in shackles. And even if she could break free, her captors would certainly chase her down and kill her.

Why would no one help her? Couldn't anyone in the crowd see that she was being forced to go somewhere against her will?

"Stand back. The doors are opening," the computer-generated voice said as the three of them waited by the tram door.

The trio was third in line to enter the tram. Claudia studied the men. They were facing straight ahead, and the muscles on the side of their faces were taut. There was death in their eyes, and she knew it was hers. As her fingers grew numb, she began to wonder if her death would be long and painful, or quick.

The door to the tram was narrow, allowing only one person at a time to enter. When the door opened and the other passengers had entered, the brown-haired man led the trio into the tram car with his right hand still around Claudia's left bicep.

"Stand back. The doors are closing," the computerized voice said.

The metallic voice awakened her survival instinct, and Claudia realized that it also gave her an opportunity for escape. Perhaps her *only* opportunity. It was a small window of hope, but she had to act quickly. She placed the heel of her right foot in the crevice between the tram and the platform floor for leverage and pulled backward as hard as she could, like she was the anchor in a game of tug-of-war. Her backward movement created enough momentum to cause the brown-haired man to stumble backward toward the closing door. The forearm and elbow of his right arm extended through the door while the rest of his body was still in the tram car.

"What are you doing!" he yelled as the doors began to close. Claudia watched as the sliding metal and glass doors slammed together, trapping the man's right arm between them. The man screamed out in agony and released his grip on Claudia's arm.

Claudia and the other man tumbled backward. Landing on top of the heap, she heard the *thud* of the black-haired man's head hitting the concrete floor. The impact caused him to let go of Claudia's duffel bag, and it slid a few feet away.

For a fleeting instant Claudia felt freedom. She righted herself and stood to run. Almost instantaneously a hand grabbed her left ankle, causing her to fall hard again. The man began to pull her toward him, groping aimlessly for any part of her body he could reach. Claudia refused to surrender as easily as she had before. Now at least the odds were one to one. But she knew the other man would only be caught in the sliding door of the tram for a few more seconds. If she didn't escape now, she would never escape.

Her only weapon was her right foot, so she kicked wildly at the man's head as he dragged her body closer to him. She found her voice again, and over and over she screamed, "Let go of me! Let go of me!" The platform was empty, and the passengers inside the tram stared out the windows at her struggle for freedom. Despite her assailant's attempts to deflect her attacks with his left forearm, Claudia continued kicking. Soon she found her intended target. The sole of her shoe landed squarely on the bridge of his nose. Blood gushed from his nostrils and flowed over his mouth and down his chin.

When he released her ankle to clutch his broken nose, Claudia struggled to her feet again. She grabbed the nearby duffel bag and ran toward the escalator leading to the upper level.

Claudia knew it would only be a few moments before one or both of the men were giving chase. Every second was precious, and she didn't have time to wait for the slow-moving escalator to transport her, so she bounded up the escalator like it was a stationary staircase. It seemed like an eternity, but in a few seconds Claudia reached the top.

She looked back briefly. The brown-haired man was helping his partner to his feet. He was pointing with his uninjured arm toward the escalator on which she escaped. Blood covered the front of the partner's white golf shirt.

Claudia stepped off the escalator into a horde of passengers who were trying to find their boarding gates in T concourse. She frantically glanced right and left, trying to determine the better avenue of escape. She knew she could hide in the crowd, but for how long? How long would it be before they found her? And when they did find her, they'd kill her. She was sure of it.

The exit door of the airport was to Claudia's left, and she considered taking that way of escape. But she had to get to Memphis, and that meant going in the opposite direction of the exit in order to board her flight. Gathering her courage, she began running toward her departure gate.

Then, out of the corner of her eye, she saw an oasis. "Officer!" Claudia shouted over the crowd noise and headed straight for him.

They met in the middle of the wide concourse, pedestrians passing them on all sides.

"May I help you, ma'am?" the officer asked politely, but Claudia noticed a hint of apathy in his voice.

"Two men were fighting down below," Claudia exclaimed, pointing frantically toward the escalator.

She knew she had the officer's full attention when his expression changed.

"Both are tall," she explained breathlessly. "One has brown hair. The other, black hair. And he has blood all over his shirt. I saw them just a few seconds ago, and my guess is that they're still down there."

"Thanks, ma'am," the officer responded. "I'll handle it from here."

The officer dashed toward the escalator, simultaneously retrieving the walkie-talkie that was clipped to his belt. Claudia couldn't hear what he said but assumed he was calling for additional officers to assist him. She stepped into a gift shop next to the Starbucks and waited to see what would happen. It took only seconds before two additional airport security officers appeared and hurried down the escalator.

CHAPTER THIRTY-ONE

Jackson-Madison County General Hospital, Jackson, Tennessee

Courtney Reed was transferred to a private room on the third floor after spending most of the morning in the ER. Being in a hospital had to be unsettling for Courtney. It was a strange place to her, Jake knew. For that reason he decided that either Rachel or he would be in the room with their daughter at all times.

Jake dimmed the lights in room 351 to make the atmosphere more conducive for rest. Courtney was finally asleep. It had taken a mild sedative to induce the sleep, but it was necessary. The doctors had said that sleep was an important part of the healing process.

When Rachel went to get a sandwich from one of the vendors in the basement, Jake was left alone with Courtney. He sat on the edge of her bed and gazed at her angelic, petite face. Occasionally she would scream out in her sleep, and he would try to comfort her. He knew the trauma from her harrowing night would take several months—maybe even longer—to overcome.

A full spectrum of emotions bolted through him as he watched her chest rise and fall as she breathed deeply in sleep.

Again he felt it—the one emotion he always kept hidden from everyone. It was fear. What had happened to Courtney scared him. It terrified him, down to the core of his being. He didn't fear for his own safety or his own life. But no one could mess with his family.

He knew exactly what the note on Courtney's nightstand meant, he finally admitted to himself. Whoever terrorized his daughter had also killed Jesse Thompson. And they had threatened to do worse than that to Jake's loved ones if he told anyone what he knew about the Thompson murder, which Jake knew meant the documents he had obtained from Earline Thompson.

What Jake couldn't determine was the source of the threat. Was it Edward Burke, the vice president of the United States? Or Dalton Miller? Or the FBI? Or maybe someone even more sinister than any of them?

All Jake had ever wanted was to keep Jed McClellan off death row. He never meant for anyone to get hurt, particularly his own child. But there she lay. Her little body bruised and battered. Her psyche damaged. The pediatric psychiatrist had assured Jake and Rachel that children were amazingly resilient. But how could Jake be sure that this night wouldn't haunt Courtney for years to come? And, if she did recover emotionally, how could he ever forgive himself for allowing this to happen? In his own home?

Jake's self-pity was interrupted by a light rap at the door. He turned his head toward the noise.

"Come in," he said in a low tone, barely louder than a whisper. He didn't want to do anything to wake Courtney. She was finally resting peacefully.

The door opened slightly and Naomi McClellan entered the room. She was the last person Jake expected to see.

"Ms. McClellan, what are you doing here?"

"I overheard some nurses on Jed's floor talkin' and knew I needed to come down. How's she doin'?"

"OK," Jake said wearily. "It will take awhile for her to get over the terror, but otherwise she'll be fine."

Naomi tiptoed to the side of the bed opposite where Jake sat, and peered down at the sleeping child. "Jake, does this have somethin' to do with Jed?"

Jake knew that Jed's case was the only explanation, but he hadn't quite pieced everything together. So he simply replied, "I don't know, Ms. McClellan. It might."

"Is it because Jesse was Jed's father?"

"I don't think that's it," Jake said slowly. "I think it's something with a much larger scope."

Jake hoped Naomi wouldn't pursue it any further. He couldn't tell her about the documents from the bank or even the money at this point. Those conversations would have to wait.

"How are you doin'?" Naomi asked, her eyes sympathetic.

Jake's gaze fell back on his delicate daughter as tears welled up in his eyes. For some inexplicable reason he felt as though he could share his soul with Naomi McClellan. Maybe it was because she was facing a similar struggle in her own life.

"I'm not doing so well," he responded. "I don't know how you manage to be so strong when you're with Jed. I can't stop believing that what happened to Courtney is my fault."

"You can't blame yourself," Naomi advised. "There are some strange people in this world, and there ain't no explainin' why they act like they do sometimes. Jake, let me tell you somethin'."

Jake turned his head away from Courtney and focused his attention on Naomi.

"You've gotta believe that there's some greater purpose in everythin' that happens. Somethin' greater than me and you both. God knows what's goin' on down here. And you've gotta believe that he's in control of everythin'."

"I've heard you say that before, but I don't understand how that's possible. How can anything good come from what happened to my daughter? How can God allow something like this to happen to such an innocent child?" Jake pointed his hand at Courtney as she slept. "I just don't understand it."

"Stop being a lawyer," Naomi instructed. "You're not gonna understand everythin' about God. That's why he's God. But he has a plan. And everythin' that happens, good and bad, fits into God's plan."

It all still seemed implausible to Jake.

"Don't you worry, Jake," Naomi advised, patting his hand. "God's in control, and that means your daughter will be all right."

Hartsfield-Jackson International Airport, Atlanta

Claudia waited in the gift shop until she saw the officer she'd talked to and the other airport security officers escorting her two assailants off the escalator and into the terminal. She covered her face with a magazine so her pursuers wouldn't see her. She strained to hear above the noise what, if anything, was said between the security officers and their captives.

"Officer," she heard the man with blood on his shirt say, "I'm telling you for the last time. We're with the FBI."

"And I'm telling you I don't care," the officer retorted. "You can take it up with the lieutenant."

When Claudia heard her assailant say "FBI," she couldn't move, much less run. Her feet felt bolted to the floor. Her mind screamed, *FBI! Why is the FBI chasing me? Why did they attack me?*

Those two men had been watching Hudson's house at Hilton Head for weeks, she remembered. What was Hudson involved in that interested the FBI? So far she was finding more questions instead of answers to the ones she had already.

She couldn't wait here any longer. Her instincts told her to run to her car and drive away as fast as she could while she had the chance. She could just leave and forget that any of this had happened.

But something inside her wouldn't let her run this time. She had to keep going. She had to find answers to her questions, and she hoped the answers to all the questions, the old ones and the new ones, could be obtained from Attorney Jake Reed.

She checked her watch. *12:15.*

Her plane was scheduled to depart in thirty-five minutes. She picked up her duffel bag and began to quickly make her way to gate B-27. She knew she didn't have a minute to spare. Twenty anxious minutes later Claudia arrived at gate B-27 just as the last passengers were walking down the Jetway. After handing her boarding pass to the attendant, she followed an elderly couple into the airplane. She felt confident the two FBI agents who had been following her were still being detained by airport security, but she nervously scanned the faces of the passengers already on board. No one appeared to pay her any attention. She located the aisle that corresponded with the number on her boarding pass, placed her duffel bag in the overhead storage compartment, and settled down in her window seat.

In a few minutes the pilot announced over the intercom that they were next in line for departure. *It can't happen soon enough,* Claudia thought. The sooner she got as far away as possible from the two FBI agents, the better.

Within minutes the airplane taxied to the end of the runway. Claudia watched out the small window beside her seat as the plane accelerated. She saw the scenery race by faster and faster, until it eventually transformed into blue sky and white, fluffy clouds. The flight to Memphis would be an hour and thirty minutes, and she would be that much closer to reconciling the events of the last two days.

The seat beside her was empty, and the man in the seat near the aisle was preoccupied with the contents of his briefcase. She glanced quickly at him and then returned to staring out the window. She surmised that he was a business traveler and was probably returning home to a wife and family. She repeated the word in her mind—*family*. The sound of it aroused a warm feeling inside her that tingled throughout her body. But, at the same time, it also caused feelings of sadness and despair. The contrast of emotions was not lost on Claudia. She realized she would probably never have a family of her own now that Hudson was gone.

When she had fled her mother's house all those years ago, she had such grandiose ideas. She wanted a life far removed from the quiet nights under starlit skies that, as a teenager, she considered boring and useless. She wanted a life where every moment was full of exhilaration. And most of all she wanted a life away from her mother. But what she found instead was a life full of emotional valleys and loneliness, of continual disappointment and unhappiness. For the first time since she'd left her mother's house, Claudia began to realize that the things she thought would bring her happiness left her empty. And that the true happiness she sought for so long had been there all along. She simply chose to ignore it.

She said the word again in her head—*family*. This time the warm feeling filled every cavern of her body, overshadowing the feelings of sadness and despair. For the first time in several days, she allowed a smile to crease her lips. Her only concern was whether her revelation had come too late.

CHAPTER THIRTY-TWO

Hartsfield-Jackson International Airport, Atlanta

The security office was in the main terminal behind a nondescript door immediately past the Delta Airlines ticket counter. Lieutenant Parker Mitchell, head of airport security, watched as two angry-looking men were led through the door to the office area and instructed to sit in the interrogation room across the hall from his office.

"What's that all about?" the lieutenant asked as the arresting officer entered his office.

"Two guys fighting in the lower concourse," the officer replied. "Get this. They claim to be FBI agents."

"FBI agents?"

"I thought you would like that one. They claimed they were on some kind of undercover assignment."

"Did you get their names?"

"Yeah." The officer removed a small notepad from his shirt pocket and read the names to his superior. "Osborne and Moyers."

Lieutenant Mitchell rubbed his chin thoughtfully. Osborne and Moyers's claim would be easy enough to verify. "I'll call an old friend of mine to check out their story. You keep them busy for a few minutes."

As the officer left, the lieutenant placed a call to FBI headquarters in Washington, DC. Even after several years away from the place, he could still remember the number.

"This is Lieutenant Parker Mitchell with Hartsfield-Jackson International Airport in Atlanta," he announced to the receptionist who answered the call. "I need to speak with Deputy Director Armacost."

"Parker Mitchell," Charlie Armacost said affectionately. "I haven't heard from you in years."

"It has been a while," Lieutenant Mitchell replied. "How have you been?"

"I'm fine. And you?"

"I'm doing fine, but I need your help with something."

"Anything," Charlie responded.

"I've got a couple of guys in detention down here who claim to be yours."

"What are their names?"

"Osborne and Moyers."

"Hold on a minute, and let me check."

Charlie pushed the hold button and dialed the extension for George McCullough. "George, I've got an old friend of mine on the phone, Parker Mitchell. He's head of security at Hartsfield in Atlanta."

"I think I remember him from when he was with the Bureau. Wasn't he on your team in Panama?"

"That's him. He has a couple of guys detained who claim to be working for the Bureau. Their names are Osborne and Moyers. Check them out, and tell me what you find."

Charlie then returned to his telephone call with Parker. He didn't mind taking the time to help a friend, even in the midst of the Thompson murder investigation. They talked about old times and how things used to be with the Bureau. In a few minutes George was in Charlie's office, and Charlie immediately noticed the disconcerted look on George's face.

"Let me put you on hold for a minute, Parker." Charlie pressed the hold button and lowered the receiver from his ear. "What is it, George?"

"You're not going to believe this. We do have two agents named Osborne and Moyers. They're assigned to the Boston field office. But they were placed on special assignment, and the only thing the assignment file says is top-secret. There are no reports in the file. No memos. Not even any orders."

"Who made the assignment?"

George hesitated before answering. "Saul Sanders."

Charlie slowly returned the receiver to his ear and pressed the Hold button again. "Parker, did they say what type of special assignment?"

"My officer hasn't been able to get that information out of them. One of them asked if any of our officers had seen a blond-haired woman, and the officer recalled that a woman matching the description pointed him in the direction of your guys."

"Where is the woman now?"

"Security tapes show her boarding a plane for Memphis."

Memphis! Charlie glanced up at George. "Parker, here is what I want you to do. Release Osborne and Moyers, but don't tell them where the woman went. Don't let them review your tapes or any other information about the woman. I need to force their hand. I can't tell you what all this is about, but it's not good."

"I understand," Parker replied. "We'll handle it exactly as you've asked."

Charlie hung up the phone and turned to George. "We may have just caught the break we've been looking for. If my instincts are right, Sanders should be getting a call anytime now. See what you can find out."

Apollyon Associates, Inc., lower Manhattan

"We lost her," Saul Sanders reported when Randolph Winston answered the call.

Saul's voice sounded cowardly . . . as if fear filled his every bone.

And the man had a right to be afraid, Randolph thought viciously. "What do you mean you lost her?" he screamed.

"I mean she got away, and we don't know where she went. And she has the packages from McAdams with her."

"You idiot! How could she have escaped? I thought you had your best agents on this assignment!"

"They were detained by airport security in Atlanta. By the time they convinced security they really were FBI agents, she had boarded a plane. We're looking for her now, but at least one hundred planes departed Hartsfield during the time my guys were confined. She could be anywhere."

"Did you say she boarded a plane?"

"That's right. Her car is still in the airport parking lot. So we know she didn't drive away. The only other possibility is that she got on an airplane."

"Wait a minute," Randolph instructed. He activated the computer on his desk and, with a few keystrokes, logged in to the Cannibal software that his company's engineers had developed over the summer. He searched through the data bank until he found a user identification for Claudia Duval; then he traced any purchases she'd made in the last two days.

"I've got her," Randolph said, after a couple of minutes in the Cannibal software. "She purchased a ticket for a flight to Memphis." A few expletives raced through his mind as he realized she must be on her way to see Jake Reed. "It departed Atlanta at 12:55, and is scheduled to land in Memphis at 1:28 central." He looked at his Rolex watch. "That's thirty minutes from now. Saul, get someone to the Memphis Airport immediately. There's not a minute to spare."

"I've got it," Saul said. "1:28."

"And Saul, don't disappoint me again," Randolph warned. "If she gets to Reed, everything might blow up in our faces."

"I understand." Saul's voice sounded even weaker than when the conversation began.

Randolph was certain that Saul understood the implication of the threat.

Jackson-Madison County General Hospital, Jackson, Tennessee

Dalton Miller stood outside the automatic sliding glass doors that opened to the ER. He spoke to the visitors and employees who entered, searching for information about Jake Reed's daughter. He loitered the length of time it took to smoke three Marlboro Lights before he located the paramedics who had transported Courtney Reed to the hospital. They initially refused to discuss it with him or even acknowledge they had transported her. Medical confidentiality, they said. But two Ben Franklins bought the information he needed, and he retreated to his rental car in the parking lot to call Shep Taylor.

"Shep, something big is brewing," Dalton said hurriedly when Shep answered the telephone. "I don't know what it is yet, but it has got to be big."

"Dalton, slow down. What are you talking about?"

"Somebody broke into Reed's house last night and terrorized his daughter. The paramedics told me the girl was gagged, and her arms and legs were tied to the corner posts of her bed." He paused. "Somebody is trying to scare Reed."

"How's she doing?" Shep asked.

Dalton could tell from Shep's tone that the question was sincere—that Shep was genuinely concerned about Courtney's well-being.

"The paramedics said her wounds were superficial and should heal in a few days. They also said she cried all the way to the hospital. I'm sure she was terrified."

"Somebody sure is going to great lengths to keep Mac Foster from winning the election. But attacking a little girl is going too far."

"That's what I was thinking," Dalton replied. "I just hope Reed doesn't think it was me. I'm the only one who has had any contact with him that I know of."

"Have you talked to Reed?"

"No, I thought that would be too risky. I didn't want him to think I had anything to do with what happened to his daughter."

"I agree. Stay out of sight there. I don't want us to be the catalyst for anything worse happening. But I think it's time to call your contact with the Bureau and bring him into the fold. Tell him everything we know."

Dalton ended the call with Shep and immediately called George McCullough at FBI headquarters. "George, this is Dalton Miller."

"Dalton? You shouldn't be calling me here."

"I know it's risky, but we need to talk. It can't wait until we have a more secure line."

"All right, Dalton. What is it?"

"Do you remember our meeting a few weeks ago at the Flying J?"

"I remember. What about it?"

"What I didn't tell you that day is that I was working for Mac Foster."

"I can't say I'm surprised, but why was that important enough that you risked calling me at my office?"

"That's only the beginning. I've been in Jackson, Tennessee, for the last several weeks."

Dalton could sense that George's interest was piqued. He knew that George quickly calculated there could only be one reason why he was in Tennessee. The Thompson murder.

"What are you doing there?"

"The same thing your agents were doing here. Looking for a connection between the Thompson murder and Vice President Burke. I know your guys pulled out of here, but there's something going on I think you should know about."

"What is it?" George asked eagerly.

"Somebody broke into Attorney Jake Reed's house last night and terrorized his daughter. We think it has to do with Burke."

"Why do you say that?" George inquired.

"Who else would have motivation to keep Reed quiet?" Dalton went on to tell George everything he knew about Edward Burke, Jake Reed, and the Thompson murder.

"I don't see how any of it ties to Burke," George commented after Dalton finished his recitation.

"I know," Dalton conceded. "That's where we need your help."

"What do you want me to do?"

"We want your help in pinning this on Burke."

Dalton hoped that George would take the bait and help the Foster campaign expose Ed Burke. But hope was all he, and the Foster campaign, had at this point.

"Dalton, I'll see what I can find out from my end and call you back as soon as I know something. I can't promise anything."

"That's fine, George. But tell Armacost that I have it on good authority that if this breaks before the election and Foster wins, there'll be a nice promotion for the two of you."

"I'll tell him," George replied. "But I don't know if it will matter."

CHAPTER THIRTY-THREE

Jackson-Madison County General Hospital, Jackson, Tennessee

Rachel was back in Courtney's room, where with Jake she watched Courtney as she slept peacefully. It had been over an hour since she cried out in horror. They both sat quietly. On the outside Rachel appeared calm to Jake, but he knew that on the inside her mind raced in a thousand different directions. Jake wasn't surprised when Rachel finally broke the silence.

"What is going on, Jake? Why did someone do this to Courtney?"

"I don't know," he replied solemnly, without taking his eyes off Courtney.

"There must be a reason why someone broke into our house, Jake."

Jake could feel her glaring at him.

"Tell me what's going on," she demanded.

Jake still couldn't look into Rachel's eyes. If he did, he knew he would have to tell her. He wouldn't be able to hide from the longing in her eyes. He thought he had to keep the truth from her, for her own protection. He was the father and husband, and he had to protect his family. He had to be the one who took control of the situation. Looking at Courtney, he knew he was failing miserably. But he still couldn't tell Rachel.

"I don't know what to tell you, Rachel. I don't know what's going on myself."

"Jake!" she screamed in frustration.

Courtney shifted in her bed in reaction to the loud sound of her mother's voice but didn't awake.

"Jake," Rachel continued in a softer voice, "I've got to know what's happening."

Jake turned and looked at Rachel. He could see in her eyes the glittering of tears and the struggle for control. And that's when it hit him. He had not only failed at protecting Courtney, he was now failing miserably at protecting Rachel. He thought he was protecting her physically by not telling her what was happening with Jed's case, but it wasn't physical attacks from which she needed protection. It was emotional ones. Jake could see that she was scared. Scared of the unknown. Even if what Jake told her was horrible, it would be better than not knowing at all. Those sad blue eyes pulled the truth from him.

"It involves Jed McClellan," he began. "I thought it was going to be a simple murder case, but it has turned into something much larger than that. I'll tell you what I know, but I'm as confused as you are." Jake told Rachel everything from Dalton Miller to the assassination to the FBI. Rachel sat in complete disbelief as Jake described the events of the last few weeks. He told her that Jesse Thompson was Jed McClellan's father and that Earline Thompson paid $2 million to keep it quiet. When he finished, he waited for Rachel's response, but she said nothing. The next few silent minutes seemed like an eternity to Jake. He didn't know what else to say.

"I'm scared," Rachel finally whispered.

"I'm scared too," Jake admitted.

FBI headquarters, Washington DC

Charlie Armacost wasn't surprised when George McCullough burst into his office without knocking. Things were moving rapidly, and there was no time for an invitation. Charlie anxiously awaited every report from George. He refused to take any calls from anyone else. After the incident at Hartsfield, the Thompson murder case had taken on a life of its own and had become paramount to everything else. All other cases would have to wait.

"What do you have?" Charlie asked as George raced into the room.

"Osborne and Moyers called Sanders just like you thought they would. The call came in at 1:50 p.m. eastern time. Then Sanders placed a call—and guess who he called?"

"Winston," Charlie replied confidently.

"You've got it. At 1:55 he placed a call to New York. We traced it to Apollyon Associates. Sanders and Winston talked for three minutes, and then Sanders called our office in Memphis and dispatched his private plane to Atlanta. No flight plan was filed, but my hunch is that he sent it to Atlanta to retrieve Osborne and Moyers."

"I bet your hunch is right. He's bringing Osborne and Moyers back in and hopes to do it without our finding out. Keep your eye on that situation, and make sure Sanders knows you're watching. I want him to know that we know about those two. It's the call to Memphis that bothers me. The blond woman Parker identified has something, or knows something, and Sanders is trying to get whatever it is from her. We've got to get to her first."

"I agree, but how? Sanders has the jump on us, and Parker said she left Atlanta almost an hour ago."

"Are Boyd and Simon still in Memphis?"

"I believe they are."

"Sanders has more Bureau agents on his side than we realize. We need to find out who he called in Memphis."

Charlie reached for the telephone to call agents Boyd and Simon.

"Before you call," George interrupted, "there's something else you need to know."

"What is it?" Charlie replied.

"Someone broke into Jake Reed's house last night. The intruder attacked his daughter. She's in a local hospital recovering."

"It's getting out of control. We've got to stop it now before anyone else gets hurt." Charlie dialed the number for the FBI field office in Memphis. The office was located in the federal building on Front Street, only a few steps from the Mississippi River.

"This is Deputy Director Charlie Armacost," Charlie stated when the receptionist answered the telephone. "I need to speak with Agent Boyd."

"Hold, please," the receptionist replied. "I'll page him for you." It took less than ten seconds for the agent to respond to the page.

"Agent Boyd," Charlie heard as Ron took the call.

"Ron, this is Charlie Armacost. We need you and Jerry again on the Thompson murder case."

"What do you need us to do?" Ron inquired. Charlie could hear the eagerness in the agent's voice.

Charlie briefed Ron on the latest developments in the Thompson case. Although there wasn't much time to go into any great detail, he did tell him that Director Sanders was involved and probably Vice President Burke as well. He also asked Ron whether he had seen any suspicious activity among any of the other agents in the Memphis office.

"Not until a few minutes ago," Ron responded. "It was the strangest thing. Agent Phelps received a call, and then he left like a bat out of Hades. He didn't tell anyone where he was going."

"I'll tell you where he's going. He's on his way to the Memphis Airport. We've got to find her before Phelps," Charlie advised, referring to Claudia.

"Our only chance is to intercept Phelps at Memphis International," Ron strategized. "If he leaves the airport with her, we'll have no idea where to find them. But we haven't got much time. Her plane is scheduled to land in a few minutes."

"You and Jerry get over there immediately," Charlie replied. "Take her into protective custody if you have to. But I want her safe. Whatever it takes, I want her safe. She knows something, and I've got to find out what it is."

"We're on our way," Ron responded.

En route to Memphis International Airport

After Agent Boyd ended the phone call from Charlie Armacost, he motioned for Agent Simon to follow him. They raced out of the rear of the downtown federal building, putting on their dark suit coats in unison, and climbed into a brown four-door sedan parked near the back door. Ron sat behind the wheel, while Jerry took position in the passenger seat.

Ron updated his partner on their assignment as the sedan sped out of the parking lot, into the alley, and onto Riverside Drive, which ran parallel to the Mississippi River. The tugboats, barges, and M-shaped bridge that traversed the mighty river quickly disappeared behind them as the car accelerated down Riverside Drive and onto the ramp leading to the I-240 loop that circled Memphis. The drive along the southern section of the I-240 loop from the downtown area of Memphis to the airport typically took twenty minutes. Agent Phelps already had a ten-minute head start, so Ron and Jerry didn't have a second to spare. Ron wove the sedan through the early afternoon traffic at speeds sometimes as high as 100 mph. Although they didn't know the blond woman's name, if Charlie Armacost was even partially right, the continued existence of America as they knew it hinged on their reaching her before Phelps.

Claudia Duval stared out the small oval window of the airplane and watched the Memphis skyline grow larger. Only in the last few minutes had she been able to slightly calm her nerves after the ordeal in Atlanta. Still she repeatedly scanned the interior of the cabin for anyone who might be watching her.

Soon she felt and heard the landing gear lowering as the pilot maneuvered the plane slightly south of the airport for a south to north landing. In less than ten minutes the plane would be on the ground, and she would be exiting through the Jetway. Her pulse quickened as she realized she was getting closer to the answers she desperately needed, but she wasn't sure whether the sensation was excitement or fear.

Memphis was familiar to her. She had been there numerous times. It was almost like going home. Her mother's house was only a thirty-minute drive southeast of Memphis, barely across the Tennessee–Mississippi state line. Claudia caught herself wondering about her mother for just a minute and then shook the thought from her mind. *I don't have time for this right now,* she told herself. *I have more important things to worry about.*

The airplane came to a stop at gate B-12, and Claudia removed her duffel bag from the overhead storage compartment. Nervously she followed the other passengers as they exited and soon emerged from the Jetway into the waiting area. She was greeted by the smiling face of a

Northwest female employee welcoming her to Memphis. The rental-car counter was near the terminal's exit, and she hurried through the crowded airport in that direction.

Memphis International Airport

Agent Jonathan Phelps stood in the front lobby of the airport near the large electronic marquee that displayed the times and gates for all arriving and departing flights. He appeared as though he was just another passenger, trying to determine whether his plane was on time or not. But the location of the marquee was the perfect vantage point from which to look for Claudia Duval. He knew her plane was already on the ground, and to exit the airport, she had to walk past the marquee.

The wall to his left was lined with ticket counters: Delta, US Airways, Northwest, American. Most of the major airlines provided service to and from Memphis International. The main door leading to the parking area was to his right. He knew Claudia didn't have a car in the parking garage. She either had to exit the building through the main door to a waiting taxi cab or rent a car from one of the car-rental companies, which were behind him. Either way he would be able to see her.

The description of Claudia Duval he'd received from Saul Sanders was minimal. Blond hair, blue jeans, a sweatshirt, and a burgundy duffel bag was all the information provided. There hadn't been time to receive an e-mailed picture of the woman before he left his office. But how many women in the Memphis airport could even come close to matching the brief description he had? He shouldn't have any trouble locating her.

He scanned the crowd but tried to avoid making eye contact with anyone. Hundreds of people littered the lobby area. Business travelers mainly. Men and women in suits pulling luggage or briefcases on rolling carts. He saw tourists, parents with small children, women of all ages and sizes, but none were Claudia Duval.

Finally he spotted a woman whose appearance matched precisely the description he'd received from Saul Sanders. He watched her as she reached the top of the incline leading from the B concourse, entered the lobby area, and then passed through. She walked within three feet of the agent's position, but she never noticed him. He watched her with his eyes, never turning his head until she was behind him. Then he turned and trailed, staying several feet behind Claudia, his vision fixed on the back of her head.

Jonathan followed Claudia to the Hertz rental counter. After securing a car, she began to hurriedly walk toward the exit on the south end of the lobby that led to the rental-car parking area. He resumed his stealth pursuit, closing the distance between them before she reached the exit. As the sliding door opened, he simultaneously grabbed Claudia's left shoulder and thrust the business end of a small caliber pistol into the lumbar area of her back.

"Keep walking, and don't make a sound," Jonathan whispered forcefully into Claudia's right ear.

Claudia gasped at the unforeseen attack.

He kept a firm grip on her left shoulder to prevent her from turning to face him and so he could quickly cover her mouth if she chose to scream.

But with seemingly little resistance, she followed the instructions and kept walking through the door.

The sedan containing agents Boyd and Simon screeched to a stop in the traffic lane reserved for taxi cabs immediately in front of the main door to Memphis International Airport. The agents leaped from the car, and Ron flashed his FBI identification badge at the airport security officer who rushed at them while Jerry entered the terminal through the automatic sliding doors. The airport security officer was quickly satisfied, and Ron followed Jerry into the terminal. He found Jerry frantically scanning the top of the crowd for Agent Phelps or Claudia Duval, or both.

Ron looked in the opposite direction.

"I've got them!" Jerry pointed at the exit leading to the rental-car lot.

"I see them too," Ron responded, looking where Jerry indicated. "I'll follow them through the door. You see if you can get around in front of them."

Ron took off, running through the crowded lobby in pursuit of Phelps and Claudia, knocking several passengers to the floor in the process. As he reached the sliding door leading to the rental-car lot, Ron reached beneath his suit coat and drew his 9mm pistol from the holster he wore under his left arm. The doors opened automatically, and he burst into the late October sunlight. He saw Phelps and Claudia thirty feet in front of him, walking across the asphalt-covered aisle between two rows of cars.

"Let her go!" Ron screamed, raising his pistol and aiming it at their backs.

Phelps turned toward the sound of Ron's voice and spun Claudia around in front of him. Moving his left hand from her shoulder, he slid it under her chin, clasping her throat in the bend of his elbow. It was a maneuver on which all agents were trained—to use someone's body to create a human shield.

When Phelps pointed his own gun at Ron, Claudia yanked at her assailant's arm with both hands in a vain attempt to free herself.

"Let her go, Phelps, and nobody gets hurt!" Ron screamed again, his voice even louder than before.

And then he heard Claudia plead with her captor, "Please let me go. Please let me go." The words began to spill from her mouth as she implored Phelps for her freedom.

But the agent didn't respond. He continued to drag Claudia backward through the parking lot. Ron could see the fear in Claudia's eyes. He had seen it before. It was the fear of death.

"I said let her go!" he ordered Phelps.

"Go away, Boyd," Phelps finally replied. "This doesn't concern you."

Phelps fired a warning shot that ricocheted off the asphalt near Ron's feet. Ron lunged between two parked cars and peered over the hood of a blue Ford Taurus as Phelps continued dragging Claudia through the parking lot.

Claudia began to scream hysterically. A high-pitched scream. She thrashed her body uncontrollably, trying to free herself from her bondage. Her pleas for freedom grew louder and louder.

"Shut up and be still!" Phelps shouted at Claudia.

But Ron could tell from Claudia's movements that she wasn't going to comply. She was hysterical. Her thrashing and screaming intensified.

"I said, shut up!" Phelps yelled and raised his gun to Claudia's right temple.

"No!" shouted Ron from behind the blue Ford Taurus. He left the safety of his metal bunker and began to run toward Phelps and Claudia, with gun drawn. "No!" he shouted again.

Phelps lowered his gun from Claudia's head and pointed it at Ron. Ron knew he couldn't fire at Phelps for fear of striking Claudia. But he had to stop Phelps from harming his prisoner.

A gunshot sounded above Claudia's unrelenting screams.

Certain that her death was near, she began to scream more frantically.

Another gunshot came from a different direction.

Almost instantaneously Phelps's grip around her neck loosened. With her arms and hands covering her head, she crumbled to the asphalt.

CHAPTER THIRTY-FOUR

Jackson-Madison County General Hospital, Jackson, Tennessee

"How do you feel?" Rachel asked Courtney.

Courtney's eyes were barely visible through the slits between her lashes. She forced her lids to open further until her precious blue eyes were fully visible. Jake knew that the sleep—even if drug induced—had been good and needed. She rolled from her side onto her back, and rubbed her eyes with two small fists.

"I feel OK," came the delayed, groggy response. Courtney tugged at the corners of her lips and made a barely audible *smack* as she tried to lubricate the inside of her mouth. "I'm thirsty, Daddy."

Jake poured water from a Styrofoam pitcher into a plastic cup and handed it to Courtney. "Here you go, honey." Gently he brushed wisps of hair away from her forehead.

He was so thankful that Courtney hadn't been hurt any worse than she was. But thankful to whom? To God? *Did God take care of Courtney last night and protect her from greater harm? Does God really concern himself with every detail of every life of every person on earth?* Jake wondered.

All he knew for certain was that his little girl, although bruised and battered, was going to be OK. And for that he was thankful.

There was a light knock at the door.

"Come in," Rachel invited.

The door opened slowly, and a well-dressed man entered the room. He was handsome. Midthirties. Dressed like a lawyer. But Jake knew all the lawyers in town and didn't recognize this man. *How did he get by the sheriff's deputy?*

"Mr. Reed," the man began, extending his hand toward Jake in greeting, "my name is Michael Hall. I'm a pastor here in Jackson. I hope I haven't come at a bad time."

Jake shook the pastor's hand. "Not at all, Reverend. This is my wife, Rachel, and this is Courtney." He motioned in Courtney's direction.

Reverend Hall walked to the side of Courtney's hospital bed and took her hand in his. "It's a pleasure to meet you, Courtney," he said, directing his full attention to her. "Your schoolteacher goes to my church, and she asked me to visit you. How are you doing?"

"I'm doing fine," Courtney replied bashfully.

"That's good. We've been praying for you, and I hope you get better." Reverend Hall looked at Jake and Rachel. "Is there anything we can do for you or your family?"

"That's very kind of you," Rachel responded. "But I think we're going to be OK."

"Good," Reverend Hall replied. "If you think of anything, let me know. We want to help in any way we can."

"Thank you," Jake replied politely. He knew Reverend Hall's offer was sincere, but what could the reverend and his church really do for Jake and his family? "We'll remember that."

"I don't want to take up any more of your time. I know that Courtney needs her rest. But before I go, would you mind if I had a word of prayer with you?"

"Sure," Rachel said before Jake had an opportunity to speak. She lowered her head and closed her eyes before Reverend Hall began his prayer. Courtney closed her eyes too.

Jake lowered his head as Reverend Hall began speaking, but he didn't close his eyes. He stared at the white, sterile floor under Courtney's bed. It had been quite some time since Jake had heard a prayer, much less said one himself. He was afraid to close his eyes. Afraid of what he might see as he looked inward.

"Dear Lord," Reverend Hall prayed, "we thank you for this child and for her life. I pray that you will give the doctors and nurses the wisdom to treat her injuries. And Lord, we may not always understand why things happen in our lives, but we know one thing with certainty. We know that you are in control of every situation . . ."

There it is again! The realization smacked Jake right between the eyes. Reverend Hall said the same thing as Naomi McClellan! "God is in control." Hearing Reverend Hall's words stirred an emotion in Jake that he had never felt before. He couldn't explain it. He felt an urging to do something, but what?

He glanced at Reverend Hall, Rachel, and Courtney. They all looked peaceful with their eyes closed, praying. The feeling Jake had inside was anything but peaceful.

What is going on? he asked himself.

". . . and most of all we thank you for your Son, Jesus Christ, who died on the cross for our sins. In his name we pray, amen."

Jake raised his head after Reverend Hall finished his prayer.

"Thank you for letting me visit with you and your daughter," Reverend Hall said again as he shook hands with Jake. "And Courtney, you get well so you can return to school. I know your classmates and teacher miss you."

Courtney smiled brightly at the attention.

"Thank you for coming by," Rachel said.

"Yeah, thanks," Jake mustered. He was still struggling with an understanding of Reverend Hall's prayer and the emotions the words had elicited inside him.

"Are you OK?" Rachel asked him after Reverend Hall left.

"I think so," Jake replied. "It's just that Reverend Hall said the same thing that Ms. McClellan has been telling me. 'God is in control.'" He hesitated as the words evaporated. "I still can't comprehend it."

"That's easy, Daddy," Courtney explained. "God knows everything. My schoolteacher told us one day that God even knows how many hairs we have on our head. If he knows that, then he has got to know everything else."

"I guess so," Jake said.

Maybe Courtney's psychological wounds will heal after all, he thought with a flood of relief.

"Why don't you try to get some more rest?" He turned to Rachel. "I'm going to check on Jed."

Jake exited Courtney's room and informed the sheriff's-deputy sentinel that he was going to the seventh floor to visit Jed.

"Just don't leave the hospital without telling me, Mr. Reed," the deputy commanded.

"I won't," Jake assured him as he headed toward the elevator. He had to find Naomi.

Memphis International Airport

Claudia continued to scream hysterically as the lifeless body of her assailant slumped to the asphalt behind her. The man who had been in pursuit was also down, but alive, lying in front of her. From the side, a third man ran toward the wounded man, his recently fired pistol still in his hand.

"Stay here!" he shouted as he passed Claudia. "I'm with the FBI!"

FBI? she thought wildly. *That's what the men at the other airport said they were.*

Who could she trust?

If he was FBI, was the wounded man lying on the asphalt thirty feet in front of her also FBI? His body writhed in pain as he clutched his bleeding left shoulder and the FBI agent attempted to stop the bleeding. Hearing him say "FBI" had terrified Claudia even more, if that were possible. With survival her only thought, she gathered her bag and rental-car keys and fled from the sickening scene of death and injury. Through her blurred vision she frantically tried to identify her assigned rental car—what she perceived as her only chance of escape.

"Stop! I said stop!" the uninjured man yelled at her. She fumbled with the keys but finally started the ignition of her rented Infiniti Q45. As she sped out of the parking lot, she could see the FBI agent in her rearview mirror, helplessly giving chase on foot.

Claudia sobbed and swiped tears from her eyes as she tried to clear her vision enough so she could see the road. It wasn't long before she merged onto the I-240 loop around Memphis and then onto I-40 east toward Jackson.

The events of the last few days seemed almost unreal. They were so confusing. And worse, the closer she got to the truth, the more dangerous everything became. At least two people were now dead, and she'd almost been the third. Someone didn't want her to make it to Jackson, Tennessee. But who? And why?

Claudia wanted to turn the car around and drive as fast as she could in the opposite direction. That was the safer course.

Take the easy way out, she told herself. *Give up before you end up like Hudson.*

But something inside her wouldn't let her quit. She could feel it. It was larger than her fear and larger than whatever evil force was trying to prevent her from discovering the truth. As she drove, she repeatedly glanced in her mirror to see if anyone was following her. Satisfied with her escape, she noticed the green sign on the side of the interstate indicating that Jackson was sixty miles away. She would be there within the hour.

Jackson-Madison County General Hospital, Jackson, Tennessee

Jake knocked softly on the outside of the door leading to Jed's hospital room and waited for an invitation from Naomi or Ruth before entering. He found each woman in her customary position on opposite sides of Jed's bed. Jake knew that neither woman had slept much in the last several days. Their faces were lined with exhaustion but also with determination.

"How's he doing?" he asked in a low tone, as if the sound of his voice might awaken Jed. He shook his head inwardly at the irony. That would be the one thing for which everyone had been praying—for Jed to awaken.

"No change," Ruth said. "But we ain't givin' up. How's your daughter?"

"She's going to be fine. Thanks for asking. We'll probably go home tomorrow."

"That's good to hear," Naomi stated. "I wish we could say the same thing. But it'll happen one day soon."

Jake hated to pull Naomi from Jed's bedside, but the emotions he felt during Reverend Hall's prayer wouldn't go away. The only person he knew he could discuss it with was Naomi.

"Ms. McClellan, may I talk with you for a few minutes?" Jake inquired.

"Sure," she replied. "You want to talk in here?"

"Perhaps we can go for a walk. It won't take long."

Naomi didn't hesitate. "All right, Jake. I'll be back in a few minutes," she told Ruth as they left Jed's room.

"What is it, Jake?" Naomi asked as they passed the nurses' station and headed toward the elevator.

"I've been thinking about something I've heard you say, and I want to ask you about it." The doors to the elevator opened, and Naomi and Jake boarded.

"Is it what I told you about Jesse Thompson in your office that day?"

"It has something to do with that, but not exactly. You told me that God was in control of every situation."

"That's right. He is."

The doors to the elevator opened at the first-floor lobby area, and Naomi and Jake exited into a group of people waiting on the next available car. They began walking down a long, sterile corridor in the direction of the hospital cafeteria.

"Ms. McClellan, I understand what you're saying, but it doesn't make sense to me. A pastor came to visit my daughter today. A nice gentleman. Apparently Courtney's schoolteacher goes to his church, and she asked him to visit. He prayed for Courtney, and in his prayer he said the same thing I've heard you say: 'God is in control.'"

"Jake, you've gotta stop thinkin' like a lawyer. It's faith, Jake. Faith."

He still didn't get it. What was he missing?

"Let's step in here," Naomi suggested.

Jake noticed that they were standing in front of the small hospital chapel. He entered the room at Naomi's suggestion. The chapel was void of other occupants. Jake saw that a stained-glass window covered much of the rear wall and depicted Jesus Christ on the cross. Two abbreviated church pews provided sitting space, and Naomi motioned for Jake to sit down.

"Let me ask you somethin', Jake. Are you a Christian?" Her brown eyes focused intently on him.

Jake stiffened. "That's a strange question. Of course I'm a Christian," he said, slightly defensive.

"How do you know?"

"I just do. I'm a good person. A good father and husband."

"When did you become a Christian?"

"I've been one all my life," he retorted. "Why are you asking me these questions? All I wanted to know was what you meant when you said God is in control. That's all."

"And I'm tryin' to tell you. It's the faith that comes with bein' a Christian. Do you see that image?" she said, pointing at the stained glass. "Bein' a Christian means you believe that Jesus Christ died to save you from your sins and that you have given your heart and soul to him. Until you do that, you'll never understand what I'm talkin' about. Without him you'll die and go to hell."

Jake looked at Naomi, and their eyes met. Was she right? Turmoil raged in Jake's soul.

"If you died right now, Jake, do you know for certain that you'd go to heaven?"

That strange feeling Jake had when he heard Reverend Hall's prayer returned, but this time it was magnified. It was indeed an urging to do something, but what? His face turned ashen, and his body trembled slightly.

"It's the Holy Spirit," Naomi said.

"What is?"

"That feelin' inside you. It's the Holy Spirit beggin' you to accept Jesus Christ as your Lord and Savior. Do you want to do that?"

Jake lowered his head and spoke softly. "God doesn't care about me. If he did, he wouldn't have let my parents die when I was just a boy, and he wouldn't have let that monster hurt Courtney." He looked back at Naomi, and his heart began to harden as he thought about all the things that had impacted him all his life. "I've made it this far on my own," he told her, "and I don't need God now."

Standing up abruptly, he hurried out of the chapel.

After Jake left, Naomi McClellan got on her knees.

"I'm tryin', Lord," she whispered heavenward. "I'm tryin'."

CHAPTER THIRTY-FIVE

FBI headquarters, Washington DC

"She got away," Simon reported to Armacost after the unsuccessful attempt to capture Claudia Duval. "And worse, Ron took a round in the shoulder. He's in transport to a local hospital."

"What about Phelps?" Charlie asked.

"I had to neutralize him after he fired on Ron. Our guys have control of the scene, and we'll make sure the place is clean before we leave."

"My guess is she's on her way to Jackson," Charlie surmised. "That's the only logical destination."

Charlie noticed George standing in the door with a peculiar look on his face. "Hold on a minute, Jerry." Charlie placed the call on speaker phone. To George, he said, "Jerry was just giving me the report from Memphis. The short version is that the woman got away, Ron's been wounded, and Phelps is dead."

"Let me tell you something else that's troubling," George replied. "Sanders's plane hasn't returned from Atlanta with Osborne and Moyers."

"I don't like the sound of that." Charlie rested his right elbow on his desk and rubbed his temples. "That plane should have been back thirty minutes ago."

"One of the mechanics in the hangar said he thought he overheard the pilot saying he was making another stop before returning to DC."

"Jerry, how fast can you get to Jackson?" Charlie asked loud enough for the speaker phone to pick up his voice.

"We're almost finished here, but there's no way I can catch up with her. She's got an hour's head start. She's probably already there."

"Sanders has outmaneuvered us," Charlie said to George. He leaned back in his chair and focused rather despondently on the ceiling. "Jerry, get to Jackson as quick as you can. I just hope we're not too late."

En route to Jackson, Tennessee

Claudia exited I-40 at exit 80A and merged into the southbound traffic on US Highway 45 bypass around Jackson. Hudson had written Jake Reed's address on the package with his name on it, and Claudia had obtained directions from a service-station attendant at the intersection of Old Hickory Boulevard and Highway 45 bypass.

The traffic lights along the route to downtown Jackson were all favorable, and Claudia reached the court square within fifteen minutes of leaving I-40. She found the law offices on the northwest corner and parked her car across the street. She removed the package addressed to Jake Reed from her duffel bag and clutched it anxiously. After a couple of deep breaths she exited the car, crossed the street, and climbed the few steps to the front door of Holcombe & Reed, Attorneys-at-Law. She was finally entering the building that she hoped contained answers to her many questions.

"May I help you?" the receptionist pleasantly asked Claudia.

"I'm here to see Mr. Reed."

"Do you have an appointment?"

"No, I don't," Claudia admitted. "But it is extremely important that I see him."

"I'm afraid Mr. Reed is not in the office at the moment. Would you like to speak with his secretary?"

"That would be fine."

"May I have your name?"

"Claudia Duval."

Law offices of Holcombe & Reed, Jackson, Tennessee

"There's a lady here to see Jake," the receptionist told Madge Mayfield, "but she doesn't have an appointment."

Madge frowned. "Did you tell her Jake isn't here?"

"I did, but she said it's urgent that she see him. When I told her he wasn't in, she asked to speak with you."

"Did she tell you her name?"

"Claudia Duval."

"Claudia Duval," Madge repeated, running the name through her memory bank. "That name doesn't ring a bell with me. I'll go up front with you and find out why she needs to see Jake."

When Madge opened the door to the lobby, the woman who was waiting looked up. Immediately Madge caught her distraught expression.

"Ms. Duval," Madge said calmly as she crossed the lobby, "my name is Madge Mayfield. I'm Mr. Reed's secretary. Is there something I can help you with?"

Claudia stood as Madge approached. "I really need to see Mr. Reed. I have something to give him."

"I'll be glad to give it to him for you," Madge offered.

"I really need to give it to him personally. Do you know when he'll be back in the office?"

"I don't know when he'll be back. He's had an illness in the family, and he may be out for several days." Madge wasn't about to tell this mysterious woman what had really happened to Courtney. "Do you mind telling me what this is about?"

"I wish I knew. All I know is that a friend of mine passed away a couple of days ago, and his dying request was for me to deliver a package to Mr. Reed. He said it had something to do with a group called the Federalists."

Madge bantered with the idea of telling Claudia to come back on a later day, but something inside convinced her otherwise. "If you'll excuse me, I'll try to call Mr. Reed."

"I really appreciate it," Claudia replied, appearing relieved. "You don't know how important this is to me."

Jackson-Madison County General Hospital, Jackson, Tennessee

Courtney was sitting up in bed drinking a can of Sprite through a straw and eating a serving of fruit when Jake returned from his meeting with Naomi. Rachel was sitting in the green vinyl chair near the window.

"Hi, Daddy," Courtney said cheerfully as Jake entered the room.

"Hi, sweetheart. You appear to be feeling better."

"I am," Courtney replied. "I can't wait to go home."

"I can't wait either," Jake said. "Perhaps the doctor will say it will be OK to go home tomorrow."

"I hope so," Courtney replied.

"Let's not rush things," Rachel cautioned. "She needs to get as much rest as possible, and this is probably a better place to do that than at home."

Before Courtney or Jake could respond, the telephone on the bedside table rang loudly.

Startled, Jake grabbed the receiver from its cradle before the second ring. "Hello," he said as he raised the receiver to his ear.

"Jake, this is Madge. I hate to bother you."

"It's OK. Courtney is feeling better, and we might get to go home tomorrow." He winked at Courtney and directed a sly smile at Rachel. "What's going on at the office?"

"That's why I called. There's a woman named Claudia Duval in the lobby. She said she has a package for you, and all she could tell me was that it had something to do with a group called the Federalists—"

"Did you say *Federalists?*" Jake interrupted.

"That's what she said. Does that mean something to you?"

"It might." Jake remembered that the documents he received from Earline Thompson contained references to an entity called the Federalists, but that name hadn't really meant anything to him . . . until now.

If this lady knows something about the Federalists, she might also know something about who murdered Jesse Thompson. And, more importantly, she might know something about who attacked Courtney.

"Is she still there?" Jake asked.

"Yes. She's in the lobby."

"Don't let her leave. I'll be there in a few minutes." Jake hung up the phone and turned to Rachel. "I need to go to the office. Someone is there to see me, and it might have something to do with Jed's case." He caught

Rachel's eyes, attempting to send a message between his words—that this visitor in the office might have something to do with who attacked Courtney. "I'll be back in a little while," he said as he left the room.

"I'm going to my office," he announced to the sheriff's deputy stationed outside Courtney's room. "I have a meeting in fifteen minutes."

Jake watched as the deputy relayed the information over his radio to the patrol car in the hospital parking lot. "Deputy Laymon is outside," he told Jake. "He'll escort you to your office."

Law offices of Holcombe & Reed, Jackson, Tennessee

The drive from the hospital to Jake's office downtown typically took ten minutes. With Deputy Laymon's escort, Jake made the drive in seven minutes flat. He slid the Volvo to a stop in his customary parking space and darted through the back door to the office and directly to Madge's desk. The deputy remained in his patrol car in the rear parking lot.

"Where is she?" Jake asked before Madge had an opportunity to volunteer the information.

"I put her in the front conference room and gave her a soft drink. She's waiting on you there."

Jake took two cleansing breaths and walked calmly up the narrow hallway to the spacious conference room across the hall from the front lobby. Jake knew that in the building's previous life as a funeral home, this room had been used as a bereavement room for ministers to meet with distraught members of the deceased family.

"Ms. Duval," Jake said as he entered the room. "I'm Jake Reed."

A glimmer of a smile appeared on the woman's face. But she certainly appeared to be under stress.

He took a seat nearest her. "My secretary said you need to see me."

"That's right, Mr. Reed."

"Please, call me Jake."

"All right, Jake. Please call me Claudia. I have a package that a dear friend of mine asked me to deliver to you. He's dead now, and his last request to me was to make sure you received this package."

"Who was it?"

"I knew him as Hudson Kinney. But his real name was Milton McAdams."

Jake attempted to register either of those names with any matches in his memory bank. "I don't recognize either of those names, Claudia. I'm sorry."

"Did you hear about the man who was struck and killed by a cab in Times Square a few nights ago?"

"I vaguely remember seeing something about that on the news."

"That was Hudson—I'm sorry—Milton."

"All right." Jake nodded. "But what does that have to do with me?"

"Before he died, Milton wrote a letter to me, and in it he said he was involved in something terrible that he couldn't describe. He also told me that I should bring the contents of a locker at the airport in Atlanta to you." She handed a manila envelope to Jake.

Jake took the envelope, noticing that it felt like it contained a video. The envelope was addressed to him. His anticipation grew as he slid his index finger into the crease of the flap and ripped through the top of the envelope. He removed the videotape and laid it on the table. He and Claudia both stared at it for several seconds before either spoke.

"Mr. Reed . . . *Jake*," she corrected herself, "Hudson, or Milton, or whatever his name, was more than a friend to me. He was my entire life. When he died, a part of me died too. But now I need to move on, and I can't do that until I put this whole ordeal behind me. The reason I'm telling you this is because I want to watch this tape with you."

"I don't know, Claudia. There may be some things on the tape that you don't need to see."

"Please, Jake," she begged. "I've been through quite a lot of turmoil the last few days. Just today I've been chased by the FBI—twice—and I was almost shot not more than two hours ago. My life has been turned upside down. I really need some answers, and I think seeing what's on this tape will help me with that."

Jake studied Claudia's face. He could tell she was hurting. Yet other than what she had told him in the last ten minutes, he knew nothing about her. He didn't know where she had come from or where she was going. But he felt a connection to her. He felt drawn to her. Like fate had brought the two of them together at this point in time for some purpose greater than both of them. It didn't matter what was on that tape. If she wanted to see it, then so be it. Who was he to stop her?

"All right, Claudia. We'll watch it together."

Jake stood and made his way around the end of the table to the bookcases on the other side of the room. A twenty-seven-inch television connected to a VCR sat on the shelf that separated the bookcases above from the cabinets below. He pressed the Power button and fed the mysterious tape into the mouth of the VCR. Then he retreated to his seat, with the remote control in hand.

The screen flickered, and then the face of Milton McAdams appeared. Claudia began to cry quietly. The image of Milton was only from the waist up, and he sat behind an executive-type desk in an office somewhere. After a couple of seconds of silence, Milton began to speak into the camera.

"My name is Milton Hawthorne McAdams. Mr. Reed, if you're watching this, then it is safe to assume that I'm dead." Milton grimaced at the thought of his own mortality. "Claudia, my dear, if you are there, I want to tell you how truly sorry I am that I have put you through all this."

Claudia's crying increased in volume, but Jake refrained from intruding on her privacy.

"I've made some mistakes in my life," Milton said, "and I'll have to pay the price for them. My only hope is that you, Claudia, are not forced to pay for them as well." Milton stared somberly into the camera for several seconds before continuing.

"Mr. Reed," Milton continued, "I'm a partner with two other men. Their names are Pierce Montgomery and Randolph Winston. The name of our partnership is the Federalists. What I'm about to tell you will surprise and shock you, but every word of it is true. Please use this information as you see fit. I don't care what you do with it. It can't harm me since I'm already dead." Milton smirked slightly at the morbid humor. "The reason this information is important to you is because it will help you prove the innocence of your client, Jedediah McClellan. You see, my two partners and I ordered the assassination of Jesse Thompson. Your client had nothing to do with it. But I'm getting ahead of myself. Let me start from the beginning . . ."

For forty-five minutes Milton bared his soul. He described how the Federalists came into existence. He talked about the relationship with Edward Burke, the fund-raising scheme, and, most importantly to Jake, the murder of Jesse Thompson. He explained the Federalists' plan to take over the world. Milton didn't leave a single stone unturned.

"One last thing, Mr. Reed. You need to be careful. Randolph Winston is ruthless, and he will not let anything stand in his way of obtaining world supremacy. He will kill you if he has to."

When Milton paused, as if to emphasize his last statement, Jake understood the warning.

Milton concluded by stating, "Good-bye, Mr. Reed. I hope you are able to use what I have told you. Claudia, if you're still there, good-bye, and remember that I love you. You are the only woman I have ever truly loved . . . and I wanted to spend the rest of my life by your side."

When the screen went to static, Jake pressed the Off button and laid the remote on the table. He and Claudia didn't speak during Milton's tape, and Jake didn't know what to say now. True to Milton's prediction, Jake *was* both shocked and stunned. He'd known it wasn't Jed who had killed Jesse Thompson, but he'd never dreamed the murder was part of such an elaborate scheme as the one described by Milton McAdams.

He leaned back in his chair and studied Claudia. Had the videotape of Milton provided the answers she needed so desperately? Her gaze was still fixed on the television screen.

"Claudia, do you have somewhere to stay tonight?" Jake asked, suddenly feeling a depth of compassion he didn't know he had.

She turned her head from the empty television screen toward the sound of Jake's voice. "No, but I'll be all right."

"I'll be glad to help arrange a place for you to stay. You need to rest after the day you've had."

"That's very generous, but I don't think it will be necessary."

Although he'd only met her an hour ago, somehow he felt her pain, her uncertainty, her confusion. And he was concerned. "What are you going to do? Where are you going to go?"

She took a shaky breath. "I'm not sure what I'm going to do right now, but I'll be fine . . . really."

"Are you sure? Because based on what Milton said, it seems that your safety may be in jeopardy."

"I don't think it can be in any more jeopardy than I've already experienced today." Claudia smiled slightly, as if trying to lighten the serious situation.

Jake smiled too. If all she said was true, then she was right.

"Seriously," Claudia continued. "I'll be fine. I think I'm going to go home."

How well Jake understood the draw of home. He escorted her to the front door, thanked her for coming so far to bring him the tape, and said good-bye. He watched as she crossed the street and departed in her silver Infiniti Q45.

Then he retreated to the conference room and rewound the tape of Milton McAdams. He watched a few minutes of it again, trying to piece everything together. The F-PAC documents. Ms. Lacy's photographs. The note beside Courtney's bed. The videotape. The things Milton McAdams described caused Jake to shiver as the reality of it all began to sink in.

If the remaining Federalists find out that I have this tape, they'll kill me. Or, worse, they'll kill my family.

Jake's gut instinct was to take the tape of Milton and destroy it. But he couldn't. If Milton McAdams was telling the truth—and Jake was convinced he was—then Jake had to do what he could to stop the Federalists and their evil plan. But how?

He stopped the tape, rewound it to the beginning again, and ejected it from the VCR. Tape in hand, he returned to his office.

"Madge," he called, "hold all my calls."

"OK. What did Ms. Duval want to see you about?"

"I can't tell you right now," he replied as he started to close the door to his office.

"Was it about Jed McClellan?" she inquired.

He closed the door, pretending not to hear her last question. Removing a few books from the bookcase behind his desk, he exposed a small wall safe. Only he and Barrett knew it existed. He spun the combination lock until the door opened and then placed Milton McAdams's video safely inside.

"She's leaving Reed's office now," Saul Sanders heard Agent Osborne say. Saul was in his office at his house, receiving regular updates from Osborne and Moyers. Guessing that Claudia would head to Jake Reed's office, Saul had directed the two agents to conduct a stakeout at Jake's office. They had been in position less than an hour when his hunch paid off.

"She's empty-handed," Bill continued. "I don't see either of the packages she retrieved from the Atlanta airport."

"I bet she left them with Reed," Saul replied. "Those packages are more important than she is right now. Stay out of sight, and tonight see if you can find them. We'll take care of Ms. Duval later."

Saul knew it was a gamble to let Claudia escape, but a calculated one. He guessed that the packages were delivered to Jake Reed, and Claudia Duval was no longer an immediate threat. The damage to Burke and Randolph—and to Saul himself—was contained in what he believed Claudia left with Attorney Reed.

Saul knew he had failed Randolph miserably up to this point by allowing Claudia to reach her destination. His only hope of redemption was in locating and delivering to Randolph the mysterious packages.

After he hung up with Bill, Saul slowly opened the bottom right-hand drawer of his desk and removed a bottle of liquor he kept for moments such as this.

CHAPTER THIRTY-SIX

Law offices of Holcombe & Reed, Jackson, Tennessee

After the video was secure, Jake thought about the information he now possessed and became enraged. He wanted to scream at someone, or hit someone, because of the terror they had made his daughter go through. The problem was that he didn't know who to hit. Then Jake remembered that the only person he had given a copy of the bank documents and the photographs to was Drake Highfill. That meant Drake must have a connection.

Jake dialed the number for the district attorney's office. "This is Jake Reed for Drake Highfill," he said when the receptionist answered the telephone.

"Hold a moment," she replied.

In a couple of seconds Drake Highfill was on the other end of the line. "Jake, what can I do for you?"

"I suppose you heard that my daughter is in the hospital?"

"I heard about that from Sheriff West. How's she doing?"

"She's going to be OK," Jake replied, and then it was time for the attack. "You realize it's your fault?"

"My fault?!"

Jake could hear the surprise in the usually obnoxious attorney's voice.

"How's it my fault?" Drake nearly screeched.

"You're the only person to whom I gave the photographs and a copy of the documents from Jesse Thompson's bank. The animal that attacked my daughter left a note saying if I told anyone what I knew, then the next time I wouldn't be so lucky. Who do you think told him that I knew something about the murder?" The rage in Jake's voice began to build.

"I don't know," came Drake's meek defense.

"I do. It was you. You told him, didn't you, Drake?"

"I didn't tell anyone," Drake insisted. But there was a quiver in his voice.

Jake went in for the kill. "I don't believe you. There's no other explanation than the fact that you told someone. Was it Vice President Burke? Was that who it was?"

Drake did not respond.

"It doesn't matter," Jake continued. "Whoever it is, I want you to tell them something else. Tell them that it takes a real big man to attack a little girl. Bunch of cowards. They wouldn't come after me. They had to attack my daughter. And you can tell them something else. Tell them I know about their secret."

"What are you talking about, Jake?" The old haughty Drake was back. "Why don't you just settle down and go home and rest for a while? It's obvious that the attack on your daughter is making you crazy."

"I'm not crazy. I've never been saner. You call whoever you talked to before and tell them that I know all about the Federalists and their arrangement with Ed Burke. They'll know what I'm talking about. And you tell them to call me immediately. I want to meet the person who would attack an innocent, defenseless nine-year-old girl."

"Jake, you're crazy. I don't have any idea what you're talking about."

"I didn't expect you to admit to it, Drake. You just do what I told you."

Jake slammed the phone down without saying good-bye, leaned back in his chair, and took a deep breath. He'd wanted to scream at someone all day, and Drake Highfill was definitely a deserving recipient.

The Lowell Thomas State Office Building, Jackson, Tennessee

Drake Highfill wiped the cold sweat from his forehead as he replaced the telephone receiver. The palms of his hands were clammy, and both arms were shaking nervously from the startling revelation he'd just received from Jake Reed. Jake was right. His phone call to Vice President Burke had started the chain of events that had resulted in the attack on Courtney Reed. Now Drake was in too deep, and he knew it. He could only think of one thing to do, and that was to call Ed Burke and tell him about his conversation with Jake Reed. He calmed himself for a few more minutes and then dialed the number he had been given to reach Vice President Burke.

Ben Tobias answered.

En route to New York City

Ed Burke and his campaign staff were thirty thousand feet above central Kentucky on their way to a campaign rally in New York City. Ed still wanted to steal the state from Mac Foster. He was sitting with Ben Tobias in his private cabin in the rear of the jumbo 747.

Just then Ben's phone rang, and he answered it. Clasping the phone with both hands so the person on the other end of the line couldn't hear his conversation with Ed, Ben said quietly, "Drake Highfill is on the phone. Do you want to talk with him?"

Ed remembered Randolph's admonishment and thought for a minute about not taking the call, then decided he needed to. Based on his last conversation with Drake, he knew Drake wouldn't call unless it was important.

"I'll talk to him." Ed reached for the telephone. "Drake," he boomed into the receiver, "is everything OK down there in Jackson?"

"I don't know, sir," Drake admitted. "I just received a very strange telephone call from Jake Reed. Perhaps you can make some sense of it."

"What did he say?"

Drake gave a verbatim account of his conversation with Jake Reed. The color left Ed's face when Drake mentioned his name and the Federalists in the same sentence.

"Did he say why he wanted someone to call him?" Ed asked after Drake finished.

"No, sir. He didn't. Just that he wanted to talk to the person who had attacked his daughter."

Ed wasn't certain, but he assumed Randolph had hired someone to scare Attorney Reed. If so, Randolph had made a tactical mistake. The attack had caused just the opposite reaction. Now Jake Reed was on the offensive. He was attacking rather than backing down. Ed couldn't afford to allow Jake to make random telephone calls like the one he'd just made to Drake Highfill. He didn't need any bad press this close to the election.

"I'll take care of him," Ed advised. "And Drake, don't say anything to anyone about this. I'll handle it."

"What was that all about?" Ben asked when Ed terminated the call.

"There are a lot of things going on that I haven't told you about, Ben. And I don't have time to discuss it with you now."

Ben's brows furrowed. "Ed, you've got to tell me!"

"After the election, Ben. After the election. Now, if you'll excuse me, I need to make a phone call."

Ben was astounded, and his face tensed. "You want me to leave?"

"That's exactly what I want you to do. I'll tell you all about it after the election."

Ed watched as Ben slung the stack of reports he was working on into the seat beside him and stormed out the door into the main cabin of the airplane. He slammed the door as he left, and Ed locked it from the inside.

After Ben left, Ed was alone in the rear cabin. He wasn't prepared to handle this type of situation. If he called Attorney Reed, that would be an admission of his involvement with the Federalists, because Jake would know that Highfill had called Ed. If he didn't call, then Reed might contact the media, or worse, the Republicans, and that was the last thing Ed needed. Ed was certain of one thing, though. Attorney Reed had damaging information that had to be neutralized. As much as he despised the thought, the only real option was to call Randolph.

Apollyon Associates, Inc., lower Manhattan

All Randolph's time was now spent confined in his office at Apollyon headquarters in Manhattan. He hadn't been to his own home since the night Milton was murdered. He had eaten some and slept even less. He knew that whatever Milton left for Claudia had made it to Attorney Reed because of the incompetence of Saul Sanders and his agents. But he also knew that Edward Burke was comfortably ahead in the race for the White

House. The pressure from both realizations weighed on him, and he looked haggard from the wear of it. Of the two, what drove Randolph more was the conviction that, at all costs, Burke had to win.

The prohibition against Burke calling Randolph directly had long since been repealed, so Randolph wasn't surprised to find Ed on the other end of the call that rang into his private line early Friday evening.

"Randolph, I've received some troubling news from my contact in Jackson. He told me that someone attacked Attorney Reed's daughter. Do you know anything about that?"

Randolph was too exhausted to disguise the truth from Ed any longer. "Somewhat," he replied. "I ordered that Reed be neutralized, but I didn't specifically direct how it was to be carried out."

"Well, you may have awakened a sleeping giant."

"How so?"

"I know you told me not to talk to Drake Highfill anymore, but I just took a call from him. He said Reed called him and said he knew all about the Federalists and my arrangement with you. He didn't say how he knew, but he was insistent that we had something to do with the attack on his daughter. Whatever he knows is dangerous, and we must do something before he goes to the media."

"Everything is under control, Edward," assured Randolph. "Don't you do anything. I'll handle it."

"Just like you've handled everything else, Randolph?" Ed quipped.

"What is that supposed to mean?" Randolph's voice was icy.

"It means that I'm tired of the way you 'handle' things. If you had simply left Reed alone, he would have never realized the importance of the information he obtained from Jesse Thompson's widow, and we would not be in this mess. But now he knows that it's as valuable as gold, and he intends to use it."

His own exhaustion and Ed's insolence caused Randolph to react in a way entirely out of character. His comments were usually calculated and carefully selected. But he was beginning to detest Edward Burke as much as Ed detested him.

The words simply came out. "Just like Thompson tried to do."

"What are you talking about, Randolph?"

"Thompson tried to use the connection between the Federalists and you for his own gain, and it cost him. He was skimming money from our F-PAC accounts at his bank and tried to extort twenty million from us to keep our connection with you a secret. We couldn't let that happen."

"You mean that you had Jesse Thompson killed?"

"Not just me. Pierce and Milton were involved."

"And Milton?"

"I did that one all by myself," Randolph bragged.

"You idiot!" Ed screamed. "Are you insane? Don't you see what you've done and what you've caused me to become? I'm an accomplice to murder."

"Don't act naive with me, Ed. You knew this was a dangerous game when you decided to play it. We're ten days away from world supremacy. Isn't that what you wanted? Isn't that why you jumped at our offer to buy the presidency for you? So don't act like this is some great revelation. All the obstacles to our goal have been eliminated, and that is exactly what you wanted."

"But I didn't know one of those 'obstacles' would be my friend."

"Is that melancholy in your voice, Edward?" Randolph asked sarcastically, but his voice quickly changed to anger. "You're as weak as Milton, and I can't tolerate weakness. If I didn't need a puppet in the White House, you would be the next to go. It seems as though Mr. Reed will get that distinction, though."

"You can't continue to kill people. That road will eventually lead back to us."

"By then it will be too late. You'll be president, and I'll be untouchable."

"This is not what I bargained for, and I'm getting out. I'm going to withdraw from the race. That is the only way to stop you."

"That's very noble," came Randolph's sarcastic response. "But you're not going to withdraw. It would take someone with courage to take such an action, and you don't have any. You don't think I chose you because you were strong, do you? You were selected because of your weakness. Because you could be manipulated and bought and corrupted. And besides, if you do withdraw, it will mean certain death for you, your wife, your family, and everyone around you. I've planned for every contingency, Edward, including the possibility that you might get nervous one day. No, you're not going to withdraw. You're going to do exactly what I tell you to do. And I'm telling you that you're going to continue just like this conversation never took place. Do you understand me?"

Intentionally, Randolph used a tone of voice that one would use if giving instructions to a wayward child. Randolph knew Ed would respond accordingly. And he was right.

"I understand, Randolph," a weak voice said, "but I don't like it."

"I don't care if you like it. Just do what you're told."

Randolph slammed the phone in Ed's ear.

En route to New York City

Ed slowly closed the lid on Ben's wireless telephone. He tossed the phone on the leather seat across from him and rubbed his face and hands with his palms. For a moment the only decent ounce in Ed emerged, and he thought of calling Jake Reed to warn him of Randolph's impending assault.

But the urge soon evaporated. Instead he sat there, thirty thousand feet above the earth's surface, feeling sorry for himself.

FBI headquarters, Washington DC

Saul Sanders shook the glass tumbler that a few seconds earlier was filled with an imported Scotch, and the slightly melted cubes of ice rattled against the side of the glass, and each other. It was the third such glass he had converted to empty in the last fifteen minutes, and the bottle was still over half full.

Earlier in the day he had felt victorious over his nemesis, Charlie Armacost. But now one of his most loyal agents was dead at the hands of Armacost's subordinates. Although he still had two agents in place, he had not been able to prevent Claudia Duval from reaching Jake Reed.

He had failed. Worse, he had failed Randolph Winston. Randolph was ruthless, and Saul knew it would not be long before he would pay for his failure. Just as Jesse Thompson, Milton McAdams, and undoubtedly countless others had paid for theirs.

Saul filled a fourth glass when the startling sound of his telephone ringing caused him to slosh some of the intoxicating liquid onto the top of his desk.

It could only be Randolph, Saul knew. So he sipped his Scotch, staring at the phone, not wanting to answer it. Perhaps if he avoided it, reality would never find him. He knew, though, that inevitably he would have to face Randolph, or someone hired by Randolph, so he lifted the receiver from its cradle after the fourth ring.

Apollyon Associates, Inc., lower Manhattan

After his telephone conversation with Ed Burke, Randolph made his next move quickly, dialing the number for Saul Sanders. Saul's incompetence was virtually unbearable to Randolph, but he still needed him. At least for now. Saul's wages for his incompetence would come after the election, Randolph decided, and he relished the thought of it.

"Saul," Randolph began in much the same condescending tone of voice he'd used with Ed. "You've disappointed me. I just got off the phone with Burke, and he told me that Reed now has enough information to link Burke with me. We don't know what it is, but obviously the information came from Milton in the package delivered by Claudia Duval. Do you understand how grave the situation has become?"

"I understand," Saul replied meekly.

"I can't tolerate failure, Saul. Not only did you allow Ms. Duval to arrive at Jake Reed's doorstep safely, but apparently, you did a poor job of scaring Reed. Otherwise, he would never have told anyone about the Federalists. Your services are unacceptable."

He paused to see if Saul would try to defend himself.

There was only silence on the other end of the line.

"But I'm going to give you an opportunity for redemption," Randolph said magnanimously.

"What is it, Randolph?" Saul asked.

Randolph heard the mixture of hope and anxiety in Saul's voice.

"Let's be certain of one thing. I cannot tolerate any more mistakes. If you fail me this time, there'll be no more chances."

The only way to convince Saul to carry out this final assignment would be to give him hope, as false as it might be, that all would be forgiven, Randolph thought.

"I'll do whatever you need me to do," Saul replied. "I realize the importance of Burke's being elected, for all our sakes. Just tell me what it is you need."

"Reed must be eliminated, and it must be done immediately. Whatever Milton left with that woman made its way to Reed, and he intends to use it against us. I can't let that happen. Whatever it takes, I want Reed eliminated."

"I'll take care of it," Saul responded confidently. "I still have assets in place, but if I have to, I'll handle it personally. Don't worry, Randolph, I'll take care of it."

Randolph knew this would be Saul's last assignment for him. Soon, after Burke's election, he would arrange for Saul's demise. It had taken years to assemble the resources for Saul's destruction, but Randolph maintained a few key contacts of his own.

At some point in the not-too-distant future, Saul would be met with an untimely heart attack, a mysterious one-car accident, or perhaps a "self-inflicted" gunshot wound. How it happened wouldn't matter to Randolph. Only that it was done, and that a failure had received his reward.

As he ended the call with Saul, Randolph smiled at how easy it had been to manipulate Saul into complying with his need to eliminate Jake Reed. Saul would do whatever it took to kill Reed, simply because Randolph wanted it done. The FBI director's loyalty was now driven by a desire to survive.

And Randolph knew that was the greatest motivation of all.

CHAPTER THIRTY-SEVEN

En route to Mount Pleasant, Mississippi

The drive from Jackson through the autumn-colored terrain of southern Tennessee and north Mississippi to the sleepy community of Mount Pleasant, took Claudia almost an hour and a half, but it was worth every second.

She stopped in front of the red-brick, ranch-style house. It was just as Claudia remembered it. The small, covered front porch, the one-car carport, the faded brown shutters. Fifteen years ago they meant something completely different to her, but now they evoked emotions in her that she never thought she would feel again. Two grand oak trees and a tall pine tree watched over the small house from the backyard, beckoning her closer.

The gravel and sand crackled beneath the slow-rolling tires as her car crept down the driveway and stopped behind her mother's car.

Claudia put the car in park and sat there, soaking in the beauty of something old that was now a new beginning. After several minutes she overcame her emotions, exited the car, and walked to the door. The distance was only about twenty feet, but it had taken her fifteen years to walk it.

"Mother, it's Claudia," she said as she opened the door and walked in without knocking. She was finally home.

Jackson, Tennessee

Agent Simon arrived in Jackson an hour after Claudia Duval had left and began his systematic search for her. His first stop was the Holcombe

& Reed offices. Not seeing her rental car parked anywhere nearby, he checked the parking lots of several hotels on the off chance she might still be in town. Without the manpower that came with a full-blown investigation, he knew his chances of locating her were slim. Officially there was no investigation, and it was incumbent on him to tarry alone in the search for the mysterious woman, and Osborne and Moyers.

He also checked the McKellar-Sipes Regional Airport to see if the Bureau airplane assigned to Saul Sanders was still there. It wasn't. He checked with the rental-car companies at the airport to see if any employee recalled seeing two men matching his description of Osborne and Moyers. The desk clerk at the Enterprise counter recalled renting a blue Chrysler Concorde to someone matching the description of Bill Osborne. After Jerry flashed his FBI credentials, the clerk gave him the car's tag number, and with that lead Jerry began searching Jackson for their rental car. Again, a slim chance of success.

By midnight he was exhausted and needed a place to rest. Although he still had the key to the old jewelry store, and the rent was paid, he couldn't afford to be seen there. Any activity at the old jewelry store would be certain to arouse suspicion. So he checked into Room 125 at the Sunset Motel on Highway 412. It was off the beaten path, and he used his fake identification when he registered to make sure no one could identify him. Safely in the room, he called Charlie Armacost and George McCullough.

"No sign of the woman, or Osborne and Moyers," Jerry advised when Charlie answered with his speaker phone.

"Sanders's plane returned to Langley at seven fifteen eastern time," George added to the conversation. "But the only person on board was the pilot. He wouldn't talk to any of our people about where he had been. I'm sure Sanders had already warned him about talking. If we assume that he took Osborne and Moyers to Jackson, then they're still there."

"I agree," Charlie said. "If we're right, that means they still haven't found what they're looking for. But what is it? If she's nowhere to be found, then she either must have given whatever it is to Reed or at least told him about it. I think we have no choice but for you to talk to Reed. You've got to convince him that he must turn it over to you, and you've got to talk to him before Osborne and Moyers do."

"I agree," Jerry replied. "I'll get some rest tonight; then I'll locate Reed in the morning. I just hope we're not too late."

"Me too," Charlie responded. "Me too."

Henderson, Tennessee

"We searched the entire office and found nothing," Moyers reported to Saul Sanders early the next morning. He and Osborne had retreated to a motel in Henderson, fifteen miles south of Jackson. Based on the reports they received from Memphis and Saul, they knew that Charlie Armacost would have agents looking for them. Staying in Jackson was out of the question.

"We were in the building for almost four hours last night," Al Moyers continued. "We looked in every desk, every filing cabinet, and every closet, and we didn't find anything that resembled the packages we saw her with at Hartsfield."

"Perhaps he took them out of the building," Sanders suggested.

"I don't think so," Bill replied. "We watched him when he left yesterday afternoon for that very purpose, and he didn't have anything in his hands. Either she didn't give him anything, or he's got it hidden better than we think."

"The packages have got to be there," Sanders reasoned. "It doesn't make sense for her to go all that way and not give one or both of the packages to Reed. Besides, Reed told Burke's contact that he had something linking Burke with the Federalists. That call came in after she left his office. That's too coincidental. He wouldn't have called if he didn't have something, and it had to come from Ms. Duval."

"We didn't find it, but we'll look again tonight."

"Keep looking until you've searched every square inch of that building. And whether you find anything or not, Winston wants Attorney Reed eliminated."

Reed residence, Jackson, Tennessee

Courtney had been discharged from the hospital shortly after lunch, and Jake was glad to bring her home. Over twenty-four hours in the hospital had been long enough. Jake and Rachel helped Courtney as she gingerly walked up the short flight of steps into the house.

"Jake, someone's pulling into the drive," Rachel said.

Jake turned and saw the two cars as they approached. "You go ahead and get Courtney settled," he told Rachel. "I'll see what's going on."

Jake could see Deputy Butch Johnson and another man as they exited their respective vehicles simultaneously and walked toward him.

Jake emerged from the garage. "What's going on, Butch?"

"This guy is with the FBI," Butch announced. "He said he needs to talk with you. We checked him out, and everything came back legit."

"I'm Special Agent Jerry Simon with the FBI," the man said as he unfolded his credentials and showed Jake his identification badge.

Jake bristled immediately. "FBI? What do you want?"

Ever since Jake had discovered his office was bugged, he'd had little use for the FBI.

"Mr. Reed, we know that a woman visited you yesterday with vital information that may have an impact on the outcome of the presidential election."

Jake rested his foot on the rear bumper of his car and crossed his arms over his chest. "I don't know what you're talking about," he said defiantly.

"Are you denying that she was in your office yesterday?"

"I can't tell you when, or if, a client visits my office. That would violate attorney-client confidentiality."

"Let's cut to the chase, Mr. Reed. We have reason to believe that you have possession of information that is pertinent to an ongoing investigation. I'm demanding that you turn that information over to me immediately."

Jake still didn't know whom he could trust. His intuition was that this visit from an FBI agent was in response to his phone call to Drake Highfill yesterday afternoon. If he was correct, there was no way Jake would give him the tape.

"Do you have a search warrant, Agent Simon?" Jake knew he didn't and knew he couldn't get one. It was Saturday, and the agent would have a difficult time finding a judge who would sign the warrant, particularly since Jake hadn't committed a crime.

"Don't be foolish, Mr. Reed. You're in over your head. Look at what happened to your daughter," Simon said, waving his hand at Jake's house. "They'll do worse than that if they think you can do anything to interfere with their plan. These men are ruthless. If you help us, we'll make sure you and your family are protected."

Jake planted his feet firmly on the ground in an immovable stance. "How do I know you're not the one who terrorized my daughter?"

"You don't. But do you think I'd be standing here talking with you about this if I had been?" The agent paused. "Let's be honest with each other, Mr. Reed. We both know that you have something I need. The question is whether you're going to give it to me or not."

Jake almost relented. Almost.

But his haunting distrust of the FBI wouldn't let him comply with the agent's request. After all, the FBI had bugged his office, and based on what Claudia had said, they had also kept her under surveillance for weeks. And worse, had almost killed her. The answer was no, Jake told himself. There was no way he could entrust the Milton McAdams tape to the FBI. The tape was too important.

"Like I told you when this conversation started, Agent Simon, I don't know what you're talking about. I don't have possession of anything that might be of interest to you. So, if you'll excuse me, I need to go inside and check on my daughter." He turned to Deputy Johnson. "Butch, get this guy off my property."

Jake turned his back on Agent Simon and began walking toward the door that led from the garage into the house.

"You're making a big mistake," Simon called as Jake pressed the button that operated the garage door. It began to descend, blocking Simon from entering the garage. Simon crouched as the door lowered and shouted at Jake one last time. "You're making a big mistake!"

CHAPTER THIRTY-EIGHT

In the vicinity of Jackson, Tennessee

The owner of the used-car lot walked toward Osborne and Moyers when they exited their rental car. He slid a cigarette from the pack in his shirt pocket, lit it, and smiled slyly as he approached.

This transaction would be easier than Bill first thought.

"You guys looking for anything in particular?" the owner asked in an exaggerated Southern drawl.

"My son's sixteenth birthday is this weekend," Bill replied. "And my friend here is helping me look for a pickup for him."

He and Al had visited virtually every used-car lot within a fifteen-mile radius of Jackson over the weekend looking for a truck that would fit their needs. Late Sunday afternoon they had spotted the navy Chevrolet Silverado truck with tinted windows for sale at this used-car lot. The business was closed, so they had contemplated simply stealing it. But that would have meant that the police would be looking for it, and they didn't need to take that chance. They'd decided to come back during business hours and use some of the Bureau's money to purchase it.

"How much do you want for this truck?" Bill asked. He walked slowly around the outside of the vehicle, as if he were actually inspecting it. Yet he and Al already knew it contained a modified engine for increased horsepower, and that was all that mattered to them.

"That one may have too much muscle for your boy," the owner warned.

"You let me worry about that," Bill quipped. "Just tell me how much."

"Five thousand dollars," the owner responded.

"Do you take cash?"

"I like that even better," the owner said with a smile.

Bill gave a fictitious name for the title and registration. The processing of paperwork by used-car dealers was notoriously slow, and by the time the fiction was discovered, it would be too late. Within thirty minutes of arriving at the lot, the two agents were on their way with the last item they needed to eliminate Jake Reed.

Law offices of Holcombe & Reed, Jackson, Tennessee

Jake went to the office late Monday afternoon to check the mail and return a few phone calls. He stayed well past sundown, dictating replies to correspondence that had come in while he was out attending to Courtney. The rest of the staff, including Barrett, left well before he did.

"I've got about five more minutes of dictation," he informed Rachel when she called to check on him. "Then I'll be on my way home."

"Be careful," Rachel admonished.

"I will. Butch Johnson is waiting in the parking lot to follow me home."

"All right. I'll see you in a few minutes."

Jake finished his dictation, turned out the lights, set the alarm system, and exited the office for his car. He waved at Deputy Johnson, who sat in his patrol car at the entrance to the parking lot. When the headlights on the patrol car flashed, Jake knew Deputy Johnson saw him.

Jake could faintly see his breath in the dark autumn sky as he exhaled and opened the car door. The heated seats in his Volvo were finally needed. He slid his wireless telephone into the mount on the dash and activated the hands-free option before backing out of his parking space.

Jackson, Tennessee

"That must be the all-clear signal," Moyers said to Osborne. They waited in their newly acquired Silverado in a vacant parking lot a block and a half south of the Holcombe & Reed law offices. He'd seen the red taillights of the patrol car when he flashed his headlights at Jake.

"Reed must be coming out," Al continued. "Let's go."

Bill stomped the accelerator, and the truck sped from the vacant lot toward the Holcombe & Reed offices. The sudden acceleration pressed Al against the seat. Their instructions from Saul Sanders were explicit. Jake Reed had to die.

"That's his car," Al said as he saw Jake's Volvo stopped at the edge of the parking lot, preparing to exit. "We've got to eliminate the deputy first."

The truck slid to a stop beside the patrol car, and Al rapidly fired two muffled shots into the driver's-side window. He saw the deputy try to un-holster his service revolver, but he didn't even have time to scream. The shattered glass from the window covered the deputy. Both rounds from Al's gun had struck him in the head, killing him instantly.

Al knew that Jake couldn't hear the shots just twenty feet away be-cause of the pistol's suppressor, but he knew that Jake had witnessed the entire surreal scene. As Jake's car sped past, the right-side tires on the sidewalk, Al fired two shots. The second shattered the rear window in Jake's car.

"We can't let him get away!" Al screamed. He was thrown against the dashboard at the abrupt change in direction as Bill shoved the transmission into reverse and smashed the accelerator to the floor. Fifty feet later he swung the rear of the truck into the first available alley and simultaneously slammed the transmission into forward.

Jake's fleeing Volvo was barely a block in front of them, and they gave chase.

Jake's first thought, after realizing he was under attack and that Butch Johnson was most likely dead, was to reach the police station or the sheriff's department. Then he realized he was going in the opposite direc-tion from both.

"I've got to lose 'em," he muttered to himself. "Or they'll kill me too!"

He made a hard left turn at the first intersection, even though the light was red, and slid across the oncoming traffic on North Highland Avenue, almost striking a Lincoln Continental broadside.

Behind him, car horns blared as his pursuers evidently made the same maneuver.

"Stay with him!" Moyers yelled. He hung his arm out the passenger-side window and fired two more shots into Jake's car. The first finished off the rear window, and the second lodged in the front passenger's seat.

Jake screamed and tried to duck his head below his seat while keeping it high enough to see through the front windshield. The prey and his pursuers sped north from downtown, and Jake frantically wove in and out of the traffic, sometimes crossing the centerline as he tried to rid himself of his attackers. All to no avail.

Three more shots sounded. Two pierced the trunk of his car, and the third ricocheted off the roof.

The speedometer in Jake's dash pointed at eighty as he approached the intersection of North Highland Avenue and Windy City Road. He glanced over his right shoulder to see how close his attackers were and returned his gaze to the front just in time to see the rear of a Pontiac Grand Am rushing at him. He yanked the steering wheel hard to the right, barely missing the back right corner of the Grand Am, and slid into a right-hand turn onto Windy City Road.

"You idiot!" Jake screamed at himself.

Windy City Road, outside Jackson, Tennessee

"We've got him now," Osborne said. "This road leads out of town."

"Ram him!" Moyers yelled as he continued firing shots at Jake's car, trying either to strike Jake or at least one of the tires on his car.

"What?"

"Ram him! Run him off the road!"

Bill accelerated, and the gap between the Silverado and the Volvo narrowed quickly until he was able to ram into the rear of Jake's car.

As soon as Jake realized he'd made a big mistake—traveling away from the safety and protection of the lights and crowds of the city—he frantically dialed *9-1-1* on his wireless telephone.

At that same instant, his Volvo was violently rammed from behind. The force of the blow caused Jake to almost strike his head on the door pillar. The wheels on the right side of his vehicle slid off the pavement onto the shoulder of the road as gravel and dirt scattered wildly behind him. Instinctively he jerked the steering wheel back to the left, and the car resumed its original path. Jake pressed the accelerator as hard as he could, trying to distance himself from his attacker, and finally completed his distressed call to the Emergency 911 dispatcher.

"E 911. What is the nature of your emergency?" a calm voice asked.

"Someone is shooting at me and trying to run me off the road!" Jake screamed at the small microphone affixed to the driver's-side sun visor. He peered in his rearview mirror and realized he had not created much of a cushion between him and his pursuer. The headlights were again drawing closer at a great speed.

"Sir," the female dispatcher began, "can you tell me who you are and where you are?"

"My name is Jake Reed! Please call Sheriff West!" he pleaded. "This is Jake Reed, and I'm heading north on Windy City Road. Please call Sheriff West!" he repeated frantically. He looked in his rearview mirror, and all he could see were headlights. "Here he comes again!"

The truck rammed hard into the rear of Jake's Volvo again. This time Jake could feel the front bumper of the truck lock onto the rear bumper of his car. At speeds greater than 80 mph the assailants' truck began to push Jake's car, and Jake knew he was helpless to prevent it.

"Sir, are you there?" the dispatcher said. "Mr. Reed, can you hear me?"

Jake couldn't respond. His mind tried to force words of distress through his mouth, but no sound resulted. He gripped the steering wheel, trying to control the direction of the car, and the knuckles on each hand turned white from the exertion.

Another shot must have struck his right rear tire, blowing out the rubber. In two short seconds Jake lost the battle for control of the car, and despite his practically standing up on the brake pedal, the Volvo began to veer off the right side of the road. The smell and smoke from rubber burning against asphalt filled the night air as Jake tried unsuccessfully to stop his vehicle.

"Sir, can you hear me? Mr. Reed, talk to me!" the dispatcher said.

The only audible sound Jake finally made was a horrifying scream associated with impending death. Both vehicles were still traveling at a high rate of speed, and in an instant Jake's car was completely off the road. He was being tossed around in the driver's seat, screaming, but caught a glimpse of the shiny steel guardrail to the bridge that traversed the Forked Deer River less than thirty feet in front of him. His only reaction was to jerk the steering wheel to the right, farther away from the road.

Jake's car broke loose from the front of the truck and bounded past the guardrail. He had no hope of stopping.

As the Volvo careened over the embankment to the Forked Deer River, thirty-five feet below, an image of Rachel and his three children appeared in his mind . . .

CHAPTER THIRTY-NINE

E 911 dispatch, Jackson, Tennessee

The Emergency 911 dispatcher heard the last few seconds; then the line went silent. She had heard pleas for assistance on numerous occasions before, always after an accident or crime had occurred. Never had she been listening when the person on the other end of the line died. She lowered her head momentarily before resuming her responsibilities.

"Sheriff's department, come in. Over."

"Sheriff's department, go ahead," replied the night dispatcher.

"This is E 911 dispatch. We had a call from a motorist on Windy City Road. He sounded as though he was run off the road by an assailant, and then the line went dead. He asked for me to call Sheriff West and said his name was Jake Reed."

"Did he say where he was on Windy City Road?"

"Negative. He was only able to tell me he was going north."

"I've got it. We'll send a patrol car."

Windy City Road, outside Jackson, Tennessee

"Look out!" Moyers screamed from the passenger's seat as the truck slid to a noisy and dusty halt just before it, too, would have plunged over the embankment into the Forked Deer River. He and Osborne peered through the front windshield in some disbelief as to how the events had unfolded. They had not intended to push Jake over a bridge, Al knew, but the end result satisfied their need. Their plan had been to shoot him, execution style. Either way, he was dead, and that was all that mattered.

Unable to clearly see Jake's vehicle from this position, and scared to pull any closer to the river's edge, Bill shoved the transmission into reverse and stomped the accelerator. Al bounced around in the passenger side of the truck as it leaped backward onto the asphalt. He nearly slid onto the floor as Bill brought the truck to a screeching stop; then before it came to a complete rest, Bill slammed the transmission into drive and smashed the accelerator again. He stopped in the middle of the Forked Deer River Bridge, and from there Al was able to see only the taillights of Jake's Volvo near the surface of the water. The car was pointing straight down, and within a few seconds the taillights also disappeared from sight.

"It's done, Sanders," Al said when the FBI director answered the call from his wireless phone. "Jake Reed is gone."

"Are you certain?" Sanders inquired.

"As certain as I am about anything. We just watched his car sink to the bottom of a river with him in it. There's no way he survived."

"Good, Al. That's good. That should be the end of our problems."

In the distance Al could hear the faint sound of an approaching siren.

Bill immediately extinguished the exterior lights on the vehicle.

"We've got to go," Al told Sanders.

The two agents drove away from the scene in the opposite direction of the approaching siren, with the headlights off, using only the glow from the full moon to illuminate their path. Soon they were far enough away to turn the lights back on, and they continued until they were safely away from the crime scene and its aftermath.

Reed residence, Jackson, Tennessee

Rachel looked again at the green numbers on the microwave clock in the kitchen. *7:35.* She'd expected Jake fifteen minutes ago, but there was no sign of him.

"I wonder what your daddy's doing?" she playfully asked Jeremy. "We better call and check on him to make sure nothing has happened." She dialed the number for Jake's wireless phone.

"The wireless customer you are trying to reach is not available at this time," the recording began. "Please try your call again later."

"That's strange," she mumbled and pressed the redial button. Again all she heard was the recording.

Windy City Road, outside Jackson, Tennessee

Deputy Billy Laymon drove slowly along Windy City Road, scanning the roadside ditches on both sides with the spotlight affixed to his patrol car. Dispatch had tried to reach Deputy Johnson on his radio but hadn't received a response. Deputy Laymon knew that all on-duty deputies had been mobilized to look for Deputy Johnson and Jake Reed. Since Billy wasn't finding anything, he called back to the dispatcher on the patrol car radio.

"Are you sure 911 said 'Windy City Road'?" he questioned. "'Cause I don't see anything."

"She said Windy City Road," the dispatcher responded. "Keep looking. I'll send another car out to assist."

"Wait a minute. I think I've got something here." Deputy Laymon looked closer at the road. "There are some skid marks in the northbound lane, just south of the bridge. Let me see where they lead."

He drove slowly, following the marks with the headlights of his patrol car, and panning the drainage ditch on the right-hand side of the road with the spotlight. The tread marks were visible for approximately one hundred feet before veering sharply to the right and leaving the roadway.

Deputy Laymon stopped his patrol car at that point and traced the ruts with his spotlight. He had worked enough traffic accidents to be able to estimate the speed of vehicles, and he knew from these markings that the vehicle that made them must have left the roadway at an extremely high rate of speed. When he determined that the ruts led directly toward the bank of the Forked Deer River, his heart sank. The drop down to the water was at least thirty-five feet.

"Dispatch, you better call for paramedics 'cause this car's in the river. And while you're at it, call the sheriff. If this really is Jake Reed, he's gonna want to know."

Holcombe residence, Jackson, Tennessee

"Barrett, this is Rachel. I hate to call you at home."

"You know you can call me anytime," Barrett replied. He was in his kitchen preparing a cup of hot chai tea when Rachel called. "What is it?" he asked as he poured the hot water from the teakettle into a porcelain coffee mug and began stirring.

"It's Jake. He should have been home by now, and I'm worried about him."

"I'm sure everything is all right. Have you tried his wireless phone?"

"I tried but couldn't get an answer."

"When's the last time you heard from him?"

"About an hour ago. I called him at the office, and he said he would be leaving in a few minutes. He should have been home thirty minutes ago."

"He has a deputy with him, doesn't he?"

"He said Deputy Johnson was waiting on him in the parking lot."

"I bet he's OK. Probably stopped somewhere and left his phone in the car. I'll make a few calls and see if I can locate him."

"I appreciate it, Barrett. With everything that's happened, I'm more than a little worried."

"Don't be. I'm sure everything is fine. I'll call you back when I know something."

The first call Barrett made was to the sheriff's department. Dispatch connected him directly to Sheriff West's patrol car. "Sheriff, I'm looking for Jake, and the dispatcher said I needed to talk to you. What's going on?"

"We're looking for Jake, too, Barrett. We got a 911 call from him that shots were fired, and someone was trying to run him off the road. Billy Laymon found what appears to be where a car left the road near the Forked Deer River Bridge on Windy City Road. It matches what Jake said on the 911 call. Paramedics and divers are on their way to the scene, and

I'm on my way to Jake's house to talk to his wife."

"I'd better go, too, Sheriff," Barrett replied.

"That's probably a good idea. We found the deputy assigned to protect Jake dead in his patrol car behind your office. He was shot twice in the head."

Barrett grew pale. He set the porcelain mug of hot tea on the kitchen counter with shaking hands and stared out the kitchen window over the sink into the night.

"Barrett, you still there?" Sheriff West asked after several seconds of silence.

"I'm here," Barrett replied. "This doesn't look good, does it?"

There was a heavy sigh from the sheriff. "No, it doesn't."

Reed residence, Jackson, Tennessee

Rachel knew it couldn't be good news when she saw both Barrett Holcombe and Sheriff West at her front door. She began to cry immediately. Both men tried to console her, and Sheriff West provided the limited details of what they knew.

"They've killed him," she said through her tears after Sheriff West finished.

"Who, Rachel?" Sheriff West asked. "Who are you talking about?"

"The same people who broke into our house and attacked Courtney. Jake told you about the note they left threatening us, but he didn't tell you everything. But now they've killed him and Butch Johnson too."

"Did Jake know who it was?"

"Not exactly. And I don't know everything. But it had something to do with Jed and Jesse Thompson and money and Vice President Burke."

"Does anybody else know about this?" Sheriff West asked Rachel.

"I don't think so. I know he didn't tell me everything he knew. He always keeps things from me because he thinks it protects me."

"I'm going to double the officers outside your house until we find out what's happening. Whoever did this to Jake may come looking for you if they think you know something."

"Sheriff, do you think Jake's really dead?" Rachel asked.

The sheriff removed his hat. "I'll be honest with you, Rachel. It doesn't look good. Until we know for sure whether that's Jake's car in the river, I can't answer that. We have divers in the water now trying to look for it. But it's dark, and the water is murky. It may take awhile before we can know for sure."

Sheriff West's answer caused Rachel's crying to intensify, and Barrett wrapped big, fatherly arms around her.

After a few seconds of crying on Barrett's shoulder, she pushed herself away. "I've got to tell the kids."

Barrett looked concerned. "Do you think that's a good idea?"

"They've been asking for their daddy all night, and I'm not going to let them go to bed wondering why he's not home. I think they need to know."

She walked into the den, where the three children were sitting quietly on the couch. They could sense the seriousness of the moment, and the redness of their mother's eyes told a story that none longed to hear. But hear it they must.

Brett was the first to seek answers. "Why are the police here?"

Rachel didn't correct him. She knew that, at his age, he couldn't appreciate the difference between the sheriff's department and the police department.

"Does it have something to do with Daddy?" Courtney inquired.

"Yes, it does." Rachel knelt on the floor in front of the couch and placed her arms around the outer legs of Brett and Courtney. Jeremy sat between the two. "It seems that Daddy may have been in an accident on his way home." Her motherly voice was soft, calm, and reassuring.

"Is he all right?" Courtney asked.

Rachel knew that the last thing Courtney needed after her ordeal was the mental anguish of being told of her father's probable demise, so she answered cautiously. She didn't want to concern the children any more than necessary, but she also didn't want to give any sense of false hope. "We don't know yet," was the best reply she could muster under the circumstances.

"I want my daddy!" Brett began to cry. His voice got louder and louder with each weeping repetition of the phrase.

Jeremy joined the conversation. "When's Daddy going to be home?"

"Soon, honey," Rachel replied, gazing into Jeremy's tender eyes. "Daddy will be home soon."

Brett's crying soon caused spontaneous crying in the other two children. There was nothing else for Rachel to do than to pull all three as close as possible and hold them as they cried for their father. "It's going to be all right," she whispered, fighting back more tears of her own. She squeezed their innocent bodies tighter and tried to be as brave as she could be. "No matter what, it's going to be all right."

Rachel looked over the tops of their heads at Sheriff West and Barrett, who stood in the doorway leading from the foyer into the den. Neither man spoke, but each raised a hand to his eyes and brushed away tears.

Hampton Inn, Jackson, Tennessee

"We are live at the scene of a one-car accident on Windy City Road, north of Jackson," the young female reporter from the local network affiliate said as the ten o'clock evening news began. "Just over my shoulder you can see the lights of emergency vehicles. Moments ago divers with the Tennessee Highway Patrol located a car resting on the bottom of the river, and rescuers are now trying to hoist the vehicle from its murky grave. The car is believed to be that of local attorney Jake Reed. Attorney Reed is the defense attorney for Jedediah McClellan—"

Dalton Miller didn't hear the rest of the report. He didn't need to. The mention of Jake Reed's name was enough, and the news was not good. He reached for his cell phone and dialed the number for Shep Taylor.

"Shep, this is Dalton. We have a problem."

Windy City Road, outside Jackson, Tennessee

After Rachel's parents arrived, Sheriff West and Barrett traveled to the accident scene. Huge floodlights were erected to assist with the search, and the accident scene—authorities were still calling it that—was completely illuminated. Rescue workers, sheriff's deputies, and curious onlookers littered both sides of the river. Sheriff West knew that everyone there hoped the car on the bottom of the river was not that of Jake Reed, or, if it was, that it somehow, miraculously, contained his living, breathing body.

Sheriff West and Barrett now stood on the bridge over the Forked Deer River, watching as the wench on the front of the wrecker strained and rattled and cracked and shook as it tried to pull Jake's car from beneath the water. The wench's motor revved at such a high pitch that Sheriff West thought it might burn the motor up. He knew that the divers were unable to see inside the automobile and couldn't confirm whether Jake's body was inside. Everyone waited anxiously.

It seemed like hours to Sheriff West, but after several minutes the tail end of Jake's car broke through the water's surface. After several more minutes the car was completely on the riverbank, and rescue personnel ran to open the doors. The front of the car was crumpled and mangled, and the driver's-side air bag hung limp over the steering wheel. Water and debris washed out when the doors were opened, but there was no sign of Jake's body. The leader of the rescue team turned toward Sheriff West on his lofty perch and signaled to him that no one was inside.

"Nothing," Sheriff West said so Barrett would understand the signal from below. "We'll begin dragging the bottom and searching the banks in the morning for his body. There's no way he could have survived. If the impact didn't kill him, the temperature of the water did."

Jackson-Madison County General Hospital, Jackson, Tennessee

From the green vinyl chair in Jed's hospital room, Naomi McClellan saw the same news broadcast as Dalton Miller had seen. Her reaction to the news was completely different. Her concern was of eternal consequences.

"Don't let him be dead, Lord," she whispered prayerfully. "He ain't been sanctified yet."

CHAPTER FORTY

Forked Deer River, Jackson, Tennessee

Sheriff West set up a command center at sunup Tuesday morning near where Jake Reed's car was pulled from the Forked Deer River. He sent boats and divers into the water, while reserve deputies, with bloodhounds in tow, trudged through the underbrush along the riverbank in overcoats and rubber boots. All were looking for the body of Jake Reed, attorney-at-law.

Sheriff West saw Barrett when he arrived and motioned to the deputy at the edge of the crime-scene tape that it was all right to allow Barrett to enter. The sheriff was receiving a report from the leader of one of the search teams as Barrett approached.

". . . and we've searched both sides of the river a half-mile down stream. The dogs haven't had the first hit on a scent. Do you want us to go over the same area again, or expand farther downstream?"

"Double-check the area you've covered," Sheriff West replied. "The divers don't think the current is strong enough to have carried the body very far. We'll have plenty of daylight this afternoon to expand the search if we need to."

"I take it you've not had any luck yet," Barrett commented after the search-team leader retreated to carry out the instructions.

"Nothing," the sheriff said, shaking his head. "We haven't found a shred of clothing, a shoe, or anything. He's probably still in the water somewhere, hung on a stump or an old log. We'll find him."

"Any leads or clues as to what happened?"

"Deputy Laymon is still taking measurements and photographs, but it definitely appears that another vehicle was involved. I've got four deputies interviewing every resident and business owner from here back to your office. Several motorists reported a high-speed chase last night, and the detectives are interviewing the last of those witnesses this morning. The first ones we talked to reported seeing Jake's car being chased by a dark-colored Silverado truck."

"What about the deputy who was killed?"

"I met with his family this morning," Sheriff West responded. "It was tough. There's only been one other time in my career that I had a deputy killed in the line of duty. Deputy Johnson had been with the department for twelve years. He had a wife and two kids. It'll be tough on them for a while. How's Jake's family?"

"They're pretty distraught, as you can imagine. Her parents are at their house. They're still holding out hope for a miracle that he's alive somewhere."

"If Jake Reed's alive, it'll be a miracle."

Jenkins's residence, Georgetown DC

It was early Tuesday morning, a week before the presidential election, and Bryan Jenkins was already working his telephone, trying to find a lead story for his next issue of *The Jenkins Report*. A 1985 graduate of Georgetown University, Bryan had developed quite a following for his weekly politically conservative Internet newsletter that he published out of his second-story flat in the Georgetown area of DC.

"Bryan Jenkins," he announced as he answered the telephone on the desk in his bedroom.

"Is this the Bryan Jenkins that publishes *The Jenkins Report* on the Web?" asked an unfamiliar male voice. Most of Bryan's informants were anonymous, but he recognized the voices of his regular callers. This was not one of them.

"That's me. How can I help you?" Bryan asked with pen and notepad in hand. By and far, the majority of calls he received were useless, but occasionally one delivered interesting information.

"You've got that backward, friend. It's me that's going to help you," came the confident reply.

"I'm listening."

"You remember the friend of Vice President Burke's who was killed back in the summer?"

"Vaguely, but go on."

"It turns out that it was a planned hit by a group of Burke's supporters."

Bryan feverishly scribbled out the words of his anonymous informant in his self-styled shorthand and at the same time tried to keep the caller from hanging up too soon. He regularly traced his calls so he could try to locate the source of anonymous calls and determine the credibility of the information. One tactic he often used to prolong a conversation was to fain disbelief.

"Come on. You expect me to believe that someone associated with Vice President Burke was involved with a murder? What do you have to substantiate your claim?"

"The dead guy was involved with some of Burke's fund-raising. He saw something he shouldn't have seen, and they took him out. That's the only explanation."

"The authorities have someone in custody for the murder, don't they?"

"He's just a fall guy. He didn't do it, and the evidence will come out soon enough to prove it."

"What else do you have to back up your story?"

"I'll tell you what. If you don't believe me, then fine. I'll take my story to someone else. But you need to find out why the FBI had two undercover agents in Jackson, Tennessee, for several weeks after the murder. That'll answer some of your questions. And I'll tell you something else: did you know that the lawyer who was representing the fall guy was killed in a freak car accident last night?"

Bryan stopped writing and stared across the room. Everything the unidentified caller had said to that point couldn't be verified. But now the caller had finally said something Bryan could at least try to corroborate through other sources.

"How can I get back in touch with you if I need any further information?" Bryan asked, hoping to get the name and a telephone number of his informant.

"You can't. If I think you need anything else, I'll call."

With that, the line went dead just seconds before the trace was complete. Bryan double-checked the tracer to see if it had recorded a location for the incoming call and then immediately began checking wire reports to find the story about the dead lawyer. He would work through the day, trying to confirm his informant's information in time for the publication of his newsletter Wednesday morning.

Jackson, Tennessee

Dalton Miller checked his watch after hanging up the pay phone outside a convenience store on the north side of Jackson; he was sure he had disconnected before any tracing machine had time to locate him. He drove back to his hotel room to await further instructions from Shep. They were playing a dangerous game, but it was the only hope they had this close to the election, now that Jake Reed was dead. The mainstream media wouldn't run the story Shep and Dalton wanted them to run, but perhaps they could get some mileage through *The Jenkins Report*.

Jackson-Madison County General Hospital, Jackson, Tennessee

Naomi McClellan knelt down beside Jed's bed as she had every morning since Jed was admitted to the hospital. As always she prayed for Jed and his doctors, but today she added something extra to her prayer that had become necessary after last night.

". . . And Lord, please be with Jake's family. I know how difficult it is when family is hurtin'. Lord, do I know. But I know you got a purpose for everythin', and there's a purpose for what's happened to Jake. But if there's any way, Lord, any way at all for him to be alive, please let him be. He ain't done nothin' wrong. He ain't asked for any of this. I know you can do it if you want to, Lord, and I'm asking you to. Not for me, but for Jake and his family. He's got those three precious little children, and they need their daddy . . . just like Jed's need him. Take care of both of them. In Jesus's name, amen."

Forked Deer River, Jackson, Tennessee

L. C. McClure's family had owned the bottom land near the Forked Deer River east of Windy City Road for the last one hundred years. And if it were up to L. C., it would be in his family for the next one hundred years as well. It had always been good farmland. The ground was fertile, and being near the river meant that the crops were rarely in need of water. Year after year, cotton or soybeans or corn had taken root in the fertile ground and produced a plentiful harvest. The land had provided food for his family's table and also generated revenue to purchase other necessities. Even when times were desperate and all the surrounding land was barren and dry, life always seemed to spring from this plot of land.

This year's winter-wheat crop looked good, L. C. thought to himself as he circled the field in his brown-over-tan Chevy pickup. The green plants were almost ankle high, creating a stark contrast with the dormant surroundings.

Every once in a while someone still asked L. C. what his initials stood for, and he would just look at them and shrug. His birth certificate simply read L. C. McClure, and his parents never told him anything different. He guessed they had used all the names they could think of on the seven children who had preceded him and simply couldn't think of another when he was born.

He stopped at the south end of the field to check the fence row for holes or weak sections in the barbed-wire fence that separated his crop from the neighbor's pasture. If the neighbor's cattle managed to get into his wheat field, they could destroy the entire crop overnight. His trusted friend, Hunter, a five-year-old redbone coonhound, leaped from the bed of the truck when it came to a stop and began to sniff for territorial markings left behind by other dogs.

L. C. checked the entire south fence line and, after fifteen minutes of pulling and tugging on each section, was satisfied that everything was secure. Returning to his truck, he heard the short, choppy, repetitive yelps from Hunter in the distance, somewhere on the other side of the field. It sounded as though the dog was near the river's edge.

He probably has a squirrel or raccoon treed, L. C. surmised. "Come on, Hunter. Let's go, boy."

Hunter was typically obedient, and usually returned upon being summoned by L. C. But this time he didn't return as instructed. L. C. whistled loudly in an attempt to get Hunter's attention and followed that with a louder, sterner call for the dog's obedience.

"Hunter, you'd better come here!"

Again the dog ignored its owner's call, and the constant barking continued. L. C. growled under his breath and stomped toward the disobedient dog.

"I'm gonna hafta teach that dog a lesson," he mumbled.

As he reached the tree line that stood along the river, L. C. could see Hunter near a pile of brush at the river's edge.

"Hunter!" he screamed. "Come here!"

Hunter never stopped barking and never turned to acknowledge his master. L. C. continued stomping toward Hunter. Along the way he picked up a medium-size limb that had fallen from one of the trees. A couple of whacks should get the dog's attention. His vision was so focused on the dog and the punishment soon to be delivered that he didn't look at anything else until he was within five feet of Hunter.

And then he saw something unusual on the ground. At first he wasn't certain what to make of it, but then he realized what was protruding from under the brush pile.

A shoeless leg. A man's leg.

Now that his master was there, Hunter stopped barking and looked intently at L. C.

L. C. knelt down and removed a few pieces of driftwood from the brush pile, exposing the body of a young man.

"That's gotta be the man they're looking for," he whispered to himself.

Stumbling to his feet, he ran toward his truck. Once he slipped on the steep embankment and almost tumbled backward into the river. Righting himself, he reached his truck and made the call that all of Jackson had been waiting to receive.

Reed residence, Jackson, Tennessee

"He's alive!" Barrett exclaimed when Rachel answered the phone. "He's alive! A farmer found him along the riverbank. He's unconscious, but he's alive."

Rachel didn't hear the balance of Barrett's statement beyond the first pronouncement of life. She screamed in relief, and the rest of the family rushed into the room. She smiled, happy tears streaming down her cheeks at the good news.

"He's alive!" she told them excitedly.

In unison, her parents, Courtney, Brett, and Jeremy all cheered, and then quickly quieted down so Rachel could finish her conversation with Barrett.

"Where is he?" Rachel asked.

"He's on his way to Jackson-Madison County General Hospital by ambulance. He should be there in a couple of minutes."

"I'm on my way."

Jackson-Madison County General Hospital, Jackson, Tennessee

The emergency room buzzed with activity after the call came in that Attorney Jake Reed had been found alive. The paramedics relayed by radio Jake's vital signs and injuries to the waiting ER staff. Everyone's biggest concern was hypothermia, and the battle to save Jake Reed's life soon moved from the ambulance to the emergency room.

Word about the newest visitor spread like wildfire through the confines of the hospital and soon reached the seventh floor. One of the day-shift nurses knocked lightly on Jed's door and stuck her head in far enough for Naomi to see her. "They found Jake Reed, Ms. McClellan," she said softly. "And he's alive."

"Thank you, Jesus," Naomi replied and clutched her hands together under her chin, as if she were praying. "Thank you."

Rachel arrived at the hospital only minutes after the ambulance had delivered Jake. She burst through the sliding-glass emergency-room doors, demanding to see her husband. Two nurses, who knew what she was going through, because they had seen it so many times before, calmed her down and took her to a private room where the attending physician could meet with her after Jake got out of surgery. It had been a horrible few hours, but finally she was able to rest. Jake was alive, and that was all that mattered.

"Jackson-Madison County General Hospital," the receptionist answered.

"Yes, ma'am, this is Blake Joyner with NBC news in Memphis," lied Agent Sam Chambers. Saul Sanders had instructed him to check and verify that Osborne and Moyers had, in fact, completed the assignment. Sam spoke with a manufactured Southern accent. "We're following up on a story about attorney Jake Reed. Can you confirm whether he has been admitted to your hospital?"

"Sir, we cannot give out patient information."

Sam quickly realized he wasn't going to get any information from the receptionist, and she probably didn't have what he needed anyway. "I understand. Can you connect me with someone in the emergency room? Perhaps they can help me."

"I'll connect you, sir, but I doubt they'll help you either. Hospital policy prohibits the release of patient information." Before Sam could respond, the receptionist transferred the call to the emergency-room nurses' station. Other calls were ringing into the switchboard, and she was too busy to speak any longer with someone from the media.

"ER," said a nurse at the emergency-room admissions desk when Sam's call rang through.

"This is Blake Joyner with NBC news in Memphis. I'm trying to get an update on Mr. Jake Reed's condition for the twelve o'clock news."

"Sir, I'm sorry. I can't give out any information about a patient."

"I understand the importance of maintaining patient confidentiality, but can you at least tell me whether he is a patient at your hospital, or not?"

Sanders residence, Arlington, Virginia

"What do you mean he's alive?!" Saul Sanders screamed when Agent Chambers called him with the report he'd received from the hospital in Jackson. Saul was hiding out at his house in Arlington and planned on staying there until after the election. He didn't want to see Charlie Armacost or Randolph or anybody. "How can he be alive? Al assured me the job had been done."

"I don't know what Al saw or thought he saw, but Jake Reed is by no means dead."

"I can't believe this is happening," Saul said. He rubbed his forehead in an attempt to ease the pain.

After a few seconds of silence Sam asked, "Director Sanders, are you OK? Do you need me to do anything?"

"That's OK, Sam. I can handle it from here."

Saul replaced the receiver on the telephone and opened the top right-hand drawer of his desk to reveal a small, nickel-colored .38 caliber revolver. He removed the loaded revolver and laid it on top of his desk. As he stared at the cold metal object in front of him, he wasn't certain he was brave enough to do what needed to be done. He thought about his life and the poor decisions he had made during it that had brought him to this point in time. He also thought about what he would do if he could go back twenty years and start over. Those decisions would have been different, he told himself.

But would they really? Would he have done anything differently? He wasn't sure he knew the answer. Perhaps he'd never have agreed to join forces with Randolph Winston. Or would he?

Randolph, he repeated in his mind, chuckling at himself. He had grown to despise the name and the person associated with it, yet now Randolph filled every crevice of Saul's mind. How could he have been so stupid? There was nothing he could do about it now, he told himself. There was no going back, and that meant he had one final decision to make. Did he wait on Randolph, or did he do the job himself?

It took only a few seconds for Saul to settle on an answer. No longer would he allow Randolph to make decisions for him. He would decide his own way of dying. He slid one bullet into the chamber of the pistol and raised it to his temple. Randolph would never have the satisfaction of seeing Saul tortured and killed.

CHAPTER FORTY-ONE

Jackson-Madison County General Hospital, Jackson, Tennessee

"Ms. Reed, I'm Dr. Lawrence," the man in white said as he entered the room where Rachel was waiting. "I'm the attending physician for your husband."

"Is he going to be OK?" was Rachel's first question. She would have plenty of others later, but the most important one came first.

Dr. Lawrence sat down in the chair beside Rachel and took her hand. "He's been through quite a bit of trauma, Ms. Reed."

Rachel searched the doctor's eyes for the answer she desperately wanted.

"But, yes," the doctor continued, "I think he's going to make it."

Rachel began to cry softly. The kind of cry that came not from fear or pain or sadness, but from releasing her pent-up anxiety. "Can I see him?" she managed.

"He regained consciousness a few minutes ago and is still pretty groggy. But I think it will be all right for you to see him. I want to warn you, though, Ms. Reed. It's not a pretty sight. His head is bruised and lacerated from the impact, and he's got a compound fracture of his right leg. The seat belt probably saved his life, but it left a lot of bruising on his chest and abdomen. We also repaired some internal bleeding, and it may take awhile for him to recuperate. But he's alert now and asking for you. So come on—I'll take you to him."

Rachel followed Dr. Lawrence through the halls of the hospital to the intensive care room, where Jake was recovering from surgery. She saw him through the window in the door before entering and began to cry again.

Not tears of sorrow from his battered appearance, as terrible as it was, but tears of joy. Jake really was alive, and she could see it with her own eyes.

The door of the IC room opened, and Jake Reed slowly, painfully turned his head.

Rachel, his wife, entered. She approached the side of the bed and leaned over the rail. "How are you doing?"

Through his swollen eyes he could see her wiping away tears from under her eyes with one hand, and he felt her stroking his hair with the other. Rachel leaned over and lightly kissed his forehead.

"I'm going to make it," he whispered, attempting a smile. "How do I look?"

She cocked her head. "Well, you're not going to win any beauty contests for a while."

Jake chuckled and winced. "Don't make me laugh. It hurts too bad."

"I'm sorry." Rachel smiled. "You had us all worried, you know. We were afraid we lost you." She caressed the side of his face.

Yet even as gentle as Rachel's touch was, Jake grimaced from the pressure. It would take awhile to heal, he realized.

"I'm sorry, honey. I know you had to be worried." His words continued to be soft in sound, but painful to deliver. He paused briefly to shift from one position to another, trying to find one that was less painful. "How are the kids?"

"Scared to death. My parents have them now. They know you're all right, but they want to come see you. I think that will do them more good than anything. Especially Courtney. When I told them you were in an accident, I saw that same fear in her eyes that I saw the morning after her attack."

"Maybe they can come later when they move me to a room. I need to see them too."

"I don't know what we would do if you had been killed."

Rachel's words caused Jake to recall the last conversation he'd had with Naomi. If he had died last night, would he have gone to heaven? He admitted to himself that he didn't know the answer. He shifted again in his bed, still trying to find the most comfortable position. Finally he realized there wasn't one. Momentarily exhausted, he lay quietly, reflecting on where he was and his weakened condition.

"Why don't you rest for a while?" Rachel suggested. She moved to a vinyl-covered wooden chair in the corner of the room.

"I'm fine," Jake assured her. "I don't want to sleep right now. There's something else I want to talk to you about. It's something I've been thinking about lately, even before last night. But almost dying made me realize that I'm not going to live forever."

Jake turned his head away from Rachel, toward the opposite wall. He wasn't sure how she would react to what he was about to say, and he was afraid to look in her eyes to find out. "I've been having this feeling that there's something missing in my life, and I can't put my finger on it."

"Are you talking about the conversation you had with Naomi?"

How had she recognized what he was going through? Jake turned slowly back toward Rachel. "That's part of it. That day she and I walked to the chapel downstairs, she asked me a question that I don't know the answer to. She asked me whether I would go to heaven when I died. I don't know the answer to that question. Do you know if you'll go to heaven when you die?"

"Yes." Rachel raised her head in confidence. "I know that I'll go to heaven when I die."

"How do you know?" he asked in an almost pleading tone.

"Because I've asked Jesus to come into my heart as my Lord and Savior."

Rachel's words echoed through his mind.

For a few minutes, as Jake struggled with Naomi's question and Rachel's answer, the only sound in the room was the hum of the IV monitor.

"You remember Reverend Hall, the pastor who came to see Courtney?" Rachel finally said. "I passed him in the hallway when Dr. Lawrence brought me to see you. He may still be in the hospital. He can probably answer some of your questions. Do you want me to see if the nurses can find him?"

The inner battle for Jake's soul raged. Part of him didn't want to see Reverend Hall, while the rest of him yearned for his questions to be answered.

"I'll have the nurses page him," Rachel said when Jake didn't respond.

A few minutes after Rachel asked the nurses to page Reverend Hall, Jake heard a light knock at the door.

Reverend Hall, still looking like a lawyer, entered the room and closed the door behind him. "I heard about your accident, Mr. Reed. I'm glad to see you doing well."

"It has been a trying few days," Rachel interjected.

"Yes it has," Reverend Hall acknowledged. "And how is little Courtney doing?"

"She's doing very well. Thanks for asking."

"Tell her I said hello, will you?" Reverend Hall hesitated, then continued, "The nurses said you asked to see me. Is there anything I can do to help you?"

"Reverend," Rachel began. "Jake and I talked about what would happen had he died. We talked about what would happen to the kids and me, but we also talked about what would have happened to him."

"I don't know whether I would go to heaven or not," Jake interrupted. He was unable to keep quiet any longer. The words erupted from his mouth like they had been trying desperately to get out for a long time.

"Let me ask you something, Jake. May I call you Jake?"

"Certainly."

"Are you a Christian?" the reverend asked, his green eyes intent on Jake's response. "Because if you're a Christian, then you *will* go to heaven when you die."

"Sure, I'm a Christian." Jake shrugged.

"How do you know you're a Christian?" the reverend asked.

"I don't know what you mean. I've just always been one."

"What I mean is, do you recall a specific time in your life where you prayed to ask Jesus Christ to become your Lord and Savior?"

Jake searched the recesses of his mind for an event such as the one described by Reverend Hall but couldn't find one. Still, the battle raged.

"Reverend, I believe in God," Jake defended. "I always have, and that makes me a Christian. I may not go to church all the time like I should, but I'm going to do better at that. So, yes, I would say that I'm a Christian."

Reverend Hall bowed his head. "That's not how it works, Jake. Until you recognize that you're a sinner, that your sins will result in your spiritual death, that Christ died for your sins; and that, without Christ, you'll spend eternity in hell, you cannot be a Christian. Think about what would have happened if you had died in that wreck last night. Without having accepted Christ as your Lord and Savior, you would have died and gone to hell. That's what the Bible teaches, Jake." He shook his head in an expression of awe. "For some reason your life's been spared, and you've been given another opportunity."

Jake swallowed hard, trying to calm himself. From the beginning of his conversation with Reverend Hall until now, the rate of his heartbeat had steadily increased until his heart felt like it was ready to explode. There was a strange tingling all over his body—the same feeling he'd experienced with Naomi in the chapel.

"It's the Holy Spirit, Jake," Reverend Hall said calmly.

The same words Naomi had used, Jake thought.

"The Holy Spirit is making you feel the way you feel right now," the reverend continued. "He wants you to accept Jesus Christ as your Lord and Savior. The question is, do you want to become a Christian and be certain that you'll spend eternity in heaven?"

Jake recognized Reverend Hall's words as being similar to the ones Naomi had spoken. He also knew that he could no longer lie to himself and those around him. He wasn't a Christian, he finally admitted to himself. He wasn't a Christian, but at that very moment he wanted to be a Christian more than anything else imaginable.

"Yes," he whispered as tears streamed from his bruised eyes. "I want to be a Christian."

"I had hoped that would be your answer, Jake." Reverend Hall smiled broadly. "I want you to repeat a prayer with me."

And Reverend Hall led Jake through a simple, yet purposeful, prayer. In the prayer Jake repented of his sins and prayed to accept Jesus Christ as his Lord and Savior. He couldn't remember the last time he had prayed. But with his head bowed and eyes closed, Jake prayed, and it felt right.

When he finished praying, he raised his head, opened his eyes, and smiled. The smile felt different. It was the kind of smile that could only come after a person's entire life had been changed. Just as Jesus Christ had changed Jake's. And Jake knew it. He was finally a Christian.

Rachel, Reverend Hall, and Jake visited for several more minutes before Reverend Hall departed. Rachel walked with him to the elevator. After Rachel and Reverend Hall left, Jake began to think about all the terrible things that had happened and tried to determine who was responsible for it all. He wanted to believe that responsibility lay at the feet of someone associated with Edward Burke. But was Burke himself responsible?

And what involvement did Dalton Miller and the FBI have? Mr. Miller was the one who had told him about the FBI, and that had been accurate. He also knew about the F-PAC documents Jake had received from Earline Thompson before Jake had told Drake Highfill about them. How did Mr. Miller know about the documents that quickly? And for whom did the PI work?

The attacks on Jake and his family had happened only after he'd talked to Drake Highfill and after the visit from Agent Simon. He surmised that Highfill and Miller weren't connected.

But what about the FBI? Whose side were they on? There were two possibilities. Either Mr. Miller was trying to scare Jake into helping him, which didn't seem likely from what Jake had seen of the man. He didn't seem the type. Or Edward Burke was trying to keep Jake quiet. Obviously the F-PAC documents and photographs of the murder scene were important to everybody, but the only person he'd told about the Federalists was Drake.

Agent Simon hadn't told Jake what he was looking for or what information he thought Jake possessed. That meant the FBI probably didn't know what that information was. If Simon was connected to Burke, then he would have known that the information involved the Federalists. Since he didn't, that meant he wasn't involved with Burke. And that pointed to Burke as being the one behind the attacks. Although Jake tried to convince himself of that fact, it was all still very confusing. Especially in his groggy state of mind after surgery.

Jake finally determined that there was only one way to find out for sure who was responsible and at the same time try to stop Burke from being elected. When Rachel returned from escorting Reverend Hall, Jake asked her to find his wallet.

Five minutes later she returned from the nurses' station with the remainder of Jake's personal belongings. He removed a waterlogged business card from it and used Rachel's wireless phone to call the number. Although the phone number on the card was barely legible after its soaking, Jake was able to get the number right on the first try.

"Mr. Miller, this is Jake Reed. Do you remember me?"

"Jake Reed?" There was a pregnant pause. "I thought you were dead."

"Perhaps I should be, Mr. Miller. But I'm alive and well."

"I must say that after our last conversation I'm a little surprised to hear from you."

"I'm a little surprised to be calling. If this were a week ago, I wouldn't be. But a lot of things have happened in the last week, and I've decided that I want to talk to you. How quickly can you be at the hospital?"

"I'll be there in ten minutes."

CHAPTER FORTY-TWO

Omni hotel, San Antonio, Texas

Shep Taylor barely slept after receiving Dalton's call just after ten o'clock Tuesday night. He knew he'd been grasping at straws when he'd told Dalton to leak information to Bryan Jenkins. But this was different. Jake Reed was not only alive, he held the key to exposing Edward Burke.

Shep could hardly contain his excitement when he, Jack, and Mac met for their Wednesday-morning planning session. He wasn't certain how Mac would react, but it was too late for that now. Events were already in motion, and nothing Mac could say or do could stop them.

"Before we get started, I've got something I need to tell you about," Shep began. He turned to face Mac, because there was no need in hiding from his actions at this point. "Mac, this will come as a shock to you, but immediately after the Democratic Convention I hired a private investigator to investigate Edward Burke."

"You did what?" Mac exclaimed in disbelief. Shep could see the anger in Mac's face as he slammed a folder full of papers on the coffee table in his hotel suite.

"Just hear me out."

"I don't want to hear you out," interrupted Mac. "I have always run my campaigns aboveboard, and I don't plan on changing now. I can't believe you would do something like this, Shep." Mac glared at Jack. "Did you know about this?"

"I only found out about it a week ago," Jack replied, his voice timid.

"Don't blame him for any of this," Shep insisted. "I made this decision on my own, and I didn't tell you or Jack about it."

"I'm astounded, Shep. What did you hope to accomplish?"

"At the time, I was hoping to find some information about Burke's fund-raising. That's what we talked about that night in Miami. But what we found was bigger than any of us ever could have anticipated."

"What are you talking about?" Mac asked.

"I'm talking about conspiracy and murder and money laundering and attempted murder, just to name a few."

"Are you saying that Edward Burke's been involved in some type of criminal activity?" Mac asked, suddenly much calmer than he was a minute ago.

"That's exactly what I'm saying. We now know that evidence exists that ties Burke to all those crimes I mentioned." Shep provided all the details to Mac and Jack, beginning with the murder of Jesse Thompson and ending with the telephone call he'd received from Dalton last night.

After Shep finished, silence blanketed the room. Mac and Jack appeared stunned. Shep knew that this information was significant enough to alter the outcome of the election, even at this late date.

"I don't condone what you did, Shep," Mac scolded. "But now that you have this information, what do you suggest we do with it?"

"Like I said, we only know that the evidence exists. Until we have our hands on it, we can't do anything. If they don't already, the FBI will soon have the same information that I just shared with you. I'm hoping they will take action, but I can't be certain they will. So we wait and hope that the news breaks soon enough to help us. If not, we may have a president in the White House who is an accomplice to murder."

"When do you think you'll know something?" Jack asked.

"Today. No later than tomorrow. The PI has a junior-level contact inside the FBI. He's on the phone with him as we speak. We know we can't talk to the director because the director is loyal to Burke. But we think the deputy director may be friendly. If our hunch is correct, the deputy director should be on his way to Jackson, Tennessee, this afternoon. If our hunch is wrong, we're in trouble."

"Anything we need to do?" Mac asked.

Shep had thought long and hard about what he would say to Mac if the conversation went the way it had. It wouldn't have surprised him if Mac had forbidden any further involvement by his campaign team. But he hadn't. For whatever reason, he hadn't.

And Shep understood. He understood that Mac realized that the exploitation of this information was his only chance at winning the presidency. *Things happen for a reason*, Mac was always saying. And Shep understood that Mac realized that maybe, just maybe, the reason things were happening the way they were was because he was supposed to be president. Mac Foster, a God-fearing, Bible-believing man, was supposed to be president. Shep liked the sound of that, and he knew that Mac liked it too. So when Mac asked what they needed to do, Shep was prepared with the answer.

"I'm already booked on a flight into Jackson. I want your authority to do whatever is necessary to make sure this information about Burke is released to the public."

FBI headquarters, Washington DC

George McCullough rushed into Charlie Armacost's office with the news he'd received Wednesday morning from Dalton Miller. He and Charlie already knew that Jake Reed was alive based on the reports from Agent Simon. Jerry had kept Charlie and George informed on the search for Jake, and they had carefully watched the developments in Jackson. George could tell that Charlie struggled with the realization that the Bureau's failure to take Claudia into protective custody, or to even intercept Agents Osborne and Moyers, may have almost cost Jake Reed his life. But now George was armed with the information that would put an end to the whole ordeal. How to tell Charlie where he got the information was a different story.

"Charlie, have you ever thought that one day you might be the director of the FBI?"

"Sure I have. What agent worth his salt doesn't think about that possibility? But with Edward Burke in the White House, it's not going to happen anytime soon, and I'm not getting any younger."

That was the answer George hoped to hear. He also hoped that Charlie would respond to the rest of what he was about to say in a similar fashion.

"Charlie, over the last several months I've been in contact with a representative of the Foster campaign." George saw the look of surprise on Charlie's face and defensively held up both hands, palm side toward Charlie. "Before you say anything, let me finish. My contact is a private investigator named Dalton Miller who was hired by the Foster campaign. He's been in Jackson, Tennessee, for about as long as we have. He called me this morning with some interesting information. It turns out that Attorney Reed has confided in Miller and confirmed that he has tangible evidence that connects Burke with Randolph Winston and the Thompson murder."

"Did Reed say what the evidence was?"

"He wouldn't say. Only that it was enough to convict, and that it was in a secure location."

"What help do Foster's people want from us?"

"They need our help in obtaining the information from Reed and releasing it to the media."

"Why don't they leak it themselves?"

"They need us to do that."

"Why does it matter?"

"It's the credibility factor. If it comes from them, then the media and the voters may question the credibility of the information, and Burke may still win. If it comes from us, then it carries instant credibility and will spread like wildfire throughout the country."

Charlie leaned back in his chair, clasped his hands over his flattop, and stared at the ceiling. George sensed that the pieces to the puzzle were snapping into place in Charlie's mind.

"That's why you asked me if I wanted to be director?" Charlie redirected his eyes from the ceiling back to George.

"That's it. We assist Foster, and you'll be named director."

"You realize the risk, don't you, George? If it fails and Burke wins, we're finished."

"The way I see it, we're finished anyway if Burke wins. You told me before that the whole world will change. I don't like that thought. The world isn't perfect, but I like the way it is now better than the alternative."

"So you want to help Foster?"

"I don't think we have a choice."

George knew Charlie was right. They didn't have a choice. With Burke as president the whole world would indeed change. He didn't know the magnitude of the changes planned by Randolph Winston. But it was enough motivation for him, and he knew it was motivation for Charlie as well, just to keep Burke out of the White House. He was evil, and he had to be stopped.

George finally received the answer from Charlie for which he hoped.

"I agree, George. We don't have a choice. It looks like we need to go to Jackson and find out what's going on."

"I guessed that would be your response, and I've already ordered the plane to be waiting on us."

En route to Jackson-Madison County General Hospital

Agent Simon was waiting with his government sedan when the Bureau-owned Learjet carrying Charlie Armacost and George McCullough touched down at McKellar-Sipes Regional Airport. Agent Boyd was still recuperating at the Regional Medical Center in Memphis from his gunshot wound. The three quickly traveled to Jackson-Madison County General Hospital, and after showing their FBI credentials to the sheriff's deputies patrolling the facility, they were escorted to see Jake Reed. Everyone—hospital staff, patients, and visitors—stopped and gawked at the three men with closely cropped haircuts and trench coats as they strode through the hallways. A buzz of conversation rose up in their wake.

The deputies led the three FBI agents to Jake's room, where they found Jake and Rachel alone.

Jackson-Madison County General Hospital, Jackson, Tennessee

"Mr. Reed," the lead man said as a trio of trench-coated men entered the hospital room. "My name is Charlie Armacost, and I'm the deputy director of the FBI."

"With everything that has happened, I can't say that I'm surprised to see you."

"This is George McCullough, the assistant deputy director," Mr. Armacost said, pointing toward the second man. "And I think you already know Agent Simon." Mr. McCullough and Agent Simon nodded in the direction of Jake but didn't say anything. They remained stonefaced.

Evidently the deputy director was going to do all the talking.

"Yeah, I know him," Jake replied. "He's probably the reason I'm here."

"I assure you that's not true. We're here because we received a call from Dalton Miller."

Jake knew from that statement that Mr. Miller had conveyed his message to the right place. He was still cautious though. "Go on."

"Mr. Miller called Mr. McCullough and told him that you may have information that is pertinent to an ongoing investigation concerning possible criminal activities conducted by Vice President Edward Burke and others. Is that true?"

"I'm not sure I want to answer that question, Mr. Armacost. How do I know I can trust you? You've bugged my office and had me under surveillance for weeks. That doesn't make you very trustworthy in my opinion."

"I'll take the blame for that, Mr. Reed. We knew that an international assassin was in the country, and the Thompson murder too closely resembled the assassin's typical modus operandi. Keeping tabs on you was the only way I had to keep track of what was happening without arousing too much suspicion."

"And the attacks on me and my family?"

"Like I said, we didn't have anything to do with that. I have a real good idea who did, but it wasn't us."

Jake closely studied the eyes and faces of the men in the room, then caught his wife's eye.

Rachel nodded slightly as if to say she believed what Charlie Armacost said.

"Satisfied?" Mr. Armacost asked.

"Satisfied."

"Good. Now back to my original question. Is it true that you have information pertinent to the investigation?"

"I have several things, Mr. Armacost, but I guess you probably already know about most of them." Jake saw the deputy director's sly grin but knew he wouldn't confirm his suspicions. "But what you don't know about is a video that I have. Until now only two people besides me knew of its existence. And one of them is dead."

"A video? That's very interesting, Mr. Reed. But I bet it's not half as interesting as what's on the tape. Am I right?"

"You guessed it. The contents of the tape are, shall we say, very revealing about a certain prominent political figure."

"I assume you mean Vice President Burke?"

"Right again."

"When can we have this tape?"

"That depends." Jake pursed his swollen lips.

"Depends on what?"

"On what I get in return."

The FBI man's eyes narrowed. "You know I could have you arrested for obstruction, don't you, Mr. Reed?"

"I know you won't do that, Mr. Armacost. It would take weeks for you to get the video."

Jake could tell from the look on the deputy director's face that he was resolved to meet the demands.

"What do you want, Mr. Reed?"

Everything was falling into place for Jake. He lay helplessly in a hospital bed with a broken leg, but he had the upper hand on the deputy director of the FBI. It was a wonderful, powerful feeling, and he savored it ever so slightly.

And then he made his demand. "Until we know that everyone involved has been apprehended, I want around-the-clock protection for me and my family, in addition to that being provided by the sheriff's department."

"I believe we can handle that without any trouble," Mr. Armacost replied and glanced around at the other agents to make sure they understood as well.

"That's not all."

"What else?"

"One million dollars."

"That's going to be more difficult."

"That's the deal, Mr. Armacost. Take it or leave it."

"Without more information about the contents of the video, I can't make that kind of deal with you. I need more to go on."

"Like what?"

"Like what exactly is on the tape."

"I'm not going to tell you what's on the tape, or where it is, until we've got a deal. But I will tell you who's on the tape."

"That's a start."

"Milton McAdams."

Jake noticed that Mr. Armacost cut his eyes toward Mr. McCullough, who was standing on the other side of Jake's bed.

"I take it that you recognize the name," Jake said.

"Let's just say that you've tempted us, Mr. Reed. But I need to know what McAdams says on the tape before I can agree to pay what you're demanding."

"Looks like we've got a problem, Mr. Armacost. Because I'm not showing anybody that tape until I get one million dollars."

"Done," said a voice from behind the FBI agents. The three agents turned toward the voice, and Jake could see through the crowd that two men were standing in the door. One of them he recognized as Dalton Miller. The other was unfamiliar. The unfamiliar one stepped forward through the FBI agents and spoke to Jake.

"Mr. Reed, I'm Shep Taylor with Mac Foster's campaign. You provide that tape to Mr. Armacost, and I'll guarantee you that you'll get the money you've demanded."

It was over, Jake realized. He had made the right decision in contacting Dalton Miller. He turned his head toward Rachel, who was standing beside his bed in stunned silence.

"Rachel, call Barrett and tell him to meet Mr. Armacost at the office. There's something in the safe behind my bookcase that he needs, and Barrett knows the combination."

Orlando, Florida

Ed Burke, oblivious to the developments in Jackson, was wrapping up a campaign stop in Orlando and walking back to his limousine when the question came.

"Mr. Vice President," the female reporter with Fox News screamed above the crowd noise, getting Ed's attention. He stopped just before entering the opened rear door of the car and turned to the horde of reporters that followed him.

"Mr. Vice President, there's a story in *The Jenkins Report* today that says you were involved with the murder of Jesse Thompson and the attempted murder of the attorney who was hired to defend the man accused of killing Thompson. Do you have a comment?"

Ed's staff had already seen the report. Daily they read every article, story, and report written about Ed in every publication in every city around the country. So he had been briefed on the story in *The Jenkins Report*, and the appropriate response had been prepared.

Ed delivered it perfectly. "It is totally absurd to think that I had anything to do with either of those events. Mr. Jenkins publishes an extreme right-wing publication, and this time he has gone too far. I trust that the people of this country will see the report for what it is, and that is a desperate right-wing attack on my candidacy at the eleventh hour of the campaign. My campaign already has lawyers working on filing a defamation lawsuit against Mr. Jenkins." Ed looked straight into the bright lights and television cameras and, with as much conviction as he could muster, made one final, convincing statement. "And to make sure nobody is confused about what I'm saying, I categorically deny everything contained in Mr. Jenkins's report."

Safely inside the limousine, Ben Tobias said, "I hope that's the last we hear about that ridiculous report."

"Me too," Ed replied, but he was worried. He knew he'd just looked into the eyes of millions of voters and lied. It wasn't the first time he had lied. But he knew that the truth was right behind him. He didn't want to think about the consequences if it caught him before the election.

Next Tuesday can't get here soon enough, he thought.

CHAPTER FORTY-THREE

Jackson-Madison County General Hospital, Jackson, Tennessee

Ruth joined Naomi at Jed's bedside Thursday morning for their daily vigil. Naomi knew that she and Ruth were the only ones in the world who still had some hope for Jed, but even their hope had begun to dwindle. Naomi said her daily prayer and thanked God for Jake's rescue and salvation. Now if he would only perform a miracle for Jed, she prayed.

"Good morning," Jed's doctor said to both ladies as he entered Jed's room on his morning rounds. "How's our patient today?"

"'Bout the same, I guess," Ruth responded. "Things don't look good, do they?"

"No they don't, Ms. McClellan," the doctor said honestly. "We probably need to start thinking about moving him to a long-term-care facility. We've done about all we can do for him here, and we need to discharge him from the hospital. You're not going to be able to take care of him without some help."

"I've been afraid of that," Naomi replied. "I wish we could take him home."

The doctor checked Jed's pulse and examined his eyes as he continued talking to Ruth and Naomi. "I don't think that's a good idea. He's going to need around-the-clock attention, and you're not equipped to provide that for him. The best thing for Jed is a long-term-care facility. My office can provide you with a list so you can begin evaluating them."

Naomi continued to watch the doctor as he moved around the side of the bed to check the monitor that measured Jed's brain activity—or more accurately, the lack of it. She knew he did it more out of habit than in anticipation of anything new being reported.

"What's this?" he said as he ran his index finger along the printout that had accumulated overnight. Naomi could hear in his tone an element of disbelief.

"What is it, Doc?" Naomi asked.

"This report is showing brain activity."

Sheraton hotel, Orlando, Florida

"What's Armacost up to?" Ed Burke asked Ben Tobias as the two of them and Millie gathered around the television in Ed's hotel suite to watch the press conference scheduled to begin in ten minutes. Ed didn't usually watch press conferences, but relied on his staff to brief him on what was said. He was concerned about this one, though. More concerned than he let on to Ben and Millie.

"He's probably going to talk about who's in charge at the Bureau since Sanders committed suicide," Ben reasoned.

"He can't do that," Ed retorted. "That's up to President Harrison and the attorney general. Armacost doesn't have anything to say about it."

"If that's not it, I don't know what it could be," Ben replied, looking perplexed. "We don't have anybody close enough to Armacost to find out. We'll just have to watch and see."

Ed didn't like the thought of not knowing about something before it happened, and he didn't have a particularly good feeling about what was taking place. Nervously he perched on the edge of the sofa in his hotel suite and stared at the television as the press briefing began.

FBI headquarters, Washington, DC

Shep knew that late the previous night Deputy Director Charlie Armacost had announced to the media that he'd be conducting a press conference at ten o'clock Thursday morning from the briefing room at the J. Edgar Hoover FBI building. It had been Shep's idea to put out the advance notice of the press conference.

Saul Sanders's body had been discovered Wednesday evening by two FBI agents who went to check on him when he didn't arrive for work at his FBI office on Wednesday. Shep knew that the media anticipated Charlie would talk about Sanders's death. But that wasn't the kind of information the media would get. It would certainly be a surprise . . . for everyone.

FBI technicians had worked through the night, splicing together several copies of the tape of Milton McAdams to distribute to the media at the press conference. The tape was too long to provide full copies and contained information that didn't need to be disseminated. Shep had viewed the tape with Charlie several times throughout the night, and together they had decided which portions to incorporate into the edited version. It contained just enough information to accomplish the goal of destroying Ed Burke, and was brief enough that it could be shown in its entirety numerous times throughout the day Thursday on all the news networks. A typed transcript of the edited version of the McAdams tape was also prepared for the print media so they could immediately get it onto their Web sites and run it in Friday morning's print edition.

Shep knew that in the life of a political campaign, the Thursday before a Tuesday election was a crucial day. Every campaign in every election, from local elections all the way to presidential elections, feared the Thursday before a Tuesday election. Shep knew it seemed rather silly to fear a particular day, but the reason was simple: if there was any election-altering news, it would break on Thursday. After weeks and months and years of campaigning, it was strange to think that an election could be altered in a span of time as short as five days. To the general population it may not seem like a sufficient amount of time to accomplish anything. But those who worked on a campaign, like Shep, knew it was the perfect day for news to break—good or bad. It was a long enough period of time for the news to be fully disseminated to every part of the country, but too short a period of time for the other side to respond.

Yes, Shep thought, Thursday was the perfect day for the beginning of Edward Burke's demise.

The briefing room at the Hoover Building was filled to capacity, and white light heated the stage when Charlie Armacost stepped to the podium. When Charlie began to speak into the bank of microphones, Shep smiled. Although it was Charlie's first press conference, he sounded like he'd given thousands of them.

What a great FBI director he'll make, Shep thought.

"Ladies and gentlemen, my name is Charlie Armacost, and I am the deputy director of the FBI. Yesterday we discovered the body of Director Saul Sanders in his Arlington, Virginia, home. There did not appear to be any forced entry, and the investigation into his death continues. I believe of graver concern to the American public was a different discovery my office made yesterday, and it is that discovery that I want to talk to you about today."

On cue, several members of Charlie's staff emerged from different doors around the briefing room and began to distribute the edited video-tape and transcript.

"My staff is distributing copies of a videotape that I'm going to play for you in a moment. First, I want to tell you how we obtained this tape, and what you can expect when you view it."

Shep listened as Charlie gave a brief recount of the developments over the last three months. When Charlie was finished, the entire room was surprisingly silent. Everyone sat in quiet anticipation of the forth-coming videotape.

"And now I want to show you what we have named *The McAdams Tape*," Charlie announced.

The lights dimmed as Charlie pressed the Play button on the remote control, and Milton McAdams's face appeared on the television monitor positioned beside the podium. Reporters from every major broadcast and print media watched the edited McAdams tape that Shep and Charlie had prepared overnight. Shep knew that the Federalists's conspiracy had now been exposed to the world, and with it, Ed Burke. Charlie allowed the tape to play for fifteen minutes before pressing the Stop button on the remote control. After the screen went black and the lights brightened, Charlie continued his prepared remarks.

"As you can see, Mr. McAdams described activities by Mr. Winston, Mr. Montgomery, and Vice President Burke that threaten the highest levels of national security. We don't know at this point the accuracy of all

Mr. McAdams's statements, but my office has opened an investigation into this matter to determine the full extent of the involvement of the people mentioned in the tape, including Vice President Burke. We have confirmed that part of the tape is in fact accurate, and that is why we believed it appropriate to allow you to view it. We are now trying to determine the whereabouts of Pierce Montgomery and Randolph Winston. We will provide more information as the investigation progresses."

Charlie left the stage to choruses of "Mr. Armacost, Mr. Armacost," as reporters tried to ask him questions.

But Charlie ignored them. Nothing further needed to be said, Shep knew. The damage to Edward Burke's presidential aspirations was done.

Bern, Switzerland

It was 5:00 p.m. in Bern, Switzerland, and 11:00 a.m. in Washington, DC, when Pierce Montgomery's Learjet touched down at a private airstrip north of the city. He knew he could claim political asylum in Switzerland and escape extradition to the United States.

Exiting the aircraft, he strolled toward his waiting Rolls Royce limousine, which would take him to a chalet he owned in the Swiss Alps. Just before entering the rear of the car, Pierce spotted a similar limousine. As it drove slowly past Pierce, the rear window of the car lowered and a face was revealed.

The passenger smiled at him as the car passed.

It was a face that Pierce had hoped he'd never have to see again.

EPILOGUE

Hilton Head Island, South Carolina

It was Tuesday, Election Day, across the United States, and the Reed family had been at Claudia Duval's house at Hilton Head Island since Sunday. She had phoned Jake after she'd seen the news reports from Jackson and offered for Jake and his family to stay there as long as they wanted to. She told him that the envelope full of documents Milton had left for her in the locker at Hartsfield-Jackson International Airport had transferred ownership of all Milton's assets, including Eden, to her.

Jake had decided to take Claudia up on her kind offer. It had been good for his family to get away from home for a few days. The sound of the ocean was relaxing to him, and the children were enjoying the heated pool located between the house and the beach. He could tell that Rachel was also enjoying the serenity of the South Carolina low country.

Jake had received word from Naomi that very morning that Jed was fully awake, and had actually eaten breakfast. That was certainly good news. Last Friday he had finally told Ruth and Naomi about the $2 million waiting for them and Jed at Jackson National Bank. To say they were ecstatic was an understatement. Jake was glad that now Jed would get to enjoy the money with the rest of his family.

Jake had taken the $1 million he'd asked the FBI for and received from the Foster campaign and established a trust fund for Deputy Butch Johnson's widow and his children. It was the least he could do, he explained to Butch's widow as she thanked him. He had sacrificed his life for Jake's, and Jake would never forget it.

It was now just past 7:00 p.m. eastern time, and Jake sat on the sofa in the den. His plaster-covered right leg was propped on an ottoman, and he squirmed, trying to find a comfortable sitting position. His bruises were beginning to fade, but Dr. Lawrence said it would be another six weeks before Jake would be fully recovered. Rachel handed him a glass of iced tea and sat down beside him as the evening news on FOX began.

"The polls have closed in the East," the anchor of the *Fox Report* said after introducing himself. "And *FOX News* is projecting that Mac Foster has won all available electoral votes in those states. Exit polls in the rest of the country indicate that Foster is leading comfortably in the remaining states as well. *FOX News* is already projecting that Mac Foster will win the presidency in what appears to be a landslide. Edward Burke will likely suffer the worst defeat in presidential election history. Let's go to Burke's campaign headquarters in Nashville for further coverage . . ."

Jake turned to Rachel and smiled. "Couldn't happen to a nicer guy."

ABOUT THE AUTHOR

A graduate of Union University, Jerome Teel received his JD, cum laude, from the Ole Miss School of Law. He is actively involved in his church, local charities, and youth sports. He has always loved legal-suspense novels and is a political junkie. Jerome and his wife, Jennifer, have three children—Brittney, Trey, and Matthew—and reside in Tennessee, where he practices law and is at work on a new novel.

www.jerometeel.com